about the author

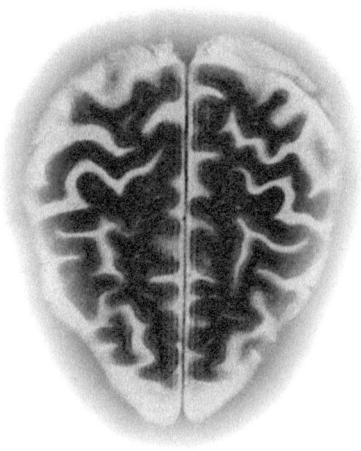

a piece of her mind

THE finest ass IN THE universe

Also by ANNA TAMBOUR

Crandolin
Spotted Lily
Monterra's Deliciosa & Other Tales &

anna tambour

T≋
p≋   Ticonderoga
     publications

to Joe Pulver,
but only if you shut up about it

The Finest Ass in the Universe by Anna Tambour

Published by Ticonderoga Publications

Copyright © Anna Tambour 2015
Introduction copyright © Jeffrey Ford 2015

All original images, including cover image and the travelling exhibition
of the magnificent insignificants, copyright © Anna Tambour 2015

Designed and edited by Russell B. Farr
Typeset in Sabon and East Market

A Cataloging-in-Publications entry for this title is available from
The National Library of Australia.

ISBN 978-1-925212-14-3 (limited hardcover)
 978-1-925212-15-0 (trade hardcover)
 978-1-925212-16-7 (trade paperback)
 978-1-925212-17-4 (ebook)

*This is a work of fiction and fact. Any resemblance to actual events or locales
or persons, living, dead, the living dead including iffy oysters on the half-shell;
diseases, the thorned, honoured, scorned, and indigestibles; or all of the above + the
unmentioned and unmentionable—is entirely coincidental, or not.*

Ticonderoga Publications
PO Box 29 Greenwood
Western Australia 6924
Australia

www.ticonderogapublications.com

10 9 8 7 6 5 4 3 2 1

ACKNOWLEDGMENTS

spread, even as you sleep. Like honey drafted by the military, all these Special thanks *have smothered sincerity, intimacy, modesty, and mystery. Help end civilisation as we know it. Your disdain could mean so much.*

Besides, this book isn't about you. It's about us. Without us *this book would not have been possible.*

—L.D., for the Contents

Contents

What I Don't Know and Do About Anna Tambour

Jeffrey Ford

I've never met Anna Tambour. In fact, I don't even know what she looks like. There's a photo of her on her website, but it's small, black and white, and my eyes aren't what they used to be. All I can vouch for is that she has dark hair, unless it's a wig. Before I started doing some research for this introduction and found out from a few sources that she lives "in the bush, somewhere in Australia," I was under the distinct impression that she lived in Tasmania in a remote location near the sea. I'm not completely sure what gave me that impression, but it seemed fitting, seeing as Tasmania is both a very real place but also one steeped in myth and lore. I partially blame my perception on the beautiful photographs she posts online of strange flora and fauna, each picture a mosaic tile from some alien biology; things I'd never seen in my vast experience lived between New Jersey and Ohio.

I compounded my inaccuracy by trying to interpret her life through her fiction, and what I imagined was an open air, one story house at the edge of a deep and mysterious jungle, the front window facing a view of the shore and the pounding surf of the Tasman Sea. Within that home, there was always a dark haired woman, sitting at a writing table, writing into existence a phantasmagorical dinner of rare delicacies—insect eggs the size of cue balls, angel faced fish poached in the sauce of a fruit that must rot before it ripens, crystalline tears, the sap of a tree, a taste that turns the mind transcendental, and for dessert, deep fried spores of the only fungus on earth with the ability to sing. All of this, of course, was prepared for her guests—an odd assortment of travelers, philosophers, cut throats, saints, and every day citizens of varying genders, from different places and different times. And there were creatures of the wild invited too—the Thylacine, lemur, humming bird, seal, and more. Those dinner parties were always resplendent, convivial, and curious.

Let's face it, I don't really know Anna Tambour. What I do know, though, is her fiction. I've been reading it since she sent me an arc of her Faustian novel, *Spotted Lily*, back in 2004. I was very taken by that book, its smooth style and the clarity of the writing, its fabulist imagination and how that resonated with the everyday, its glorious sense of humor—scatological, colloquial, intellectual— and its shrewd feminism. After reading *Spotted Lily*, I back tracked to her earlier book, a collection titled *Monterra's Deliciosa & Other Tales &*. This work contains no less than 30 pieces—stories and poems—and gave me a deeper sense of Tambour's gifts as a writer. An eclectic gathering of narratives from fairy tales to science fiction to fantasy to the subtlest magical realism to the weirdest weird, this book in addition to the novel made me certain I was reading a very unique artist. What do I mean by artist? In this case, I mean one with an idiosyncratic vision and capable, through a certain mastery of craft, of transferring to others through writing anything the imagination can conceive.

My assumptions about Tambour and her fiction were validated when in 2012 Chomu Press published her novel, *Crandolin*. She sent me an ARC but I was busy at the time and it took me a while to get to it. In the meantime it had been nominated for a World Fantasy Award and garnered quite a bit of enthusiasm. The book is a sumptuous cosmic weave of a fiction and all the wonderful technique and power of story I'd seen in the previous work was present, coming together like a symphony. The storyline was both errant and revelatory—a search through time and place for the truth about a delicious mythic dish. The narrative jumps from location to location, year to distant year, and each of these scenarios is added like an ingredient to the pot. It's only later when these ingredients start to boil together and you smell the connections cooking that you begin to understand the ingenious nature of *Crandolin's* structure.

For those of you who have chosen *The Finest Ass in the Universe* for your first foray into Tambour's fiction, you've made an excellent choice. In these 26 stories, she's at her best—streamlined yet sensuous description; humor in all its forms; spontaneous, organic invention; a magical linkage of character, voice, and style in the telling; clarity of line; the indisputable reality of dream. And, oh, those you'll meet herein—a boy reincarnated as an eggplant, a shopper looking to purchase a dead parrot, the man of the river, a wizard, a dog named Ibsen; a jeweler of unusual gems, a window dresser; the Emperor Whose Glow Will Blind You; an Orm who pops up through a toilet in Flushing—and more, many more, in settings both just round the corner and further afield from Ohio than even Tasmania.

For those of us who may not know Anna Tambour but know well her fiction, *The Finest Ass in the Universe* is a moveable feast, a 26 course dinner to be enjoyed at one's leisure. All the dishes are unique. All the dishes are mythic. Set the table. Pour the wine. Invite the Thylacine.

THE finest ass IN THE universe

The Oyster and Alice O.

Most agoraphobic oysters,
ever sweet and passive,
are torn from their homes
to slide down throats and die in gastric acid.

The lucky ones are fried in oil,
and die ever so quickly.
Others die on their opened house,
smothered in spinach, ickily.

Though one, it's told
slipped, naked from the lips it was being borne to
and fell, its silvery slither lost amongst . . .

Delacillo's was one of those restaurants people go to when they've got
something better on their minds, and it was that time in the evening
when the fug had reached its zenith: scents of crushed cat-glands and
amber, bruised orange blossom and Bulgarian rose, aged tobacco tar,
champagne dregs, powdered armpits, perfumed crotches, rich men's
anticipant breath, and the ozone of oysters by the bushel.

The band was playing something syncopated in competition with voices, glasses, dishes. It lost.

In this confusion, the oyster slipped away, with many reasons and absolutely no rhyme.

It fell upon the tablecloth, and recoiled at the harsh dryness. Seeking something familiar, the oyster leapt.

At that moment of the oyster's leap, Charles Maginnis was in the act of leaning, and at the moment of the oyster's landing just under the pearl necklace around the neck of Alice O., Mr. Maginnis's lips met the oyster in what would have been a passionate smooch, but Charles Maginnis recoiled like a backside meeting a tack.

He looked at Alice's tender neck, seeing only a champagne-tinted shimmer of pink and pearl. The girl looked alright, all right, but her flesh had tasted fishy. Well, not exactly fishy, as oyster isn't fish, but Charles sluiced his mouth with his tongue and was disgusted. You never know about a girl. He'd downed a magnum of brut and two dozen tiger-makers on the half-shell this evening, planning for a wild-one of a night, but he expected her to smell like that Shalimar he'd bought her. Maybe she'd worn it for someone else. If so, he was gonna take these pearls, too. He couldn't abide a woman with poor hygiene. "And that's what perfume's for, dammit. To drown their smell," he said.

He reached towards her neck, not knowing if he was gonna kiss her again or choke her, or grab that necklace offa her —

Alice slipped sideways fast as clear soup off a fork, stood and walked out of Delicillo's. She didn't hear Charles Maginnis's "Hey, you" and the crash of his chair as he lost his balance, nor the sodden-dufflebag thuds of him onto the floor—just jumbled percussives in the syncopated tings and crash of china, glass, slipping shoes on greasy fake marble, snared brass, brags, laughs, whines and variegated demands.

If something hadn't saved her, she'd be in Charles Maginnis's grasp, of that she knew. Oh, let's not fret about that. She'd much preferred Charles Maginnis's attentions to a trip to the dentist who had filled a molar just last week, but she'd had her fill of Charles, let alone his pearls and perfumes.

She shed a tear of frustration and one of pity.

"I've only got my brains and beauty," she could have said, and it would have been true. She was so beautiful that men went silly for her, and a few had actually probably killed themselves for her, and not just tediously threatened. And she was smart. Really intelligent. And witty.

She was greedy, no buts about it.

She fingered her neck, and found the oyster. She wasn't surprised.

Only something extraordinary could have stopped Charles Maginnis. He was a man of fierce passions, and when fuelled by champagne, oysters, and young beauty such as Alice O.'s, Maginnis was a man inclined to forget that some girls want a link in between a nice dinner in a fancy place and a bedroom afterwards—a little charm? Definitely yes, and no, if it means just more jewelry. Alice, for instance, would have . . . well, she would have made Charles Maginnis need no courage-makers, if he could have thought beyond pearls. Instead, she had needed to gracefully wrest his tongue from her neck in Delacillo's before, and had resigned herself to the tedium again, when the oyster saved her.

It wasn't that she was embarrassed. Delacillo's, at this time of the evening (early morning) was a scene of anacondic tongues, cephalopodic limbs, and a common sensibility that descended upon the place every night in the fug itself, that everything that happened here, happened here in its own reality, broken only by the break of day and its lashings of chlorine bleach and elbow grease. So shame wasn't a factor, but boredom was.

God, she was glad to get rid of that bore. For he wouldn't have done, would he?

No, she admitted as she walked under a gentle rain.

When they got to her bedroom, she looked in the mirror. The oyster was nestled in the V of her throat muscles, its silvery sheen more complex and beautiful than the white glow of the pearls.

"You want to grant me three wishes?" she said.

"That's rich," said the oyster. "Who just saved whom?"

"Am I drunk?" said Alice, pulling down one eyelid.

"Of course you are," said the oyster. "You owe me four wishes."

"Four?"

"Three, then."

Alice twiddled her fingers. "Three, then," and fell onto the bed on her back.

The oyster slapped her. "You promised."

"I promise," said Alice. "Now let me sleep."

ALICE WOKE WITH the oyster on her neck beating to the low brass whahh whahhh of Billie Holiday singing "You can get it if you try," backed up by the band music of the heater in the building's basement chugging through the pipes of every radiator in the rooming house.

"Well, hello there," said the oyster.

"Don't be too sure," said Alice, groaning.

"Look, beautiful," said the oyster, stretching itself over two pearls in her strand. "I've been patient enough in my life."

The necklace that Charles Maginnis had given Alice O., was what's called a 'collar'. The oyster squeezed its adductor muscle around the pearls ever so gently, turning the collar into a choker.

"Okay!" said Alice, sitting up. She rubbed her eyes.

"If you tell me your eyes feel gritty . . . " said the oyster, tensing.

"Alright already! I just need—"

"No you don't!"

"What?"

"A prairie oyster," said the oyster. "You were just about to say—"

Alice tossed her head in that imperious way women who make men threaten to kill themselves if they don't get their way with them do.

"You don't know me that well," she said, and in those six muscular syllables, almost popped the pearls.

The oyster slipped, gripping frantically, but Alice's skin was so smooth and the room so hot and slickening, the radiator pounding out a beat so hot that it was summertime all the time, else folks got colds down here.

Alice picked the oyster off the soft nest it had fallen on, something like seaweed, and she nestled it back in the V of her neck.

The oyster was silent, perhaps unusually so.

"They can't take that away from me," sang Billie.

"God," said Alice. "Can't get away from that woman anywhere in this town."

"I like it," said the oyster.

"Taste!" said Alice, but her eyes teared up. One drop rolled down her cheek, drew itself under the so-sure chin, followed the perfectly chiseled line of her throat, and spread upon the thirsting flesh of the oyster, a gorgeously salty wetness.

"What's eating you," asked the oyster, trying to sound tough, but really, in that instance, smitten with a strange feeling in its gut.

It must be said that the oyster had only a few days before, become a male or maybe a female, and maybe it had just changed back (in that could-be-said rather frivolous spontaneity that oysters take, with sex) at the touch of that woman's fluid. The thing is, oysters are as sensual, though the crude would just say "sexual", as any night on the town, though their wandering days are few, and only when they are extremely immature.

And this oyster had just realized that leading a sheltered life, never roaming to and fro like, say, jellyfish, limits a homebody's experience. Never had the oyster learned of this magical fluid. Such lubricity, such salinity. Deliciously luxurious, irresistibly tasty. It wanted more.

"Do you all taste as good," it asked.

"I guess," said Alice, answering noncommittally automatically, a habit she'd fallen into. She was thinking of a strong bittersweet cup of chicory coffee, washed down with another cup of same. And two fried eggs, two slabs of toast, and a mountain of grits, its crater running with butter. Already, she'd put past her, what had made her want to break into great jags of sobbing, only a moment ago. Well, she was young, beautiful, and smart. Why wouldn't she be forgetful?

And the oyster? How we judge them! As they say, "It's always better to be stupid and uncultured."

The ones we say are very good, irritate mighty easy; and though we've come to praise them, they meet the knife that pries them from their home before they learn the meaning of agoraphobic.

This oyster might have had naive taste in music, but it wasn't stupid—and it was by personal nature, lascivious. Only yesterday morning, it had been quietly feeding when it was violently tilted, its home ripped from its very foundations, let alone neighborhood. And only last night, the oyster's home had been broken into while it was supposedly healthily making some sort of a life in this uprooted abode piled just anyhow with so many others; and then the knife . . . Now it was impatient.

"Do that again," said the oyster.

"What?" said Alice.

"Bathe me in your salty stuff."

Alice blushed prettily, which made her break out in fresh perspiration.

This stuff was more concentrated, though very good. But there was too little of it.

"More of that other stuff," ordered the oyster, gripping the necklace as Alice stood up.

"I've got to get bathed," she said. "You can come with me." She unclasped the necklace, but at the oyster's scream, she clasped it again.

"You win," she said. "But better not let Mrs. Davidson see us, or she'll think I want milk in my bath."

When they returned to Alice's room, the oyster was still sputtering with indignation. It had been, oh!: lathered ("inadvertently!" Alice had insisted), dropped (when it slipped off its grip on the pearls) onto the enameled tin that was swimming with the foot funguses of one newspaperman, one divorced drugstore employee, and a girl who'd last been a girl fifty years ago; and almost sluiced down the drain, only to be pulled painfully, free. In that torrent of cascading water, Alice was too slick for the oyster to ride. That Alice had then perched the oyster in the soap dish thinking that that would do, created a scene that Alice had been obliged to sing *over*, to draw attention *from*, knowing that just across the hall, resided as if the house had been built around her, a Miss Fleeb, who was known in the rooming house, as Miss Enemy, (for Nothing Missed, Ever).

The oyster berated Alice so harshly (being itchy all over from that burning lathering stuff, so harsh, so quite unlike proper froth), that she sat stark naked on her bed, except for her pearl necklace and the oyster leaning on it jerking in little gasps from itchiness—and Alice began to cry.

She was hungry, confused, and feeling maybe a spot of guilt for half-wanting the oyster to have slipped down the drain, to oblivion.

She was unused to being properly berated. Cajoled, yes. Begged, oh my yes! Whined at, emotionally blackmail-tried. But out and out roundly chewed out till her ears were pink, not even in her dreams.

She cried and cried, and the more tears that fell, the more soothed the oyster became, though at first, the oyster only chewed her out more, as this was so wonderful that the oyster was worried lest she stop. But even when the oyster had been thoroughly cleaned of that toxic substance, and then clean, had bathed in it, turning its sleekly muscled body till its complex sheen of tarnished silver to light of the moon made the pearls look dull and pedestrian again—even then, more tears fell—enough now that the oyster tasted one, and savoured another, and then imbibed them slowly in its inimitably classy way.

No open mouth, no chewing noise. Just understated elegance. The oyster silently gorged itself, taking not just sustenance from the essence of Alice's tears, but thrill—as the private sensualist aesthete it was. And after all that drinking to which it was not accustomed, the oyster tingled with feelings. Ones that had built up till they had to be satisfied one spectacular, draining night a year, on a month with no 'r' in it.

The tipsy oyster tottered on the hammock of pearls, and almost fell.

Alice blew her nose.

"So our feelings er mushual!" it cried. "Should I do eggs or sperm?"

Without waiting for Alice to answer, without even trying to line itself up to reach the tissue that Alice had blown into, the oyster released.

Call it rash. Call it rude. But please don't say condemn it. Now the oyster was mortifiedly alert.

Alice wiped the milky substance from between her breasts.

"How many wishes have I granted you so far?" she said.

"I don't know," said the oyster. "I'm sorry to have taken liberties."

"That's quite all right. It was nothing . . . compared to—oh, hell," she cried, and threw herself on the bed.

"Come, come," said the oyster. "Tell me."

THE SIGHT OF Alice lit passions wherever she went, and all those whining men had cooled Alice's sexuality till she felt as cold as a high-class fish market—until Charles Maginnis.

He ate to get sex, had a horrible habit of extruding his mouth parts all over Alice, and it is painful to state that 'parts' is no mistake. Mr. Maginnis's teeth were large and white, but in the throes, what with his tongue and all (his eschewal of the prophylactic use of denture paste): floppy.

"But what an artist. You should see his line work," Alice sighed, unconsciously drawing her finger lightly along the oyster's back, making it shiver.

"His line work, you were saying."

"Yes. Governor Gable's nose. If only I could do that." And she sighed again.

"So let me get this straight," said the oyster. "You wish to be a political cartoonist, and he is the best in the country."

"Oh, yes!"

"And you met up with him, hoping he could teach you."

"Yes, the chump."

"You or him?"

"Him, of course."

The oyster reserved judgment, though about human emotions, it was learning so fast that it could be called an idiot savant, with a sensualist bottom note.

"And you actually fell in love with him," it asked.

Alice blew her nose again, confusing the oyster who was still bamboozled by sinuses.

"Of course I fell in love with that big lunk," said Alice. " But if you'd seen that cartoon he did with the paper bags under the . . . and his caption!"

She broke into helpless laughter.

"You're just as witty. I heard you last night, and now I understand some of it."

"Of course I am, but I can't draw."

"Let's have a look."

"You promise to be honest?"

"I promise," said the oyster solemnly.

"Hang on."

The oyster swung from the pearls while Alice pulled a large tray out from under her bed. It was filled with loose sheets of paper. She rifled through them, and pulled one out. "This might be a bit too esoteric," she said, timorously.

The oyster looked long and hard at the drawing.

"Of course, Randolph and Baggins aren't in office anymore," said Alice, "So the caption might not work with you."

"Of course," said the oyster, trying to think of something else to say. "These are humans?"

"No, they're monsters!" said Alice, tossing her head

"Then this is an excellent portrayal." said the oyster. "I've seen things back home that look much like them. Have you spent much time—"

"What," said Alice, "are you talking about?"

"Your two monsters here. Your line work on their fins—"

"Those are ears, and I wasn't trying there for caricature."

The oyster fell silent.

Downstairs, a telephone rang.

"Damnation, I'm late," Alice said, without moving a muscle.

"You can get it if you try," Billie sang, with all the sensitivity of a recording.

Alice jumped up, threw open her door, yelled "Shut that lying woman up," and slammed it.

Her chest was hot, her pearls shaking like the sea in a storm.

"Shhhh," said the oyster. " Shhhh, and sit."

"Gotta get to work."

"Nope, ya dope" said the oyster, who had learned much in the kitchen with the shuckers.

"You're the boss," Alice sniffed. "I just hope . . . Oh, I just hope . . . you see, I could . . . a bit of shade just here . . . "

She leaned over and picked up a stick of charcoal, hovering it over the cartoon.

"Hotsy-totsy, baby," said the oyster. It had to make itself feel and sound upbeat, because of what it had to say.

"If my heart could only talk," Billie sang, heartlessly.

For the truth of the matter was: at first, the oyster had been confused by Alice's drawing, thinking it a scene of last night's kitchen: two naked, helpless oysters lying on a table waiting to be thrown into a steaming pot. Now the oyster realized with its dim idiot savant mind that the pot was the State Capitol building, and the two oysters, not the State Attorney General and Treasurer portrayed satirically as two of the more obnoxious monsters of the deep, but Alice's attempts at human renditions with a bit of extra emphasis to the nose, mouth, and jaws of the men.

"Alice," said the oyster gently, but firmly. "Face it."

"I must, mustn't I?"

"I'm afraid so."

"He didn't teach me anything."

"Those who do . . . "

"Oh, oyster!" cried Alice.

"You're my egg-sprayer!" the oyster chortled. "Or do you wish to provide the sperm?"

"Eggs, dear. No matter what I wish," said Alice, surprising the oyster. "And only one at a time."

"We'll see about that," replied the oyster, surprising Alice.

So the next month ("To hell with the 'r' in it!") they wed by the light of the moon, and remain a couple. Where they are now, I can't say, but their progeny favor bayous, bays, and bars, and are changing the world more than anyone can say—from the efflorescence of cartoonists that can't draw, to the glut of poets with no reason and absolutely no rhyme.

Sometimes the oyster travels in the V of Alice's neck, but more often, much more discretely, in a place that it calls home—as dark and wet as the oyster's old neighborhood, but this has central heating, sustenance to sate a sybarite—and for a music lover, what rhythm!

Lab Dancer

That loser suckup lab assistant Eugene something had begged Libby Purfouy to watch how she worked. Sure, he'd been a bit creepy with all his obsequiousness, and so unambitious-acting that she'd had suspicions; but he had proved himself to be so careful to label scrupulously, store everything in its proper place, and keep out of her way that she had given in and let him know that she did her real work late at night, really late, "so if you're willing to watch and keep out of my way, you can come."

It was the watching that she hadn't properly thought out.

He was so attentive to her that he could have been a guide dog. It was unnatural and a bit nauseating. But this silent undemanding waiting-upon her every need was so damn useful and hell, both flattering and unthreatening. He couldn't have learned anything much from watching her. And washing up after her wasn't anything any other lab assistant saw as a path to glory.

She was working with a type of bacteriophage that had played a key role in a tubeworm's digestion mechanism when the phone in her pocket rang. At 3am, there could only be one reason. She fumbled for it, feeling scooped out in her gut. If only she had convinced her parents to move into her apartment. He could have been resting here now on a couch by the wall where she could keep an eye on him, pop a nitro under his tongue when he turned grey.

"Mom?" she said, to some reply she couldn't make out. Maybe from her mom's most celebrated on-stage self, the ostrich-tailed Lady Carlotta LaRou.

"Lady LR?"

"Doctor Purfouy?"

"Las Vegas General? Intensive Care?"

"We are sorry if this is a wrong number. We are looking for Doctor Libby Purfouy."

"I'm Doctor Purfouy. He's not . . . " She couldn't say it.

"Doctor Purfouy, we are sorry to disturb you at this hour." The foreign accent and manner would have been charming at another time, maybe a palace ball, but now the formality infuriated her as much as hospitals and their euphemisms always had.

"Disturb! He's my dad, fuck it. You've got him stabilised?"

"Doctor Purfouy, I am sorry to hear that your father is unwell, but we are calling you from the Royal Academy of Sciences in Stockholm. My name is . . . "

THE SOLEMN SWEDISH man, she didn't catch his name, must have been used to inane reactions, and had been very gracious about ignoring her crudeness when she thought he was a hospital drone. But she used all her roused skill in repressing her real thoughts once she realised that the call wasn't a prank and that in hours the world would know her (and Kadambini Bhattacharya) as the newest Nobel Laureate(s). The Nobel Prize in Medicine.

Freedom and respect. She would no longer have to pretend that the scorn of other scientists didn't hurt. After all, it's only so long you can pose as someone who doesn't give a shit when people sneer at your work, call it pseudoscience—when they damn you by your associate. Now she could walk the halls with her shoulders back, and throw herself into research that might be loopy as anything Hawkins would spout, and she would never again have to worry that her work might be considered not worth considering for funding. Hell, she could start her own institute, but what to study next?

Of course she had hoped. What scientist doesn't? And though she knew that her and Bini's discovery could, *would* change millions, hundreds of millions of lives, this Nobel had to have been singularly argued. She couldn't help thinking of the headlines. She would have to be the youngest recipient ever at 31, but then that worldly board that made the decision might have had a wry chuckle at her joke in that interview in *Science*, "amoebic dysentery isn't anything that a body can ignore, any body."

All this flashed through her mind as on another level, she maintained a short and dignifiedly friendly chat with the man in Stockholm. It seemed like she'd been covering for her whirling brain for an hour but it was only three minutes later that she thanked him politely, expressing again her surprise and humbleness, and then ended the call by saying that she must get back to work. "I usually work now when I can be least disturbed, though you can disturb me this way any time, hah hah."

He apologised again for disturbing her in the midst of an experiment, saying "I always seem to interrupt scientists in the middle of the night, and the middle of an experiment." Then he said he'd look forward to meeting her plane when she arrived for the December ceremony, that he liked to meet all the Laureates personally, and then hung up to save her the awkwardness.

She thought for a moment about Bini in Mumbai, who was probably now having a party surrounded by her department at the Institute, and would later be stuffed with sweets by her extensive family.

Maybe I should ring her. No, if she wants, she can ring me.

She dropped the phone in her lab coat and took her feet off the desk, jumped out of her chair, dumped her coat over its back, and danced—eyes closed, arms close to her sides so they didn't hit equipment, but otherwise her whole body in play.

Her ass wasn't just bossily leading her dance as it tended to. It was a real mutt of a dance in its swishes, sways, rolls and bounce—a cross between a deliriously happy dog and Las Vegas showgirl.

She sang as she danced, used stirrers as drumsticks against the glassware.

When Security called through the door, she stopped.

"It's okay, Charles."

"Roger, Doctor." He was her favourite, and as she told him, might have been a scientist if brought up in another family. "Discover something?" he asked.

"No such luck tonight."

"Can't have that every night," he said reassuringly. "Still, I'm glad to hear you keepin' up your spirits."

She left the lab and walked out into the balmy Santa Barbara night. Charles walked out with her and watched her unlock her bike. He was unhappy that she didn't let him call her a cab. "Can't have anyone followin' you," he always said. He was sweet, but old.

She answered back with "Who you kiddin'? I'm a lady scientist," which he accepted without further comment. It had become a routine between them. Anyway, Santa Barbara is such a village of a place that she would have jogged home if it didn't make him way too nervous.

The moment she got under the covers, she remembered Eugene, and shrugged. He'd heard other phone calls from her, reminding her dad to take his pills. Other phone calls with hospitals. He must have left as soon as the phone rang.

Sleep was impossible and it was too early to ring her dad and sister. Her stomach felt like a filled and tumbling washing machine

She made herself a cup of coffee and dumped in, after a hunt, a dash of vodka that someone had given her. It was—interesting. As interesting as any of her own cooking.

So she got on the web, to distract herself with something mindless and silly.

And wow, this should be good. Something that from the headlines looked to be more viral than H5N1:

Who Says Scientists Don't Have Big Brains? Do This To My Test Tubes, Baby!

By the time she got to **Lab Laureate Shakes it Up**, she was gasping for air.

That little shit! His name was there in the brh corner, copyright. Sure, he'd been pirated probably a million times by now, and America hadn't even woken up, but he'd sold the first rights to someone, or tried to. She tried not, but couldn't help but read, an interview with him.

"She's a really nice lady, you know . . . Yes, she IS kinda weird . . . No, in regular work hours she doesn't wear shorts to the lab . . . No, honestly, I haven't noticed that about her . . . "

All the stories had the same quotes, so she gave them a break and looked instead, at that thing that you couldn't avoid. It streamed now into the room from her laptop, phone, and pad.

She felt sicker than when she thought her father had just died.

The screens were filled with her wagging butt.

It was apparently being sent around (when do people sleep?) stirring up a storm of words. Tweets were turning into headlines, posts, the stories that spread because they spread, turning more virulent the more they infect, changing strains to keep infection lively.

The Bump and Grind of Science
Book a Laureate-o-gram for your Bucks Night!
Chickflick makes Nobel the butt of jokes
Crap queen drags Nobel into muck
High honor, low morals
Too Young to Know Better
The Tail that Wags Science
What can you expect from a copraphiliac?
Class Ass
Gen Why Makes Alfie Nobel Roll in Grave
This Nobel Laureate will take her Prize money
in 20s, in her G-String

She forced herself to pick up a scalpel, plunge it into her arm, and strip out her veins. Actually, she forced herself to go offline. It felt like all the pain of a torturous death without the result one should expect: the peace of oblivion.

She hid in bed, even from devices that she couldn't cut off.

People rang to be let up. She put cotton in her ears. Tried to read a biography of Madame Curie, a stupid idea; then a collection of Judy Horacek cartoons, which didn't work. Then had such a long shower that her skin pruned but still didn't feel clean. Slept, woke, took a lot of food to bed, ate till she felt worse, tossed cartons and wrappers to the floor, curled up and passed out again. Had another shower, got in bed and tried to sleep again.

At 3PM she gave in and peeked. Some pollster sleaze "news agency" that would make the most of it, was making headlines with its snap poll.

Not only had 78 percent of women said that they would rather be known for having the "finest ass in the universe" but that they'd prefer that to getting a Nobel in Medicine.

The top headline in Google News: **Experts debate latest laureate's lack of visible pantyline**

At six she rang her parents in Las Vegas. He answered the phone. "How's tricks?" same as he always did, making his little joke at the expense of science. He'd been an electrician and off-season magician in the casinos, and had come out of retirement to work himself to a heart attack, so proud he'd been of his daughter going into science, and not only that, but performing "tricks" that could maybe make real magic, as antibiotics had. He had followed as well as he could, the scientific basis of her work, as well as the social side; her lead role in the development of what one report called erroneously, "beautiful poo." He had always believed her brilliant. "My little rabbit," he'd called her, and she would wiggle her imaginary puff of a tail.

She was only wiggling now with shame. "I'm so sorry, Dad," she blubbered.

"What's that, Bunbun?" he said. "You can do it. If that experiment failed, you've got to . . . "

He didn't know. He didn't look at trash.

"Dad, shut up before the waterworks come again. Mom, are you on the other phone?"

"Of course, Libby. What is the problem? You can always come home if everything's bad there. Horrible place, California."

"Geez, Mom. I wonder what you'll say when you go to Sweden. And Dad . . . Dad," She stifled a hacking sob. "You're forbidden to have another heart attack until at least next year. You've got to see me on stage, picking up my Nobel Prize."

One phone dropped, and Libby heard her father whooping up a storm, stamping on the linoleum floor. She could only imagine his saggy butt flopping in its trousers.

The other phone went dead after a quick "Love you, Libby, Gotta make sure Dad doesn't overdo."

Libby laughed till she cried. The most unreal thing in her life had just pulled her mom, for the first time in years, out of unreality.

Her mom had never understood why she wanted to work at what were often lower wages than a hotel maid in Las Vegas, let alone with "even more dangerous filth." And Libby's father had been so proud of her wanting to be a real scientist, but never understood how she could "do experiments with someone in another building," so she hadn't mentioned to them now, had never mentioned Kadambini Bhattacharya. She could just imagine her mother's reaction: "How can anyone live with a name like that?" Anyway, Libby didn't know what even her father would think of her working with someone in India, especially after she brought back at 18, not that boyfriend he had warned her about (Todd dumped her the first time she couldn't hold her shit), but a case of the runs that almost killed her, and certainly changed her life.

She and Todd had been on the Grand Trunk Road, in a bus that was so crowded that she was sitting on her pack on the floor in the back, when it happened. She'd been trying not to vomit from the heat, the diesel fumes coming in the open windows, the jerky way the bus driver sped, swirved and hit his horn; the miasma of India—crushed-together humanity, an intimacy of natural body odours and spices; and on this bus which must have carried three times the stated passenger limit, one passenger limit at least (and most of the floor) filled by huge bags of onions that many of the passengers were carrying to market.

Suddenly she forgot her nausea. She desperately needed the bus to stop. She had to get out. Todd was jammed in beside her, sitting on his own pack, his face streaming sweat but his head bobbing to what was streaming through his earphones. She grabbed his arm and he looked at her with annoyance—not that he could have done anything with that mass of people, goods, and those hundreds of kilos of onions between them and the door.

With a slight grumble that only she would have been able to hear, her bowels didn't wait. Like a silent fart, the air was blasted with stench. But this hadn't been a fart, and the smell wasn't rich. It was unbelievably acrid, poisonous. And it was wet. People turned to look accusingly at Libby and Todd.

Libby's seat felt horribly warmed. Before she had a chance to think about whether the shit had gone through her underpants and into her khaki cargo pants, her bowels spurted out another liquid explosion. She clenched her sphincter, but that was as effective in stopping the flow as trying to shove a cork back in a bottle of champagne.

She squirmed but couldn't really move, and neither could anyone else.

Someone nearby yelled a few urgent or angry words, and they were passed up along the passengers till they must have reached the driver. He beeped his horn even more wildly than he had before, and slewed to a stop cutting in between a camel caravan and a lorry.

All around her, people shifted. Bags of onions were pulled aside, and she saw that the bottom of one of them was soaked.

The bus door opened up front with a rusty sigh.

Todd jumped up and space was somehow made for him. "I'll get you something," he said, rushing out. She couldn't see him but heard him say "Excuse me" a few times, and then a bunch of other people got up, more and more of them in the front. She couldn't get up. Anything she could clean up with, cover herself—it was all in the pack, the pack which was now soggy with stuff that had run down its sides and wet the backs of her legs. She'd moved her legs away from the pack though that moved more stench out into the air, and now some short hairs on the back of her calves were being lightly pulled, as from a drying facepack.

People were saying things to her, but no one spoke English so she did all she could think to do—smile shamefacedly at them and motion an apology. She had to wait till Todd came back with a sarong or something, something to cover her and her pack so she could get off the bus and somehow, clean up.

Her gut cramped again, and her bowels let go again, this time with a long hiss and series of pops.

She almost slipped off her pack, and couldn't look at anyone, but the whole bus erupted in yells.

Someone poked her in the kidneys. Another pulled her arm. People pressed away as she was poked and shoved to a standing position. They gave even more space for her pack that she had to pick up and carry, dripping, toward the door. Someone pushed her out, and she fell to the dust beside the road, her shit-frosted pack hitting her head.

Todd was nowhere to be seen. His pack! *The bus took off with his pack while he's looking for something he can buy, something to help me off the bus*, but then she remembered a detail of him leaving—he'd casually slung his pack over his back.

Oh yes, Todd and shit were inseparable—and they certainly had changed her life. As had the kind doctor out with his family in his funky old Indian car that had been cared for with love but that he poo poohed with an Indian headshake, saying, "Increase of material comforts, madam, does not in any way whatsoever conduce to moral growth."

For a few more minutes, she forgot about her current disaster. But she had to call her sister in New York.

"Calm down, Juliette," she said, which only opened up a fresh onslaught of accusation.

Juliette Adorina, an opera singer in the chorus at the Met, had been having her late breakfast, with headlines. She was livid. "Do you remember that tomorrow is Saturday and you promised to take Clare for a week while I tour?"

Libby had forgotten. Clare was due in LA airport at 11PM. "I've not forgotten at all," she snapped. "Don't worry about her, and have a good tour."

She hung up cutting her sister off in the middle of something that sounded nasty.

THE STEWARDESS MET Libby, Clare in tow. "Such a beautiful child," she said. "She was such a pleasure."

Clare smiled shyly at the stewardess and took Libby's hand. In Clare's other hand a theatrical mask dangled from a cord. She was wearing a cloak that matched the mask, thick green velvet with an elaborate gold toggle. She might have stepped straight from the stage at the Met.

Libby snorted when they were out of earshot. "You should be illegal, you're so enchanting."

She stopped and blew up a red balloon, handing it to the child. It was really something she had done for herself, thinking it might make her feel more festive. But she'd forgot to bring string, so it looked more than anything, like something biological.

Clare took hold of the balloon. "D'you bring anything decent I could change into?"

"Sorry," Libby said. "C'mon. You'll just have to suffer the looks till we get to my car."

"You should know, sweet cheeks."

Libby swung round.

"You've seen?"

"Who hasn't?"

"Has your mom—uh," She tried not to badmouth her sister even though Juliette obviously felt no such scruples.

"Mom wouldn't have known. I saw it first and showed her. I didn't know she'd go ballistic. It's a hoot."

They were walking fast, and had almost made it to the car park.

Libby looked down at her ten-year old niece, a strange one, that. The halogen lights were so strong now at midnight that they made human skin take on the sick gleam of hot dogs in a gas station. Yet the girl was, even in this setting, almost impossibly beautiful, as innocent looking as a day-old chick. Her talk, however. She could have posed online as a thirty-something with too much experience to remember. Libby could almost believe in reincarnation, listening to this child. Clare had the rather bored mien of a 19th century courtesan who wore her victims like a train. Her wit was channelled through a 21st century Mae West. Libby hated thinking what the girl would grow up to be. Life was so full of falseness that Clare couldn't help but have a face creased by total cynicism before she was 17.

At 10, however, she gleaned from the meanest nastiness, the most sophisticatedly innocent fun. She was a hoot to be with. She broke from Libby's side and pulled the mask on. "What level's it on?"

"C3. Be careful."

"I'm a nutcracker." Clare tripped ahead, leaping and twirling as she ran. With that mask over her eyes, her glossy hair streaming over the snap and flow of her cape, she could have been a prima ballerina on Mars, so misplaced was she in this mundanity.

"You mean you've just hibernated? Like, been literally in the dark? Not communicated?"

"Would you?"

They were sprawled on pillows, polishing off a package of oatmeal cookies.

"Give me a break," Libby said. "Tomorrow I'll catch up. Work my whole life for what? To be turned from a fool who disgraces science by my crackpot ideas, to now, a chick with an ass."

"Will you grow up already?" Clare rolled over, her child's bottom covered in faded flannel. With her thrift shop pyjamas she looked like some Christmas appeal poster. It was one of her affectations, a fad that Libby catered for, their little secret. In New York Clare was always dressed in the most theatrical getups. She was already a fashion chameleon in the pages of *Vogue*, and not in children's clothes. Libby was her escape in so many ways.

Libby changed the subject. "Want to do microscopy now, or sleep?"

"I've got some disgusting stuff to look at, yeah. But that's for later in the week, if there's a chance. But I don't think there will be."

"I've got enough food for us to stay here till you leave."

"But you won't have the time."

"Don't."

"Too late. Nah nah nah nah NAH!"

Libby waved her iphone in Clare's face. On it was a headline:

India explodes in rapture

Libby grabbed for the phone but Clare was too fast.

"From the *Times of India*," she said. "Hundreds of thousands of Indians celebrated in the streets today as they cheered the first Indian woman to win a Nobel prize; and not only that, but the prestigious Award for Medicine. Many view this as the first time in living history that an Indian who is proud to be an Indian, in India, has become a Nobel Laureate. Today Kadambini Bhattacharya was announced to be the latest Laureate along with her co-winner who also worked on the discovery, American Libby Purfouy. Dr Bhattacharya has dedicated the past thirty years of her life to fighting the scourge of amoebic dysentery and now thanks to her, not only will the poor millions in India (and in many other countries) no longer lose their lives let alone their work from this debilitating infection, but, she adds pointedly, 'so will many tourists.'"

Clare looked up. "Should I read on?"

Libby nodded.

"We found the modest woman, who looks like a simple grandmother, at her pocket-sized office in the venerable Institute of Sciences in Mumbai. She said that she was pleased and humbled by the Prize. She also said modestly that she couldn't have achieved the breakthrough without the help of the brilliant young scientist who shares the Award, Dr Libby Purfouy, who Bhattacharya considers a 'daughter of Lilavati' and affectionately thinks of as the 'child I never had'. For this dedicated professional had to forsake the joys of having her own children in the quest to do good for the nation and the world. She was instrumental, however, in helping other women to work in sciences in this country. And she is almost militant in her insistence that India is a place to stay in to make discoveries.

"When asked if she would move to, say, Harvard, like other Indian Nobel winners who had moved abroad years before they won, she answered with a touch of anger. 'Why? If Indians hadn't saved their bacon, both American IT and biological sciences would have dried up like a smear of yesterday's dal. And any cursory glance at science papers in America would tell you that our unpronounceable names are everywhere, not just the USA but the world. We must have been doing something right, or they would not have wanted these exports of ours.' Your reporter thought that this little woman had subsided, but Dr Bhattacharya had only paused for breath. 'Many people have said that Harvard is heaven,' she said, 'but you've got be dead to be in heaven. Besides,' she said, adjusting her mango-and-lime sari, 'Heaven's got too many rules. I'd hate to have to dress in widow white."

Clare stopped because of a sound that her aunt made, but Libby waved her hand to continue.

"Dr Bhattacharya is a fine mixture of fiery-eyed militant and jolly joker. Every morning she can be found amongst the devotees of laughter, making seriously raucous noise for thirty minutes under the gaze of the Taj Hotel. Of her choice to not marry, she referred quite irreverently to Gandhi, by saying, 'He devoted himself to a cause and made his own children and spouse suffer. I make no one suffer when I work through the night, nor have I needed to learn how to make good lime pickle. I'm afraid that I even burn chapattis. But as Auntie, my family gets the best from me and I can give to them, and the nation.'"

"Does it end there?"

"No, but don't you want me to find what everyone's saying about you now?"

Libby made a grab but Clare slithered away and continued.

"This reporter asked Dr Bhattacharya what her reaction is to the erroneous conviction of millions of Indians, that she is the 'first Indian woman' to win the Nobel, when in fact, as we reminded her: Mother Teresa of Indian citizenship won the Nobel Peace Prize in 1979 for what the Nobel committee called her '*work in bringing help to suffering humanity.*' The good doctor raised an eyebrow. This seemed to be her comment but then she delivered what might have been a mini lecture. 'The discovery that Dr Purfouy and I have made is only a pixel in the bigger picture. India's problems are really no different to those of every nation's, indeed, of the world. Clean water and sanitation can only be achieved by civil action, just as you can't clean up corruption by scientific discovery. Did you know that

France's water was a source of disease and result of corruption until really quite current times? There is no reason why wealthy Parisians shouldn't be yearning to drink, say, bottles of Mother Ganges water instead of wealthy Indians guzzling Perrier.' Her eyes flash when she talks, and she has an especial scorn for bottled water, which she says only keeps an inadequate system propped up in its inadequacy while making crores of ruppees for big-business bottlers.

"Her work has been supported by grants from the National Science Academy. When asked about how much she has received in contrast to her colleague in the USA, she said that she didn't know, but that she had done much better than the American scientist, receiving perhaps a tenth of the funds that the American would have been able to get. 'But we cost so much less here so we can do so much more with less' is how she explained the discrepancy.

"When asked again if she would consider going to the United States, she said that she is not interested in trying to find cures for mortality in the wealthy over-eighties or cures for wrinkles in the under-forties. When asked if she considers herself a radical economist, as some have labelled her for fighting all attempts to patent her and Purfouy's breakthrough cure, that eyebrow rises again, like Shiva's trident. Then she delivers a big belly-shaking laugh. This is one Auntie you don't want to cross."

Clare looked up as smoothly as a newsreader. "I always wondered why you never told me much about her before. Now I know. She's pretty awesome. Let's see what else—"

"At 3AM? It's way past your beddybyes."

Clare bounced onto her feet. "How about ice cream?"

Libby blushed. She had bought a carton of Clare's favorite, but it vanished between her bouts of escapist sleep. She picked up her keys. "Let's have an early breakfast."

Clare stuck her feet into a pair of slippers with a bad case of mange and pulled a hoody on over her pyjamas.

"Stop," she said as Libby opened the apartment door. Clare tweaked the curtain. "As I suspected."

Libby slammed the door so fast that Clare giggled. "They're just douches out there with cameras, not a disease."

"I can make eggs."

"With what you make them do," said Clare with a shudder, "I'm not surprised persuasion hasn't worked." She tossed her pack to Libby. "Lucky one of us plans well. Open it."

Clare always travelled light to her aunt's place, since Libby was entrusted with keeping all the clothes that Clare loved wearing. This time, however, Clare's little carry-on pack was stuffed with drab used men's clothes, a Budweiser baseball cap, a half-tube of glue and a scruffy beard-and-mustache.

"You don't look half bad," she said after she'd stuck the facial hair on her aunt.

"How?"

"I sorta divined. Lucky I saw the stuff while I was still at school. First time I've ever got anything worthwhile from going to the School of the Performing Tarts."

They made their escape with Clare bent over under a blanket—a groaning sick child being taken to the hospital by her loving sleep-deprived dad.

The paparazzi and "news teams" were on wait, not watch at this hour; but didn't pay the two more than a glance, not even considering the man as someone who might know the woman.

Libby drove to a 24-hour donut place on Carrillo Street, and then to Clare's favorite picnic place. Resting the cups of hot chocolate and coffee on the stones, and dipping into the big paper bag, they sat in the cemetery, taking their time working their way through cinnamon-sugar, jelly-filled, Boston cremes, and Long Johns. They ate and drank to the sound of waves, till their presence had been noted by the seagulls, who got three donuts.

Libby folded up the trash. "Do you want to walk on the beach?"

"Why would I?"

Libby wondered how Clare could bear to be out here so—naked. Clare had left her phone at the apartment, and didn't even act jumpy. She must have left it purposely, a state of being that Libby had never reached, though when Libby thought about what she got from the thing, a new state of sick panic took over her stomach again. Clare said nothing now, seemed oddly self-sufficient. Again, Libby thought it both weird and natural that this child could possibly be her best, probably her only friend.

"Libby," said Clare. "Have you ever been to India?"

"A long time ago. I got very sick."

"That's a no-brainer."

"Hey, young lady. What's all this about?"

"Go to a place like that, and what do you expect?"

"Eat a school lunch and get sick from FDA-approved pink slime, and what can you expect?"

"Okay, okay, I'm sorry. But what happened?"

"I got sick, is all. And it made me think of how we need to do something to stop this kind of thing."

"Oh."

"Good we cleared that up."

"No we didn't. You're harder to open than a giant clam."

Libby flushed. Sometimes it seemed that life was one long series of embarrassments. The doctor—she never did catch his last name, and his first couldn't have been Sandy, but that's how she remembered him—the doctor must have been tortured by his quandary, where to take this foreign visitor to whom he had apologised so profusely for his country having "poisoned" her with its "unsanitaries".

"Our hospital is having a shameful state of unrepair," he said over the poisonous blurts of Libby into the back seat of the car. Libby groaned at the image of some hellish hospital, and the thought of being abandoned there terrified her. "Can't you just take me to your place?" It was either there or dying, she almost didn't care anymore. Her stomach hurt so much that she put herself to sleep, an ability she had always had when she needed to escape.

Whereever the family had set out for on their drive, Libby had never known. She was installed in a high, airy, room darkened by the huge mango tree that hung over the old house and the dense, flower-filled front garden. The walls inside and out reminded Libby of sweated-into shirts. They all had rough, ugly lines of stain where no paint would adhere, but mould and mildew congregated. The smells inside the house were such a mixture of decomposition and flowering, spice and rot, scented talcum powders and powdered sandalwood and incense, ripening fruits, mice, sewers, and warm hot bread. The whole family smelt quite deliciously edible.

He was extremely worried about her diarrhoea, but when she refused to let a stool sample be analysed, he then carefully explained that there were two kinds of this "discomfort, one of which is most serious because the little creatures, parasites that you cannot see but drink your moisture can be the undoing of you. We must keep your insides moisturised."

"Anything, just get me well," Libby said, mumbling "so I can get out of this shithole country." He went out and brought back sachets of rehydrators that tasted vile but looked legitimate, emblazoned with the names of international drug firms. And he prescribed and his wife made, drinks that they begged Libby to take even though she cried into her hard pillow that she couldn't stand the stuff: gingery, peppery salty buttermilk, some weird pulped fruit stirred into boiled water; ground pomegranate rind in milk, something so yuk that she demanded to know what it was. Rice porridge that smelled like Christmas cookies but was essentially, thin, cool hot cereal. Three days later, the doctor asked if she would like him to take her to a hospital.

"God, no."

"Would you like me to take you anywhere else?"

"Home."

She was a sullen patient, silent when she wasn't weeping. She felt gypped by pretty much everyone and everything. Todd had dumped her. Her dad had been right. She had no business going off with the jerk, to some dump of a country where she was probably gonna die, too sick to go off by herself to the American consulate to get help and a ticket home. Not that she knew how to do it anyway. Everything was just too hard.

The family must have bent over backwards for her. She had to be taught how to use the squat toilet correctly so as not to dirty it, and doctor and his wife had been particularly fluttery about their arrangements. "You will be so happy when you again have recourse to your sparkling American commodes."

Everyone in the family, and the two dessicated servants, were always washing, themselves and everything else. Libby could hear the splash of water on floors, rain of water-can on paths and garden. The ambient sound in the air was a mix of birdcalls, crush of people and traffic frighteningly close on the road outside the gate, but close, inside the environs of the humble home, a constant sweep of brooms that looked like movie props for a fantasy. The doctor's wife woke before dawn and set out fresh flowers and food gifts on the little shrines in various places in the house. One morning, Libby padded out to the kitchen and saw her praying to the elephant god. In a corner, a mouse was nibbling on a flower petal. That was when Libby realised how hard it must have been for the woman (Libby never did get her name) to gently explain so many times that Libby should be careful with her food, not to let any lay around.

Libby was getting stronger, almost able to keep food in long enough to properly digest it. One morning she squatted over the toilet and finally felt a civilised movement coming out when her buttock was lightly brushed by a giant rat leaping up and out.

The doctor drove her all the way to the American consulate in Mumbai. He didn't let her out of his sight until the US Marines had opened the gate for her.

She couldn't get away from him fast enough. That last look of his, a smile that showed most of his big white teeth.

The consulate had seen too many dumped teen-age girls who were also disgustingly sick to be anything but coldly efficient, not bothering to veil their disgust. A reassuringly American member of the staff got hold of her dad and advised him how to send money for Libby's ticket home. Somehow, that added another dimension to the experience. "You come from Las Vegas?" the staff member asked, though he already knew. Then he copped such a clever and fast feel that she knew it was a game of his, one that he couldn't lose. She was fixed up with enough Lomatils ("They won't cure you, but will make it easier to get home. We advise you not to eat anything but bread or rice and to drink lots the water on the plane, and wear sanitary napkins. And definitely, no alcohol!") to stop up a diarrheic horse before being got rid of on a nightmare of a flight back to the States. But the nightmare continued when she landed. American hospitalisation-admittance, a bout of hospital "care", and then "treatment". She never did know if she got well finally, from exasperation.

She went back to college, not aimlessly but with a passion. She felt possessed—both better and worse than boy-fever, she had never guessed how emotionally draining science would be. Her highs and lows she kept to herself, but it came out in fidgeting at school and work; and when she got home, dancing till she dropped.

The doctor began to appear in her dreams, begging her to forgive his country, himself. One night she woke up, her pillow soaked with tears. She'd seen his smile again, was just as furious as when she'd fled from it, but this time she looked upwards from his lips, and she saw his eyes, his broken eyebrows.

That face, the lying mouth, the truthful eyes and brows—it was the same as that of a student from India who was attending the same lecture she was. He had asked a question, one that she had wanted to ask but hadn't had the gumption to. "I just explained that," said the professor, "but maybe you don't understand English."

A few titters could be heard, and the eyes of the room were on the student. He broke into a smile was almost as wide as the doctor's. Libby felt like yelling at the professor, but didn't do anything. Instead, this smile of the student's made her spine crawl. The lying mouth, the honest eyes: pure shame. Not shame that she had felt in her life, but a shame on behalf of someone else, someone who needs it but is lacking. A shame that should make the other person suffer agonies of embarrassment, but it's not meant that way, anyway. It's a smile of almost Christian charity—*I'm dying for your boorishness*—without the superiority. The professor was smiling too, perhaps in relief. He'd certainly avoided answering a tough question.

But the doctor's smile had an added dimension, Libby saw in the aftermath of her dream. Fear.

The doctor. She didn't even know his name. She hadn't even asked for his address, let alone his telephone number.

Sometimes she wished that she had been able to tell Bini, but she couldn't. How could he be found again. Even if he could be, what if he was dead? What if he had died—of shame?

Ah, well. Strange how things work out. India—the whole country—had become a place of blanked-out thought to Libby, till Bini contacted her because of that "unscientific" paper that Libby had written. Libby and Bini had joked in emails that Bini had Indian foresight that she applied every morning with her finger. Bini had offered to send Libby a pot of instant foresight. Bini was, in fact, so understanding about so many things.

"You're such a great sigher," said Clare.

Dawn had broken. They walked hand in hand to the car. The traffic was almost nonexistent this early Saturday morning, but Libby's street was now parked out with cars and vans. She could only find a spot two blocks away. They entered the building as unnoticed as they had left.

"Back to work," said Clare, as if they were co-workers and this a normal day.

They searched on Libby's laptop. *The Hindu* ran an interview in which the journalist praised Dr Bhattacharya for her nationalism, only to be lectured at about nationalism, a sentiment that she called "the diversion of a government that sits on its nitamb".

"See?" said Clare. "If it hadn't been for you, I would never had learned a new word for ass. But shit, look at this!"

India was now the top story in all media, with new stories coming in by the second. Twitter was a cacophony. The place was indeed exploding. Literally millions had taken to the streets in spontaneous demonstrations. Night must had fallen there, and the sky was alight with not just lights of many colors, but exploding fireworks. They showered millions and boomed like armies of joy—set off by civil servants, fathers, mothers, children. Libby thought it must be just like that festival she had wanted to see, but hadn't been able to stay for, way back when. And everywhere there was dancing.

Someone buzzed the apartment, yet again. "Aunt Lib," whined Clare, who had jumped up, only to be grabbed by the ankle.

"They can all wait."

"Coward." Clare pulled what she though of as an ugly face. "But no shit. I'll scream if you don't look through your messages."

There were hundreds of them, but in the midst, there were five from Bini, each more worried than the last, but in Bini's inimitably gentle way, not showing it. The last one read, "Dear child, I know you must be so busy with interviews to contact me, but let me again congratulate you on your brilliant win. We would not have achieved anything without your wonderful intelligence and creativity. And without you getting sick in the first place! Please don't let your sensitive soul get the better of you at this important time. Remember that what counts is not what the crowd says about you, but your own sense of worth that only you can weigh. your loving Bini"

Clare was busy on her own iphone. "Cool! Wanna see this story on Fox? It's titled Nobel Disgrace: The Anti-American and the Lab Dancer."

Libby laid down her phone and blew her nose.

"It's too stupid," said Clare, "but heh. Oh you've *got* to see this."

"Not another YouTube."

"Not just here. It's from some science place, but like . . . it's everywhere!"

Under a banner that said "Daughters of Lilavati" about two dozen women stood together on a stage. The streaming subtitle said Scientists Scientists Scientists. Most wore saris or salwar kameez, but some were in western dress. They bowed solemnly, then broke their line—into dance—smiling like mischievous starlets, moving like houris. They were colourful as a garden, and in their dipping twirling dance they waved beakers, petrie dishes, goggles, rubber gloves, kidney dishes and bladders. They used lab coats like veils and scarves, and threw themselves around with joy and in such close cooperation, the riot was carefully calibrated abandon. Suddenly, in the midst of them, Dr Kadambini Bhattacharya burst through, in a gold-bordered pomegranate-red sari. She moved her stuff like an overripe Bollywood star.

Libby's eyes were already flooded, but then Bini and the troupe broke into what the subtitle streamed—*The Purfouy Boom Boom*.

AUTHOR'S NOTE: *This story was written before seventeen-year-old Malala Yousafzai (a Pakistani) and Kailash Satyarthi (an Indian) were jointly awarded the 2014 Nobel Peace Prize. The inclusion of Kailash Satyarthi was widely seen as a peace message from the Nobel committee, to India and Pakistan. He is one of many people and agencies in India working in the field of Indian children's rights. He remained so unknown even after the gala ceremony in Oslo, that a few days later, lawmakers in the Assembly of his home state of Madhya Pradesh heaped plaudits for the win on industry minister Kailash Vijayavarghiya, citing "his humanitarian work". As NDTV reported, "The minister was not fazed or embarrassed at the case of mistaken identity. He explained that the confusion was caused by the fact that he is more well known in the state than the Nobel laureate."*

Strange Incidents in Foreign Parts

It was the year that Roald Amundsen, "last of the Vikings", successfully navigated the Northwest passage; the year that Huckleberry Finn and Tom Sawyer were banned from the Brooklyn Public Library; that millions of hearts beat time to "Wait till the sun shines, Nellie" and "How'd you like to spoon with me." The year that Greta Garbo was born and Jules Verne died. The year that Frank Branston, son of Violet and Cuthbert Branston, was a ten-year-old boy who lived at 87 Mulberry Street, Fentonville, Illinois, in the land of candy corn—and at that moment it was five minutes past six o'clock Halloween suppertime, and he had just laid down his fork. In his impatience to trick-or-treat, a part of him stuck out its lip and shut its mouth hard, refusing to let him eat the clod of rutabaga on his plate. And though he felt a satisfaction that made his earlobes glow, he also wanted to box that bad part of him's ears. Why hadn't it waited for *tomorrow's* rutabaga clod?

"Franklin's got bellyache if anyone asks," Violet Branston ("the flower of Fentonville") declared. Cuthbert was in the doghouse for forgetting to fix the porch step till it broke. His son looked hopelessly to him for the indignation someone needed in this house, someone besides Frank's mother, who ran on enough het-upness to run a riverboat to the moon. Frank's father, the ex-sailor, now seller of sensible shoes, sat looking at nothing, like a dead catfish. Frank's father avoided his son's eyes, but couldn't avoid his wife's.

Compliant Cuthbert (who was once called 'Cutlass', and who'd always hated rutabaga, but never in front of his wife) marched son up to son's room, where father wordlessly left the stoic, heartbroken boy, who threw himself on his bed. But moments later Cuthbert returned, finger on lips, and handed Frank a book, "Parvel's Adventures and Voyages in Strange Countries and Foreign Parts, with Many Incidents & Curious Beliefs". Like the other two surprise books Cuthbert had given Frank, this was all about places marvellous and far from Fentonville, and it was a secret between them, to be stored, hidden in a place that Cuthbert had secretly and expertly constructed in the boy's bed. With a pat on Frank's head, Cuthbert left, closing the door. Frank hid the book. Moments later, Violet Branston flung open the door to see her boy kneeling praying by his bed. Not sure she was happy, she shut the door and turned the key with a click whose smoothness was positively self-satisfied.

Of all the what-for, caster-oiled, last-judgement hell's-high-water punishments she could have conjured up—and Frank was convinced she spent most of her time conjuring—this ruination of his Halloween took the blue ribbon.

"I hope your chin grows rat hair! That your hands grow tails!" Frank cursed under his bedcovers, and he added a few choice ones for that mountain that would wait till he ate it or Kingdom Come. Though he was no high-pants boy, and his hair wouldn't take a licking and stuck out around his head anyways, he cried on his bed like a baby—a baby just old enough to cry without disturbing.

Eventually, he went and stood by his window, watching the children come. He heard their knock, the *trick-or-treat!* and then he watched them walk away. He heard them mutter, and then clatters like hailstones. By tomorrow, those clattering things would be all over the street, and people would step on them unawares, they'd crunch underfoot with a frightening *crack*. And if it was a grownup who done it, why he'd step away smartly, worried it was old Mr. Farley's glass eye.

His mother's homemade treat, again this year, was the trick in trick-or-treat. Horehound drops. Made with lots and *lots* of horehound.

OF COURSE THE beggarly trick-or-treat, the unhealthy feast of Halloween offended Violet Branston's sensibilities, but when Frank was five, Cuthbert argued cleverly to let their son do what every other Fentonville child did on that one night. "What would the Hammersmiths say, pet? Violet thinks Fentonville's not good enough for her son? Violet's worried Alma cooks poisoned treats?"

The Hammersmiths ran the town's social calendar, Alma Hammersmith prided herself on her sarsaparilla divinity, and Violet Branston would die if she were excluded from Alma's annual strawberry social.

So for five years, Frank Branston had trick-or-treated, and he looked forward to Halloween with the keen anticipation of a boy whose mother believed in food that provides regularity. Not even the Little Lord Fauntleroy costume Mrs. Branston made for him put saltpetre on his tail.

All that mattered to Frank was the trick-or-treat. Mrs. Brenner's popcorn balls, the Cooper family's rainbow-striped salt water taffy; fat licorice sticks stamped with initials fancy as some riverboat gambler's stickpin; corn kernels that tasted like corn *should*; humbugs that would break your teeth if you didn't suck them slow; candy apples that stabbed your tongue with cinnamon; exotic salted almonds from the Goldsteins; and best of all, a great big bar of Giegerhopf chocolate, wrapped in silver foil.

Frank made those treats last as long as he could, which being a boy, and one who couldn't take chances, meant one gorgeacious night. Come dawn, even the last humbug was only a memory.

Now memory was all he had to suck on, as suddenly, the Revelation came upon him like one of Reverend Woodley's lightning bolts. *Next* year, Franklin Branston would hand out candy—the shameful horehound drops. Trick-or-treat for him was dead forever. There was nothing ahead for him in life.

Then he remembered the book, which on any other night, he would have been gorging on. He un-secreted it and took it to the window, where he could stand and read in the new streetlamp's light. He opened randomly—a private superstition.

Tonight he learned about the Hindoos and their wheel of life. How if you're good, you won't die and go to no Temperance Meeting heaven, but get whirled around by the wheel and flung out as someone else. It reminded him of what his father told him about the roulette wheel on the riverboat. As a Hindoo, his honesty would be valued about that abomination on his plate. And as his reward, he would be turned into someone good. He thought of his father, and knew this was a message from him. Would they meet? If only his father hadn't hurt his back . . . Together they'd sail . . . But wait! There was a hook attached to this wonderful future, just like in everything. He'd have to die! What dang use was that?

He put the book away, but . . . "Please," he said, looking towards his bed, and he bowed to it and uttered a gibberish prayer that he made up on the spot, *please fling me back as a pirate.* In the meantime, his feet were icicles. They hurt so bad they felt good, the misery of his body keeping company with his mind.

Eventually, all the other children were safe in their beds, eating. The street light now lit up the late-night life. Frank watched a cat play with a horehound drop. He heard the *clink.* And then another cat appeared and challenged the first. And then a raggedy tom swaggered in, and there was a no-sidelines, all-in-for-everything banshee-wailing all-out-brawl, and it was just wonderful; and then at the sound of a window opening, all the cats skedaddled. Frank was too cold to move, though he was just looking now at an empty street. Then all of a sudden, he felt sore inside. Sore as a woke-up bear. So sore at all those cats having their freedom, no one telling *them* what to do. Frank felt so sad and sore at everything but especially at those cats, that all he wanted to do was go out and get him one of those cats, and . . .

He opened his window when he should have been sound asleep dreaming nightmares at his refusal to eat God's food. He climbed up and knelt on the windowsill and leaned out and grabbed the branch of the mulberry tree. Wrapping his fingers around its comforting limb, he swung away from his window, but his right foot caught and unbalanced him, and he lost his grip, and fell away from both branch and window, onto a piece of broken copper gutter Cuthbert Branston had forgotten to fix, a very sharp piece.

Of course Frank died. But since he'd never believed in any hell worse than he already knew, and was, as his mother never ceased to remind him, no Christian, he died as he believed most recently—as a Hindoo. And since he'd been a bad boy (not about the rutabaga mash—heavens no—but about wanting to harm creatures), the wheel of life spun him round and flung him out as an nascent fruit of the exotic East—a baby eggplant in Trinkamalee, Ceylon.

THAT WAS THE first of a long line of eggplants. They don't have much scope for change in the hierarchy of the living, being such passive players. So that eggplant suffered a typical eggplant life. Death at the prime of life, by pickling-suffocation. The next eggplant ended life as a torture of slow drying. The next, born in the cool hills above Isfahar, was licked to death by flames. Then there was . . . oh, you're probably not interested in the details, other than the fact that each eggplant born from the death of the last was flung out into a different Foreign Part, another someplace exotic, though every place is exotic to someplace else. They saw the world, this line of eggplants, but what can an eggplant do about it? And so they were flung out as other eggplants.

AND SO IT went, eggplant unto eggplant, till we get to the latest eggplant incarnation. This one we find sitting amongst a pile of eggplants at a Sydney harbourside-neighbourhood fruiterer's. It had no distinguishing marks. Just a general shine of health and a hefty weight, and it was bought.

Late that afternoon, the woman who chose the eggplant picked it out of her shopping bag in the kitchen of her waterfront home. As she touched her chef's knife, her mouth prickled with anticipated taste—a recipe she planned to test. She drew the blade across the taut flesh. The purple skin resisted—went *squuuueeek*, but when the wound was still only a surface gash, she suddenly remembered. It was her *a cappela* performance night. There had been a change of date. She washed the knife and dried and oiled it, and put the eggplant, slashed-side down, into a wooden tray along with a dozen flame-orange tamarillos and six long-stemmed artichokes. She took out a frozen container of aioli, a loaf of crusty filoncini, and a container of calamari stuffed with eggplant caponata and gorgonzola cheese, all homemade. She wrote a note for Ned, their son. "Singing tonight. Dinner's on the counter. Barfi in the sweet tin for puds." She felt a tiny twinge at his disappointment last night.

Earlier in the week, she and Quentin had forbidden their son to attend last night's inaugural Halloween party at Ned's school. Quentin had said no by proxy, being tied up with a case in Goulburn, so the No had caused her to get all the bad vibes. "It's not Australian," Geoff had said immediately, *exactly what she had said*, and he almost had a cat on the phone when Kath had added, "He wants to go as Spiderman."

"He can go with his head in a bucket, or not at all," Quentin barked. Quentin Kelly's most brilliant professional (and private) move had been to name their child after an outlaw. His chambers had edge, it got him a swag of front-page clients, and gave him, above all, panache—the larrikin who pissed on the system. But he knew, *go as Ned Kelly or not at all* meant that Ned wouldn't go. Game, match, and set. Kath felt as viscerally against the school's imposition of yet another capitalist cultural-imperialist import as her husband, but it was harder on her, as she had to face-to-face.

"What's so Australian about that stuff you sing, your agurella or whatever those shithouse weeds are. Your *stinkyfeet* cheeses! Your quack dong fish sauce fad. Your *Tuscany* food trip!" Ned sneered, and he picked up the pashmina draped over the sofa, and held it up. "This," he announced, "in *Australian*, is only a nanna's shawl!"

Last night, "Halloween" evening—when the school's party was being held and Ned and his mother were stuck at home together because Kath's personal trainer had cancelled at the last moment, Kath thought about the boy. She'd once thought that a child would be a confirmation. As mother and son avoided each other, Kath tried to remember, confirmation of what?

So when Ned came home today, he slammed the door. Everyone at school had talked about the fun they'd had last night, and he couldn't get their fun out of his head. He saw his mother's note. She wouldn't come home till midnight, earliest.

He checked out the vegetable tray. He picked it up and took it to their jetty on the waterfront.

First, the artichokes, he planted between the open slats. With an oar, he whacked their heads off one by one. The tamarillos, he stomped on. The decking looked like a bloodbath when he'd finished. Then he picked up the eggplant and shoved it into his shirt. The eggplant was *the* worst of all his mother's revolting vegetables and disgusting fishy things. And now she was in the eggplant section of her recipe-testing for her next book. Just remembering the smell of that last test, reeking of silver-polish stink of cooking eggplant, made him want to chunder.

He threw the oars into the rowboat tied to the jetty and jumped in, his belly tight with the protruding fruit.

It was a warm summer night, and he rowed strongly with a ten-year old boy's anger. He rounded the bend and set out for the open waves, choppy with blustery wind. He rowed till he was tired, and settled his oars. The eggplant, he pulled from his shirt. He held it as if it were a footy ball, and then he stood in the boat, and smashed the eggplant as hard as he could, at the sea.

The eggplant's buoyancy and the strength of the wind made the sea's surface hard as a calloused hand. That hand grabbed the eggplant and tossed it back, hard, right at Ned's stomach. He lost his balance and fell out of the boat, gulping for air and swallowing sea. As he grabbed for the boat's side, sharp clinker edges cut into his knees, as the rowboat bucked against him. By the time he flopped back in, he was holding back tears. The eggplant floated *wongk wongk* against the seat. He picked the thing up and sat down. It's knife-cut had split open, showing the bruised pale flesh as a large bloodless gash. Somehow, his tears began to flow. His fingers gripped the eggplant, fingertips into the gash. He had never actually touched an eggplant before. It was firm as his own thigh, warm as his own flesh, cool on the outside, warm underneath . . .

As night fell and the ferries in the distance turned into black caterpillars on golden legs, he turned practically invisible, a boy in the dark, bent over an eggplant, holding it like a like a hurt pet. The wind died and the boat bobbed gently now as he cried over the eggplant, and talked to it as to a friend.

And thus the eggplant, *that* eggplant that had been fated, it had thought, to live a passive life—that eggplant that had never *felt* like an eggplant, nor ever wanted to feel the way an eggplant *should*— that eggplant and that boy Ned met. And the boy Ned rowed back safely and ate the dinner his mother had prepared, and he ate it alone—that is, *alone* in the yesterday meaning of the word. And afterwards, alone he buried the eggplant in the back garden under a heavy stone, in a private ceremony.

And when the eggplant died there, as it soon did, calmly and without pain, the wheel spun round and flung out a baby boy, into someplace exotic.

Marks and Coconuts

"I wish to buy a dead parrot."

The pet store owner rubbed his St Christopher. The first customer of the day always made him superstitious, and this guy's suit, watch, and smell reeked money.

"Yes, sir! Any particular type?"

The customer considered. "No."

Joe Lansby hooded his sometimes too honest eyes, and walked to the window display. "You deserve something special," he called, to no response.

Joe shrugged and carried the cage to the counter. "It's just off the boat, if you know what I mean. An Election Parrot from Australia. Still a bit jetlagged, but it'll sing opera in a week, if that's your thing. Or maybe Shakespeare?"

The customer looked at the bird, and back at Joe. "Did you hear my request?"

"You wanna parrot. Or maybe a croc?" Joe pointed to the tank with the alligator.

"I said 'I wish to buy a dead parrot.' "

Joe shot his cuffs, forgetting that he was wearing a sweatshirt emblazoned with *Apsk to Psee our Psittacines*. "Between us, sir," he said, "You look like a diplomat, and this bird is a diplomat. You can tell it anything, it won't leak."

The customer didn't even smile.

Mentally, Joe shoved a wad of chewed Bazooka up this jerk of a tightass. He was getting annoyed. "You want something cheap? They don't really suit—"

"Perhaps you didn't understand. I. Wan-na. Dead. Parrot."

"Dead?" Joe grabbed his St Christopher. "You from the Health Department? Sorry." He banged open the till.

The customer slapped the counter, startling the parrot, who let out a sound like a smoke alarm. "Have you heard nothing, even when I translated? I wish to buy a dead parrot. Have you one, or not?"

"Mother fuggity," Joe muttered. He was sure that later today he'd step on a crack or walk under a ladder. "Mister, you wish to find yourself a taxidermatist. Or a shrink."

He pulled the current *Fortune* out from under the counter, opened it beside the parrot's cage and gave it all his attention.

The customer walked around the store, Joe's eyes shadowing him. This whacko made his skin crawl with superstition, but maybe the customer wasn't a nutcase and was just another con artist. Joe thought of a mantra that he had chanted to himself in former times while wincing at the bill for clothing himself at Brooks Bros: "Clothes make the thief."

The customer stopped at every parrot's cage, and there were many. Joe's uncle Theodore had built up a fine reputation in smuggled psittacines. From Cape York, there was that dull-eyed but brilliantly red and blue *Eclectus roratus*. In the largest cage, a tall black *Probosciger aterrimus* regarded everyone as a prime minister does, back benchers. With that beak, it looked like it took its Scotch neat and wasn't picky over blend. There were parrots from Patagonia, Madagascar, a swathe of tropic islands, the Congo and the Cameroons, Zanzibar, and even from Theodore Lansby's apartment, because Joe's uncle was presently in the state that the current customer had expressed his wish for, in a parrot.

That Joe's uncle had dropped dead at exactly the best time for a relative to do that in Joe's life, was an act of providence that strengthened Joe's faith in Luck coming at the right time if he kept wary of things like ladders and cracks, and kept in touch with his St Christopher. On the day that Joe shredded his last Leap business card, formally winding up a very special hedge fund that unaccountably failed, whomp! Uncle Theo dropped dead.

Joe was a great believer in Cause and Effect, and this fortuitous death just strengthened his belief. He had always regarded himself as a great Cause, and so, it seemed, had Uncle T.

Theodore Lansby had indeed thought highly of his nephew back when Joe was Little Joe. But in the years that followed, bad times hit Joe time and again. Theo had secretly made his Will out to Joe, in case the boy was brought down yet again by life's unfairness to the true creative-business artist. If Uncle Theo had known that Joe had managed to secrete a cash-for-emergency-bribes stash of considerable worth, he would only have admired him more.

And so, the day the pet store came into Joe's hands, Uncle Theo smiled from wherever and chided himself harshly over his disappointment that Joe couldn't tell a Hyacinth Macaw (*Anodorhynchus hyacinthinus*) from a South Island Kaka (*Nestor meridionalis meridionalis*), nor give a shit about his ignorance.

To Joe, the birds and all the rest of the smelly stock were goods, the customers marks, and the fact that prospective marks who preferred talking in taxonomic names expected to pay sky-high prices, wasn't worth the work, as far as Joe figured. Joe was not only used to turnover in goods and schemes, but in customers. By 4:00 on the first day of Joe's tenure as new owner, Theo surveyed Lansby's Pets from the place that he could do nothing, and his nose prickled at the foreboding air. He reminded himself that Joe's preferred stock had always been intangibles that cost Joe nothing, never needed care and feeding, and didn't shit on anyone except the customers, safely after purchase. Wadya expect? a voice said to Theo, as he watched Joe yell "Shut your faces" to the chatting stock.

Theo was feeling the ropes then himself, new to everlastingness, and he couldn't tell if that voice saying Wadya expect was his or from someone else.

"Wanna play canasta?" said a lady with clacking dentures. Instantly, Lansby's Pets evaporated, and he wiped his brow. Canasta? Not only that. This was nothing less than an infinity of widows and Florida in eternal August.

T HAT EPISODE WAS not only two weeks ago, but in the Hereafter. And time is money, so Now:

In the store, the customer had spent the past five minutes peering into cages. He stopped in front of a smallish wire tower housing a pair of smooching *Nymphicus hollandicus*es. He bent his neck so that his head paralled the cage floor. They bent their necks, too, and the lower two of their eyes looked at the cage-floor covering, while the upper two eyeballed him.

"Hey, mister," said Joe. "Vamoose. Go lose yourself on the sidewalk with the looneys. Dead parrot. anyway! What made you come in here for one?"

The customer straightened and smoothed his tie. "Why wouldn't I?"

"From Lansby's Pets?" Joe lifted a forefinger. "Lemme guess. Because you're short of a washing machine. Or maybe want a ticket to Timbuktu." That amused Joe. "Fly Dead Parrot Airlines. Hey—"

"Considering," cut in the customer, "that you and your guests here in this happy hostelry devote all of your reading time to business journals, I would think that you, of all pet shop owners, would not only understand but leap to satisfy a wish to purchase a dead parrot. I hand you an untapped niche market, and what do you do?"

Joe hung his head. There was something to this guy, not to mention the old truth, "The customer is always right." The door jangled and a rush of cold air hit Joe. The customer had almost flown the coop.

Joe flung open the door of the *Eclectus roratus* (the jetlagged parrot on the counter) (to its delight), grabbed a peanut (to its surprise) and with his other hand, stuffed a stray feather down its open mouth. All this took 0.348 of a moment, all of which was paralleled by the customer's left calf muscle contracting as his foot left the—

"Sir," huffed Joe, grabbing the door. "I think we have just what you are looking for."

The customer, known to his local shopkeepers in a more formal clime, as Mr Tershire, turned. If he had worn a monocle it would have flashed, if he had let it. But he wasn't that kind of guy. A muscle might have pulsed in his big square jaw, if he were another. His pupils might have contracted, but he considered that also, vulgarly demonstrative.

"My time is valuable," he said mildly.

"So is mine!" said Joe indignantly. That was his best line, and it bugged him that this . . . this—mark—yes! had stolen it. "He won't leave Lansby's Pets," Joe vowed silently, "without buying something for at least $19.99, not on markdown."

"We can't be too careful," he said, another line he loved. It had worked so well to sell high-yield short-term-futures at the Preventative Care Practitioners Convention in Cleveland only five years ago.

Joe led his customer to the counter where the cheated parrot looked out from behind the bars with a look that wasn't perky. "Take this parrot," said Joe.

"This parrot isn't dead," said the customer. "She isn't even contemplating suicide."

Joe waggled his finger at the man. "This is a do-it-yourself dead parrot."

"Oh!" said the customer.

"Oh yeah," Joe guffawed. Suddenly, he felt on top of his game. This was the first time he'd had fun in this hellhole of boredom.

"How much is she?" asked the customer. "I don't see a price tag."

"Of course not. Who dangles price tags on companions?"

The customer nodded slowly with his eyes closed, like a cockatoo listening to Chopin. "Yeah," he drawled badly. "So how much dya want for this here DIY?"

Joe rocked back on his heels. "Well," he said. This weirdo foreigner flustered him. A bird in the hand, but a flighty one. Close the deal! "Seven K, and I'll throw the cage in free."

"How do you calculate that?" (no fake accent) "What is the cage worth?"

"Five K for the bird," Joe said, his voice loud in his ears. "Three seventy-five off for this beautiful cage. Only two K for the optional extra."

"What optional extra?"

"The DIY."

"Only two thousand?" Joe's mark dropped into a crouch. From somewhere, the sound of what Joe thought was an adult Galloping Iguana but was really an Australian goanna, specifically, a young *Varanus giganteus*'s slithering erupted.

"That animal needs its nails clipped," said the, uh—"Defend yourself, man!"

Somehow, the facts have eluded mentioning till now, that: 1) the customer, mark, uh—Mr Tershire, ran marathons for relaxation and was the only entrant of any nationality in Unbeatable Banzuke ("where the only constant is the bitter taste of defeat") ever to complete the impossible Handstand Pogostick Hop #3 course; and 2) Lansby's Pets was 20 steps from Nazir's Hot Dog & Pretzel stand, Now with Chocolate Chip Baklava; and 3) Joe Lansby's greatest weapon and his greatest enemy, was his mouth.

"Please, mister," begged Joe, grabbing the biggest thing he could find to fend off this crazy person. Joe wondered if this guy was from the UN or had some other diplomatic immunity.

Joe imagined himself being murdered and Mister Muscles here moseying out of any conviction, probably flying back to London with a dead parrot, obtained for free. It gave him reflux just thinking about it. "Just my luck," he said, brandishing the cuttlefish bone.

Tershire snatched it from him and instead of throwing the $5.95 On Special This Week Only item to the floor where it would have shattered, placed it carefully in its basket.

"You're not as stupid as you act," he said. "I've got a business proposition."

"Oh, yeah," said Joe. But he was interested. The customer not only reeked money, but had a confidence that had not been undermined by cruel fate. This guy had gotten rich, somehow.

"You don't know anything about birds, do you?" asked the rich guy.

Joe's mouth grinned idiotically, the traitor.

"Nor animals . . . No, I didn't think so. It's a wonder they're alive."

"I take good care of them!"

"Yeah."

"Hey, mister. You want me to sic Big Beak over there on you?" Joe pointed to the parrot he thought was a Coconut Cockatoo (the Prime Minister), a bird he had wished sold or dead as soon as he took over the shop. That beak could snip out car bodies, and no way was he gonna clean its cage, let alone give it fresh fruit. As a matter of fact, the monster scared him so much that he couldn't sell it because, as he'd learned to his dismay, you can't sell a parrot to a customer unless you are willing to take the parrot out of its cage.

Tershire strolled over to it. "This *Probosciger aterrimus*? You are this bird's benefactor of . . . what is this? A hot dog bun crust poked in from the top? That, sir, is not the way to make a friend, unless, of course, the parrot's mother fed it thus."

He pulled out his impeccably folded pocket square, opened it and then the cage door, and proffered the parrot a macaroon. The cookie was taken tenderly. Tershire turned his back before the bird launched into a speech.

Joe looked at his watch. 11:30, and no sale on the horizon. "You wanna talk business. Shoot."

"To the point," said Tershire. "You want to be successful, as your reading shows. It is obvious that this establishment was created by someone else and that you are merely owning it, frustrated by your position as owner, yet yearning for greater opportunities, at which time you fully expect to seize the opportunities with both hands, and make a killing."

Joe gaped, gripping his St Christopher in a stranglehold.

"You know what a niche market is," continued Tershire, strolling over, striking a match against the counter, and lighting up a fragrant cigar against 27 assorted borough, city, and state regulations. It smelt wonderfully of warm peat fires, pineapples, and a hint of suntan oil.

The *Eclectus* breathed in deeply. Tershire opened the cage door, and the parrot, a greatly imaginative bird, fell headily in love. She climbed to his shoulder and gently chewed his ear.

"It's touched you, you buy it," snapped Joe.

"Shut up," said Tershire.

"Sorry."

"Accepted," said Tershire, massaging the parrot's skin under an uplifted wing. "As you know, you have this pet shop, yet it's just a pet shop. People come in looking for something they expect and you expect them to expect. You either have it or you're fresh out of it. Boring as washing dishes."

Joe's eyes moistened. "Gosh."

"Yet you look at that magazine, and what do you see? Successful people with new ideas."

"They get all the luck," Joe whined.

"Shut up!" Tershire barked.

"Hey," snarled Joe, "I don't like your tone."

The Prime Minister walked out of his cage, menacingly.

Joe gulped.

"And before I start," said Tershire. "I'm leaving now if you're going to kick up a fuss about investing that money you've got stashed away."

THEY SUBLET THE premises and moved to an area where big money roamed the sidewalks, hunting, opening up, in an ex-bookstore with the personality of a warehouse: Marks' Exclusives.

In that arid wasteland, they made an adventure jungle. Parrots filled the air with whistles and screeches, pirated songs, light opera, and snatches of oratory. Sleek and portly goannas floorwalked silently, only rising on their tails to look without comment or display into the eyes of bargain shoppers and other bogus clientele, never making a crass or flashy move, and never accosting you with perfume atomisers.

In Marks' Exclusives, you'd never find bargains. You'd never see price tags. *Ask for anything*, was Marks' in-the-know slogan. They wouldn't have it, but they would sell you something *Just for You.*

Joe thinks of those days as his happiest yet, and hopes there will be others. He had his teeth freshly capped for that picture on the cover of *Fortune.*

But Fortune doesn't last forever. That 92-year-old woman who came in looking for Age-fighting MegaMiracle Mushroom Skin Serum and left, having purchased a five-year torrid affair with a chiropodist, with all the trimmings, was the undoing of Marks' Exclusives.

That woman, Mrs. Alberquist, talked, and talked . . . and yesterday Joseph Francis Lansby was arrested for selling futures with unlicensed chiropodists.

To be fair to Luck and forgiving to St Christopher, Joe had it coming. Tershire saw good in Joe, but it was all potential. "Just for You," was what Tershire taught Joe, or rather, thought he taught. That was the oldest line in Joe's markbook. The reason Tershire oozed class was that he truly believed in exclusivity. "Just for You" meant something to him, and wasn't a variation of "It's you. You'll see after it stretches."

Another difference between the partners was Tershire's cynicism versus Joe's belief. Customers need leadership, according to Tershire.

But Joe actually believed somewhere in his best parts, when it suited him: "The customer is always right."

So when Mrs. Alberquist's three bridge partners came into Marks', fresh from her funeral, Joe could not put their demands off, though supply and demand made this a tough nut to crack.

MR WOOLSLEY, AS he is now known to his shopkeepers, is at this moment choosing a coconut, under expert advice.

"I love you," says one advisor, tonguing his ear.

"A little too green," the tall dark one says stertorously.

The Walking-stick Forest

It started like this. When the blackthorn trees were bare, Athol Farquar would pollard them—sawing them down to their gubbins, pruning them almost to the ground, just low enough so that, once the raw winter passed, a great number of new branches would shoot up quick, in a vertical panic of desperation while the sap ran strong. Come spring, there Athol would be in the thicket that was the forest, tying up (with soft woollen twist) the short young fresh-fleshed pinkies to the rods, and from that moment on they could push up all they liked, but every movement was caught and bent to measure.

Every day Athol would come, his woollen bonds stuffed in a pocket of a vest he'd made from his ancient khaki jacket; a girdle of wires loosely wrapped around his waist, and ready in his left fist, an ingenious set of grips he'd forged to shape the discipliners themselves, be they wire, iron, or his sculptured cages of beaten tin. Often he was bare-chested, his hands and arms hardened from years of smithing, so the thorns that could kill with a scratch were nothing to fear. Or maybe they were, but he didn't pay them any more heed than he did the feisty rapier-sharp branch tips everywhere that he hadn't pruned, which could have flicked his cheeks or eyes open. It was almost as if he enchanted the blackthorn. Thorns were his caressers. Branches bent to his will. And he loved bringing up his creations so much that many a moonlit night he spent bending, moulding, tending, admiring and listening, hearing and smelling the night breath of the forest.

The fact is, the pure air suited him. The sloes that the unpruned branches grew, purple and sour as a preacher's face, suited him too; so every autumn, after the first frost, he'd fill a few sheepskins with the firm fresh plums and eat his fill before their skins lost their face-powder bloom. He macerated the rest of his pickings patiently till his sloe gin was devilishly smooth. He'd start his day with a drop of it in his mug of tarry tea, drunk surrounded by his forest.

The young trunks couldn't help but grow, yet every day their own wills were subjugated more, till they were no longer something you'd think should have thorns and leaves but something leaping, roaring, splashing, slithering, dancing, moaning. Nothing so mundane as a tree, let alone a many-trunked bush. When a blackthorn walking-stick-to-be grew to this stage in life, he cut it. Farquar did almost no finishing after that. Even his seasoning and colouring was done without what he considered cosmetic abhorrences—painting, staining, shellacking, gluing pieces on. The only additions he ever made were: to the tip, he fitted a metal cap, robust but finely made as any goldsmith's ring; and occasionally—to finish snakes, women, that sort of thing—he would inset eyes he made of the whisky-coloured cairngorm stone that only he knew underlaid the walking-stick forest.

Yet for all his ability to propagate treasures more unique than a Fabergé egg (which any master goldsmith can duplicate) he wasn't vain about his gift, but moved, and ever more secretive. On some nights, bent over the blackthorn, his chest hurt like that of a lover's, as he felt something from the forest that he could never explain. Trust? On a fateful day in the hell of 1915, he'd seen a chair made of contorted tree limbs; and in the ruins of a church found a pearl shaped like a sheep, and a shard of an ivory saint, its halo still proud. From them grew his plans to make walking sticks that looked alive, if he survived. He had prodigious skill and ingenuity, but had set out with modest aims, little imagining how the forest that he loved and protected bristled with life in ways he could never fathom. Take two of his masterpieces: a man petting a dog, and two playful lovers. Natural development? Bah! There was something preternatural going on. The blackthorn that grew at his guidance into such impossibilities trembled at his touch like a filly eager to be bridled.

Athol Farquar called no man master, and certainly didn't bow to any god. He made his quietly famous sticks to order—never setting his discipliners on a shoot he didn't know the future master of, and the shape this little innocent would grow up to be. He demanded to be paid first, and what he charged was so outrageous, he was heavily sought after. But he would only accept a client and an order if they met his unpredictable criteria. He made his considerable fortune on a few men and women who had everything, so they couldn't get enough of his sticks.

These were collectors such as Mr. L———, who'd made his boodle in khaki dyes. His baronic front hall bristled with walking sticks, whangees, pikestaffs, shoot sticks that folded out into stools; tippling and sword canes; and though his taste ran to music hall, an opera cane whose head glittered with diamonds.

He was particularly proud of two vicious knot-ended clubs, "A shillelagh and knopkierie," he was fond of explaining. "See this shillelagh with its head, like an Irishman's, filled with lead? The effect of this, like its simple African cousin here: Indistinguishable! Tap a man's head and you can scoop his brains out with a spoon."

His ballroom looked like a museum—rows of glass cases filled with walking sticks made of precious metals, woods, and jewels. One find, he'd moved to his safe because he was not sure of it anymore after some nasty tittering by other collectors. The seller, a drinking buddy on that cruise ship to New York in 1920, had sworn: "It's fair dinkum or strike me dead. Bavarian unicorn horn."

All of Farquar's customers had huge collections. Each begged to see him as soon as they found out about him, as if he had a cure for the incurable. He dealt with their fevers calmly but firmly, just as he did the most willful shoot or thickest trunk in his blackthorn thicket. When collectors yearned for Farquar, they wanted something as *different* as when the engorged gourmet wants, at long last, simply a drink of water.

Athol Farquar's sticks were prized, like the holy grail, for their purity. Made only of the blackthorn, a wood as humble as the Saviour's cup and crown. And no matter how elaborate the design, a Farquar walking stick was never whittled. If it looked as if its head were a ram's horn, or a running dog, or a woman, that was purely a delusion caused by the natural development of the blackthorn when taken into hand by their maker.

There were some sticks Farquar made that he didn't sell. These were working sticks—crooks he gave to the shepherds in the hills surrounding his little forest. For McAlister, he made a double-handed crook so that the old man could lean on it. Athol Farquar bent the length of this stick to complement the bow-shape of McAlister's bandy legs, the result being that if you saw him at work peering out along the slopes, you'd think, *Now, what a fine specimen of a man. They grow them well in these wild parts.* Grayson liked to snag a sheep from the belly so as not to break a leg, so his stick had one great scoop atop, wide as an unshorn ram. Young Stephenson would want something sharp and fancy to twirl in the village on a Saturday night. Athol Farquar didn't ask any of the shepherds first. He just thought he knew and made the sticks without consulting. Then he gave them out—and to each shepherd, something happened once the first touch of hand to wood was made. Somehow it became a part of him, as necessary as his legs.

These weren't sentimental gifts. The shepherds and Farquar had a relationship that each wanted to maintain. Sheep in the blackthorn would be a danger to themselves, even without his disciplining rods and wires making the forest into a nest of traps. And sheep eating the tender shoots of blackthorn would cut each walking stick in the bud. So he maintained a fence against the sheep, a combination of hedge and sharp banks, so that they'd stay on the grassy slopes and not venture into the forest. The triangle of the forest formed a V, the broad part at the top rising up to the rounded mound where McAlister tramped in every weather. The two sides of the V were valleys. Stephenson roamed the slope on the other side of the valley to the right, and over that hill. Grayson's land was on the left, his rise levelling out to become the closest thing to a plain in these contoured hills. The nearest village wasn't much to talk about. A day's drive by ass-cart, a brisk morning's tramp for Farquar. There was also a scatter of haughty houses within view of the slopes, not that the shepherds nor Farquar had anything to do with the foreigners who tended to rent them, Londoners and such, the villagers said. Neither the shepherds nor Farquar nor anyone in the village had one of those motorized contraptions, though it was already 1924. Young Stephenson wanted one with all his heart but the only way he'd get out of being a shepherd was if he wanted to 'herd' wild cattle. Some Laird out Auchencruive way who thought to turn rubbish into gold was offering mad amounts of money to skilled shepherds to civilise them, for the cattle were not only stupidly ferocious but used their horns like bayonets. He fancied his looks, but no matter how hard he scrubbed himself, he smelled of sheep, and therefore, failure—whereas a man with engine muck under his fingernails wafted the City, adventure, romance, escape.

"The daevil is ut made that," McAlister would say, laying on the brogue whenever he saw a vehicle, though there were precious few that made their way up to these parts, the roads being what they were, and the reasons, fewer. It wasn't the contraptions he objected to. They'd not bothered him in the War. More, the people who swanned around in the beasts. And everyone here agreed.

Not one of the people who craved Farquar's canes put a thought to where he lived, nor imagined his precious forest any more than a one of them had ever put a thought to, say, some tree that provided ebony, or the men who cut it. All correspondence was through the postmaster at Blair Atholl, a man who might as well have been a priest when it came to confidences. Farquar was so strict about meeting his clients in various remote inns and waysides he designated, that one tin-can magnate broke a leg leaping from a train and a moving-picture actress came down with quite useless hysteria.

Farquar's wealth grew as great and discreetly as his fame. He had, however, the habit of thrift. So in every hole he made by pulling up a lump of cairngorm stone from his hidden warren of mines under the blackthorn roots, he stuck a dumpling of soil filled with the old-fashioned dosh he demanded: pre-1917 gold sovereigns.

No one local thought of him as anything more than a poverty-stricken craftsman, actually someone even poorer—because he had not even one rough Highland sheep—than the crofters who spent their winters weaving hoary lichen-dyed tweeds that were prized by Lairds, Lords, and those who with war fortunes, were paving their way to obtaining a Title. The crofter-weavers never knew what power they had, if only they'd learned worth, but the middlemen-buyers who made the rounds of cottages were fierce as wolves, and always bought with their lips curled.

So there Athol Farquar was—as there and unnoticeable as his thicket—and as uninteresting, anyone would have told you. What did he look like? A necessary face. His body? It wasn't ailing. Otherwise, what decent person looked at a body?

She watched him from the point just below the forest, the point of the V, that deep watercressy place where the spring came out to run down between the two long-sided hills. She'd found and followed that spring, up past its calmness, up where it narrowed and rounded over rocks, up, her feet numb from the frigid waters where its banks were too steep to walk beside it, up towards its secret heart; into a region that half-comforted her with its secrecy, its terror. All around, the forest loomed—a tangled blackness that if rendered by an artist, must be something from a madhouse where the food might be rationed but not the ink, black accented with brilliant, dancing white. The moon was a searchlight. A light breeze made the forest sound like mice in a box of chocolates.

She had left home at the first call of the owls when the moon was already full, and now had been crouching, her ballet slipper-shod feet perched precariously in the stream. She was taking a drink of water from her dish of hands when she heard come, a man. He stopped just far enough away that she could see his khaki vest and his bare muscular arms.

She watched him bend forward toward a branch, and just then, a cloud shifted. Moonlight cut them sharply into silhouettes. Her heart jumped. That branch looked like the reared-up head of a dying horse. The man held its neck while he reached down and . . . what? Was he pulling something up? He straightened out partly and kicked the ground in the area his hand must have been. Was he kicking something out or pushing something in? She couldn't see. Then he turned away and disappeared into the messy blackness. She could hear him—creak, crackle, snap. He was tightening a wire here, stroking a green shoot there and nipping a leaf between his fingernails, not that she could see. As carefully as when she'd crept down the creaking stairs, she crept up the slippery bank . . . and was caught.

The more she struggled, the more thorns found a purchase. First it was her skirt, then the silly flounces in her jacket. Its uselessness annoyed her so much that she'd hated to take it, but as with all her clothes, she had no choice. And now her hair had shaken loose, pins scattering into the branches like so many other spiky shoots. Her unfashionable, wild, waist-length tangle was caught, spreading with each movement to be an ever-larger web.

"Farquar," she called. "Mr. Farquar!" You *idiot*, she thought. It had to be him. Why did I wait?

She tossed her head and barely missed a thorn in the eye, and now her hair was so trapped that she couldn't move. He was too far away now, the forest too dense. She couldn't hear him at all, only frightening noises in the depths of night. The moonlight and small sounds only made everything look leering. There might be wolves here! Are there any wolves anymore, or are they just in stories? Tears flooded her eyes. Her cheeks mottled like a child's. She wrenched as hard as she could, which only served to tear some hair from its roots. "You *ninny*!" she yelled, which helped a bit.

Suddenly he was there, in front of her, tsking. "What a muckle you've made." His voice was deep but rough, his fingers gentle but skilled, and soon she was free. "Put up your blasted hair," he said, handing her some twists of worsted. She hesitated and he turned her like a top, grabbed the great soft mass, wrapped it and bound it as expertly as some Roman maid.

But that was just craftsman's luck. Since the War, he'd not been this close to another woman—to trouble.

His confusion soothed her, emboldened her. "You're Mr. Farquar?"

"That I am," he said without thinking. His instant reflex was always the honest response. And after that, he rarely said anything, not that he knew what to say now, with this—this girl up here, in the secret place—in the middle of the night. If 'twr a man . . . Farquar being the ex-blacksmith he was, one reason he kept to himself was his temper. In war, it had helped being able to beat a man's brains in with one blow. In his regiment, they'd bet on him, till he stopped their fun and took, instead, to poetry and keeping by himself. Now this girl here.

"My father," she said, ignoring his scowl, "will be up here tomorrow morning. . . . This morning."

She was so matter-of-fact, he forgot she was a girl. "How can he?"

"He's hired a detective and I heard them talking."

"What do you want?"

"To warn you." She didn't act like a woman. She spoke simply and her eyes didn't bat at him.

"You don't know who I am."

"I know who my father is. Richard Galveny."

She was so straightforward, yet she bristled with life. He pulled her skirt free of another thorn. Richard Galveny. The name rang no bell.

"My name is Rose, not Cairngorm."

"So what does this have to do with the price of cheese?"

"He wanted you to do the Rape of Cairngorm. You refused . . . Scratching your head won't help you, but will this?"

She posed, with her head turned away.

"Aye." His gut clenched. Richard Galveny. Richard. The man who had signed in a scrawl, and introduced himself as "Mr. Galveny."

They had met at Garnshiel Bridge, that humpbacked thing along the old military road linking the two historic garrisons of Braemar and Corgarff, a place of Galveny's choosing—"for romance," he'd said in his letter. "Do please indulge me," he'd written. "I'm besotted with history." Farquar had believed him.

Farquar was waiting when his client arrived alone, driving himself in a motorcar. Galveny stopped the beast on the top of the hump and invited Farquar into the pines on the wild side of the bridge. The man was impeccably dressed, softly spoken. "Lovely day, don't you know?" he said, and it was his voice that charmed Farquar. A voice made for poetry. The man also respected history. Farquar had been somewhat tense all morning, berating himself for breaking his own rule, indulging a client and putting himself out to meet at a place of the client's choosing, though it wasn't, to be honest, any problem for Farquar, who loved this country and had relished the ramble. "I think you'll appreciate," said Galveny, "the level of verisimilitude I demand. History and romance, don't you know. Can you copy a picture from life?"

Farquar nodded reflexively, a little miffed at the doubt, but he was used to this sort of thing from clients. "You'll think it's alive."

Galveny pulled the picture out of his breast pocket and held it in front of Farquar.

This girl—the one in front of him now—was the one in that disgusting picture.

Even when Farquar had thought the woman in that staged rape photograph a whore, he'd been revolted by the—the decency of the man.

Farquar had refused Galveny in two words, both filthy. Galveny made a gentlemanly threat in return, murmured in the voice of a mellifluous poet. Farquar had said he'd need to think about it. He told the truth. He needed time. He walked over the bridge and stood looking up at the bleak, blank-eyed stone inn. There wasn't a soul around. Galveny's motorcar waited like a patient dog, in the middle of the bridge.

Galveny had found himself a seat in the pines on a low stone cairn. When he saw that Farquar was returning, he rose and primly brushed off the seat of his Highland heather-tweed trousers—cut in that London tailor's presumption of a Scottish baron's kit. As they drew close enough to see each other's eyes, Galveny laughed.

"So it's settled then," he said, and his handsome, politely annoyed, bland, upright-as-a-judge expression changed to one of mischief, like a boy stealing a pie from a ledge. "You're a rogue, you are," he laughed. "How much do you plan to skin me for, you canny Scot?"

"Just this," said Farquar, and caned Galveny's face till he would never look respectable again. Then he took the picture out of Galveny's pocket and walked off while the man was still rolling around on the soft bed of pine needles in pools of his own making.

This was not the only instance of Farquar refusing to satisfy collectors. He'd had to discipline a few, mostly because they got greedy and had to have more of his canes. Or because they asked him to tell them secrets about or in some other way undermine the success of other fanatics who craved his works. Galveny, however, had been unique. The man was a monster, and this girl . . .

She was looking at him, not saying anything. Not being hysterical or making a scene like women do. Yet she was both young and, undoubtedly, a woman—in full bloom. She was, it hit him, the most beautiful woman he'd ever seen.

"Why did you come?" he demanded, suddenly suspicious. Why *would* she come?

"Why wouldn't I?" she spat. "I know what you did. He's coming to *kill* you. He's hired a man called Skulley. D'you know him?"

"Who doesn't in these parts? He's lucky to be alive."

"And Skulley's got a dog."

"Aye, that brute."

"We've got to stop them."

"Why?" Bloody hell, why? "So I caned your old man," he said. "I didn't *save you* from anything. Coming up here, it could have been the death of you." Farquar's voice had gotten louder and rougher by the word. "Why *did you do* this mad thing!" He looked ready to punch her.

"How could I not!" she shot back. "You knew nothing about me. And he's rich as Croesus, and still you . . ." Her eyes, liquidly bright, gazed into his. "And to thank you. And to meet you. And I love you."

It just came out, and as it hung in the air between them, they knew that it was true.

Hie, she'd already bashed what he knew about women to smithereens.

"We've got to kill him first," he said.

"Of course." She took his arm and he didn't flinch. "But what about Skulley? And the dog?"

"Don't take mind o' them gorse-heads. That cur won't come within miles of Stephenson or Grayson. Their sheep could jump in his mouth and he wouldn't gulp. They're the shepherds up here, and that dog's back has met their crooks. And Skulley, he thinks the forest is haunted."

She made a sound like a turtledove. She was *chuckling.* "That wouldn't have anything to do with you scaring the daylights out of a person, would it? That rearing horse!"

An eerie but comforting feeling came over him, of knowing her before, as if she'd been Curlew. Two loners, they'd formed an inseparable bond when they were thrown together in the Second Battle of Ypres, during one of those times in May 1915 when men lost their minds merely from the sound. Just before a push, they read poems to each other, then climbed out and tried not to drown in the holes or get shot while they did their duty. On one relatively good day, at a hellish place named in soldiers' humour "the corner of Joy and Crucifix Streets," where the ground squelched as much with rotting bodies as sucking mud, and bones poked up like stubble, Farquar was in the lead, pulling a horse he planned to shoe. Curlew was pushing from behind. Curlew slipped and fell, spearing himself through the eye on a split arm bone.

This girl was looking at him now, smiling somewhat indulgently. "Get a move on," she said. "I never imagined you as a daydreamer."

SKULLEY HADN'T LIED. He knew these parts and before the quilt of morning fog had lifted, he, with his dog, led Galveny up through the fields of violet harebells, as gorgeous as any spring bluebell but so contrarian here in the kind of cold that chills the bones. Not that Skulley noted, and Galveny walked streaming muttered curses at the ankle-twisting outcrops of limestone and wet grasses, slippery as ice. Up they tramped, passing dead nettle, gorse, stepping on heather and other sharp-scented herbage, till they reached what looked to Galveny to be an impenetrable leafy wall.

"Down," whispered Skulley. "Crawl through."

Galveny was just going to say, "Are you mad?" when he saw the tunnel, little more than rabbit-size. "Crawl," Skulley hissed behind him.

Galveny took his gun off his back and shimmied with it under him, he imagined, just like soldiers had. His jacket back tore and so did one sleeve. He would have liked to demand part of Skulley's pay back when this adventure was over, but he didn't plan for there to be a Skulley capable of listening then.

More than an hour later Galveny, standing in the stream, drank water from his hands, tried to stop them from shaking and failed, and reshouldered his scratched, muddy, new game-shooting rifle. He also held, concealed in his breast pocket, a beautiful palm gun handcrafted in Germany; and in his sock, a knife with a medieval hunting scene of hound and hart.

He was soaked to the bone from first the thick fog, then the drizzle, and increasingly, his own cold sweat. He'd been abandoned and couldn't have turned back if he'd been paid a million quid. He had thought that Skulley would lead him within spitting distance of Farquar's back, for Galveny's armaments were obtained specifically for this event. In fact, his fighting skills were as good as his sense of direction. The man always thought himself quite the navigator, though he could get lost in a steam bath.

His face was a painter's inspiration: the nose as wheezy as a bulldog's, flat-profiled but puffed, textured and coloured at the sides like two bunches of lightly trodden grapes. The cheekbones were off-kilter, and the mouth—with its tattered lips and not enough bone to attach false teeth to—the mouth was a dribbling gape. His voice was no longer that of a thespian but a whisper-loud, hoarse lisp, so many letters unable to be formed in the wreck of a palate that his anger in how they came out only made him a thing unreal, an abomination of a man. Indeed, he'd even frightened the servants in his exclusive little London club. His fellow connoisseurs all cut him off. He was alone. He only had his daughter; for his wife, after that beating, instantly fled to her mother's house, where she divorced him. He looked, she said, like some thing in a War veteran's Home. No one who should expose himself. It enraged her and every one of her friends that he didn't think of their sensibilities.

And his face had only grown uglier and more determined while he hunted for this Farquar. Galveny travelled light, renting through agents, for a season or a few weeks. His possessions: three bags, one trunk, and his daughter. No collector would tell him anything, and only a great deal of money to an Edinburgh detective agency led to him being certain enough to move to the staging house that was luckily free and only ten minutes' walk from his guide, the scoundrel poacher Skulley who'd demanded cash up front. Damn Scots. Can't trust a one of them muckheads. But Galveny had paid up like a lamb. He had no choice.

He rubbed his sleeve against his forehead, only succeeding in scratching his eyelids with grit. Proper daylight would come soon enough, he told himself. Then the forest would be his hunting ground. Ah, you think you're clever, you gorilla—you're an animal living here, with your pretensions. Everything's money. You're no better. And little do you know a Galveny. We remember everything.

He splashed further along the creek, bloodying his knees, chin, elbows on the moss-slick stones, cursing and vowing as he went. His voice had kept him company ever since he'd realised: he'd been deserted by even the dog; and he hadn't the faintest idea where he was, or his path back. Meanwhile, the forest he'd expected to get lighter got even darker—and that sky that wouldn't stop pissing on him didn't help. As he rushed forward, his gun hitting the back of his head at every fall, the scenery closed in around him ever more oppressively, reminding him cruelly of some play he'd had such fun at years ago, some murder mystery that gave him a frisson of fear that lifted when the lights went on.

His eyebrows dripped, blinding him. His ruined lips he could never properly close dripped tears, sweat, dirt, and snot into his mouth. He stumbled up the stream. There didn't seem to be a way into this forest, this intolerably contrarian place that Farquar lived in—"Like a fucking dog!"

Cursing was the only thing keeping Galveny going when at last, in the crotch of the forest, in its deepest darkness, a shaft of light or sound or something alerted him to a way to escape from the stream itself. He grabbed at a tangle of jutting roots and pulled himself up the bank.

On land again, in this bit of clearing, he felt a new man. He was reaching behind to take his gun off his back when his arm stopped in midair, then dropped. He felt four years old again, some *nothingness* grabbing at his back like those nights when his father locked him out on the crumbling window ledge for being naughty.

He ran unseeing, forward into the forest, because suddenly—he had to run. Arms out, eyes screwed shut, he ran straight into the middle of a mob of walking sticks in their adolescence. A rearing horse, a woman brushing her hair, a unicorn, two snakes entwined, and a chipmunk.

Two vinelike ends of some disciplining wires caught him, one by an arm, and another by the back of his neck. Another, unaccountably, looped around his waist. And as he struggled, more wires confoundedly found their way around his torso, ankles, wrists. He wrenched left to free himself, and one very sharp wire slipped, ever so discreetly, into his left ear. Any movement he made only drove it further in.

"Farquar," he screamed. "Farquar!"

Of course he sounded, with no teeth or much of a bottom lip, rather comical, like a ham actor playing a raven.

The screaming only managed to drive the wire deeper down his ear canal.

Then it punctured his eardrum with a burst of purest pain, shoving out the childish fears.

He saw blackness and a brief flash of light, like being in an alley when a kidnapper wags a lantern. His thoughts slipped back to other good times, sights and sounds. A girl crying had squeezed a tear out of his Sir One-Eye. He grew strength from that, and even felt his other senses gaining heightened sensitivity. For after all, his right ear was still sound, and his limbs, though bruised, were sound—*and*, he reminded himself, *with patience comes reward.*

A gusty wind must have settled over this mountain, making the trees thrashing all around take on the oddest character, creating the strangest phantasms of sound—a horse's neigh, just behind his elbow. Assorted chitterings all around.

Indeed, the forest seemed to come alive with sounds, now that he noticed. There were too many to count, but his ear picked out one above all, and strained for it. Low and regular, rough and deep: a woodsman's saw. No. A man's voice—lifting, falling . . . lift, hold, down in a long stroke. Then again and again, in some drawn-out rhythm that threatened to never end, like the bugger was reciting old-fashioned poetry. Interminable. No distinct words, of course.

What could make that? Wind shoving two branches back and forth against each other, back and forth . . . till suddenly the air stilled, as if for a moment's silence.

And so close he would have bet his life on it—quiet but deep: "Would you like to hear another?" followed by a soft coo like some bird.

The man's voice had to be Farquar, the primitive bastard! So this was his sense of humour. It *had* to be Farquar. Galveny was thinking fast. Stabbing Farquar in the back now was impossible, and gunning the man down would have needed that poacher to do the work. The only thing for it was to return the next night, alone. Not entering the forest, of course, but by skirting its edges, Galveny reckoned he could set fire to the blighted place, with Farquar trapped in it proper, like an ape in a cage.

Galveny opened his mouth to demand release when something tickled his right ear, and into it poured a warm, moist, low, musical, pitiless chuckle.

His mind, already crazed, shattered. The wire in his left ear drove in further.

Maybe he closed his eyes—he was beyond knowing.

He felt the fetid breath of the forest drip into his every pore.

He heard the swishing hiss of a cobra.

The yipping of a fox.

The love-gurgles of turtledoves.

Strains of a current craze-song for a fox-trot, words and music that bore into you.

A man's conversational syllables, deep as stones dropped in a well.

A ripple of woman's laughter.

But perhaps his last feast of sensations was of smell—that most restoring of all cups—a cup of tea with a kick in it. His nostrils dilated. *Hot with a drop of something ineffable—sweet, rough, strong.*

BITE AND BURROW, swell and rot. The flesh is weak, but the rods have never weakened. His skeleton is held bolt upright in that impenetrable tangle.

The Jeweller of Second-hand Roe

Honoré Barrot, the *bijoutier*, as he was called, was the most uncelebrated of his trade and proud of it, as his life depended upon secrets as surely as a spy's. In the tubercular gloom of a Paris cellar, he worked standing inside a square of trestles. On the planks to his right and back his materials crowded, piled in anything that could hold them—wicker baskets, stoppered crocks, bowls, *Le Matin*. At his elbow, a tower of china plates threatened to topple. Empty wooden trays were stacked on the floor. He worked in a fever. Observe his eyes—those whites, yellow as yolks; their cast: ecstatic as a pilgrim.

He moved precisely, this great bull of a man. His hands, coarse and quick as a mastiff's mouth.

Take the plate he was arranging at the moment. A swallow's nest, only partly toyed with; a triangle of ray with Périgueux sauce; a marbled slab of jugged hair; and a diamond of quince paste that he scraped free of gravy with the knife that hung from his neck. The final touch: a spray of disinfectant. He used no chopping board—it wasted time. Trimmed bits, he dropped in a wooden bucket. He wiped his fingers on his waistcloth in the act of choice. If sold today, this plate of bijoux could make the jeweller rub his hands. If tomorrow, perhaps touched up, he could smile. If the next day, nothing to sneeze at. Every made-up plate will sell, even if he has to sell it as scraped-off messes wrapped in old news.

If, on a summer's day, you were to somehow find his workshop, even if your nose could see through the emerald glaze to the rainbow on the ray, your eyes would crave these beauties. Or maybe sounds seduce you—*boudins* of pheasant *á la Richelieu*, a *lettuce*, almost fresh. No? Then come here. You might be amongst M Barrot's most exclusive clients. This cutlet lay before the President of the Republic. See his marks? The price? If you need to ask, don't ask. Only for genuine bourgeoisie.

But before I continue, perhaps the world has changed so much since all this happened that you are confused. Put in the bald terms of today's brutal world, Honoré Barrot sold second-hand food. You cry "horrors!"? Perhaps you turn up your nose at eel! When I was a boy, the *bijoutiers* flourished in a certain level of society, as did the *belles de jour*.

THE BIJOUTERIE WAS a family affair. Three sons kept supplies and deliveries constant. Olivier, the oldest, drove the anonymous covered cart. The giant Thibault acted as loader along with younger brother Claude. Little Etienne was the *bijoutier*'s apprentice. Rats were his responsibility. He watched gravely, this little prune.

They earned enough to call themselves *bourgeoisie*, but their rooms—bare, even of a china shepherdess.

They dined upstairs, sitting around the stove. Their food was old bread and a soup that Mme Barrot made of whatever her husband gave her for the pot. She stirred with a big wooden spoon. They ate with horn spoons. All the metal cutlery had been swallowed, except one large knife.

Olivier, Thibault, and Claude ate with the appetites of oxen. Etienne and his father, delicate artists, ate like stuffed birds. *Food?* *No!* That blood-ruby glop of stewed quince, the carved-moonstone whorl of a boar's snout, a slice of tomato with a good facet. That endive nibbled by the mistress of the Minister of Finance—stark, on its white plate, as a diamond in platinum claws.

In this business where discretion was the key, and volume the oil, back doors opened all over Paris, from restaurants to the finest homes. The three oxen moved in regular rounds: cooks, housekeepers, storesmen, restaurants, households, stalls, workshop, cooks—the money they collected they delivered, every sous, to their father.

Three young men who gained no joy from Art. Why would they work like beasts? The family shared a passion—all except Mme Barrot upstairs, as busy and close to the father and sons and yet self-centred, as a blackbeetle.

"Speak of the devil!" people said when Mme Barrot ventured out. Women tossed curses. Men pretended they hadn't seen her, but watched her every move. *Will my wife? mother? daughter? sweetheart? catch it, too?*

Virginie Barrot. She cleaned as much as a Dutch housewife, but not to be closer to God.

A bootnail. A rustflake. She picked the stove poxy. She ran as many errands as a mother mouse, but like the mouse, stole close to home. The dressmakers called to each other from doorway to doorway when she opened her door. The man who repaired pots in a little cubbyhole, crossed himself and clacked his shutters to.

The subject was never discussed between man and wife, though the Doctor was called upon one night. The umbrella-repair man banged on the door next day, and against all custom, let himself in and barrelled down the stairs, demanding to be paid for three spines that vanished from his workshop the day before when Mme Barrot paid him a visit on the pretext of obtaining a price to fix her umbrella—an umbrella, moreover, that she didn't produce.

Jeweller and umbrella-fixer settled accounts with no demur from the jeweller. "She'll pauper you, my dear Monsieur Barrot," the umbrella man said once the coins were in his hand. The *bijoutier* led the way up and out, taking cordial leave at the door—to prying eyes, a courteous call between tradesmen. Overhead, he heard the shuh shuh of her twig broom. He clompered sloppily down again the better to hear only his wooden shoes. *One more who deems my wife unrespectable—and he, an umbrella fixer!*

If a person who pocks a stove for bits of rust is a thief, then Mme Barrot was a thief even when she didn't steal umbrella spines and pins. The setting meant nothing to her: family, neighbour, gutter, slops. Shiny, dull, new, old, valued and corrupt—in ecstatic furtiveness she sought, found, swallowed and sought for more even as her throat convulsed upon the latest load. The gossip was that she stole for gluttony, that her life revolved around eating, that she ate the family poor. That was the say. Proof? That huge belly, those slippery eyes. She was certainly not with child. *And* the Barrots dressed disgracefully—*and* the Barrot household! Bare as the Bastille! *Shameless*, they called her, and they shook their heads for her family.

Most men and some women in this shoulder-to-knee, look-up-her-skirt neighbourhood disgusted the gossips. They added nothing to the gossip stew. Perhaps they had gone to Mme Dumont's funeral. She fell to starch, the laundress's temptation. The flower-making twins ate their teeth out, from vinegar. Their neighbour, the lace-maker Mme Roule lived alone with a baby after losing her man through her unmentionable lust.

The plan, agreed between the young men and their father, was to expand business as fast as they could, saving like the proverbial ant. With an addiction as advanced as hers, Dr Donnedieu had said, she would need a month in his sanatorium, or more.

A normal woman would have been a harridan. After all, every woman in the neighbourhood had a fiendish ability to calculate. Virginie Barrot never asked for money, and had not for many years visited the cellar. "She never sticks her nose in my business," her husband once bragged, but whether her reason was disinterest, delicacy, or shame, neither he nor his sons could tell.

It is hard to understand how her sons, not to mention her handsome husband (yes! Several women planned to claim him) could have loved her, but they did. The husband and the three big ones remembered her as she was. The woman they described was not that thing upstairs, forever sweeping or picking on the stove, or when she stirred the family's soup, dribbling bits from the spoon to the pot as if she hoped to find a finger. Etienne dreamed of the beautiful woman his father and brothers loved.

But first she'd have to go. Father and Etienne worked tinged with the fever of the cellar; the three oxen, with the fever of desperate haste.

They were *that* close when one morning at the busiest time, the health inspector called.

A breech of the law is common as piss against a wall, and for an inspector, a Cause to Close is easy to find as a blinking eye. Down in the cellar, the inspector coughed. His eyes dilated. The *bijouterie* was not illegal, nor was it strictly legal. The health inspector's nose quivered, smelling what he most loved.

His visit set them back at least a year.

To THE SOUND overhead of Mme Barrot picking at the stove, her husband and sons met. The three big ones tried to walk their anger off, but it was too much. Thibault, the second son, who dwarfed them all and was hopelessly in love, smacked a trestle. The board jumped and the china towers toppled—a bombarde of shards. Splinters leapt everywhere. He burst into tears and knelt.

For wordless minutes father and sons crawled over the floor dropping *pink*, *clink*, *crack*, china into a bucket. When they'd picked up what they could see, they swept with their hands. Then they fished through the food—feeling for sharps in chops, tarts, legs, pastes, soups, sauces, ragouts and soggy puddings.

Sniffling, Thibault felt something in a bowl of quince. "Zut!" He flung it to the floor.

"Where are you, you devil's claw?" *Mind how you move, oaf.* He sucked his finger as he crawled.

There, dotted with ruby syrup: a diamond brooch.

Although they called him "the jeweller", **Honoré** Barrot had no experience of gems that didn't rot. But he knew that quince. It had sat before the President at a restaurant as discreet as M Barrot.

He never considered returning the brooch. As laundrywomen say—*Them who must wear pearl buttons make tailors live on promises.* He would make discrete inquiries, and sell it.

He wrapped it in a clean rag and stowed it in his pocket, his mind stirred to dizziness.

That night he climbed into bed beside his wife just as he did every night, but instead of falling asleep exhausted, he tossed, schemed, fretted, calculated the minutes till morning and fretted more. *So many minutes! What use is night?* He knew he could not close his eyes, but soon enough, he snored.

SHE HAD EATEN no metal for four whole days. His jacket and trousers hung from the peg on the door, intolerable temptations. She hated herself for doing it, but she had to look. Perhaps a sous . . .

A horrible beast chased him through the dark green forest. Trees hampered his every move. The shaggy thing opened its mouth, its stinking mouth.

"Ouf!" That dream again. He turned over, snuggling up to . . . damp sheet.

"Virginie!"

She held the only metal thing she'd found. At the sound of her husband's roar she shoved it in her mouth, gulped, and fell to the floor.

FATHER AND SONS are yellow as rancid tallow in the light of the lamp down here. The father has stopped talking, even to say "Virginie." Etienne keeps his tongue between his teeth and his mouth shut. Thibault can't keep his clogs still. You can hear his teeth grind his moustache.

(She is upstairs, revived with cold water by her husband, who carried her to bed and tucked her in as if she were a child.)

"Doctor!" The third son, Claude, copies his oldest brother, to the curled lip.

Their father had wanted to rush to Dr Donnedieu. Always before, they spoke of the doctor as a saviour, an eminence whose kindness—

Now, this jaundiced light.

"Trust him?" Olivier asks. "Trust?" he laughs.

"And what assurances did we ever have?"—Claude.

"To operate is too dangerous."

Their father shakes his head. He sits on Etienne's stool, his head between his hands.

Olivier and Claude put their heads together. Thibault stands in the middle of the room. He kicks the floor as if he's breaking down the door to hell. Etienne slips his hand between his father's, against his father's scratchy face.

Claude's throat grates. The gob he spits is big as a plum, and green.

His father, who could thrash a man to paste if he'd a mind to, doesn't even look to see where it lands.

Claude and Olivier stare at the glob as if it were alive.

"There is only one thing for it," Olivier announces.

"No!" says father Barrot, but his 'no' is muffled in his hands; and anyway, his oldest and third sons have already run up the stairs.

"Wait," cries Thibault. "I'm the strongest."

"No!" Father Barrot shoves Thibault out of his way and mounts the steps. As he opens the cellar door, his "Stop!" shakes the window.

Thibault and Etienne look to each other.

"Stay here," Thibault says, and follows his father.

FORGIVE ME IF I told you more than you wanted about some things, and elsewhere, left your jaw hanging. That is how I remember it—pieced together from scraps, I who was only a small apprentice, but already a ratcatcher.

The next time I saw Maman, she was laid out in the front room.

The neighbourhood came out, to a gossip, for her procession. The splendour of the spread laid out for them when they returned from the funeral must have filled the gossip-pots to bursting.

I have the Certificate, signed by Dr Emile Donnerieu. *Self-inflicted Injury by Virtue of Insanity (Class, Female Hysteria; Subclass, Pica).*

The rest, you must put together yourself.

There were many sounds overhead. I stayed downstairs, more out of fear than obedience. Beast sounds. Strange, terrifying. Fights? Sobs? A fight, I think. Then there were footsteps and the front door opened and slammed, and an hour or so later I heard a horse and wheels, unfamiliar voices, one possibly the Doctor's.

Finally, Olivier came down the stairs. "Maman is in heaven," he said.

Discretion must be in my bones. I was ten years old before I asked Papa what happened that night. "She did it for us," he said.

I made Thibault tell me.

By the time he got there, he said, it was all over. She was on the floor, her guts tangled out all red and blue, Olivier and Claude swearing to Papa that she'd done it herself. The knife was beside her.

THE DAY PAPA died I took over, at my brothers' insistence—not a moment too soon. Yellow gaslights had given way to electric white. The Barrot *bijouterie* such as it was, of basket and cart, fit old Paris.

The Barrot concern soon fit a modern army. Under my guidance, the Barrot family rose to the heights of discrete wealth. If you haven't heard of us, that is well. *Discretion*, as Papa used to say, *is the greater part of good business.*

Poor Papa is lucky to never have known one thing. That brooch he treasured and never sold, that brooch that he recovered himself while Maman was still warm (I pieced that mess together)—that diamond brooch—paste!

So long ago.

Forgive this old man for his garrulousness—this vulgar need to divulge to you, so far from us that it doesn't matter. Before I end, two gems from my father:

Family is all.

Love is sacrifice.

AUTHOR'S NOTE: *A large second-hand food trade flourished in nineteenth-century Paris. This story is a peek into the euphemistically named 'jewellers' and their 'jewels' at an upper level of this complex, tiered system. A more detailed view, down to the 'coal miners' who traded in third-hand food was impossible, as the scene would be totally unbelievable to modern readers, not to mention reading like it was written to be gratuitously disgusting.*

High Life

Many of the people who call the neighborhood we'll call 'Mary's Corner' home, had spent years out of the little district, seated two blocks south at Tang's. This is where they not only ate their hot meal of the day but where Joe and his wife Lily didn't think in terms of seat rent.

Popular menu choices at Tang's were Egg Foo Yung (thick huge flying saucers accompanied by boats of tasty brown sauce), Beef Stew (rich and chunky with tender beef, carrots, and greens served on rice), Baked Apple, Tapioca . . . —a plain old-fashioned assortment of dishes all made on the premises, most of it for the last 20 years by a hulking cook you could see through the open kitchen door. He looked like a star in a B-grade horror movie of the 1930s, his head always stubbled and scarred with ringworm's many angry red moons.

Tang's did have rules. You couldn't bring bottles in. You could talk to yourself, but had to keep it down, and weren't allowed to yell. And there was no credit, though Tang's would cash your pension check and not take any commission. Tang's had quite a turnover, and there had been times when men up to no good came in to steal the take, or to leave without paying. You were lucky if you were sitting there, so you could watch. The cook would dry his hands on his apron and emerge holding the cleaver that he used to chop beef bones. Sometimes a new customer or a table of them would eat and leave, thinking that, like one who was challenged politely said, "Chinks ain't got no guts." These customers found then that, not only were they wrong, but sometimes there were other customers who found this talk objectionable. Tang's regulars had over the years, used their fists, boots, and once (a lady regular) a bowl of chili with saltines in the face, to object.

The best thing about Tang's, to some faithful customers, was the way you could actually eat hot food there if you couldn't chew. Onion cream soup, macaroni and cheese soft and fluffy as a pillow, warm applesauce with cinnamon sauce; and on those foggy days that sink into your bones, if you got there at 11am, *warm* tapioca flavored with something none of the customers would have guessed. Lily insisted that the star anise was never dropped from the recipe, though it added to the cost. She swore it helped against rheumatism. And Tang's was known for really special service, if you had a problem with soup or drinks because your hand shook. The next time you'd order, your food and drink would be served in sippy mugs, with no comment. Some customers from Mary's Corner area, Miss Simmons and other retired ladies, loved Tang's best for the lighting. In another setting, it might be termed "soft and romantic." Tang's had other regulars, mostly tradesmen, some who ate two meals a day at the place every day of the year.

The building that housed Tang's was nothing for architects to speak of. Large dark windows and an unlit hoarding that just said *Tang's*, although in 1980 a slogan was added—*since 1926*.

It hadn't been Joe and Lily Tang's choice to close the place that Joe's father had opened before Joe was born. But they not only couldn't fight progress; they were congratulated by many on their good fortune. Some other restaurant owners made snide remarks about them, about them having such an odd menu. About Joe's father having abandoned the neighborhood, about them "throwing good rice to bad dogs" in that place of theirs. No one knew quite how much the Tangs had made on the deal, but the talk was, from twenty to thirty million.

It's hard to see Tang's in the mind's eye there now, the big barn of a building splayed out on that busy corner, its rickety balcony making it seem like a Wild West saloon that had confidently moseyed out of a time machine to plonk itself on this street and then go all senile.

The transition from Tang's to gaping hole, to shielded building site—to the tight well-lit self-contained 24/7 stylish urban-living, discriminating shopping, provisioning, coffeeing and dining district that it is now—was probably slow and frustrating to the developers but as speedy and past-erasing to everyone else, as a straightening in a road. Within weeks, weeds grow through the old way and you can't remember where that curve was—not that you feel a loss. What purpose would there be to remember?

There would be even less purpose now, guidebook writers would say, to step back in time almost four years to when Tang's existed, to venture those two blocks to Mary's Corner, an area treated by guidebooks as invisible (which always means *dangerous*) possibly because its residents have all seen things that are invisible to the civilised, and from the look of them (now that we have done the purposeless and unwise)—still do.

There's Gunther Kroll smoking a cigarette with surprising gracefulness, considering how smelly he looks. He saw his first moose breaking out of a wall poster in 1970 while living in an experimental college—a few houses bought cheap in a working-class black neighborhood in Portland—where college professors experimented with fresh young things and philosophies, and played with hash, mesc, increased consciousness and open marriage. His eyes are in such a constant state of agitation that if they are the windows of his soul, it's a relief that he curtains them with dark sunglasses.

Miss Simmons, the retired biology teacher, creeps by. She holds her right hand against her face in a rather screen-queen pose. Under the hand is the scarred hollow that was her cheekbone.

By the corner itself, sunning themselves against the window of the corner store with its sign painted on the glass—*Triumph*—are Karel Vlachova and his cat Tesla, who sits on his lap in his wheelchair. Vlachova wears a sweatshirt that says in a rainbow of letters *Stairway to Heaven*. On a shelf above his head is a velvet bedstead such as you might think a tiny Sultan would roll around on. The shelf is fringed with tiny bulbs. Vlachova's head is tilted backwards and in motion, as if he's doing some sort of yogic neck-muscle stretch. He might be looking at something up there, up at the sagging mess of wires and hanging dead-eyed traffic lights, sad as a rest-home's Christmas tree.

Whenever lost tourists, having walked left two blocks from the Square instead of right, accidentally arrive here, Mary screams

"That's my curb," and they skedaddle back to one of the several luxury hotels rimming the Square. Or say you are one of those tourists who now need post-traumatic-shock treatment more effective than a brief escape to your hotel before your next foray out. Amongst these name-brand five-star pleasure houses are equally high-end name-brand clinics that are quietly busy, but will always fit you in. There you might work off your shock by spending $100,000 or so on, say, a timepiece that, if the ads are right, you'll never actually own. Or, if you're more of an individualist, one block *north of the square*, that's up *that way*, you'll pass the Vanutina Skin Resort, Levis, the famous McArties Bar and Grill with all those pictures of stars on the wall; and just past McArties, a delightful little stretch of tiny galleries, cutting-edge jewelers, and Mon Dieu, which you might have been looking for on your misguided trek, for you haven't lived if you haven't had their absinthe-bacon ice cream (rated Throw-yourself-off-the-cliff in Romer's Guide to To-die-fors).

But say you're not a tourist. Say you belong around Mary's Corner but sometimes stroll out with your collar up on a rainy night, just window-shopping so to speak (with an umbrella you scored). Before anyone comes after you, says something to you, go back to Mary's Corner, back to that neighborhood.

Across the street are some buildings that seem to be used as storage by other businesses somewhere else. Amongst these are two establishments. See Girls says one—it has glass silhouettes of women flanking the door. From the shape of the women and their hair curves, they are dames, each not a day older than 75, caught at their best in 1945. The next-door establishment says Peep Show and advertises its attractions with brown-tinged photos that look vintage 1960. One of these establishments is active. The other is now boarded up. The one that is working has a clientele that must go to sleep early, or not feel safe to be here in the dark. Its busy time is afternoon.

On the busy side of the street, at the corner itself, just behind screaming Mary, is Mr. and Mrs. Park's store, Triumph. It's got windows facing two ways, but neither is used for display except for signs that say "No checks cashed" and "Please don't ask for credit" and "Coke refreshes." Next to Triumph is Silvers Pawn—in the neighborhood so long that no one can remember when it wasn't. If you're looking for a 9k gold lucky horseshoe ring with or without a diamond chip, Silvers Pawn is the place to get it, as well as that accordion you can't live without. The window display is so ever-changing that it is one of the neighborhood's sights.

When the residents of the Brandon Hotel (two doors down) come out to buy say, two cigarettes at Triumph or just to escape the cockroaches in their rooms (the lobby of the Brandon lost its chairs and couch some years ago, as well as carpet. Now there's an expanse of worn linoleum broken by the manager's desk and a cigarette machine) Silvers Pawn is always worth a stop, a gaze, a dream. There's stuff in the window that you can't imagine why, like a dozen eggplants. That you can't eat.

For food in the neighborhood, you must go next door, to Triumph, where you can buy a can of spaghetti or beans, or instant noodles in a cup and use the sink in your room to add hot water, or if you are living on the street, the Parks are happy to give you the hot water from a flask they keep in the store for just that purpose. Triumph and Silvers Pawn are in a couple of three-storey buildings that lean together like an arthritic married couple standing waiting for something they dread, now that it's too late for their dreams to come true.

ENOUGH OF THAT diversion. You'll just have to remember the sights, for even with a guide, you would be advised not to show your camera. Let's get back to the present, and a different neighborhood.

Three years have passed since Tang's closure. Joe Tang often has nightmares about the customers. He hadn't been able to tell them, had not trusted himself not to break into tears. Lily said she was superstitious. So on one Tuesday Charles (the cook) was bringing out a purring Tesla from the kitchen . . . and that night, the wreckers did their work and the gaping hole was surrounded by fencing that sported a picture of the glorious shopping center-to-be.

Money! It frees and complicates.

Charles had been seriously ready for retirement, and was generously provided for. He bought a houseboat up somewhere in Northern California, and often sent Joe and Lily pictures—some of the local scenery but many more slightly blurred ones that he had set his camera to take—Charles catching his breakfast off his houseboat deck, his growing young cat on his lap.

Joe and Lily paid off all the children's loans, student and otherwise, lectured a couple of them on managing their money, and gave each of the children $100,000. But that still left so much that it was an investment headache, and a growing problem every time the children rang, which they had begun to at such great frequency and in tones of such unprecedented similarity that Lily said to Joe one night, "Don't you think it's odd that Eleanor and Jonathan communicated with each other?"

"I'm afraid not. We're ready for the meeting, aren't we?"

Lily nodded, both thrilled and frightened.

"Of course, you'll have to explain," said Joe. "You did most of the work."

"No, darling." They were sitting on a park bench in a scrap of green on a back street in Chinatown "You can't chicken out."

Wafting out from behind them, from a dimly lit room on this steep block, came the sharp energetic clicks of mahjong tiles, along with sporadic flurries of excitement sounding remarkably like happy laying hens.

A week later, on the third floor of that same building, above Seng Yan Grocery and Jade Peacock Jewelry, the Tang family was sitting around a large table, together for the first time in ten years.

"I always said this job of mine in Las Vegas was temporary," said Eleanor, at 26, the youngest. "Now I can go to New York to be in the right place for auditions."

"And what will you do between times?" asked her mother.

"We're not going to pay you to do nothing," said her father.

"I don't do nothing in Las Vegas. There's plenty of dancing I could do in New York."

Actually, she had planned to move to New York following some of the other girls when she heard of the money they were making, doing Ironic Burlesque in the Wall Street district. But when the bottom dropped out of the market, the girls all came back to Nevada. Now some worked, making even more money, at Kitty Ranch.

"We'll pay for your retraining," said Joe Tang. "Thank you," he said to the ancient waiter who was doing the rounds of the table, filling cups from a fresh pot of tea.

Eleanor put her hand up. "Diet Pepsi here."

The teapot dribbled in midair, and the waiter jerked it upright. "Sorry, miss," he said, though only the tablecloth had been splashed. He seemed rusted in place, stuck with a stupidly willing smile.

"You know there's no soft drinks here," said Lily.

The waiter straightened as much as he could. "No worries, Mrs. Tang. I get downstairs."

He rushed out as fast as he could, and four minutes later, came back with a cold can of Diet Pepsi, a glass and a straw, apologizing profusely for the wait. The family had not exchanged a word in the time he'd been gone.

"Thank you, Arthur," said Joe.

"You're welcome, Joe." Neither man made eye contact.

The place was packed at 9AM. Although every table had tea-drinkers, many of the people weren't eating. They were chatting or reading newspapers, some printed in Chinese.

A squeaky wheel announced the arrival of the trolley laden with dim sums, scallion pancakes, steamed buns, sponge cakes. The family (all except Eleanor) took some, including Alessandra, Richard's wife. She wielded her chopsticks with the same politeness as everyone else in this room, though she was the only non-Chinese. Richard had introduced her to the place (and his parents) seven years ago as "my parents' hangout. You could call it the restaurant-owners lounge, cum retirement home. I hope you don't have an allergy to MSG."

Although no one in the family was hungry, there was a pretence of serious eating amongst those who had chosen a selection, a lack of comment about the one who had waved her hand dismissively; and the children caught up with each other with talk that was somewhat stilted, as if they had rehearsed it. Finally Lily said, "Joe," and arranged her chopsticks in the *I'm finished* position.

"The sale was so successful," started Joe, startling Lily by his abruptness, "that some of it, we would like to plough back."

"Stop," said Eleanor. "I can't breathe here."

Her older sister hit the table with a fist. "Enough histrionics, Elly!"

"No, she's right," said Jonathan. Eleanor was sitting beside him. "You look like two million bucks," he said under his breath. "Dad," he said, "This is too important a meeting to take place here. Elly, where would you feel comfortable?"

She screwed up her face. "We haven't booked, but I bet they'll squeeze us in if we get out there now ... Yes, they've got great service."

"Where?" Joe asked blandly. Under the table, he was crushing the starched tablecloth in a fist.

"Benson's on the Square. I could use a drink, and they have a superb Afternoon Tea. It should be nothing to get them to serve it to us now."

"It should be nothing," said Caroline, in perfect imitation. "Give me a break!"

"Be reasonable," said Jonathan. "Benson's is just what we need. Someplace neutral."

"Neutral!" exploded Lily.

"It's okay," said Joe. "We'll need two cabs," he said to Jonathan.

"Meet you outside," said Jonathan, taking his phone out of his pocket. "Wait for me," said Eleanor. The other children followed them out.

"Do you have enough money?" Joe asked Lily.

"I'm sure I do. If I have to, I'll use the card."

Joe paid the bill in cash, but had a small argument over the Diet Pepsi. The waiter had not included it on the bill, and wouldn't take any money for it.

45 minutes later, they were all in the lobby lounge of Benson's on the Square, arranged in a semicircle on a couch, and perched in little decorative iron chairs around a few tables that the children had pulled close. The Royal Afternoon Tea (with a glass of Pommery Brut Champagne) was not actually available till the afternoon, but Eleanor, who did look like two million bucks and was wearing a watch worth probably $50,000, had talked to the manager, who'd talked to someone else, and Benson's was going to make an exception for this party of 6.

Ten minutes later, a handsome young waiter arrived with a tray of glasses of champagne. "At last," breathed Eleanor, giving him a movie-star smile. She clicked glasses with Jonathan, and they both drank.

"You can start, Dad." she announced. "Tea will come while you talk. God, I'm famished. Don't leave those bubbles to go flat, guys."

"Piss off, Elly."

"Hey," said Richard, making a time-out sign. "Get real."

"That's funny," laughed Caroline. "The cosmetic surgeon wants us to get fucking real."

"Ooh, Mother Theresa's swearing!"

"I flew three thousand miles for this?"

Lily leaned towards Joe and whispered in his ear, "I love you."

"Children," said Lily. "Enough. Joe, begin."

"Well," said Joe. There was no cover for his hand, nothing to grip without anyone seeing. Lily reached over and grabbed his hand, holding it firmly.

He cleared his throat. "As you all might realize, your mother and I didn't exactly decide to sock money into property when we had to sell the family home and move into an apartment by ourselves."

Richard chuckled. The family home had been the floor above the restaurant, cold, drafty, and with such squeaky floorboards that he spent many sleepless nights under the sheets, hiding from ghosts. His parents now lived in a dinky old apartment on the edge of Chinatown.

"Geez, I thought you'd traded the old life for one in a penthouse," he quipped, grinning.

"No, dear," said his mother. "Not even a yacht."

The two of them provided Joe with the wind he needed.

"This is what we plan to do," he said, launching straight into it.

The plan was to buy the two derelict buildings that were both owned by that old pawn shop guy (the ownership records listed him as Isaac E. Silver), and to build the neighborhood center there, setting it up as a non-profit trust. A place for the poor of the neighborhood to spend the day and perhaps learn how to live, a place with cream soup and tapioca, not for free. Not for charity, which has no dignity, Caroline. No. The food would be inexpensive, but have to pay for itself. There would be check cashing available, of course, for no additional fee. As for the shops that would disappear, that would be a blessing. There was no need for Triumph anymore, not when there was now a big bright supermarket in the new shopping center. And that pawn shop. Pawn shops are disgusting little parasites. So much better to teach people to make their money stretch, to plan ahead— all part of the good training that the neighborhood center could pass out. The block was blighted, so the Tangs could be generous and give the old man a good retirement, then something safe and suitable, and there would still be enough money left over from the sale to give each child a windfall of $100,000.

"Those bums took advantage of you all our lives, and now you want to give them a neighborhood center?" The Tang's oldest girl, Caroline, a doctor in Doctors Without Borders, had the most trenchant argument. "If you want to do good for the world, help people who are refugees, help young people, help anyone, Mom and

Dad. But help someone who's worth it, not a bunch of old drunks, potheads, crazies and prostitutes."

The rest of the Tang children agreed. Richard nodded sagely, adding "Sad but true." Jonathan, the accountant with Standard & Poor's went into detail about what was wrong with the plan. Even Eleanor, whose education (training to be a ballerina) had been the most expensive for her parents and who always found her dad an easy touch, agreed with her sister and brothers, reacting with disgust and horror to her parents' idea of squandering this long-awaited boon.

The Royal Tea, by the way, had arrived, by bits and pieces. Small pots of tepid water and cups with one teabag per cup. Little dry "scones", cold as gravestones, that made Joe want to laugh or scream. Compared to his mother's famous melt-in-the-mouth baking powder biscuits, pastries that . . . He tried to control his breathing, to not let anything that doesn't matter bother him—just knowing that Lily was equally outraged helped, immensely. They both tried to keep to the important issue, telling their children this news that they had hoped would bring the family together, give the children a sense of pride, if only by association, by family connection.

"As an investment, you couldn't do worse," advised Jonathan, the accountant. "It's going nowhere. And a non-profit trust!" He shuddered. "I bet you want to call it the Joseph and Lily—"

"Certainly not!" said Lily, incensed. She didn't have to whisper here. The high-ceilinged lobby was filled with a dull echoing din that made it hard to hear, let alone make real conversation.

"Down, Mother," said Joe. They had planned to call the place Tang's Community Center, thinking of two ghosts: Joe's father and Tang's. Joe scrootched closer to Lily on the couch. They gave each other strength, but not enough.

"Dream on," Caroline said, and even with the sound distortion caused by the ambience, Caroline's intent was clear. She had made the word "dream" evoke a nightmare. Richard leaned over the table clutter and whispered loudly, "Dad, do you know there is such a thing as male menopause?" Jonathan, sprawling back in his little chair, delivered a lecture about this being a typical case of older people who come into money. "They need to have their money managed because they are so irresponsible about it. It often slips away, taken by the unscrupulous who prey on the loneliness of the retired, their fears of death. Uh," he said. "Of course you're not them, but never turn good fortune around."

All but the daughter-in-law who said nothing but looked uncomfortable, nixed in no uncertain terms, both the neighborhood center and other thoughts the parents might have along those lines, letting it be known in no uncertain terms that if even $50,000 were "thrown away on charity," the parents' new spendthrift lifestyle would be hotly disputed. Eleanor put it bluntly. "Like dirty laundry aired in court." Jonathan mustn't have thought that adequate, for he added, "I'm worried about you, Dad. Are you clinically depressed?"

"He was happy till he came here!" Lily said. "This discussion is over."

The party broke up quickly after that, the children talking about schedules, and making promises they wouldn't keep, about "catching up."

A busboy took away the mess, but neither Joe nor Lily could catch anyone's eye for the bill, so Joe said he'd go to the bar to settle up. "Just leave," said Lily. "You won't have enough. I'll meet you across the street in the park."

Joe nodded. He felt in his pocket.

"Go," Lily ordered. "I'll pay the tip. And don't ask." He grimaced, but also felt so relieved and in such perfect harmony. How many other couples could be together for so many years and be so much in synch? Money divides and conquers but can also show how much two people are perfectly suited to each other. About the tip: Both Lily and Joe resented paying it so much that they felt the imposition of it as an insult. But they would never jilt a worker. Bad service here came from the top down. But what could you expect in a place like this? As Joe's father had said, Orwell was right. Never eat in a grand hotel.

Joe was waiting for the light to change when his arm was grabbed.

"Sorry to startle you, Dad," said Richard. "I had to catch you without the others."

Richard took Joe's elbow and stepped off the curb.

"I can walk," said Joe, pulling free. When they reached the grass he stopped and faced his son.

"What is it you wish to say?"

"I, we, me and Alessandra just want to say we're here for you, Dad. You and Mom should come to LA and have a break. We've got a spare room, or there's a comfortable hotel just two minutes taxi ride away. Frankly, Dad, you look terrible. And so does Mom."

"So we could relax at or near your place?"

"Yes. You don't know what to do with yourself now. Alessandra could take Mom shopping. We could show you the sights, and you could look at my clinic, see what I'd like to do to expand. You could—"

"Thank you, Richard. And give our love to Alessandra." He turned on his heels, took a scone out of his pocket, and clucked to a pigeon.

The bill came to $372, plus the tip. 6 Benson Royal Afternoon Teas at $42ea plus a surcharge of $20 per person, for the Outside of Hours service.

Now at mid-day in the park, there was not a bench seat to be had. "Let's sit on the grass," said Lily.

They couldn't find a place that was free of people, and clean.

Lily took his arm and they set out heading towards Chinatown, taking the less busy streets, walking uphill with their backs bent.

"My baby," said Lily.

"Ours." A tear ran down his face. "Dead. What would my father say?"

"Mister CSS?"

That was the name that he had come to be known as, after he turned his thriving restaurant into a soup kitchen in 1930. He made his soup as nutritious as he always had, boiling the chickens to make rich stock, shredding them into the broth, pouring in a shower of golden noodles, and greens that no self-respecting American would be caught dead eating unless they were starving or ate the weeds unknowingly in Chink grub, making the whole pot boil furiously, then dropping in the beaten eggs. *Chicken and spit soup*, people called it, many of them men who'd eaten three squares there and paid him good money only months earlier, when the street's boomtimes seemed unstoppable, the ring of hammers to be the sound of unbeatable progress. Some of the customers were women who had also worked hard, in many positions.

Why did he do it? He said that it was because he was pulled into a shop during a cleanup of Chinamen, when he was running a little eatery in a goldmining town that collapsed soon after. The grocer was bashed to death, his cart burned, his mule butchered where he stood, just for fun. And nobody had laundered clothes afterwards in that dump of a place. That man who pulled him into the haberdashers was, as he said to his children, as Chinese as Moses.

"They don't even care about ancestors," Joe Tang mumbled, possibly talking to himself.

"Of course not," said Lily sharply. "Any more than history."

"Customers. What was the use of making the kids work in the restaurant?" Joe's right eye twitched. "What did they learn about respect?"

"Nothing," Lily thought, but she said, "We can't condemn them for wanting what every New Year's wish asks for."

"Didn't we give them better values?"

Lily didn't say but she had formed her own theories. Their firstborn, Caroline, had served in terrible places, but she acted like—Eleanor was nasty but so right. Caroline probably dreamed she was Mother Theresa. She loved administering to the powerless in some place that no one changed politically, so she'd patch up and save lives and be a face for getting more funds, but, she always argued, "Like my organization, I'm strictly non-political. That's how I can help." At Tang's as a teen, she had refused to wait on customers, and cried the time her father forced her to clean tables. Caroline and Eleanor, the oldest and youngest, had the strongest personalities of the children. Lily thought that Eleanor had become addicted to money, and was not-so-slowly falling into the trap that women less beautiful than Eleanor had, since time began. Eleanor was the most scathing about the women for whom Tang's had been a shelter. She was the worst about the retired ones, some of whom had merely been peep show professionals with tragic taste in men.

"Dreaming?" said Joe.

Without discussing it, they had walked past their apartment house and all the way to Chinatown. The closest thing that they had to 'home' now was the place where they were now too embarrassed to return to. They passed its entrance and went around to the alley, to the scrap of green, but one old man was sitting on the single bench, and another was practicing Tai Chi. They continued past and were in another minute, back on one of the frenetically busy streets.

They had separated as soon as they entered Chinatown, but Joe was dragging his feet and starting to breathe heavily. "I need to stop," said Lily, "Let's go in." She shoved the way through into the first place she'd seen that would have chairs and tables inside. It had a fishtank in the window.

"You can't be hungry," said Joe.

"Of course not. I'm tired."

They'd barely pulled out their chairs when a young man bustled over with an efficient frown. Lily ordered two bowls of soup and he rushed away.

"Give me your hands before it comes," she said to Joe. "We'll rest here, and then go."

"Where to? Our child is dead."

"You're acting like an angry ghost. But you're not dead." She ran her slippered foot up his leg. "You're not even an old man."

"Lily!" he whispered, alarmed. Anyone could have seen that. "What you on about?"

"Let's make another."

Joe looked at his wife fondly. They had always been a match made in some ethereal cloud of happiness.

Two soups were plonked on the sweaty table between them, the man twisting away in the same fluid movement.

"You flatter my sperm," said Joe.

"There's nothing wrong with *any* of your workings," Lily chuckled. "But I didn't mean that kind of child. They're too much of a heartache."

"Then?"

"Maybe we can think of something if we visit."

Lily might as well have dumped a bag of ice cubes down his back . He hadn't been able to face seeing the old site. Had banned himself from ever going back.

"I mean the place," Lily said. "You know. At the least, we could imagine the buildings whisked away in a cloud, Triumph and Silvers Pawn two bad memories best forgotten."

" . . . okay."

"Or are you tired? Too much for one day?" Lily asked this with a twinkle in her eye.

"Not unless you plan to jog there." His attempt at bluster was so half-hearted.

"Joe," she said, shoving the bowls away. "You worried you might cry if we're mobbed by our customers?"

He was. Sometimes he had nightmares about those customers living off the garbage bins outside that bright young fast-food court.

He didn't know if he'd be able to stand without bursting into tears, the love and the missing him of those he hadn't been able to say good-bye to. But for Lily's sake, and a kind of ceremonial Putting to Death of their Tang Neighborhood Center dream, he stood up. "Let's go anyway."

"Kiddo," she said, "We're not down and out. So we can't spend our children's birthright." She screwed up her mouth at birthright. "Think smoke and mirrors."

Lily had a thing about smoke and mirrors, and when the children were young, had performed magic tricks at their birthday parties.

"Maybe I can bring a moment of joy to some of them," she said.

"The man with the cat?"

"Poor him," said Lily. The man with the cat—the Tangs had never addressed nor remembered anyone by name—the crazy in the wheelchair (he never acted crazy except that he mumbled to himself, always wore the pothead sweatshirt, and had that fantastical platform above his wheelchair where they supposed the cat slept)—in short, the man with the cat had come every day for his beef stew on rice and pumpkin pie for dessert. And every day Charles would come out of the kitchen and take the cat into the storeroom behind the kitchen, where he'd feed that cat huge amounts of fresh chicken or an egg foo yung without sauce or fresh shelled prawns or a fat fishhead, and always a saucer of milk. Like an overattentive waiter, Charles would stand curved like a taut bow, watching the cat eat, and once the plate was polished he would sit on a milk crate while the cat cleaned himself on Charles' lap and fell asleep, while the man in the wheelchair ate his meal and took his time over coffee. Lily and sometimes Joe had to cook then. Nothing could shift Charles. He was crazy about the cat. The catfood was billed as "Tea, cup—20c." Once a week Charles would hand Lily a ten-dollar bill, saying "It's for the kitty."

"Let's get a fish head for the cat," said Joe.

"And a couple chicken wings."

The long walk down was harder on the knees than the walk up had been, but they strolled toward the place of their dreams in remarkably sprightly form—as soon as they were outside Chinatown, hand in hand.

GET OFFA MY curb!" Mary screams, and a silver-haired couple dressed for a luxury safari does a right-about turn, crosses the other curb and escapes walking just quickly enough that you know he's saying "Don't run, or they'll come after us." The Nikon cord is held so tightly, it pulls his neck down.

"Not safe there!" the man whispers, as Joe and Lily pass, both rather amused and disgusted by these wealthy bigots who think a person who is poor is someone out to rob them. They reach the corner where, across the street is Triumph's, and against its window, a man in an oddly rigged out wheelchair, with a fanciful cat's loft above his head edged with tiny lightbulbs. In the late afternoon, the shadows are sharp and deep, so his lap is in shadow and the Tangs can't see the cat, but the light hits the letters on his sweatshirt just so. The rainbow colors of "Stairway to Heaven" glow.

"Some things never change," says Lily, kissing Joe's ear. They are smiling and excited as children as they cross the street towards him and the woman they both remember as "the half-order beef stew lady."

"That's my curb!" she screeches at them.

They stumble back, confused. She'd never been a problem in Tang's. "She doesn't know us," says Lily. Joe is suddenly shaking like an old man.

"Ain't you the ching chongs?" says a man, pulling himself free of the wall he'd been leaning against.

"Foo yung," says Lily under her breath. She grips Joe's arm tighter. "We're the Tangs, yes," she says brightly.

"What you come here for," he says. "Need a place to stay?"

"The Brandon's full," someone else says.

"So much you know. Evelyn popped her cork last night."

"Nah!"

"True."

"Good old girl."

"No she wasn't," says Mary. "Thank god. Now what brings you two to our fair quarter?" She had pushed forward to stand in front of Joe and Lily. Her hands are on her hips. All she needs is a badge.

"We thought to visit," Lily says.

"They need sympathy," someone says.

"Don' hol' id agains' 'em," says mister sippy cups cream soup and apple sauce.

"No decent person would," says miss baked apple (Lily thinks. Joe thinks she's miss 11AM two dishes of warm tapioca please.)

"Nobody worth his salt will think less of you for failing," says someone with a voice the Tangs recognize.

"Mary," he says. She waves her arms, the growing crowd parts, and the man with the cat rolls up beside her. Mary dips her head below the platform and gives him a kiss on the cheek.

The Tangs are almost pathetically relieved that he has addressed them. Joe nudges Lily, who dips into her bag. "We brought this for your cat," she says, holding out the bags of fish head and chicken wings.

"You taking the piss outa him," someone says. "I'll knock some respect into—"

"I'll knock *you*," says Mary. "Look at their faces. You of all people should know a suck up when you see one. They're just lonely SOBs looking make friends any way they can."

"Tesla died a year ago next Tuesday," says the man in the chair.

"I'm terribly sorry," Lily says. The clouded plastic bags of gifts hang from her hand. The fish head bag has sprung a leak. It's smelly, too.

"Please don't say you're sorry for something you didn't do," says a woman.

"Life is a state of flux," says the man in the wheelchair. "But you didn't come here to learn philosophy, so what's up?"

"We had an idea," says Lily, nudging Joe. He stands like some beaten old man. "Joe here," says Lily, "felt so bad when we had to close down that he couldn't face you to say good bye."

"Don't cry." Mary reaches into a pocket and pulls out a packet of tissues. She hands Joe a fresh one.

"Good byes are always tough," says old mom-tattoo chocolate tapioca.

"We didn't have any choice but to sell," says Lily.

"See what I said," says Mary to the crowd. "The manifest destiny of capitalist scumbags. But." She winks at Joe and Lily, not in fun but in mockery. "Didn't you make enough money out of it to start a country? You want to tear down this neighborhood and plonk another restaurant here?"

"Just try," says mister chili with extra saltines. "I've demo'd since '65."

"Shut up," says the man in the wheelchair. "What exactly are you two lobbying us for?"

"Nothing!" Lily's spirit is roused. "We wanted to build you a neighborhood center with the money. Our children have objected. We came here to see if in some way, we could brighten your lives."

"Lily can do magic tricks," Joe says, so lamely that the crowd explodes into laughter, hoarse, cackling, and could-you-believe it wry.

"And what would this neighborhood center have had?" asks the man in the wheelchair.

"What would you want?" says Lily.

"A bathroom of my own," a young female voice pipes up. "Yes, yes, yes!" another grunts orgasmically.

"You two'll have room service soon enough, in Hell," says Mary, to applause. She turns to Lily. "Please don't be offended if your generosity is treated here with, uh, contempt. We tend to be too cynical here for our own good."

Mary's face feels hot. "This is why we wanted to help. We were thinking of a place that cares about you, where you could get in out of the weather." She stopped herself before she blurted anything about their plans to include a place with the Tang's old regular wholesome stuff, not a soup kitchen but a place that paid for itself, of course. With everyone here being so suspicious, she's unable to share all the joy that she and Joe had thinking of this wonderful place that these people would spend so much of their days in— in their own neighborhood center. So she says, "Where you could cash your, uh, paychecks without someone taking a commission, where financial parasites don't prey on you, where people could learn things that would make their lives easier, like, say, how to manage your money."

The corners of Mary's mouth stretch. "What a wonderful idea."

"Down, girl," says the man in the wheelchair. "Mary was an auditor."

"Auditor?"

"Don't act so astounded," she says. "If you want to find an auditor who doesn't audit, look in other neighborhoods. I *did* audit."

"My girlfriend's a whistleblower," says the man in the wheelchair.

"Ex," she says primly. "And my boyfriend here is a complete nut. Will someone get these two some seats!"

The door to Triumph had been open during this commotion, and now it opened further. A tall handsome young man comes out of it carrying two drink crates. He nods to first Mary, then the man in the wheelchair, who points to the pavement right beside Mary's usual spot. The young man upends the crates and holds out his hand to shake both Lily's and Joe's. "I'm Daniel Park. We've never met but you must be someone special. Whoever you are, you don't know how lucky you are. That's Professor Karel Vlachova."

"Ex," says the man without the cat. "Mary?"

"Let the show begin!" she hollers. "Hey you useless gawkers. Will somebody drag Silvers from his cave?"

The pavement down the block rings with footsteps and commands. Activities seem to be happening back there on both sides of the street. In the meantime, several people come up to the Tangs who, seated on the crates, now have to look up to everyone who leans over and introduces themselves. Joe is coming back to life, though in a fragile way. He seems suddenly, so old. People are treating him with a special kind of respect—they have that *Please don't drop dead here* look in their eyes, but this might also have eased their own shyness, for there are some people who come over and say they're sorry Tang's closed down, a few introducing themselves formally, two even putting out their hands to shake. One woman that the Tangs had never met, comes merely to sympathize. "I loved work," she says. "It's a terrible thing when you have no purpose any more, isn't it?"

"Sorry to interrupt, Odille," says Mary. "Karel asks if these folks need to eat now. Are you hungry?"

"No thank you," says Lily quickly, grabbing Joe's hand.

"You're a regular Mister Waterworks." Mary smiles. She hands Joe a new tissue. "You're stealing Karel's stock. He cries over the death of a cockroach."

"Thank you," says Lily.

"Don't thank me, lady. I think it's sexy. If your man cries any more, I'm gonna steal him away from you."

"Silvers is coming," people yell. "Make way."

A rumbling announces the approach of a rickety two-storey clothes rack.

A man puts his hands on Lily and Joe's shoulders, and leans down. "Don't worry if you're hungry. This'll make you forget. And we always eat after the show."

"How?" asks Lily.

"Order in, of course."

"In?" asks Joe. He seems more his old self again.

"Not in, of course, but here. They deliver here. God," he says to Joe. "You really are helpless."

"We've never ordered meals to go," Lily explains. "But how do you pay?"

"Are you implying I mooch?" His fists balled.

"Back off, Zooter," says Karel Vlachova. "She's doesn't know enough to imply. We divide the tab amongst everyone who's gonna eat, like people do at a restaurant, except with us, there's both credit and more fairness, or you're taught a lesson, and if that doesn't do it, you're out. Satisfied, Zooter? You need taming."

Meanwhile Mary had physically shoved the crowd into position, arranging people in a semicircle looking toward Mary's Corner—where she positions herself on the edge of the curb. Karel Vlachova rolls himself next to her.

On the opposite corner, by a fire hydrant, a rumpled pot-bellied little man leans over a fire hydrant.

"Mom, Dad, it's time," calls Daniel Park.

"Hit it," says Karel Vlachova, pointing like an orchestra conductor, to Mary and the pot-bellied man.

Mary reaches down, fiddles with something, then stamps on her curb.

The mess of wires above rattle, and the two dead-eyed traffic lights hanging from them come to life, flickering once, twice, and now to a rhythm—in purples, blues, turquoises, every color under the rainbow but what is supposed to be in that light—changing, not to some designated traffic flow determinator but to the beat of Stairway to Heaven, booming from the very street.

And now, the lights that were a show enough in themselves, take on a psychedelic air as the giant clothes rack jerks orgasmically, and shoots its load—out of a thousand tiny holes along its length. The rain machine stands higher than the lights so every bit of color becomes a rainbow and a million rainbows fall upon the crowd, a crowd that is now united and divided—dancing, dreaming, sighing, crying, heads thrown back in ecstasy.

"Here's spit in your eye!" bellows someone. Another bawls like a drunk. The lights above and darkness below make all the people into one moving mass. "You gotta dance," says a burly man with a face like a mound of strawberries with two blueberries for eyes, pulling Lily and Joe up as if they're stuffed toys.

Karel clears his throat. "I think they need to cool their feet, Burt. But don't you save your leather."

"I ain't got no mercy for shoes," laughs Burt. He lowers Lily and Joe gently back into their places on the crates, and skips off.

The music makes the pavement vibrate. Lily looks toward Joe, wishing they could get up and dance—privately and yet cocooned in this world.

Stairway to Heaven rises to a crescendo, and crashes to end with a spectacular display of crazily loony lights, as seductively funny and alluring as a cartoon concussion.

"Ready, Mary?" says Karel. "Daniel?"

"Yes, Professor."

"Everyone," commands Mary. "Stand back and shut the fuck up. And you two. This is for you."

The man in the wheelchair gets up out of his chair, picks up the seat cushion and hands it to Daniel Park, then picks a keyboard and some kind of metal box out of the seat, places them on the cat's bed, and messes around. Mary and Daniel watch his left hand, which rises, holds, and jabs to Mary.

She jumps down from the curb and bashes a heel backwards, hard.

Sparks pop from the curb—and now smoke rolls upwards in two long streaming curls, as from a dragon reclining in the drain, smoking a giant stogie out the stormwater window.

The ribbons of smoke are purple, yellow, green, silver and gold, an unkempt tangle that now meets and rolls with the crazy dancing rainbow of the hanging lights.

"Like New Year's without fireworks," whispers Lily. "But who needs fireworks?"

"Now?" says Daniel.

"You bet," says Karel.

" . . . It . . . works." Daniel's voice is husky.

"How could you doubt," says the professor. "Don't look at us, you idiots. There!"

Something is emerging from the curb.

There—tarnished silver, titanium blue, jade, gold, coral-orange, leaping-flame red—in a shimmering rainbow of colors something slips smoothly upwards. Up it flies in a sinuous twisting curve of a leap, up so high that it reaches the blackness where all lights are below, where it hovers, splayed out and shimmering for a moment, then arcs down in a curved fall, its shining head shaking back and forth as it snaps at smoke ribbons, gulping them, gaining even more ever-changing colors with every bite. And with a complicated twist and twirl that look to be done merely to show off, it lands heavily, but neatly on the wires.

Lily rubs her eyes, thinking this is one of those dreams where you know you're dreaming. Besides, she feels wet. Any moment now, she'll wake and need to go to the toilet. But it's still up there, looking more real than ever.

People are screaming too much to think.

"It's a fish with a pee!"

"What the—?"

"Wodehouse."

"It's a flying fish bird!"

"It's evolution."

"What am I gonna feel like tomorrow?"

"Is it real?"

"It's a trip."

"Freee key."

Whatever it is, it's being spattered by the rain machine, but that makes it take on a rainbow-glitter halo and become even more kaleidoscopically unreal as in *I'm having an unreal time*. It's looking down at Mary's Corner, stretching out, craning its neck and swaying its head back and forth, peering.

Several people point to themselves hopefully and one says "Me?" in mistake. It shakes itself, shedding a shower of shattered rainbows, and then puffs out its chest and inclines its head, singling out with its shining full-moon eyes—Joe.

And now it winks at Joe in quite a confidential way.

"Joe," you can imagine it saying. "I might have the head and neck of the fish that got away, weighed down by the pecs and wings, tail and feet, of a phoenix, but that never stopped me having fun. Hell, it gives me added swagger. Joe, let's go do something. Something totally outrageous."

"Let's," says Joe, his eyes streaming rainbows.

Baad-hin'jan and the Chickpea

His real name, it has been written, was something approaching Xzhul, but everyone called him Baad-hin'jan—eggplant. Like that smooth, agreeably plump vegetable, everyone he touched wanted more of him and thought him quite as delicious as lovers do each other's mouth. Yet every pleasure attracts those who condemn it, so this name for eggplant also means *demon's eggs*.

And so it was that physicians condemned him as poison, a causer of black bile, disfiguring and deadly growths, black spots on the face—and a stomach filled with stones like a man who stores inside, his every memory of being wronged.

So his reputation was hotly disputed, in whispers, innuendo, guarded hisses, not the least reason being that he was not a physician himself. No, he had been merely a curiosity present one afternoon on the Island of Delights when the Caliph, himself a lover of eggplant, choked on a dried chickpea that must have been missed in the smooth puree. Baad-hin'jan threw himself at the Caliph, bear-hugged him and squeezed, hard. The chickpea flew out of the Caliph's mouth as well as a prodigious mouthful of golden pastry rich with kidney fat which must have been wrapped around stiff sesame paste slathered with pureed roasted garlic and topped with an army of oil-soaked eggplant slices. Indeed, so much flew out of the Caliph's mouth that it was a wonder anyone found the dried chick pea. If it hadn't hit the visiting ambassador in the eye, this would have been another case of the Caliph's enthusiastic eating, his overexuberance often causing him to, as the saying went, paint the chamber in many colours.

So the man whose name had not been announced and who never actually mentioned his name, was either foolhardy in the extreme, brave and thoughtful, or thoughtlessly adventurous. But who can know, just as who can know the reason that in other lands, a King's heart (just as every other man's) sits in the left side of his chest when favoured guests sit to his right? A mystery as unsolvable as the reason why Baad-hin'jan didn't watch whatever came to pass as impassively as the other guests.

Due to the quick action of the strangely garbed companion/translator of the ambassador, the Caliph's life was saved and another's shortened to perhaps a half hour more, whence he was captured on a donkey he was practically beating to death in his haste to flee the city. He shouldn't have pretended to be a simple old man, not smelling as he did, of Faludhaj (the Caliph's favourite chewy honey pudding). Indeed, he was spotted not because of his scent, for no one wished to get that close. He had attracted as many bees as a hive. So instead of him being taken to the Palace to provide a spectacle of justice, an arrow was loosed upon him while he kicked the donkey. As he slipped to the cobbles, the donkey made away with surprising zeal, slipping out of its baskets filled with the stuffings that had attracted all those bees.

And so the Caliph gained no pleasure in the spectacle that was due any attempter on the Caliph's life, not that time. But the next day the eunuch who hadn't had any time, some would say, to pull off the mad lunger at the Caliph and choke him to death, was duly put to death. The eunuch did not attempt to defend himself against the fact of his standing for those seconds like a post (not that he would have been granted a voice) and died with a quizzical expression on his black-tongued face.

As to the old man, he was never spoken of, because the very insignificance of his motivation was an insult to the Caliph. But the reason he poked the chickpea into the dish of chickpea puree just before it left the kitchen, was that he despaired of his elbow having given out, after all these years, with so little to show for it. No longer would he be able to mix the Caliph's favourite chewy pudding with the zeal it needed, yet he was still only a second-class confectioner. He could not command anyone, but was himself now liable to be dismissed, thrown away like a wooden spoon that snapped. So the old man thought to kill the Caliph only because he could. He had the means to kill the Caliph, means that would be sure to miss the royal taster unless Fate was unusually playful. And so the Caliph's death afforded the old man with a merely second-class satisfaction but it was something, the Caliph dying in place of the master confectioner who the old man, who had been beaten by the master's tongue and stirring stick for years, couldn't think how to kill.

So unfair, therefore, that he sought to take his bad fortune out on the Caliph as a proxy. This insult would have earned the second-grade confectioner an especially showy death, but his petty action was *doubly*—No!— *triply* insulting to the ruler. In fleeing with all that 1) stolen pudding made for 2) the mouth of the Caliph *only*, he attracted the bees, and 3) thereby made himself unavailable for easy capture, therefore robbing the Caliph of the entertainment of justice served.

This gallimaufry of arousers of spirits that no subject wished to see resulted in a deep silence about the chick-pea miscreant, so much so that no one ever told the Caliph about this incorrigible worm.

Ah, life—like this telling, always too little or too much. I shouldn't have tarried with this worm in the telling here, but as it is said, *A Caliph can slip on a worm and break his neck*, so did this worm change the life and fortunes of both the Caliph and the man who soon was known as Baad-hin'jan, for that very day the Caliph declared him "brother," and bade him sup by his right side, a bidding that had never occurred in the Palace in anyone's tales or memory—for as everyone knows, *You can't stab a man across a floorcloth laden with dishes, but anyone who can whisper in your ear can wrap a scarf around your neck.*

First, when the Caliph called his lifesaver "brother" he hadn't meant "brother" as the Caliph had always lived (he had had all his brothers strangled with a silk scarf about which he was quite sentimental) but said "brother" in the sense that he thought this foreign guest would understand—for the Caliph felt about this odd foreigner, a trust he'd felt in no man.

And what of Xzhool, or Zzhul, or whoever he was? An incorrible adventurer, he had acted before he thought, but then again, he'd never been able to cure himself of the habit, partly because he'd never known if it were a fault or a gift. He had met the ambassador while travelling, and the other man had begged for his company. There was something about Xzhul that was both exciting and comforting . . .

& yet, an about-face. A confession: How could—some of you have asked—the bowman who so decisively arrested the guilty man, have known about that chickpea? How could he have known the motives behind the attempted murder? How could he have known that there had even *been* an attempt to choke the Caliph, in his wildest nightmare, or wish?

The old man was caught looking like a thief, his very manner attracting such suspicion that he was targeted, killed, his goods discovered after the fact, which proved the reasonable suspicion, and then the thief was as remembered as the fly you killed one day last summer between bites of a melon.

I told you about him, I suppose, because I am the eye, I am the ear—and though men pay remarkably scant attention to their lives, I am an incorrigible romantic. So much so that though the old man might have felt only fear and the comical rage of one who can do nothing to better himself, I knew what he would have articulated, if he had the sense he never knew. So in truth I must confess, no one spoke of the thief of the Caliph's favourite honey pudding because everyone knew that a lapse that allowed of that brief slip was one that demanded a correction, the one that the Caliph had imported from foreign lands, known as the 'boiled pudding'.

So now having witnessed my confection, I beg to pun, let us hasten back to the Caliph and the foreigner, that annoyingly attractive and comfortable looking, oddly dressed man who was never actually introduced and because the Caliph could hardly ask, was called by the Caliph "brother," which tickled the ruler, "bear without a nose-ring," which was too unwieldy to be fun, and finally, during a meal that the Caliph particularly relished but that his physicians decried, the name that stuck, Baad-hin'jan.

For this name suited him royally. This Baad-hin'jan gave the physicians great pain, as well as everyone else in the Palace bureaucracy. If you had heard the whispers between the chief eunuch and the chief physician regarding plans to topple, literally, this poisonous intruder, your blood would chill. Not that they thought to even pay another to put the physician's favoured Medicine to End Life in Baad-hin'jan's cup. The problem with Fate is that if you try to change it and it objects, it can turn upon you in the most vicious way. So they only fantasised to each other, but both knew that Fate would deal them Death if they were forced to take their own medicine.

Now, it amused Baad-hin'jan, for a while, that the Caliph placed him by his side. But you can only see so much out of the corner of your eye. What no one knew because no one asked, was that this strange, rash traveller with such unique skills and charm—some said *sorcery*—was a collector, a collector of observations. He'd gone from court to court, and could tell you tales of rulers who scattered rubies to the poor, the next day making a poor man eat a bag of rubies. He'd sat beside one king who cried at the beauty of a perfect flaying. He'd stroked the hand and brought a sense of perfect solace to another who was mourning his favourite songbird, eaten by a rat who'd slipped through the bars. He'd held up a king's head and fed him simple buckwheat gruel on that singularly good man's deathbed. And at the man's deathrattle, Baad-hin'jan (who was known in that realm as Balmsly) cried tears as bitter as that drawn forth from any eggplant when sliced open. For, though the ruler had been poisoned by his son, a tale all too common in Baad-hin'jan's collection—this good man being a ruler was a story so unique in Baad-hin'jan's observation that he would have thought it a fairytale, if he hadn't known it to be true.

Indeed, though Baad-hin'jan had a something about him that made anyone he touched feel incomparably good, he had no magic power, nor was he a medicament. Nor, to his dismay, could he make a ruler *be* good. He couldn't, to his despair, change anything about them, any more than he could change day into night. This didn't stop him from trying.

And so this particular caliph was, as a ruler, depressingly common garden.

But Baad-hin'jan was getting stubborn in his maturity. His spine was also getting contrary, complaining of all those rugged roads it had been knocked around on. So Baad-hin'jan determined to not think of the dreariness of this caliph who like so many rulers, fancied himself as a gourmet at the same time as shoving so much in his mouth that they might as well have been a heap of kitchen scraps. Baad-hin'jan didn't look away from the Caliph's refined sense of torture. Every ruler but one in Baad-hin'jan's observations, had thought himself an expert at meting out pain and death, and of the entertainment: a connoiseur.

And Baad-hin'jan was used to palace intrigue, had grown eyes on the back of his head and an ability to sleep wakeful. So the hate he felt from so many in the Palace just kept him warm.

Baad-hin'jan, he said to himself (for he rather liked this name) *This time you're going to change the man, and not only that. You're going to lay your touch upon everyone in the Palace, and make them serve their masters.*

A crazy idea. Insane as jumping out at the Caliph. For even the good king hadn't thought of the people as his masters. Yet if they hadn't lashed the stalks of wheat till they gave up their grain, he would not have been able to eat his fine white manchet. If they hadn't flayed their flax, he would have been naked as a newborn.

If the physicians had only known what was in Baad-hin'jan's heart, the Caliph would have relished seeing his best eagle tear it out. But hate is just as blind as love. And say that Baad-hin'jan had been wont to speak? Who spoke to Baad-hin'jan? The haters only spoke *of* him and the Caliph only spoke *at* him.

The Caliph was so rich that he only got richer, ambassadors arriving daily trailing, like comets, streams of servants bearing and leading precious gifts. Gold urns beyond measure, strings of pearls, wild-eyed zebras, elephants that would soon die of being fed too few kitchen scraps, beautiful women and sloe-eyed boys. Often the ambassador's face would be streaming with cold sweat because this surfeit brought on peevishness. They all knew the terror of a ruler's yawn.

One day while Baad-hin'jan pondered how to really change minds while he stroked the Caliph's hand during a royal attack of boredom, a new ambassador came to the fore, this one not being a genuine ambassador at all.

"The Chief Confectioner to the Court of Gufelteland" the Chief Eunuch announced (it sounded something like Gufelteland, but all far lands were so hard to keep straight, so the Palace never tried).

The man bowed, rather perfunctorily. Dressed simply, with a plain cap and a striped robe, he laid on the floor a plain wooden box.

The Caliph sat up and nudged Baad-hin'jan. "Open it, brother."

Baad-hin'jan got off his cushions and went forward. There was always a certain thrill to anything to be opened. He'd never forget the basket with the cobra.

One could never show fear, which could be taken for fear or disrespect.

He kneeled on the floor, his body between the mystery and the Caliph, and opened the lid.

"Careful, sire," said the man introduced as Chief Confectioner. "Let her rest on her bed."

Baad-hin'jan nodded, but his famous sense of touch failed to charm the red silk cushion out of the box, so tightly was it stuffed in. So instead, he held his breath . . .

"Well!?" the Caliph thundered.

Baad-hin'jan stood up carefully and turned around. In his hands could have been four broken eggs, he held them with such delicate precision.

"I can't see!"

Baad-hin'jan lowered his hands slightly, but didn't rush forward. Nor did he look at the Caliph.

"You made this?" he asked in the confectioner's tongue.

"Yes, sire. "A token for his, err, majesty. I hope to learn a few somethings from your Chief Confectioner."

"What are you saying?!"

"Excuse me," Baad-hin'jan said to the confectioner, then glanced up at the Caliph. "Most Gracious One, this beautiful gift for you is made of sugar and feathers."

"Not feathers," the man whispered.

Baad-hin'jan started. The man was not only a wonder of a confectioner, but he could listen in. If only more ambassadors realised how useful this bit of learning would have been, in saving their own skins.

The Caliph held out his hand, eager as a child.

The confectioner leapt forward at the same time as Baad-hin'jan pulled back.

The Caliph's mouth opened, but no roar came out. He was simply too astounded.

"A thousand regrets," murmured Baad-hin'jan, and from any other man, this would be pouring oil on a fire, but this was the man who had saved the Caliph's life.

The confectioner dropped his eyes to the ground and took a step back. "She is only for gazing at, sire. Even now, you should put her back."

"We must treat this gift like fine glass," said Baad-hin'jan to the

Caliph. "Why don't I put it back in its—"

Baad-hin'jan had already turned his back and was bending down to lay the mask on the cushion, so he didn't see the stormclouds on the Caliph's face.

"Give me that!"

The Caliph shoved Baad-hin'jan, and the mask fell into the box where it shattered. Now the cushion was scattered with shiny white shards, some, like a broken plate, filled with decoration, fine scrollwork of verdigris green. The feathers also, were now a mess of shiny brilliants as lovely as a rubble of jewels. Yet this had all been made by a confectioner.

"Chmmm!" said the Caliph as he held the box to his chest with one hand while his other hand grabbed and stuffed all the shards in his mouth. The confectioner watched, horrified, but not able to stop himself thinking that the Caliph's jaws sounded like a peasant's clogs on a stony path.

When the Caliph finished, he dropped the box. "You try to take too much care of me," he said to Baad-hin'jan who, like the confectioner, had stayed silent and still through the whole demoliton.

"My nightingale," said the Caliph, leaving the room. The Chief Eunuch scurried to fetch the birdcage for the Caliph's nap.

"Would you like a sherbet?" said Baad-hin'jan to the confectioner.

That night, the Caliph ate even more piggily than usual, needing to be hugged, hard, yet again. This time a glut of saffroned honey cake flew from his mouth, painting the room gold and red.

The next morning, the Caliph fell off his cushions while his mouth was full with sweets. At midday, he rejected a taste of his favourite chewy honey pudding, complaining that his mouth tasted of copper, and suddenly he voided himself at two ends. Baad-hin'jan himself put the Caliph to bed, where he stroked his hand. The Caliph's skin looked like a peach, yellow tinged with green. The whites of his eyes were tinged with blue. By the evening, the Caliph's formerly black hair had a sheen of green. He was fretful as a teething babe. "Give me a, no give me a, something! Maybe some candied eggplant?"

Only Baad-hin'jan could say No. "Not even eggplant," said Baad-hin'jan. "But I could have whipped up for you, a dozen eggwhites. That would do you good."

"There's no taste in eggwhites!" whined the Caliph. "I loved that sweetmeat. Why didn't he make blocks of it? Do you have him in the kitchen teaching our blockhead?"

"As you speak," said Baad-hin'jan, which was only a partial lie. The visiting Chief Confectioner was in the kitchen with the palace's Chief Confectioner, but the Palace's specialist was like all others—only willing to tell his secrets to another Master, possibly, after death.

And besides, the palace's Chief Confectioner was distracted. He was trying with all his wiles, to extract the secret of this rival's heavenly sugar brittle, not the silly sculpture of it, but its taste. The Caliph cared not for form, just function.

What confused him most was that he was sure he already knew. He'd made hard candy for the Caliph many times before. His sugared almonds, though not lovely as this mask had purportedly been, with its beautiful woman's face, its pure white glowing smoothness a model of complexion, its plump, rich red lips, its gorgeous face decorations, sea-green swirls cut into it like the finest of tattoos, and that ridiculously showy headpiece attached somehow to its top, those jewel-bright 'feathers', all a waste of fancy because all—all!—shattered, and indiscriminately scooped up in three greedy handfuls that the Caliph tossed into his mouth as casually as he did, stoned dates. And wasn't it just the Caliph's habit!? Only when the mess was downed did he truly notice it, miss it, had to have it, couldn't live without the stuff, the stuff that his own "useless clod of a confectioner" had never made. Oh, the shame, and *danger* of it all. Fie on being a Master. Much safer to be a second-grade, that useless old bag of bones who should have been here. Where was he?

He was telling his nemisis a lie of a recipe when Baad-hin'jan entered the kitchen and fetched the man away. Neither heard the frothing when the Palace Confectioner, out of mixed pique and terror, climbed up and threw himself into his vat of boiling sugar. That would ruin the batch!

Baad-hin'jan and the visitor walked in the Palace rose garden.

That evening the Caliph took a turn for the worse. His face looked like a lemon, his hair like fresh seaweed, his vomit was green as was his shit.

His physicians insisted on taking over, and he was too weak to resist. They opened his veins to let his blood flow, they cupped his chest, and the most ambitious of them tried to administer a suppository.

Vainly he called for Baad-hin'jan, the only man he trusted. But the whole Palace barred the man from the Caliph's chambers.

That night, the Caliph got greener and greener, and since he couldn't keep suppositories in nor food down, the physicians decided to obey what his body obviously wished. They made him drink salt water till his mouth frothed like the tide; they purged him till his other end flowed like an unstopped river.

His limbs shook like an old beggar's."All so unnecessary," they chattered, well knowing that he could hear. "An evil spirit came to live with you when that Baad-hin'jan blew in. Your father trusted us . . . " The room resounded with their grumbles mixed with the sounds of violent retching, explosions of breath-catching stench.

"Sweets!" whispered the Caliph. "Bring me something sweet."

He was too weak by then to speak up, but his wish was still Command.

"We have no sweets," said the bravest physician. "The Chief Confectioner has ruined the batch."

Indeed, they'd looked. But the Caliph must have polished off everything to hand, and the kitchen was a mess, the tiled floor being topped with a new type of honeycomb brittle, which also glistened, like the glassy candy coating on a cherry, on the ex-Chief Confectioner.

"There is nothing sweet to give you," echoed the other physicians.

"That is no answer," answered the Caliph, so weakly that it might have been his last breath.

But who could take the chance?

"Baad-hin'jan," muttered one physician to another. "Tell him to make the visitor give us something."

And so they went to Baad-hin'jan's chamber where they had asked the Chief Eunuch to keep him if he dared try to gain the Caliph's presence.

And they demanded something, something that was simple and fast. They wouldn't take a No. They couldn't be argued with. They saw the visitor's little box of tricks. They made him open it. And it was they who grabbed from his hand, the two bottles of stuff that they rushed back and mixed together, pouring the sweet stuff as he reached for it, into the Caliph's mouth.

Sweeter than honey, sweeter than sugar, shining and delicious as lovers' spit. Even better than eggplant had ever been. The sweetness of life! The Caliph's smile was beatific, his eyes filled with tears that overflowed in his weakness, of love and gratitude to these men he had so shamefully neglected.

Meanwhile, Baad-hin'jan and the visiting Chief Confectioner whose stores they had pillaged, had been bundled unceremoniously out of the Palace and been advised by the Chief Eunuch that if they valued their lives, it would be best that they make themselves unknown furthermore to the Caliph. To make sure that they would leave, a soldier who'd been left, like the rest of the Palace Guard, unpaid, was given a purse of money to see these two out of the country and across the border.

At the Palace, the physicians and eunuchs were rejoicing. Finally, the Caliph was theirs again. He slept for a while and woke with convulsions. When he could speak he complained again, like a child, that his mouth tasted like copper. He obviously needed more of the miraculous elixir. The pure white sugar of lead that the visiting confectioner had used to give such a fine lacquered pallor to the beautiful face—they had almost used it up—and as for the verdigris that had so delicately bit into the face, the same colour that the physicians had pounced upon to give that trustworthy green to the Caliph's liquid sweet, this elixir that he was now so grateful for and that had so changed their own fortunes—there was only a smidgeon left in the bottle.

They set to work, therefore, commandeering all supplies of sugar of lead from every painter in the land, and all the verdigris from them too. Within hours, such was the power of a request from the Palace, that a storeroom was filled with bags of the stuffs, enough to satisfy the Caliph at his greediest for all eternity, they joked. For they were in the highest spirits. And so to the Caliph's increasingly garbled demand for More More More sweet, they complied with beaker after beaker, taking jealous turns supporting the Caliph's head, holding the beaker itself, while he drank.

By nightfall, between convulsions, vomiting and fomentous eruptions from his bowels, the Caliph praised their loyalty, and begged for more, his craving becoming ever more insatiable, his need to wipe the taste of copper, as he described it, becoming an obsession. The marble walls and floors of the Palace rang with his demands, and the physicians were all ensconced with him in his chamber. So in the room that held the source of these cravings, bag by bag disappeared. By the time darkness fell that night, everyone who was anyone in the Palace (minus the Guards) had drunk a beaker or more, of the drink that the Caliph couldn't get enough of. Even the physicians had each drunk well in the same way that they would have eaten the best tray of the Caliph's favourite pudding, if they'd been positioned to get their hands on it.

When morning broke, Baad-hin'jan and his new travelling companion who was to Baad-hin'jan's delight, also an apothekary, were trading tales on a riverboat.

In the Palace, the Caliph's chamber was a scene. Screaming for more, he lay in a soupy pile of pillows and his effluence. He was entirely alone. Down the hall and in room after room of the Palace, dignitaries groaned, cursed, crawled, vomited, shat, and over the next few days, shook, convulsed, choked on their vomit, and in diverse ways, died in rage. As for the Caliph, he swallowed his tongue, crying, "Sweet!".

The Palace Guard held their noses as they supervised the cleanup. Then they took their pay, and command.

By the time they had sorted out who would rule, Baad-hin'jan and Onger (which was this companion's true name) were swinging in hammocks on the high seas, having taken passage on a merchant ship to the New World.

They were therefore, asleep as rocked babes when, "Hoy!"

The very boards gnashed above them, as the ship was boarded. And soon enough, both passengers found that cutthroats do carry their knives between their teeth.

The blackguard had descended like a monkey. Still perched on the ladder, a lantern in one hand. His teeth gleamed, the knife repositioned like a pipe as he glared their way: "Is there a phyzik this tub?"

Baad-hin'jan could hardly believe his luck. And he counted himself doubly bless'd when Onger flipped himself out like a pea in a pod, begging to assist.

Up deck, the boarders must have felt sore pressed, for they left with only their human cargo baggaged on the backs of two knife-suckers across the ropes that were then unhooked. The merchant ship's sails fairly sighed as it awayed.

Baad-hin'jan was burlied into the captain's cabin. The 'captain' of the pirates was in bed, moaning like a ghost. He lay on the bed with his left ear uppermost. It reminded Baad-hin'jan of a lady of the love profession who he had met in the Levant. Rising out of the tangle of black, curly hair—the lobe, the colour of a damask rose, was cleft like those nether lips. In the depths, a glint of gold winked at Baad-hin'jan, thrilling him to his core.

This head blackguard was wonderful afflicted.

Behind Baad-hin'jan, Onger the apothekary rubbed his hands.

The Eye of Nostradamus Summit

The rarefied air of Coprahaagendas swirled and separated into zones, like vinegar whisked into milk—an acrid miasma that puffed and seeped from the great building atop the hill.

There is only this one building in Coprahaagendas, but the singularity of this temple-high structure makes up for its loneness, not just by its prismatic colours that exceed our vision. The structure defies architecture. Figures and symbols cover it, as uncountable as they are unstill. They cling to, spring from, crawl over and *maybe are* every wall, ceiling, column, cupola, dome, grate, doorway, step and arch. Arms, wings, hooves, snouts, breasts, cunts and priapuses do everything imaginable, and more. Beings humanick and otherwise fuck and slaughter; lust and leer; look out and inwards, reach down and upwards—making and remaking this stupendous edifice into an evermore impossibility of unfathomability, to us.

Not that we would ever see this building, let alone Coprahaagendas. Our leaders have only just left Copenhagen.

In the great hall, up on the stage, the smiling pink fatty closed his eyes. With one hand, he shoved a shell into his floppy left ear, sighed, and opened his eyes so slowly that it looked like it took supreme effort—as though his gorgeously long lashes might have been made of heavitrium. They were only weighed down by reluctance. With another hand, he sniffed a water lily while he waved a mace with another hand. Finally, with his fourth hand, he lifted up a sun-polished discus so that its face, turned away from him, should make countless eyes blink.

Still, that was not enough, so he trumpeted.

And no one can trumpet like Ganesh.

"You will please be silencing," he said in his normal tone— sweet, soft and rich as caramel.

So then, despite the desperate planning, the cajoling and officiousness, the promises to fill the hall with pomp for those who wouldn't come down for anything less, that "You will please" ad hoc call to order ended up being the opening statement of this unprecedented assembly, one so important it is called merely "The Coprahaagendas Summit".

Ganesh had been chosen to chair the meeting, as he was the only one who was both significant and unhated by all. He was also a stickler for responsibility, even having given himself the task of reading Robert's Rules of Order. So although the meeting had no precedent to those assembled, he opened it almost in the manner to which we have become accustomed.

With a flourish of his trunk, he said: "I call the distinguished . . . "

Kuan Yin was first. She barely topped the podium, swaying like a graceful willow. "We are simply talking about the very life support system of this planet," she said, but since there was no sound system, practically no one heard her. Tears sprang from her eyes. Her face blotched with the passion she felt, but she had not managed to memorize any other words, so she fled from the stage in a whirlwind of peach blossoms.

Next to speak was an old man. He took forever to get there. Hands gripping two arms as if they belonged to a walking frame, he was led through by a translucent young woman and a scruffy young man. Once the old man's hands had been transferred to the podium, however, he leaned on one and picked the other up and pointed it as if it were a staff and he were Ruler of All.

Behind and to the side, Ganesh made silent patting-down motions with his trunk while trying to glare at the assembly, a bad choice.

"The time for hesitation is over," the old man screamed. "Smite—"

"Bwahhh!" blared Ganesh, but though he trumpeted so loud he bruised the delicate inside of his trunk, he couldn't shush the troublemakers, who must have been waiting just for this. The very walls reverberated mirth.

The young man and woman grabbed the old man's elbows. "My pulpit," he snarled, gripping the sides with hands that were stronger than they looked.

A blast-ray just missed him.

"Take his gun!" ordered Ganesh.

But Xenu is no evil intergalactic warlord for nothing. His hand flickered at the two hulking giants (blue- and red-faced respectively) coming for him, and faster than a blast, he had his hands full of their body parts and was stuffing them in his frog-wide metallicate mouth. Then, like any frog, he used his thumbs to push the flailing legs in.

A roar rent the outrage. "Who let Xenu come?" demanded Seth. He jumped forward, foam dripping from his long curved snout. His man's arms stuck out awkwardly from his overmanly chest, his muscles ridiculously engorged. But it was his erect tail, high as a sacrificial flame, that really showed his rage.

"You're always angry at something," said Astarte. But Seth paid no mind to this interjection from a goddess who was only half-risen-from-the-dead—she of less worth than a barley offering. Only Sita, the pallid former beauty who had also been married unhappily (but at least she wasn't murdered like me, Astarte had always thought resentfully) and the blue hippo nodded. Astarte's heart flooded with love for her newfound friends, but the three of them might as well have existed in another universe, so noticed were they in the tumult. Indeed, this first agreement in the summit missed being a historic moment, as it was never noted.

Ganesh pointed to Saraswati. "Did you not say to me that everyone says that Nostradamus predicted nine-eleven?"

"Almost," she said. "The numbers are countless. This is why we must agree to my plan."

"What is this 'my plan', my lotus blossom?" rumbled Thoth beside her, baring his baboon's teeth.

"Hoo hoo hoo," piped Hanuman. "Their first fight!"

Up on stage, Ganesh had difficulty holding back his tears. He couldn't keep his ears from flapping as he motioned to Ogiuwu, who had been standing at the foot of the stairs to the stage, smiling smugly.

Ogiuwu sauntered up sure as a death after treachery. His footsteps were naturally slippery and red—the spoor of this God of Death.

Even his voice is scary. "The clock is ticking," he said.

"Good planets are hard to come by," called Xenu.

A low wet sound of hmming and umming began. Ganesh, powerless spectator to countless kitchen arguments, rubbed his stomach in agony. *From mixed agreement and disagreement flows digression, into the river of aggression where everything is lost—* Anarchy threatened to flood the assembly, yet again.

A fixed grin on his elephant face, Ganesh waved his big head slowly, panning the crowd. The noise grew louder, the mixing of the deities more bodious.

Just when he thought he was defeated, he genuinely smiled and pointed to someone Ganesh recognised from the nametag pinned to the delegate's lapel. During the pre-summit publicity and arrangements, they had corresponded. Ganesh had found him to be so dry and pedantic that the savvy pink god knew this being could dry up anything.

And, Ganesh, thought, *to get this unprecedented Summit properly launched, plans made and agreements entered into, something important must happen to get past the introducing prattle from those who don't count but who could make trouble.* He had to steer the Summit past them, and into the flow of the discoverers of the EoN Crisis.

He had to get everyone to listen to Saraswati (whose very name means "flow") and not just look at her, for though she is a goddess of learning, her beauty is apt to swamp her message, especially in the minds of those who do not value reason—and seeing that the assembled have an absence of reason to thank for their existence, *how,* Ganesh asked himself, *can anyone defend reason?* As Saraswati had said when she and Thoth announced their discovery and called it the Crisis of All Time, "We must fight this with collective reason. It is a dangerous tool, but the only one we have."

Ganesh had agreed then, but now, up on stage, looking out at everyone who is anything—the movers and shakers—he thought it his greatest challenge, not to argue for reason, but to stop the sniggers when she and Thoth soon appeared together. *Will they be listened to, or rudely gestured at? Will the severity of the crisis bring minds to thought, or will gossip and crudity take the fore?* For Saraswati and Thoth are an item these days. Matched brain for brain, otherwise he sometimes baboon shaped and at other times an ibis where his head is, but a man everywhere it counts.

All these worries flashed through Ganesh's mind in the half-moment before the devil's hooves flashed like patent leather. With one leap over two rows of beings as if they were only rocks, the devil clattered to a stop, just behind the podium. As if that weren't enough, with a theatricality that simply brooked no inattention, he shot his long-nailed hands from two impeccably tailored cuffs.

"The pace and scale of the threat may now be outstripping even the most sobering previous predictions," he said, impressing the assembled by his lack of notes for a statement with so many words. He gripped the podium and leaned forward, as professional as a preacher.

"If we don't act now," he said, dropping his voice to a whisper, "if we lose sight of our goal. If we don't find the eye of Nostradamus. And destroy it. I repeat: If we don't find that eye of doom, *and* all its tinctures, it will be irretrievably—"

He pointed to a clump of red-bearded giants having fun punching each other. "That means, for all of you un-studious ones. If we don't do something at this summit, what we live on will be lost. We'll starve to death. We'll be destroyed." He pointed his hand at the podium. "It—" Scratch! "Will—" Scraatch! "Be." *Sssscccrrrraaaaaatch!*

He turned his red eyes on Ogiuwu. "Too late, even for the strongest." The little devil had not met this god before, but that hadn't stopped this devil knowing about Ogiuwu and this god's growing strength. For years, the devil's dearest hope had been that Ogiuwu would live long, suffering fate worse than death. O, this devil might be little, but his heart is big and jealous.

"Even you!" he pointed. "The great Ogiuwu. You'll cause as much quaking as the feathers from a dead hen's egghole."

Ganesh was astounded. He had never guessed the depths in the foppish little fiend. But the devil worked the miracle. The assembled had watched him, spellbound, and remained silent after he leapt down with a stylish flick of his tail.

Ganesh took control again. "The summit is finally tracking!" he cried, and couldn't help dancing a few steps. His stomach jiggled so happily, you'd think it had just received a ball of ghee-and-coconut offerings.

Ganesh felt a little giddy, but calmed his tone. "I predict," he said, looking as down to business as his pinkness could, "that history will be made. Coprahaagendas, *we* will be coming to agreement and save our world."

"So you are a seer now?" quipped Hanuman, who was slapped so hard for his wit, the monkey god spent the rest of the summit practicing his arts of thievery.

A S MEETS LIKE this are meant to do, committees formed and met. But the assembly wasn't formed of delegates other than in name. Each attendee was an individual, representing the self. Each self shared the common fear that brought this unprecedented meeting into being but each had a private interest to feed, not to mention a curiosity to slake. Few had met many if any others in the panoply, and there were many hopes that others might not live through the cataclysm to come—a fate that each hoped to have the strength to survive, but none held the certainty.

So each had come to this assembly, not necessarily believing the pushy invitation "The time for hesitation is over," but enough alarmed by this possibility that the frightened outnumbered the morbidly curious.

There were only three committees expected to actually do any work. The plan was that they would come up with three proposals, hopefully the same, but close enough that a quick meeting of their chairs would then sort out the differences. The proposal would be presented to the Summit. There would be instant concordance, and the plan would be immediately implemented. The only problem that Ganesh, Saraswati and Thoth had fretted over was the delegation of responsibilities. There are so many jealous gods.

One of the problems that occurred instantly when the delegates sat around their tables was that Coprahaagendas has no laid-on food. The air whirred. There was a constant flitting off from the place. Angels, gods, goddesses—practically everyone breathed snatched offerings, wiping their lips of blood, sweat, butter and chicken. This annoyed other delegates trying to work, and made the three chairs of the most important committees angry. Each chair tried to hold that unconstructive emotion in, but it made them testy in their duties.

So Saraswati pretended not to see the foppish devil raise his finger while she explained the need to think laterally to solve this most dire threat to the world in history.

"I say," he said, and jumped onto the table, swishing a clump of papers from her hand. "You're all talk. If this is such a clear and present danger," he said, smoothing his moustache, "why don't we just take them out with extreme prejudice. Isn't that what you call it? And neutralize the threat?"

The tortoise opened one eye, and shut it so eloquently that Saraswati felt grateful.

"We would have," she said.

"You?" someone laughed.

"What'd the devil say?" boomed someone.

The devil stood up on his hind legs. "That someone should have damned well crushed 'em!"

"Tell me where!" Thor stomped forward. "I'll grind their bones."

"No bread," screamed Hanuman, leaping from shoulders to heads.

In another room, Ganesh was having the same problem. And in another, Thoth was wishing he could crawl back amongst the dead.

The truth, which they were having difficulty getting across, was that the Institute and all associated had proved as impossible for them to find as Coprahaagendas is to mortals. They couldn't even find the banks that must get those vast riches. Every purchase made of FutureSeize is impossible to trace. The route dissolves into the air of the internet as surely as the smoke from a sacrifice grows invisible, even though the blood leaves stains.

O, if killing had been easy, they would have done it. Not the three of them, to be sure, but Ram, for instance, had been let into the knowledge early, and had been disconsolate when he had learned that he could not just do it.

Thus, this conference, for which the edifice had been built, something that should be recognised as the achievement that it is. For this building is made of contributions from every delegate, offspring created for the purpose. The idea (a gem thought of by some god of war) was that if all the living Otherworldies are to meet in one place for the first time in history, each delegate must feel protected by an army of faithful minions. So each delegate sent the minions on the moment agreed upon (another unprecedented agreement) and the building that sometimes looks like a temple in Southern India and at other times, like a writhing Parthanon, and at all times quite like the new Scottish Parliament, exists as a shining example of cooperation, on the hilltop of Coprahaagendas, a hill appointed for that purpose.

— II —

BUT WHAT, YOU might ask, *is* this great threat?
Saraswati and Thoth had been playing on that other otherworldly world, the internet, when one of them (they were too much in love to remember who) found it—the source of the EoN Crisis.

The news was in an online newspaper sponsored by the Global Institute for Future Certainty. It seems that a team from the Institute opened up a wall in the ruins of a church in Galinoxy, "a region that has in history, times been rule by Goth, German, Frank, and Cossack." In those ruins, they found a small box once sealed in bands of iron. They opened the box and found what only one man in the team ever truly thought they would, though the others doubted.

"The team leader, who for obvious reason, must remain anonymus, is found the stoled piece of the great Knower of the Future—Nostradamus. There are many falsenesses about his body. He was not standing up. But his body was dig in the French Revolt and beary again. Our team set out to find the parts that peoples thoughted to be so value, they were take from his box."

The article was short, as are all the news stories in the newspaper of the Global Institute for Global Certainty, but the text was large and illustrated by many small pictures full of drama and colours.

The gist of this article, and all the others in the newspaper—was that the team found a reliquary in a sealed glass bottle. Unlike other reliquaries—gruesome sentimental keepsakes all—this piece in a bottle is the very source of the greatest power in the world. This is the Eye that Can See the Future, the right eye of Nostradamus, an eye reputed to be twice the size of any normal man's, but Nostradamus was never any normal man.

By the time Saraswati and Thoth had read the articles four times, and looked at all the pictures just as much, and picked out to read yet one more time, every article that talked about the special offer of FutureSeize™ and "how, for this short time only, you can obtain your own piece of the future, for you and your family, forever"; they were rolling on the floor locked in embrace, stinking of jasmine and jism, wet fur and fear.

After a cooling drink, they resumed their studies.

Of course, they didn't believe that the offer was for a short time only. But as Saraswati pointed out to Thoth, who had never known housekeeping: "This Institute is not quite Ghandian, as it must fund itself to continue to do good works. But it is undoubtedly subsidising this great gift."

"Not to the masses," said Thoth, who'd been raised to higher consciousness by his current love.

Saraswati rolled her beautiful eyes. "I am so happy that you see this. However, remember our stays in Mumbai and New York— where we posed as a tourist and her pet?" She stroked his coat. "How many times have we pondered distribution."

Thoth somersaulted away and clutched his knees. "Only few mortals can ever share the good."

Saraswati sidled over to him. "I am thinking it is a natural law of physics." She closed her eyes and chanted, "Take for yourself your future." This was a rallying cry in many of the special offers. Other consciousness-raising reminders related to the state of corruption, secrecy, and selfishness common to government, officials, and "the people who control power".

"So this?" Thoth pointed to the screen.

Saraswati started. Sometimes she thought Thoth *too* analytical.

"This special offer," said the god who had watched the pyramids go up. "Even if the tincture is affordable at a reduced eight times $89. 95, it will be bought by how many, can we estimate?"

Saraswati licked her lips. She loves big numbers.

"And used at the suggested dose," interrupted Thoth, who was rewarded by a little crease between Saraswati's silken brows.

"Two, point three five nine billion for the first quarter," said Thoth in a rush, looking at Saraswati uneasily. She smiled. "Approx," he added.

WHEN SARASWATI AND Thoth looked back on this little discovery session filled with fearful love, they called it the Calm Before the Full Cataclysm Realisation (dubbed by the EoN Crisis Steering Committee, the CalBeFuCatR).

They threw themselves into the work of reading all the news from the Institute. Each article in the Institute's FORWARD SEIZED

CHRONICLES not only illustrates the value of the Eye, but proves how valuable the tinctures taken from it are.

The couple's suspicions about the side-effects to people taking this drug were only displayed to each other in that perfect state of communication that is current love. So they spent several weeks alternating reading, worrying privately and reassuring each other aloud, and rolling sweatily over Saraswati's petal-strewn marble floor.

The clincher was the day Thoth ventured off the Institute's site, hitting first, the headline "Nostradamus and Gurus leaving the body"—about the Guru Osho, and his relationship with Nostradamus. In an advanced state, "Osho could be seen with his eyes fixed in the middle of his brow." And Osho predicted he would "dissolve into the body" of his followers after death. Furthermore, those predictions of Nostradamus were noted (chapter and verse!) yet the teachings of the Vedas, the Mahabharata and Ramayana, and even the most common New Age Book of the Dead—all ignored. Instead, the guru declared: "Government will always fail as long as its root to the cunning, political mind remains uncut."

"Listen to this," Thoth said, breaking into Saraswati's study of some problem. His throat convulsed, so he could only point.

Only that morning Saraswati had been telling Thoth of the time Lord Krishna changed the time of sunset to give Arjuna a no-risk opportunity to kill Jayadratha. And Thoth had fed her in turn, some delicious bit of treachery he remembered between, who was it?—not that the story mattered. They called these incidents "soup", made as they are from what they'd labelled in a lovers' brainstorm: "The Essence of Power".

Now Saraswati shrugged one shoulder. She slid over to look at whatever Thoth . . . and instantly forgave him for breaking her train of thought. A moment later, they were both crying with laughter.

Yet a moment after, Saraswati wiped her face. "He is not too ignorant for followers. That lie!"

Thoth tried to compose himself, but couldn't. "He says, therefore." He straightened his back and dropped his eyes, taking up the guru's pose of knees out, legs folded, hands upended on knees. Without the guru's robe, Thoth looked so tempting that Saraswati's laughter would have rung with delight and fun.

Not now. "He expects his followers to believe that he posseses some magic scythe! That with a sweeping statement, he cuts down what is, and ever has been?"

Toth sighed. "I only told you to see the dimples in your cheeks."

He stretched himself out on the floor and licked the deep curved base of Saraswati's back. "Don't trouble your mind with such . . . mmm, nonsense. This so-called guru knows no history."

Her buttocks twitched. "Nor any present, in any world!"

Toth slid away, not just wounded that she did not respond to him, but peeved that she sweated about a *man*. He sat up with his back to her, and stared at nothing. "Perhaps," he said, bored with this silly guru and his ignorance-spreading. "Perhaps to followers, to say is to know." He felt a bit soiled saying something so stupidly vaccuous, but his scorned tongue needed the pleasure of annoyment.

She was silent. Thoth hoped she was trying to find a way to end this and get back to making love. Always a generous lover, he planned to say *yes* to anything she said, and then take her divine feet into his hands.

"To his followers, to say is to know," she repeated. "If they are buying!" She grabbed Thoth's coat so hard that she made a bald spot on his back. "See there on the screen? He too, is selling."

Thoth turned.

"Whoever buys this tincture," one said, "has no need for us," the other finished, putting in stony terms what they both had airily worried might be true.

. . . and their hands found each other, and their eyes saw each other, through the mirrors of their tears.

THROW AWAY YOUR false beliefs!" cry the ads. This call to action sits next to those other calls, irresistible to the mortal:

"Lose 5 to 15 inches in one day"

"Cut Down 3 *lbs of belly fat* EVERY WEEK! . . . In fact it worked so well *I lost* 8 stubborn pounds of *fat in 3* short weeks!"

"Regrow your own crown."

"With this secret of successful lovers, you can have so many, you can watch them fight."

The irresistible appeal of the tincture taken from the eye of Nostradamus is explained in many different ways, such as this advertorial in a popular online current affairs magazine centred around the lives of celebrities:

"Put only one drop of FutureSeize™ in both eyes per day, and you can not only see the future, but enjoy it. Do you see yourself dead in five years from cancer? Celebrate! Get that loan tomorrow, quit your job, and sale around the world. Or take that lover you know you want. Or if your on a budget, plan well and you could happily give your neighbors what coming to them. Make your life your own. You can finally use your money yourself. Waste nothing on false hopes and silly prayers. Who will help you if you no help youself? You only have one life. Live it NOW. But act quick, or this special offer will be . . . "

THE SARASWATI-THOTH TEAM networked widely, spreading the knowledge of the threat. To make their knowledge understood by all, they had to dumb it down, first trying to explain their discovery of the Eye of Nostradamus in terms that didn't necessarily accept the power of the eye, but stressed the lack of necessity for truth, if belief sustains its popularity.

This concept was too hard to put across. So the two next tried flattery, using the most modern concepts as if everyone were up-to-date. But *meme* failed, too.

No one was the least bit frightened. Saraswati and Thoth were only laughed at. Finally, they had to sink to a slogan they hated, as both live above clichés.

"A plague is coming to us" worked when they matched it with "Our end is nigh."

Ganesh was their first believer. He instantly understood that if people could see their fate, they would not waste their time offering any bribes to gods or otherwise to save them from inevitability.

With his supreme perception, he saw a future of starved immortals wandering, not able to leave their world but doomed to die in it. Eat or be eaten? With his supreme strength, he cut off his speculative vision, but he couldn't help patting his stomach and shuddering.

Ganesh thought of the Summit, and was the principle organiser. If the firmament awarded an honour for a supreme effort made for the Otherworldly Commons, Ganesh should receive it.

There isn't, however. Not only that, but if an effort fails, should anyone receive honour for trying? That is a question worthy of Ganesh, though he has not had the mindspace to fit it in.

THE COPRAHAAGENDAS SUMMIT ended in general discord. Most delegates, it seems, just came to see the others. Some viewed each break in the proceedings as a chance for a bit of light rape and murder. There was no sense of urgency amongst the bulk of delegates, because they could not imagine a world in which the sacrifices to them stop. There was one point in the discussions, Ganesh is pained to remember, when the Summit almost reached something—a point of no return.

That was on the third day, back in the big hall, when the old man started raving again. "Smite them!" he kept saying.

He meant the whole mortal population. A clean sweep.

Saraswati bustled up to the podium. "We do not have that luxury. Focus, please!"

The old man's son raised his hand meekly. "Perhaps He could remake them."

Ganesh lost his temper. He made the mistake of stamping his feet, which jiggled his stomach and made his fat pink trunk slop back and forth.

Hanuman led the laughter. "Cleanliness is next to godliness," he said, always the sneaky one. "Any god who doesn't consider destruction isn't serious." And with that, he stole a pin from Kuan Yin's coif and gambolled out the great doorway, down and out of Coprahaagendas.

TODAY, ABOVE AND around us, many of the Otherworldly quake. The tables have been turned by a mere mortal, or a band of them. The problem is, the idea of targeted destruction is not something that can be contemplated, not unless the target is, as the old man wants, all of us. And he is gaining some ground amongst the short-sighted who fear but do not see.

Even the tax departments of our most feared governments can't find the Institute, nor anyone associated with it. The coffers and storehouses of FutureSeize™ are as hid, to high and low, as the Greatest Secret in the Universe.

The question, therefore, is a moral one. If every one of us in the humaworld pitches in, it wouldn't take much to save the Others' world. Just resist, if you can, that offer. Lose your belly fat instead.

But perhaps action to solve this Crisis must be led by those of us with vision, so this is a call to architects. That World-Heritage-worthy building on the hill in Coprahaagendas is admittedly designed by amateurs and is a work in progress, but dooming those amateurs to death could lead to the death of their offspring that constitute that building (where these innocents live and play, in expectation of another Summit) and the death of the offspring's offspring—first undermining and then causing the destruction and elimination of this singular Built Structure—this Grade A Listable Wonder of the Otherworld.

The Old Testacles

"Ahem," said Moses.

"Do I need to repeat myself?"

Moses trembled. "Do you need to repeat yourself?"

"DO I?"

"Do . . . No, o Lord my G-d."

"Then get—"

"Ahem," said Moses, with an understandable 90 percent temerity but 10 percent chutzpah.

"WHAT?"

God's voice loosened a boulder that nudged Moses' shoulder. His grip on the tablets slipped.

"Now look what you've done," thundered God. "No, don't pick them up yet. Speak!"

"Well, G-d," said Moses. "You know these Commandments?"

"Why should I know them? I just gave them to you."

Moses ignored the sticky shower that had just fallen on him.

"We both know, O Lord, Creator of Heaven and Earth," he continued, "that the people are having the time of their lives down there."

"Why else did I call you here?"

"Why?"

"SPEAK ALREADY."

Moses rubbed one horny toe in the dirt. "So these Commandments, to be effective, you want for them to be the best that they can be?"

"Why should I want that? I wouldn't want that," said God. He'd dropped His voice to almost silent, the calm before—

"No, G-d. Yes, you wouldn't." Moses tucked his neck into his shoulders. "But?"

"BUT?"

"Oy, let the man talk."

A blinding light dropped between the old man whose face was twisted with malice, and the merely wizened old codger, Moses.

The light transmogrified into—into . . .

"And *you*," She said, looking at the bulge that suddenly appeared in Moses' filthy robe. "You who have refused to lay with your wife because you think to lay with *Me*."

"Is this true?" asked God, flabbergasted.

Moses cocked his head and opened his hands toward God, "You'd grown tired of Her, no? And haven't your hu—uh, servants destroyed all mention of—uh, and forbidden us to—"

"TTHAT DOESN'T GIVE YOUU—"

The once-married couple looked at one another, and the female snorted.

"I admit to having made bad choices in my time," She said to Moses. "But I'm still not desperate."

"Please accept my apologies, wife of—"

"X!"

"X!" Moses hastened to correct himself.

"Now," She said, "Tell us about these so-called Commandments. And don't worry about Him."

"Well," said Moses, and suddenly all that learning he had received at the Pharaoh's court made his eyes shine with pedantry. "The first one isn't a Commandment."

She smiled. God's face was full of wrath. He was furious but powerless to change the fact that in She resides all Understanding.

"Go on," She said, like oil on bread.

Moses spoke at Her eyes, though it was hard not to get distracted by the shape of Her breasts, and the attraction of that slit of all slits, through which pours Creation. He closed his eyes, the better to spurt out, "And the next three Commandments are tautologies."

"WHAT?"

"They all say the same thing," She said, explaining as patiently as any good teacher.

"Go on," said X to Moses.

"And those plagues."

"WHAT ABOUT THEM?"

"Over these forty years, O Lord my G-d, King of the Universe, I've wanted to ask you, more and more. Why did you kill all those innocents? All those beasts who served so well. And the seed of the poor, who have no power. And above all, all those first-born of the slave girls. And why do you think we're so obsessed with gold and silver?"

God was mercifully quiet, encouraging Moses.

"And why," said Moses, "did you have to make everyone you killed in the plagues suffer such horrible deaths? All that skin peeling. And what is this Commandment about not coveting the slave of my neighbour? What makes us ex-slaves different to any other slaves?"

"So you don't want my liberation?"

"G-d forbid you should think that, Lord," said Moses, tugging at his beard. "But—"

God's beard thrashed like a storm at sea, froth tossing everywhere. He might have poured forth Words, but they were drowned by the sound of X's laughter.

God's hands clenched, He bared his great yellow teeth, and . . . exploded, catching a nearby bush on fire.

And suddenly, He was No More to Be Seen.

"About time," said X.

Moses took heart, looking to X with the eyes of an ancient ram.

"Don't even think of it," She said. "Now let's get you down to the valley below. I'll grant you a little lease on younger life so you can entertain your wife again. And now I can get back to work creating joy, and fruitfulness and understanding."

"It's been too long," said Moses, still hoping.

"NOT SO FAST."

Moses' heart skipped a beat. That was the Voice of G-d, and now that Moses couldn't look Him in the eye, He was even more terrifying than before.

"YOU," boomed He. "You were trouble from the beginning."

"And you," X shot back. "I picked you up from the gutter. My curse is that I've got bad taste in consorts."

She turned to Moses. "I picked him up on the rebound, someone so opposite from my great love that I thought he would make me forget, like dropping that tablet on your foot made you forget what you were thinking of the moment before you did it."

"Tell me more," said God.

X ignored the sneer in his voice.

"My great love—don't get your hopes up, either of you. He was another god. His favourite drink was the libation that once a month I pour from between my legs. That's why my creation-works inside are a cup. And why all my daughters have them, too."

Moses blinked. A cup inside? And that couldn't be—

"Disgusting," spat this god. Moses felt the spatter, and it stunk. God had obviously never felt the need for personal hygiene.

X gazed at Moses, then at God (He couldn't hide from *Her*). "Good thing I changed men as I did," She mused.

"What was that?" said God, who reddened with embarrassment. He hadn't a speck of curiosity in his making, but was full of forgetfulness.

"I let him help create you," She said to Moses. "Men. But he wanted you to have forty balls."

"She reduced them to two," said God.

"Only when I saw what you were planning."

"One to hold your seed," She explained. "And one to kick when necess—"

Moses looked in the direction of God's Voice with surprise and accusation.

"Enough already," He said. "I've still got SOME power."

And with that, His hands must have risen, for *whoosh*. When the smoke cleared, another old man stood in Moses' place.

"Abraham!" two voices rang out, not in harmony.

X left in a huff.

"G-d?" said Abraham uncertainly. His eyes were crusty as dried-up saltponds. His head shook like a rotten flowerhead in a breeze, and he smelt of moist death.

"You remember that Covenant we discussed?" God said to Abraham.

Abraham tried to stand straighter. "How could I forget?"

"You, too." God sounded exasperated. "Why is this night different from all other nights, that everyone's answering a question with a question?"

Abraham prostrated himself. "Blessed be He who has delivered me here."

"Now we're getting somewhere." The Voice was content. "Remember the Covenant?"

Abraham shuddered. How could he forget? He woke up one night with a voice telling him to kill his son, or he'd be killed himself. Of course he was going to kill his son, but then when he had the knife on the boy's throat, the voice chuckled, then told him that he, Abraham, had passed the first test of loyalty. There were more to come. All the voice wanted was blind obedience or death, an order so simple that even Abraham the schlemiel was able to carry it out.

"Remember," the Voice boomed now, with the terrifying confidence that Abraham remembered all too well, "how I told you that you could know certainly that your descendants would be strangers in a land that is not theirs, and will serve them, and they will afflict them for four hundred years. And also the nation whom they serve will I judge; and afterward they will come out with great possessions?"

"Yes, O Lord of the Universe who is the One and Only G-d," lied Abraham. Actually, the only thing he remembered was that someone in some unimaginably far future would have possessions greater than he did. G-d hadn't exactly showered him with wealth, an oversight that made Abraham's conjugal relations rather fraught, since he mostly either sat around daydreaming, or wanted to lay with his wife who was too busy trying to make ends meet to put up with his nonsense. Besides, he couldn't count to ten.

"That time has now come to pass, said the Lord. You will now take on the mantle that Moses shed."

"Who is—"

"Thick as two mudbricks," said X into God's ear.

"It doesn't matter," he snapped. "From now on, you shall be known as Moses. And don't look at nothing like a sheep. I'll tell you what to do."

And God, with one stroke, erased the witless countenance of Abraham and replaced it with one infinitely learned, pained, censorious, unquestionable, meshugganah as God—making him the first Priest of the Hebrews.

"Now pick up those tablets," said God, "and only throw them down when the people answer with the first question."

And Abraham who was raised from the dead to become "Moses" did as he was told.

As for his home life, X took care of that.

So he "lived" with Moses' wife for an interminability of years, till one sunset when he was finally released. And she who possessed X's Understanding lit a candle and ate some fruit and honey, for she was also blessed with infinite Outlastability.

Rocket Fantazyor

Irving Wiseman's uncle Leo dropped some magazines on Irving's bed. "Enough dreaming," he said, pulling the book from his nephew's hands and placing it on the bureau. He would have liked to toss it, but it was a book, and even more than that, a library book.

"You gotta make a living," he said.

Irving sighed, but rolled over and laid the magazines out before him on his bedspread like cards in a game.

"You got talent," said Leo. "You must have. So they're showing it, no?" He pointed like some professor in the movies, at the middle magazine.

The right breast of the woman in the underwired but otherwise unstructured pink brassiere stared at the 17-year-old. It wasn't just the woman's youth that perked those breasts, Irving knew. His uncle had told him that 64% of women, once they hit the age of 20, already have bosoms that not only fail the pencil-test, but are as perky as easy-over-light fried eggs. This woman's bazoongas were held up in their most flattering form, high as they could go. Irving didn't know but guessed the reason: those arms pulled up by the wrists clamped into cuffs on that chain pulled up over the swingbar by the scientist's assistant.

Leo stabbed that cover—*Marvel Tales*, May 1940—with his pipe. Ashes fell on the assistant's manic frown. "What have you to tell me?"

Irving opened his mouth, looking ready to recite, or yawn.

"No, that's too easy," said Leo. "What does that remind you of? And this is no bordello. What you lying down—"

Irving sat up and ran his hand through his thick curls. "The other pink job."

"And when are they not pink?"

"When they're red or chartreuse or—"

"If you can't piece these together, just how you think—"

The boy took off his glasses and pinched his nose, an odd gesture considering that without his horn rims, he looked like Michelangelo's David. "Long blade of paper-guillotine in action of cutting a brunette in half. Alright already. False underwire of round cotton-waste piping, non-adjustable rayon-satin ribbon straps, one-inch separator of same connecting bandeaux-style shallow unshaped cups. Suitable for women with no body who think they don't need fill—a twenties look."

"Better." Leo produced yet another magazine from inside his fitted suit. "This? I just picked it up."

Irving pulled the magazine close to his face. Its ink was still loud, crude. Only out for a few months, this February 1941 *Spicy-Adventure Stories*, "Space Burial" featured a screaming redhead slipping off the back of some flying bird—the important thing being that apricot sateen number with the shaped straps and wholly improbable way that the breasts could be supported. He snorted, "Artistic license. No can do. Not with that fabric and no seams."

"Now we're getting somewhere." Leo pointed to the bed. "What do you think of that one in the lineup?"

" 'The Soul Scorcher's Lair'?"

The middle-aged man with no paunch waited. After all, he had once had dreams, too. But 15 seconds was enough.

"If you think I'll let a fantazyor eat your mother's kreplach. And she a widow working her fingers off . . . "

"Hotformed lace, steel underwire, flare-banded from armpit to breast differentiators, elasticized arm straps, presumably three-hook back, D cup, black, suitable for full but firm breasts because there is still no adequate support for the average woman."

"Excellent, my boy." Leo smiled broadly, the picture of the proud uncle, even possibly, though he'd never seen it, the university professor gratified that his student had actually listened to all his lectures. Leo was proud of himself, too, for he had successfully hidden the hurt that the boy, through the callousness of youth, had dealt him. For Irving was right. That bra had been a great seller in '37—but its success had rested on the racy lace and daring black. Women don't know how to fit a bra, and this one, for all its advertised appeal, was two flimsy colanders, so the average woman's breasts were sadly earthbound or showing their inadequacy of build with an embarrassment of collapsed cups when what they needed was adequate shaping, filling, engineering, uplift.

As Irving civilized his hair and washed his face and hands, he heard his mother setting the freshly scrubbed table in the kitchen—laying it with three places for the three people who lived in that little flat in the Bronx.

He was pleased in one way that he'd made Uncle Leo happy. Of course he didn't want to hurt the man—and besides, he felt sorry for him. But he also felt a simmering anger he hardly admit to himself. To sign his life away. Yes, so Mama had started in the sweatshops at the age of nine. But still. Irving put that out of his mind while he dried his face, and dreamed for another snatched moment, of designing rockets.

What he knew of the breasts of the average woman, of *any* woman for that matter, was the sum of what he'd seen of Egyptian, Greek and Roman statuary in the Metropolitan Museum; all those magazines his uncle brought home for him to study; and Leo's own blueprints and lectures about the real things.

Irving wondered if the man, that lifelong bachelor, had ever touched the real things. He'd gone from being a tailor of men's suits, an unenviable specialty in New York in the 1930s, to a brassier designer, only because of a friendship made by Irving's mother, who when her husband dropped dead of a heart attack when Irving was only 13, went into business on her own, sewing foundation garments to fit particular women, especially those with a breast or two cut off, and opera singers.

Her constructions, all made of pink canvas, could have held cement. Their fillings felt rather like it, and never shifted. Sometimes she made shapes that looked rather beautiful to Irving, but that she inevitably had to modify for her conservative clients, who seemed to prefer what Irving thought of as the 'squashed look'. Maybe they were ashamed. He didn't know but felt frustrated for his mother, who couldn't afford that luxury.

It was she who had talked to her brother about setting Irving up. She not only didn't have the money but there was also that limit of 'Hebrew' students already reached in all the top schools. So he had to take that job Uncle Leo wangled for him, opening in January. Until then, after graduation from high school in a week (what a waste of science classes!) he was to learn the trade—designing for three dimension with two-dimensional materials, under her. Not that this training came, of course, with an opportunity to look at or touch the goods inside these constructions.

THE FIRST DAY in training he successfully ran a Singer needle through his forefinger. It was a good lesson in driving speed on the newly electrified machine. After that, he surprised himself on the thing, finding that the more difficult the curves, the more fun he had making the turns, and he grew so skilled that his mother started trusting him with ever more mountainous jobs.

The fittings were all done in her bedroom, and the clients looked nothing like, say, that blonde with manacled hands and the rayon full-torso breast-delineating underpiping but otherwise purely unsupportive cups fronting *Terror Tales*, September 1934. Most of her clients were frankly, variations on the potato or a cubist painting, even with her expert foundations giving them shape. "Today's woman," he said to her one day, "should thrust out rockets, not your matzo balls."

"So, Irving. This today's woman? She tells you this?"

Her son blushed reassuringly.

"You fantazyor," she said, patting his cheek. "Your today's woman is in the future, and she's made of steel."

But to make him happy, she let him create two designs that were quite astoundingly shaped, giving body where needed he said, but always "up and outlift". She hated wasting the canvas and thread, but kept that thought to herself. After he had constructed both models—impeccably cut and sewn, she was pleased to note—she offered them to her two youngest clients, having quickly to explain that it was just an idea. She almost lost both women.

So instead, she asked Irving to tell her of his dreams while he sewed.

It helped him to hear her sigh.

The months passed more quickly than he imagined they would, and he was doubly sorry to see them go. His mother had always been a heroine to his way of thinking. One day he would find a woman like that, he thought when he forgot that he'd be a brassiere designer, something to laugh at. So embarrassed did he feel that he refused all comers, and with looks like his and his shy, thinker's manner—he could have explored all he wanted, even the nice girls.

December came, and with it, the Day of Reprieve.

He was told there was no way he could get into the Air Corps, so he went to the Army office across the street. After interviewing him, the guy there wrote something on a piece of paper and sent him back across the street. He walked out of that office signed up for a course, launching him into the Air Corps.

With his new skills in mapmaking, he flew over Germany and then was stationed to Burma, where he learned to hate the English for their filled storehouses, meant not for the people who needed them, but for export; visited temples that he laughed to think about gracing towns in the US of A—the horror! In this alien land he felt, for the first time, the real things, if only stone; and after much encouragement and teasing, the real things with a real-life woman, who said she "love" him, but she kicked his pet mongoose.

He hadn't been surprised that the stone women on the temples had matzo-ball breasts. After all, they were ancient, weren't they? But this woman in the flesh—hers were something he had only imagined. She was soft and warm, but they could have been made of tin, they were so conical. They only confirmed, however, his thoughts that the woman of today would love to look like that, if she only could. Of course, she must have been a freak, a beautiful one but nevertheless, a fantasy come to life in flesh. Breasts like these didn't grow on women or he would have seen them on statues. They need guidance.

Not that he planned to give it to them. No siree. Now that he'd escaped, he saw—through the squalor of death and fear, the confusion of cruelties intended and unthinkingly dealt out—this war that he helped to serve—not only the opportunity but the responsibility to engineer a shining, uplifting future.

He was just having what isn't supposed to be but what many have experienced: a great war—when in a nightmare, a blonde turned up, "Dead Man's Bride" from *Terror Tales*.

On a pitiless noon when he was sitting outside his tent, a wet kerchief over his head. He had been dreaming—but only daydreaming, and sketching rockets.

"Wise guy," she cracked, as if that nut were fresh. She had a hand on her hip and one of those so-sure of herself voices that fit her cover-girl looks, on that cover. But she mustn't have traveled with a compact. Her peach-gold skin was pitted with oozing sores, one eye filled with dirt, and her skull poked out like the Andaman Islands, from a blue-tinged scalp.

Yes, Irv had been around. He noticed not only that, but that her breasts were like two flops of camp stew. Man, did she need engineering, and uplift.

She sidled around behind him and hung her head over his shoulder. "That's what I want," she said. "We all want it."

"This?" He drew the nosecone, then another one beside it, and drew straps.

"Exactly." She snatched up the paper as something precious, and held it to her ravaged chest. He was almost charmed. And she didn't smell half as bad as other unexpecteds he'd come across, unreported 'casualties', the still oozing dead.

He wondered if someone had put her up to this. "Do you know the woman in that black lace number in *Eerie*—"

"Corinne? She prayed for you! Thank her for your luck changing."

He repressed a smile. He'd always reckoned this blonde for a tale-spinner, but it was flattering nonetheless.

"Can she come here?"

The earth moved, and up from it crawled Corinne. That bra had not lasted half as well as it should have. It was even less recognizable than Corinne.

But she retained some of her strawberry-blonde set hair. It had looked to be so shellacked that its preserved curves would last in a museum.

"Dis war will end," she said through her lipless mouth. "And you will become the greatest brassiere designer there ever was."

He jumped up. They could have tossed a grenade in his lap, his heart pounded that bad. He wanted to flee into the jungle, but knew they'd follow. What did they have to lose? He couldn't lose them, so he said simply, like some dumb grunt, "I'm sorry but I'm a rocket man."

"Not on your life, you're not," said the *Dime Mystery* Maid, now to his left. He looked her over, and was unsurprised to note that her flimsy slip of a bra, that couldn't hold two flies, had slipped to her waist. Whatwith her ribs sticking out, and her breastbone and all, he had to remember what her problem was. Ah, no breasts to speak of.

Before the rest of his troop came back from maneuvers, he was surrounded by a bevy of former cover-girls, all insisting that he heed their call. Their story was that it was too late for them, but they still had their duty, which they would carry out no matter what.

"Not," the siren named Mitzi (of "Crisis in Utopia" she reminded him) chuckled, "that 'no matter what' means anything to us. We have forever. And a purpose in death."

"But why should you care?"

"Haven't you noticed that we're all young dead?" said Mitzi. "Models don't last long. But that doesn't mean we don't feel solidarity with the girls still walking the streets in flesh and bras. They don't want old-fashioned bodies. They don't want straps that fall down. They need up and outlift! And you're gonna give it to 'em, Captain."

The girls, as they called themselves, gave her the best they could with a Bronx cheer.

THEY WERE MORE persistent than gunfire in an assault. And they didn't let up for sleep or regrouping. He'd seen so much already in this war that he didn't think them any more strange than some of the orders he'd been given by Command. Nor the sights that he came upon and helped to make, because of the orders from people whose war experience was intensely spent on maps only pocked by pins.

He argued with the girls. Then he tried to reason, telling them what a waste a creative brain like his would be, to engineer brassieres, when space (and the needs of war of the future) cried out for a genius with solutions.

"But you're such a genius in this," said Corinne, giving her lacquered hair a flick, which exposed her shapely bones. "Besides, you can't deny your heritage."

"What's that s'posed to mean," Mitzi shot.

"He's a Hebe, that's all. No offense, Mitzi, but you know."

Mitzi would have flashed her eyes, but she couldn't even blink them. Instead, she said, "Captain Wiseman. Irving. Be a doctor."

"Or better yet," piped up the woman who still had chunks of her zaftig build, dug into her terrible torture marks. "A psychiatrist."

So suddenly, he had two allies, sort of.

And there was war amongst the girls till finally, he was shipped home, a month after the War officially ended.

The ship was crammed full of men but that didn't stop the girls boarding too. They weren't alone. There was a whole contingent of dead with missions, attached to both troops and officers. Irving sensed this, though they were better at hiding than any soldier he'd ever known. He never talked about them to anyone, and no one told him of the dead who stalked them. Does it take war to bring them out, he wondered. And if so, could at least there be the retribution of having them pester just as much, the idiots in Command, the civvies who made money from the war, or glorified all the wrong things about it. But he'd been around enough by now to figure that only soldiers were delivered these particular rations—these dead, all on missions.

So while the living had to come to terms with peace, war raged amongst the girls and at him—a constant ack ack about his future, all the way to New York Harbor. But not one of them advocated rockets. Even to reminisce about riding them on covers, as (formerly) bigchested Bertha L'Amour had in "Payload: Vavoom", rockets were a no-go zone. If he brought them up, the girls would sing Big Band hits—and with their torn out and rotted voice boxes, now *that* was the stuff of nightmares.

So when he walked down the plank and saw his mother, shorter than he remembered, he strode up to her and hugged her long and hard, with a grip less manly than his looks. Down the length of her back, Irving felt a new backbrace that his mother hadn't written about. "They should rip my tongue out," she would have said, rather than complain to her son. Instead, she'd sent him stories she'd penciled painstakingly, tales of her customers and the neighborhood, all to make him smile; and that 'New York cornbread' he loved—heavy round loaves of rye so solid you could brain someone with it. Most of the letters and packages from home never got to him, but one loaf arrived that when he opened the wrapping, exploded turquoise mold, not that he ever told her. Anyway, for years, nothing from him had reached home intact but the briefest "I'm doing well. This land is beautiful".

She shoved him out to arm's length, smiling and frowning at the same time. "You're skin and bone."

"Nonsense! Would you take a look at that chest size?" Leo stepped forward and shyly stuck out his hand. Irving had a double-take at how old and frail his uncle had become, but recovered in time to react with a man-to-man, eye-to-eye handshake. Leo's eyebrows and right eye sent a mixture of confusing signals. Awe? Sadness? Or maybe just professional eyestrain.

Two hours later, over the homemade gefilte fish, Irving said to his uncle, "There still a job working with you?"

Leo placed his fork on the plate and wiped his mouth. "Don't you dream any more? I can only imagine what you've seen."

"You can only imagine." Irving's laugh was muffled, like a knife ripping cloth. "You've seen it too."

On the third-floor landing, the elevator creaked. And up from the depths, in the steamy confines of that little apartment in the Bronx, the radiator clanged twice.

"So?" said Irving.

Leo reached across the tablecloth and grasped Irving's forearm.

"You can come to work tomorrow. A veteran with skills. I'll make sure they take you."

"Over my dead body," said Bessie Wiseman, splashing the chicken soup. "You must go back to school. That's an order, Rocket Man."

The radiator issued another report—this time three bangs. And somehow, somewhere around the front window, a tendril of cold from the keening wind outside snuck through, but the girls couldn't get in.

Out on the pavement this chorus of sirens pitched everything they had up at that window—wheedles, soft-soap, promises, demands—in brassy blare to rot-muffled croak, they threw their voices up at Irving.

But they knew they'd been defeated.

And Irving Wiseman did become a rocket designer, a military scientist on typically low pay and sworn to secrecy about his achievements, but happy as clams are supposed to be, and they don't complain. A clam who didn't even notice and was never told by his uncle, that while he was gone, the Conical Bra had come out, a great success, and from a competitor. It was engineered with military precision, even had maximum reinforcement.

When the girls found out, they felt so stupid about having missed it all, having gone on a mission to the other side of the world (that failed anyway) when all the action was happening at home, that they slunk back to their holes and never regrouped.

AUTHOR'S NOTE: *The pseudonymous 'Irving Wiseman' is actually my father—and the time of his life covered in "Rocket Fantazyor" predates his time machine, on which he later installed a seatbelt for my safety.*

Sincerely, Petrified

— I —

On the approach, it's the world's most unassuming national park. Not here, the jutting majesty of organ cacti, buttes, Cathedral Rocks. Though the Painted Desert is technically part of it, you wouldn't know that here in this flat, dry ex-floodplain. Only a few scattered stumps and a red brick building greet the drive-in tourist to the Petrified Forest. Within easy walking distance, everything's flat as a Roman ruin pre-restoration. The usual walk-around outdoors, though littered with surprises, lasts less than half an hour; and would for most visitors, be a visit soon sunk below memories of the shopping at Silver City, fried breads at that little place in Taos, the lonely cliffdrop down to the rushing Colorado at Mexican Hat, and those Western-movie backdrops around Moab.

What catches pretty much everyone, however, is the museum/ gift shop. It's like that thing in the Tequila bottle—the worm that bores into the flesh of cactus, deep enough to kill it.

Architecturally, the low-slung building is pure highway office, Department of Motor Vehicles. The gift shop has Navajo silver jewelry inset with paint-bright stones, string ties, belt buckles, bookends, and bric-a-brac. The petrified-wood in them is certified "from sites outside the Park, but of the same quality." For kids, there's Magic Crystals, plastic dinosaurs and rubber rattlesnakes, a Junior Scientist Guide to Rocks, unconvincing chunks of "fool's gold," and a Genuine Tooled Leather Wallet Kit. No food here, and the only drink is water from the restroom sink. Most visits would end now, but it's the rec-room size museum, oddly enough, that makes visitors stop, stare through the glass, actually read, and more amazingly, remember.

YOSEMITE, SO PHOTOGENIC that it loses nothing in black and white, was given Park status in 1906 with a sweep of the great-white-hunter president's pen. But since the late 1800s, when Wild Bill Hickok made the West interesting, experts argued about making *this* place known. Park status would draw attention to it, a damnably fool idea. Others argued that this elitist attitude was what made the East what it was—somewhere to escape from. "Our corner should have its national park," said a faction known by the watch chains stretched across their heavy tums. But all sorts of people agreed, many who would not agree with each other on anything else. "All Americans should have the same right to enjoy what only a few enjoy now," railed the Summer 1909 *Allaeompic Light*, a short-lived journal owned by two men and a woman: two naturists and a naturalist.

Yet unlike Yosemite, Pike's Peak, or Mt. Rushmore, the attractions of *this* place are portable.

Want a polished slice of *Araucarioxylon arizonicum?* Once, in the highlands, a stand of great pre-redwoods shaded tyrannosaurs, only to fall and be washed down into this floodplain where proto-crocodiles and salamanders the size of great white sharks slid amongst the cycads—before the volcanoes. After, ash fell over the logs, buried and washed through them; and then the logs and broken forest detritus slowly dried. And so, like candying fruit where the sugar permeates and preserves, the mineral-thick bath dried over 225 million years, and quartz and other minerals replaced the cellulose. Depending upon the mineral, the wood looked almost as it had in life, down to the cell structure—or altogether different. The long-grained purplish red pieces broken from the heartwood, streaked with fat-white quartz—like corned beef.

But that is by the way. What matters is that before it was a park, every year more of the petrified wood just disappeared—casually souvenired, deliberately collected.

In 1907, the first committee formed to solve the problem. And then came: War. Depression. War. Deaths and birth. The story of the committees. No agreement reached within any of these short-lived collections of geographically scattered folks who had only one common interest. Finally, in 1960, when urgently finding a solution had become a necessity given the fact that the place was becoming more known every summer vacation, the newest committee recommended a solution. Simple. Logical. American. It could not have been proposed in the days when the West was wild. No, this recommendation was a product of the post-war, Peace Corps, think-not-what-you-can-do-for-yourself time: Law.

So, in 1962 Congress legislated the Petrified Forest National Park into being, and also laid down the law about taking anything from it, other than memories and purchases from the shop.

The opening day of the park was the same day that its museum/shop opened.

WALTER R. WILDER and Hugh Krey had been on that committee and attended that last meeting at the University of Arizona. The air conditioner's noise was so loud that other members yelled louder than normal, and the meat-packing-room cold made Wilder wish he'd brought a jacket. Krey's monosyllabic scorn for law thrilled and rather frightened Wilder, who doodled something shaggy on his yellow pad, and noted: *K - Wolf eyes.*

Neither man proposed another plan. When the meeting ended with some backslapping, these men slipped out avoiding human contact—each going his separate way. On the train home, Wilder's imagination served up scenes of what would happen to the petrified forest, the . . . the final devastation. And while he couldn't visualize a lighthearted Krey, Wilder had felt Krey's frustration, and suspected that he too, was depressed enough for Valium.

PROFESSOR WILDER TAUGHT psychiatry at the University of Chicago. Dr. Krey, a geologist with a huge reputation for his work on cryptobiotic soils, was a lecturer at U of C's School of Geophysical Sciences.

In a campus famed for eccentric dressers, Wilder, an over-ripe-pear-shaped man, wore string ties: leather plaited thinner than a whipsnake, caught with a decorative silver choke. He had a collection of them and seemed to wear them according to some presentiment of what mood the day would bring. Some chokes were Navajo myth-themed: the turquoise-winged thunderbird, yellow-and-white-striped squash blossom, thundercloud—as common thematically in their homeland as caps with flaps are, in Chicago—yet the stones in these pieces were choice. Most of his chokes were simply-mounted stones, each a head-turner in its own way. One of them cried out for rye, sauerkraut, and mustard. He didn't look any sillier in his string ties than Theo Grossner (Dean of the School), who wore sandals and socks throughout Chicago's winter. Both men, however, left their pet peccadilloes in Chicago. At a conference at, say, Harvard, only their words were notable.

The living room of Wilder's apartment could have been a museum, so well had he bought and displayed his collection. The sparkling halite crystals from the Wieliczka mine—to other tastes, mere salt to be crushed. Mouthwatering wulfenite from the Red Cloud Mine in Arizona, as red as a blood orange. Great rock-candy mimetite protruding from what looked like a slagheap of burnt sugar, coming all the way from Johanngerogendtadt in Saxony where Siegfried and Kriemhild's love ended in bitterness and blood. Atacamite from Wallaroo, chrysoberyl from Takovaja, rutile from Pfitsch, and brookite from Froßnitz. The pieces showed a wide and particular taste. The Alexandrite from the emerald mines along the Takovaja Urals had cost more than its worth, but what a history. Then there were the grotesqueries. The iron-flower from the Erzberg in Styria. The writhing horse of lead. Nothing here was shaped by human hand.

His second bedroom held his books. He was divorced, with one surprising issue from the marriage—a daughter in her twenties whom he loved uncomplicatedly and who taught, of all things, home economics.

Dr. Hugh Krey was a long jerky strip of a man, in clothes he ordered when the ones he had wore out, from the Sears, Roebuck catalogue or picked up at someplace local (since he'd arrived in Chicago, *Kresge's Dollar Store was the place—cheapest and closest*). His eyes were the color of a snow-laden sky, with pinprick pupils. They disconcerted people, attracted women who loved dangerous men. Not that he was predatory. He just used women same as they used him.

Even though there was the odd coincidental interest that both men had in the petrified forest, Wilder had always avoided Krey, who hadn't seemed to notice Wilder. The psychiatrist didn't blame the man. Wilder had always shied away or been tongue-tied in front of the famed geologist—the shyness of an amateur in an expert's presence. Now at last, he had something to offer—a thought hatched from his own expertise.

A month after the Arizona meeting, on a stinking-hot September day the first week of the new semester, Professor Wilder rang the geology lecturer at work, made a wry observation about the committee's balls, and invited the geologist to his apartment "for a beer after work." The address he gave was 3C, to which Krey said, "'Kay."

Wilder had lived in the same Hyde Park apartment in Chicago's South Side for thirty years, Krey for two—a once-gracious brownstone a block from Lake Michigan. The phone call from Wilder was the first time they'd spoken. Krey wondered what beer Wilder would drink. Decided Pabst Blue Ribbon, in a glass. Which was another reason Krey always preferred drinking beer alone, but he approved Wilder's lack of chattiness, his silence when others in that committee spoke so authoritatively about the psychological effect of harsh penalties on the guilty. *He must have been laughing up his ass.* Yeah, Krey knew what Wilder was and would have been willing to listen to him, up to a point. *What came first, crazy people or shrinks?* So Krey didn't mind the invitation. It intrigued him.

WILDER OPENED THE door holding a Budweiser that he handed Krey. Then he stepped aside. "I'll get mine," he said, flicking some switches on the wall and escaping down the dark hall to the kitchen, not that Krey noticed. The stuff in the cases had caught all of his attention.

Light poured over, pierced, probed and petted the rocks and minerals. Krey walked slowly around the room, not noticing the widening wet around his armpits. The night was sweltering, and though there were no visible lamps in the room, all the wattage in those subtly hidden light sources could have fried an egg. When Wilder entered, bottle in hand, Krey was bent over, gazing, not at the picnic-table-size slice of *Araucarioxylon arizonicum* mounted on the wall, but at something in the case just to the left.

Wilder's hand squeaked against the neck of his bottle. "I'm just an amateur."

"Hn," said Krey.

"Ready for another?" said Wilder. He reached out.

"Whoa." Krey drank, one eye on Wilder, as if the bottle were a glass of milk and Wilder was his mother watching.

Wilder was in agony, awaiting the judgment of this expert. His right big toe flexed so hard, he heard the knuckle crack. His guts felt stirred with a wooden spoon.

"Thanks," said Krey.

Wilder took the bottle and scurried to the kitchen. The contents of his own bottle, he poured into a jar and put in the fridge. He picked a fresh cold one from the pack in the fridge and returned with it, hovering around Krey, not knowing if the man wanted it or not.

"That," Krey pointed, and laughed, sort of. "It brings back memories."

Wilder's laugh exploded. No "What a fine collection" or "nice stuff." No appreciative comments at all.

"Your collection must be so much better," he blurted before he could stop himself.

He mopped his face with his handkerchief. Did that disguise the redness that he felt rise up his neck? His eyes must have been closed because when he opened them again, Krey's back was to him. The man was mumbling to himself, bent over a clump of epidote from, Wilder had been told, Knappenwand in Untersulzbachtal.

His toe shredded the sock.

Krey finally turned to him. "I wouldn't say that. Different, is all. Got another beer?"

He handed it to Krey and scurried back to the kitchen.

Krey thought of his own collection, every piece of which he had personally found. A source of pride, but a limit. Display? He'd never thought that way. He'd always hoarded them. Home? His bed stuck in an arroyo that wound between buttes of books, papers, and boxes that had once held shoes, booze, artillery shells. He was almost jealous. He'd heard that some professor at the university had fallen heir to a bottled orange juice fortune, but that he continued living as he had—teaching. Krey hadn't paid attention to the name then, but remembered now: Wilder. Krey remembered how disgusted he'd been—and resentful. How he'd thought of the discoveries he'd make, contrasted with that dumbass— a fortune wasted on a drone with so little imagination, he'd continue teaching. Now, he looked again at that hunk of soberyl, and had to do something before he felt sorry for himself. Wilder was no dumbass.

He wandered to the kitchen door, where he watched Wilder pour a bag of beer nuts into a bowl. A red shell floated to the table. Wilder sponged it off before taking two beers out of the fridge, putting them and the bowl on a tray. He opened a cupboard and was looking into it when Krey entered, pulled out one of the two kitchen chairs, and sat, digging a handful of nuts from the bowl.

"Have a drink," said Krey.

WILDER LET THE bottles accumulate on the table. But by his third, his toes were still as herrings in a can, not because of the beer (straight vodka was his drink) but because of Krey. The geologist was telling of the time when the sphalerite in his pants gave him crotch rash at a Bulgarian border post, while the guards tore his rickety British van apart because they spotted a dirty magazine he'd planted on the back seat.

"But why cause them to suspect you? What about the van?"

"They're Bulgarians! I threw them a bone. As long as they didn't chew the wheels, I was happy. And I *was, very* happy. There's nothing like a bracing border search." Krey's eyes sparkled like Wilder thought a mad dog's would, terribly exciting, but odd. *Krey a chatterbox? or is he lying? and why? Does he think I don't know value? Is he laughing at me? No. He really does admire my collection. Is he a little jealous? I hope so . . .*

Krey's long legs had tipped his chair back, its front legs reared up. Wilder would have been furious if anyone else had done this to his furniture, and almost didn't notice now.

"But we still have that problem," Krey said, sitting up abruptly.

Wilder looked into Krey's eyes. He hadn't bruised the floor to be offensive.

"Decidedly." In all the excitement, Wilder had almost forgotten what he'd planned to say to Krey.

"Of course this is *your* expertise." Krey's expression was receptive, respectful, expectant.

"I wouldn't say that," Wilder smiled, thrilled beyond words. This was the first time he'd brought an expert to see his collection, and to be treated like a peer—

Krey's forearm jerked forward, sweeping salt and peanut crumbs onto Wilder's spotless floor. "Isn't behavior your specialty?"

"Certainly. Of course." Wilder felt his neck burning, wished he wasn't wearing one of those new white nylon open-neck shirts. "Absolutely."

Krey pulled a pipe, tobacco pouch, and wooden box of matches out of the left breast-pocket of his shirt, and paid them undivided attention. Wilder escaped to the bedroom where he dug a cigar from his night-table, collected the cutter and box of matches, and steadied his breath before he returned to the kitchen, where he replaced the empty peanut bowl with a heavy ashtray, and sat at the table preparing his cigar. Then he wasted a good smoke, pulling on it with as much introverted eye-avoidance as Krey, who in his absence had produced a notepad and pencil.

Krey smoked as if his pipe and thoughts were his only companions.

Eventually Wilder stubbed out his cigar stub, left the kitchen with no comment, got his own writing materials and returned with them. Ostentatiously, he took the hood from his pen.

Krey's smoke floated between them.

Wilder's big toe cracked. *I'll be damned if I break first.*

Krey prepared another pipe, and *still*, Wilder didn't say a word, but now that he *thought* about what he'd liked about Krey in the first place, his anger slipped. The man was honest. He didn't shit around. "You were saying?" he invited.

Krey knocked the pipe in the ashtray, and stuck it headfirst, in his pocket. "What'll a law do?"

"You mean, prohibiting collection?"

"Yeah. Fines, jail, criminal record, what have you."

"What's prohibition ever do," Wilder said. "The stuff'll skyrocket in price and be trucked out before you can say blackmarket."

"Normal Joes couldn't afford it. Not unless they bootlegged, or sold white slaves."

Krey's eyes narrowed, spreading the crows-feet. "Or were heirs to stinking fortunes." It was humor. He wasn't being offensive. Just signaling.

"Rotten stinking fortunes," corrected Wilder.

Wilder left for another cigar. He needed a break to get his thoughts together, as now he really didn't want to sound stupid. Now that he was sure Krey was the man he most wanted to expose them to, and to act in concert with.

Alone, Krey smiled with his teeth showing, something he never did in the presence of others.

K REY SPOKE FIRST, not even giving Wilder a chance to sit. "What does law create, doctor?"

A growl of happiness escaped the older man. "Desire," he said in the voice that had laid waste dozens of female students some years ago.

"And?" Krey asked.

"And what?" Wilder was confused, not used to questions he hadn't planted.. *Prohibition creates desire. Desire above all . . . but law, penalties, the hunt . . . the thrill of—*

"This isn't Psych 101," Krey snapped. "You can't treat me as a peer, I know, but—"

Wilder held up his pen, for silence. "The greatest motivator in the human psyche," he said, "is fear."

"Why, give the man a coconut."

"Fear" was what Krey was aiming for, in his attempt to get Wilder to think of a solution. Krey had examined his own psyche well enough, he reckoned, to know that fear gave him purpose. It distinguished desiring women. The ones married to colleagues wafted the most danger, and amongst them were the most desire-worthy, for a while. Every specimen he'd ever smuggled to his craggy but cozy little lairs bore a worth proportionate to the fear attached to its acquisition. Like neighborhoods jostling, contentment and resentment lived neck and neck in his thoughts, as they did in the nation. Money could buy anything, but for a man like him, even on a dean's salary, *if I'd been law abiding, what would I have?*

That petrified forest irked him immensely. Only obscurity had saved it from being carted away to the moneyed, as wholesale as a feedlot of steers to the Armour sausage mill, to be consumed with as much intelligence as America does its hot dogs. *That slab on the wall here . . . polished! How big is mine?* Krey clicked his tongue, comparing, remembering. His largest piece of the Petrified Forest was a 386.5 lb splitfaced-broken length of *Schilderia* (rarer than the *Araucarioxylon arizonicum*) pried out of the ground by himself and a wetback who was pathetically grateful to do it for ten bucks and a ride into Flagstaff. Three hours from home (Denver, then) at dusk on an evil incline, the last drop of oil from his rundown Ford leaked, and the pistons melted solid.

He had the hood open and was leaning over the dead engine when two singing saviors pulled beside him on the one-lane road, in a bad excuse for a truck. No more than ten words were exchanged. They took over his Ford pickup and the situation. First, they shoved the pickup into a little hide of firs just up the road a bit, the kind of place you'd expect to find, if you're alone at night, half a dead woman. They smelled worse than two drunk skunks, but next, they tossed out the cord of wood they had in the back of their truck as if the split logs were toothpicks, and they lined the truckbed with burlap sacks one of them fetched from somewhere inside the truck. Then, grinning like maniacs, they pushed him out of the way and hefted the unwieldy rock from Krey's pickup to their truck. They tossed in his pick and shovel, and tied it all down till the tires could bounce along a logging track, and the load would stay quiet as a body. Git in, said the one with the most teeth. The passenger door was opened for Krey by Eustace. Clive (he was called) rode shotgun, literally. Eustace drove with one hand on the wheel. He was generous, pulling out (with his teeth) a cork stopping a bottle that said Nehi, and wiping the bottle on his shirt before handing it to their guest. His own bottle was Heinz Ketchup. He didn't ask questions, but served up stories wrapped around homilies like "Johnny Walker's for the ladies" and "The gubermint persues happiness, to arrest it." In their youth in Kentucky, they'd made a hassled living as "distillers." Krey shook his head. The stuff was cloudy as the water in Cubatão, and twice as deadly. They hadn't been going to Denver, but since that was where he was going, that was where they went because, as Eustace said, it was a thing he'd do for them if they were up shit creek.

When they reached his embarrassingly suburban house (a university rental property), they carried in his things, keeping the burlap wrapping on everything including the pickaxe till they got indoors, where they didn't dump stuff, but asked him where he'd like each item placed. Clive folded the wrapping neatly and took it to the truck, returning with a full Dr. Pepper. Happy home, he said. So long, said Eustace, and they left. Krey knew they wouldn't take money, but he'd laid the keys to the Ford on Eustace's seat. He had just closed his door when there was a knock and Eustace appeared, dangling the keys.

HE LOVED THAT rock but not for itself. He loved the way it challenged him to think he knew something when he analyzed its samples. Within its seemingly static cells, as dead as Pluto, it encapsulated life, death, transformation. It was what religion *should* be, mushed myth to the pap of rubes. There was nothing flashy, obvious, easy about this rock, or anything in his collection. His slivers weren't biopsies, teeming with marvelous virulence. His petrified woods, like a crystal rose, globules of obsidian, every rain-pouring grain of simple salt, was *life*. Life in a timeframe that dwarfed science itself—science—the only truth worth seeking. Sure, he'd washed that hunk of stone once, but he never lost sight of what it was. It lived near his bed, covered in a patina of greasy, cat-fur-laden dust. When Denver had imploded and he'd had to move to Chicago, real moving men from Mayflower had packed his belongings with mostly silent distaste—"You got any furniture?"— until they got to *it*, leaning against the corner nearest where his bed had been. "Bud," the bigger one said to Krey, "That's a hernia. You want that mountain? You move it outn." He sat heavily on the floor. $20 each moved him and his colleague to move the mountain. Even then, once the Mayflower van's back doors were locked, the poet came back and put his hand out bold as a bellhop. "Suspicious load," he laughed. Krey meekly forked over another two fives because he didn't trust them not open the van and *look* for something to take. And the Mayflower sailed away. *Chump!* Krey threw the university's house keys into the hydrangeas. *What's to stop them?* Not that he had anything they'd know to take. *Nothing like Tiffany's here with the glass cases, everything spotless and sparkling Precious Find. I've got nothing that Money values.*

Krey thought of his cat, Punk, who only enjoyed food that wasn't his. Krey helped Punk pursue happiness. The steak on a mousetrap was the most pleasure so far. The steak on the rat-trap, Punk left. He must have considered that a trap too dangerous to play against. Instead, he watched it and ate the rat who judged incorrectly.

"Am I interrupting an internal dialogue?" Wilder smiled. "Want some eggs?" He emptied the ashtray down the dumbwaiter.

Wilder cooked pedantically, using more utensils than Krey would take for a dig. The plate he slung in front of his guest had six colors on it, and that was just the food. Until that moment, Krey never knew that parsley existed outside of restaurants. He ate it first, so as not to be rude.

They finished the meal with black stewed coffee. Proper prospector's mud. It made up for the eggs.

Wilder wiped his mouth on a linen napkin, collected the plates and stacked them by the sink. "Fear is what I was thinking of," he said as he placed a fresh ashtray on the table, and a pack of Marlboros and book of matches that said *Macello Ristorante*.

"Go on," said Krey.

"We gotta cut the balls off desire. Replace them with a special kind of fear. Know what I mean?"

"Of course."

"What?"

"Fear . . . "

Wilder held the Marlboros out to Krey, who shoved them away. "Tell me, doc."

"Dread," grinned Wilder. "That's the worst kind of fear. Dread of what will happen."

Krey blew a smoke-ring. He'd lit up without knowing what he was doing, but now he needed time. Wilder's words were what he'd thought himself, but thinking as he did, of people, he hadn't trusted himself. Sure, people are stupid, but just how stupid are they, and how do you make them fear something (he hadn't figured that brilliant *dread*)—how do you make people fear something to the point of it being *too* dangerous to ignore, taunt, steal its threat from under it and laugh all the way to the bank or wherever—if making "theft" a criminal offence only makes it more attractive, a mere mousetrap to a Punk? Krey was confused, but possibly Wilder had figured something out.

Krey snorted. "It's only property. Congress is hardly going to strap someone in the chair for stealing rocks, even diamonds at Tiffany's."

"Congress! What are they compared to gods?"

"Gods?"

"You haven't read my monographs of course, but did you happen to see the *Saturday Evening Post* of March 6, 1958. Deities of the Desert? No? A little interest of mine, you see."

"You collect myths, too? So Indians prayed to the rain god." Krey rubbed his eyes. They felt sandy. "Capture it on Kodak."

"Want some raisin toast?"

"No goddamn raisin toast. Get to the point."

"We need a myth."

"And you'll make one?"

"I thought something along that line."

"You're a regular rattler in the grass," Krey laughed. "Make toast. I'll open the window."

"I wouldn't do that."

But Krey already had. The room filled with a sickening warm fust. The washing line that stretched between Wilder's window and the apartment on the other side of the open square (garbage cans and cats' playground below) was filled with diapers.

"I wish that woman would get a washing machine," Wilder sighed, but really, he couldn't care less.

He ran his hand over the strands of hair on his dome, delighted that he'd assessed the world-renowned scientist correctly. For a while there, Krey had scared him in all the wrong ways—the man's lack of social skills, his sense of grievance, something else that left a chip on his shoulder. But looking at Krey's back now, Wilder was not only proud of his own ability to assess someone he'd only observed briefly, but felt true warmth inside. Camaraderie.

Krey's unusually small teeth gleamed—unconscious, open-mouthed admiration. Wilder was definitely not what a nice rich psychiatrist with a tenured professorship should be. *And for some reason, he trusts me.*

Krey ate his toast like a dog—fast, without chewing. He was getting it out of the way. Wilder poured two mugs of coffee.

"That dread," said Krey. "Are you talking cause and effect?"

"I never thought of it that way, but yes. Think of it as the expectation of a reaction from a previous action. Be bad and you won't get anything from Santa, or the Easter Bunny won't lay you an egg. And other myths, all implanted in the human psyche for a purpose."

"Control!"

"Egg . . . zakly. You wouldn't be a Trotskyite?"

"I'm eggnostic."

"Touché."

"So you're going to fake some story of the god who looks after the petrified forest."

Wilder waggled a finger in Krey's face. "Better than that. Fake? What *is* reality? I'll implant the scholarly records. Remember, I have a reputation."

At night in various deeply uncomfortable places, Krey had read lurid-covered rubbish to escape the weather, wildlife, and other people. He never *remembered* any of that trash as such, but . . . "I know that story of mine about the crotchrash was bullshit," he said, "I'm sorry, but it's not like I made it up. It's a goddamn cliché."

"I know," said Wilder, remembering that the man was telling the truth when he had said "your expertise." *He respects me, I think. Maybe even my collection, just a little.*

"I'm just telling you this because you've lit my fuse, but you're the expert here. You were talking dread?"

"An emotion you might regard unworthy of rational beings." Wilder wasn't being ironic.

"I've read papers in front of colleagues, too, you know." Krey poured himself cold coffee. He was actually nervous.

"I promise I won't laugh," said Wilder.

"It's eight o'clock. Don't you think we should call in sick?"

THE RING OF the telephone," said Krey. "The knock on the door. A man lives in a neat little house. He opens the door in the morning and reaches out. What should he expect? A rolled-up *Tribune* and a bottle of milk. Implant dread, and you could pay him a million dollars, he won't open that door. Ask him what he expects, and a million to one, he can't tell you. Not a rattlesnake coiled in the Sports section. No strychnine in the milk. He just *expects*. Nameless dread."

"Or as I once wrote: paranoia is the key."

"Exactly! But I don't know how to do it," Krey ended.

Wilder had put much thought into his faux myth. He hadn't reached the stage of myth invention, but telling Krey of the idea, *false myth*—had led to Krey's gestalt—and Krey had in turn, inspired him, especially Krey's idea of "nameless dread."

"Did I tell you," said Wilder, "that I'm retiring this year? That I applied for and was accepted as Director of the Petrified Forest National Park museum?"

Krey's mouth fell open.

"Don't congratulate me."

"What'll you put in it?" Krey shouted. "Petrified wood and signs? You romantic fool. You'd get more respect running a Dairy Queen."

"I did it for love," Wilder said. "And you're right. I rather dreaded that it would be hard to curate compellingly . . . until you."

— II —

"Superstitious, I wasn't," reads a penciled crumpled scrap of butcher paper. "However, more bad luck has happened to me than any one person could rationally have experienced. Take this back." It is signed, "A cynic no more, Scranton, Pennsylvania"

⋄

A typed letter on expensive blue Cross stationery reads:

To Whom it May Concern:

Please warn everybody Not to Take the Petrified Wood from the Park. My husband just died. My daughter is sick. Before he took what was nothing really, just a little pebble, we were such a happy family. I warned him but he took it anyway. He had it made into this pendant that he gave me for our anniversary. He didn't tell me that this was the pebble till he was going in for the operation. I'm a good Christian woman, so take this and bury it or something, please please please. It's more evil than the snake in the Garden of Paradise.

Yours sincerely,
Mrs. John S.
Los Angeles

⋄

A ruled page filled to the edges with words:

Before. Yes, before, I sailed my little boat on a placid sea of ignorance. Was I blissful? Oh my, yes. Before the truth floated like jetsam towards me, fouling my rudder . . .

A telegram:

> STOP THIS CURSE STOP TELL THEM
> IM SORRY STOP HERES THE STONE

A letter in German. Several in semi-American, one of which mentioned mummies and the Hope diamond. One letter with an envelope marked Beverley Hills in which a woman states that her mother-in-law "stole" a tiny piece of petrified wood on her honeymoon in 1911, but who didn't find out about the curse till 1954. "Is this (see enclosed) why my husband dropped dead at 49? Is this why my granddaughter has seizures and my grandson got a bee in his ear? Is this why I never win the lottery?"

These were only some of the great pile of letters and pieces of petrified stone in the central display case when the museum opened—all Krey and Wilder productions.

A few months later, Krey's game was up in Chicago—something about a Mrs. Everly. He took early leave and was accepted for the next year at West Virginia Tech.

Dear Hugh,
    You might enjoy the cutting.
Fondly,
Walt
ps. How are you faring so far from civilization?

The Tucson Star, Wednesday, June 6, 1963:

> ### THE CURSE OF THE PETRIFIED WOODS
> #### by Phillip Joy
> . . . Dr. Walter Wilder, the head of the museum and a noted authority on myth, had this to say: "Myths have their purpose and should, even in our scientific times, be respected, as the underlying strata of our value systems. Some myths, like this one about the curse of taking petrified wood from the park, are so old that they

predate historical knowledge, but that doesn't make them any less worthy—we know to avoid snakes without being taught at school. We instinctively avoid fire . . . "

Krey read it in his windowless office at the Tech. His door had been closed at the time, but that didn't stop his unseemly laughter traveling down the hall and penetrating the ears of at least one envious colleague.

Hugh was faring fine. He was, for the first time in his adult life, in love. And the woman wasn't even married. They walked arm in arm, under the black limbs of hickories and talked as Hugh had never talked with anyone before. Especially a woman. "I'm opening like a flower," he told her.

September 8, 1964

Dear Hugh,

You won't believe it! Letters and rocks are coming in from everywhere! Someone shipped us a whole log! These tales are unbelievable. I am going to write a book. *When The Silent Psyche Speaks the Truth*. You're a loss to the psych profession.

Walter,

A little something for your collection. Your *personal* collection!

Fondly,

Hugh

"Hugh?"

"Walter?"

"I had to ring you. I've looked everywhere. What is it?"

Krey's laugh startled Walter, it was such a rippling stream.

"Moissanite, Walt. Dropped from the heavens to West Virginia."

"It's beautiful. How can I thank you?"

"No thanks needed Walter. That's nothing compared to the beauty here beside me."

Walter heard some scuffling, and a giggle.

"Am I disturbing you?"

"Yes."

"Oh, I'll—"

"No you won't," laughed Krey. "You already have disturbed me. How ya doin', you old conman?"

"Hugh?"

"Hugh who?"

"I'm serious. My collection. You truly think it has a worth?"

"Are you kidding? I'd give my eyeteeth for it."

Walter Wilder's eyes closed. He'd wanted to hear that line for so long that he almost didn't believe it. "You really mean that?"

"Who *wouldn't*, Walter?"

"I've been thinking a lot about it. Do you know where I live out here?"

Krey hadn't asked. Wilder's letters had the park as return address.

"In a trailer," Wilder said. "The collection is in storage in Chicago. I would like to give it to you . . . Hugh?"

Wilder heard whispers on the line, then what he thought might be a door closing. He waited.

"That's almost the nicest thought anyone's ever had for me. But you can't be serious."

"You seem to appreciate it. Are you just flattering me?" Wilder's voice almost wheedled for a *no*. He couldn't know that for a moment, Krey had trembled with desire.

"The Wilder collection would make the finest museum proud. Give it to the Field, or . . . God! The University of Chicago. The Wilder Collection, in its own wing, in of the School of Geophysical Sciences."

"You really think so?"

"It *is* a fucking museum."

"You really think so?"

"Are you breast-feeding deprived or something? Yes, yes, great ballsa yes!"

"Your old school?"

"How many times do I have to—uh, except for one piece. That polished slab of petrified wood on the wall."

Walter Wilder was finding it difficult to concentrate, but he tried, through the fog of his confused happiness. "Why?"

"It's not science."

"Doesn't it show what it's like crosscut?"

"Yes," Krey admitted, "but it's beautiful. Decorative."

"I thought so, too."

"It doesn't belong in a museum, Walter."

"It must belong somewhere."

"A mafia coffeetable," slipped out of Krey's mouth. "No," he said. "I didn't mean that."

"Yes you did." But Wilder wasn't upset. "What do you advise?"

"Well . . . Arizona! The state capital. They'll hang it there."

"I'll ring the governor. And thank you, Hugh. But are you sure you don't want—"

"Part of me does, Walt. The unscientist part. I *am* part human, as you might have guessed." Krey waited for Wilder's laugh, then continued. "I only keep what I collect myself. I'm kinda proud of it. And I only collect to study it, as a scientist."

"I admire you," Wilder said, and hung up.

February 5, 1965

Hugh,

Here's a handful from our mailbag from just *this week*. You would be amazed at the tonnage we're getting back with it. Last month a 250 lb piece came by UPS. I couldn't do with it what I do with all the others, a ritual I really love. Every evening after the park has closed, I walk out under the stars and toss the send-backs out, like a farmer sowing oats. Rather like God tossing stars into the heavens.

"Dr. Wilder, please."

"Please hold."

"Wilder here."

"Fuck, Walt."

"Eh?"

"I just got your letter."

"Hugh?"

"Who else. Gimme your home number. I'll ring you tonight."

"Walter?"

"Yes, Hugh."

"You wouldn't take a body and open up the skull, and stick the hypothalamus where the fuckassimus would be, would you?"

"Whatever are you saying."

"Or reverse the liver and spleen. And have anatomy students study the cadaver?"

"Why would anyone do something that crazy? That's nothing short of despoilment."

"So why the fuck are you despoiling the land?"

"Are your underpants too tight, Hugh?"

"Look, I know what you *thought* you were doing. Your intentions are noble, but this is the problem with amateurs when they think they're doing good. What you've engaged in is . . . as bad as pop psych."

"But what?"

"The wood that comes back. Don't put it back, Walt. Just don't. You don't know where it came from, and spreading it around only despoils the body of the land. No one can study it when you do that, because you're throwing spleens around as if they belong in armpits."

Walter Wilder broke out into a cold sweat. He pinched his leg viciously, he was so angry. "God, I'm sorry. I can't pick them up. I can't undo what I've . . . what an idiot. I'll never forgive—"

"Shut up, Walter. You understand. We all make mistakes. Just don't do it again."

"Believe me, I'd have my arms cut off first. But what'll I do with the returns?"

"Anything but that. Why don't you give 'em to all those Navajo jewelers you know? They don't care where the stuff comes from."

"They don't, do they?"

"It's not in their interest to know."

"Thank you, Hugh."

"Thank *you*, Walter. I'm sorry I was a bit harsh."

"I was a slow student," Wilder chuckled. "But am I wrong in something I do know a bit about?"

"Do you know a bit about anything?"

"The human heart. Have you given yours away?"

" . . . Yes. Her name's Ann. We're getting married in June. She's making invitations. It'll be her family. I don't have any."

"Yes, Hugh. You do."

Walter Wilder wasn't surprised that there was a delay in response, and an unmanly wet sound. "I forgot to tell you," he said. "Congratulate me. I'm going to be a grandfather."

⚛

On a bleak day in April, just before the first crocuses broke through the sodden gray of autumn leaves, Ann, that was her name, Krey's love, got Stage 1 of Dying Stupidly. A scratch from a squirrel she was feeding got infected. Some days later, they gave her penicillin. Then they put her in the hospital where she got streptococcal pneumonia. From scratch to burial took a month.

⋄

'69
Merry Christmas, Hugh.
You don't have to write,
but I'd love to hear from you.

⋄

In 1971, Walter Wilder retired from his directorship of the museum, nothing that made any news stories, but a few months earlier, his granddaughter, the one he gave a rattle made of petrified stones that he'd personally picked for her from the returns, was diagnosed with encephalitis. On taking the directorship of the museum back in '62, Wilder had had his collection of string tie chokes remade into necklaces and bracelets and given them to his daughter.

⋄

"Her Majesty put on rubber boots and a Burberry mackintosh; the President changed into cowboy boots, denim jacket and Western string tie."
— "The Queen Makes a Royal Splash" by Kurt Anderson,
Time, March 14, 1983

⋄

"Sales of string ties (the "bolo", the official state neckwear of Arizona since 1973) have gone up 12,000 percent since President Reagan took office."
— *Menswear Marketwatch*, March 20, 1985

⋄

Two pages typed on an old manual:

To Whom this Should Concern
Damn you.
Nothing I did deserved this. Three deaths in my family in the past year: my parrot Rudy, our loving dog Kevin and a kitten my youngest daughter brought home when she found it crying in the snow the day after Christmas. I would be sleepless from fear if my husband's sleeplessness didn't keep me awake. These days our home, instead of a WELCOME mat, seems to have a sign on the lawn: MORGUE. No one visits. We missed the last

neighborhood party. I used to be the organizer. Do you know what it takes to organize potato salad for 150 people? My husband's manager hates him. My oldest boy's intelligence is measurably diminishing. My oldest daughter is secretly meeting a boy who has just one thing on his mind, not that she cares. When I think that only two years ago when we visited your park, she was going to be a scientist, I want to scream, but that accomplishes nothing. I tried to communicate with you, in your visitors' book, my disgust for your display of naked superstition completely inappropriate in a museum supposedly dedicated to the exploration and elucidation of natural phenomenae. I yearned then to state my true name, to speak to your staff face to face, but didn't because my daughter was so impressed with the site that she expressed an interest in working at the park when she matured. I was loath to prejudice her chances. The blessing was, she never saw that hogwash under glass—all that please forgive me. I took this absolute s**t. Yes, s**t. You need to be shocked out of your complacency. Not all of us are stupid. She wanted all of her time during our visit to be spent outside, something I was thankful for, and to which I attributed her intelligent upbringing. This sensible attitude of hers only made me more furious at that insult to science that you display in what has to be pride of place.

So just before we left, while my family were in the restrooms, I strolled outside till I found the biggest piece of petrified wood that I could fit in my handbag. I took it.

I used to keep it hidden indoors but recently buried it in a wasteland where no children play and real estate conditions are so depressed, it is safe from development unless our species spreads its infestation thoroughly across the land. WARNING: I can dig it up and send it to a lab at any time.

Why am I giving you notice? Because you should tell first. I shouldn't foot the bill to discover your sordid secret. Why did you think rational people would stay quiet forever? I won't.

You've ruined countless lives, yet you didn't have to. You could have posted signs. Something polite and decent like Please don't step on the grass—pick the flowers—run in the hallway. People are used to signs. You didn't have to slow poison us. You are, after all, not vengeful gods, but creepy little bureaucrats. Mark my words. It's only a matter of time before Truth Will Out. In the meantime: Find out how to clean up your site and DO IT, or do you have just

*as much of a clue about that as about uranium, or what they put in
Colonel Sanders' chicken spice?*

Very truly,
A. Ware
Somewhere, USA

◇

"What the—"

"Hello . . . hello . . . Is this Hugh Krey?"

"Depends."

"This is Walt, Hugh. Walter Wilder."

"Walter, do you know what time it is here? How the fuck did
you find me?"

"You didn't make it easy. It took a week. Listen, Hugh. Did you
see Reagan on TV?"

"When?"

"Last week."

"Are you kidding? This is Nigeria. And why would I want to
watch the Ray Gun?"

"Don't make fun of him."

"You aren't serious."

"If you saw his rendezvous with destiny speech you couldn't say
that. The man understands the human psyche."

Hugh reached out his toe and flicked the fan to high, now that he
was fully awake. "You can't want to talk politics."

"Did you see that picture showing the president in his string tie,
with the Queen?"

"Gosh," Krey said. "I didn't get my last issue of *Menswear Daily*.
Walter, are you seeing anyone for this?"

"This is serious. It was in all the papers."

"When?"

"Back in '83."

"Eleven years ago? I was prospecting in hell."

"The string tie was a hunk of petrified stone."

"You remember the date?"

"People here framed the pictures. You really didn't see?"

"*The Hades Chronicle* doesn't even have funnies."

"The point *is*, and *please pay attention*. Now President Reagan
has Alzheimer's. He announced it last week."

"So that's his excuse."

"You don't get it?"

"What's to get? He can't remember the Iran Contras. Yeah, I do get that."

"I'm not talking politics, thickhead. That's petrified wood from the petrified forest. I'm sure of it."

"Where?"

Wilder's sigh was louder than the crackles in the line. "His tie, Hugh. His string tie choke."

"Dr. Wilder. Good night, or morning or whatever the fuck. I need my rest. Get medicated."

◇

It's a rest home only people with money can afford. There's a pretence of dignity. One old man is sitting beside the bed of another. It's a "private room."

"I couldn't open my door," says the one in the bed. "Too afraid."

"It's no shame to be here. They do the maidwork," Krey says.

"Don't," says Wilder. "I asked you here because I want to warn you." He rises up on his sticklike arms. "Get rid of your pieces."

"Or I won't get the girls," smiles Krey. His lips champ over teeth that make a dull grinding sound, like a melamine cup on a melamine saucer that doesn't fit.

"Get *rid* of them. There might be something left in your life."

Krey laughs. "You sound like a believer."

"There *is* a curse. I just didn't believe it before."

Krey's eyes cloud. "You made it—*We* made it up, Walter. Remember?"

"I remember all sorts of things, like my Wendy and her beautiful daughter. Like that love of your life. And your career."

"Bad luck."

"Too much bad luck."

"We're scientists, Wilder! Don't you remember what you said: Paranoia is the key?"

"I also remember what I said: Myths have their purpose."

"That was between us. A joke, remember? A white lie for the good of the site. We're scientists, you and I. We *implanted*, Doctor. Please remember. Walter. Come back to me."

Krey reaches out. His arthritic hand looks like an exotic fruit that hasn't sold—something purplish and overripe. Wilder's is bones in rice paper. It is cold.

Eventually the nurse comes in. She rolls up a wheelchair with a colorful crocheted throw disguising an overthick seat.

"Mr. Wilder. It's time for your lunch. Should I tell the dining room that there will be another guest?"

Wilder turns his head to Krey. "Want lunch? We're having oysters Rockefeller, roast grouse, and some kind of gateau."

The nurse's eyes signal professional sympathy to Krey, who for some reason doesn't notice her. Then she's all business with Wilder.

"No sir. It's tomato soup and fruit cup, and a birthday cake for Mrs. Wood."

"I was jesting," says Wilder, his eyes locked on Krey's. "He's leaving."

And he does leave, quickly and wordlessly, but not fast enough before the nurse throws back the covers and exposes Wilder.

Krey drives away, slowly and very carefully. He doesn't dare stop, so he has to swallow the bile that's refluxing with volcanic violence. "We did it. We planted those expectations. We sinned against science." Krey weeps as he mistakes the fast lane for the slow one.

Don't trifle with the curse of the Petrified Forest. Steal a piece of ancient wood . . . and some version of hell on earth will surely come your way. That's what Park rangers suggest to visitors, and the hundreds of letters they've received prove it.

— Leo Banks, "Petrified with Fear! The curse of an ancient forest dogs park troopers", *Tucson Weekly*, December 15, 1997

Unfortunately, in spite of severe penalties, written and verbal warnings and the opportunity to legally obtain petrified wood, thoughtless visitors continue to steal over one ton each month.

— Petrified Forest National Park Information Page, http://www.petrified.forest.national-park.com/info.htm

The Dog Who Wished He'd Never Heard of Lovecraft

There was a man who had a dog who had—for the good part of every day—never heard of H.P. Lovecraft, though this dog enjoyed his Will Cuppy, always licking his chops over the line, "The nuthatch cannot sing and does not try."

Now this dog—and since we didn't catch his name, we'll just call him Ibsen—was a rough-haired, right-flop-eared bitser of no particular color except for the black patch around his left eye. Being a virile male of middle years whose chin badly needed a shave, one could easily have said he had a morbid cast but one would be wrong.

He could have been a cert in the movies, but if he'd ever wanted to sit at the drugstore counter to be discovered, he'd never have been allowed to, in that town—and besides, he probably would have preferred to work on the stage, though that is a speculation. The town's Players didn't tolerate children at performances and eschewed Little Orphan Annie because of Merrilee Fairweather's purported allergy.

Ibsen didn't feel the loss, and not because he was blissfully ignorant. He was self-employed, is all. And by that, we don't mistake busyness for work. He wasn't one of those dogs who spends his waking hours scratching his ears and falling over backwards after trying to bite the root of his tail, or whining to be noticed, or acting like a butler who never mentions the stench of slippers. And he certainly wasn't a dog who lives for chasing, or any purposeless expenditure.

Say Ibsen were famous and some dog were cast as him. That dog would have to learn how to sit in a loose-boned slump, tilt his head about 26 degrees, and quarter-close his eyes. As the script would direct, if a dairy farmer were to write it:

IBSEN. [*ruminating*]

For Ibsen was above all, a thinker. Sure, he read a lot (see ref. to Cuppy above), but in his limited way, he was an observer, and that limitation sometimes roiled. He often, as fall rain merrily ran down the windows, wistfully wondered whether Cuppy had been intentionally hurtful when he wrote "Hasn't everybody? [been to Ceylon]". The first time Ibsen read that unthoughtfully hurtful comment, he felt like he'd just swallowed a stone in his dogbowl, thinking he'd bolted a hardboiled egg. Though even with that provocation, Ibsen would most likely have jibed at the globetrotting life of a celebrity—all that interruption. His eyes, under that wild hedge of eyebrow, were deep wells into which his observations dropped. What did he make of all he learned? Who knows? His hairy face was as expressionless as a barber's floor.

The problem with not knowing his Lovecraft is: his master (we'll humor the man), Hylam P. Hector, lived and breathed the man *he* called 'the Master'.

It might be that Ibsen was, at heart, a contrarian, or possibly the strain of acting faithful when assaulted by the man (the 'P' stood for Pituitary, an attempt by Hylam's father, an internist, to infuse enthusiasm in the fruit of his loins, to take up his own adventurous practice)—the man who is Mr Hector to most of us and Hylam to some but who encouraged Ibsen to think of him as 'Daddy', to, where were we?

The strain, yes. Mr Hector had got in the habit, bad, of writing Lovecraft-influenced poetry. If only this disease had progressed silently, but it *would* out. Every evening, Ibsen was interrupted by a long portentous "Ahhh," followed by the dread Introduction:

"Daddy's finished."

And the poem would come out of Ibsen's master's mouth, the poem in all its rambling incoherent imperturbable interminability.

Ibsen didn't, in all honesty, consider himself capable of critical literary analysis. He would have been the last dog on earth to decry this drivel as mere pastiche. That it was as nonsensically dallying as the man who thoughtlessly tosses a ball in his hand while talking to a friend when his ball-besotted dog is at his feet, waiting, was as clear to Ibsen as the fanatic eyeglow of achievement in Hylam Hector's eyes upon finishing a reading.

So Ibsen humored the man, his master. But, like 'Pituitary', Hylam Hector's zealotic enthusiasm was inadvertently the One Surefire Method to turn Ibsen from anything Lovecraftian.

Indeed, these readings set Ibsen upon a new short course of learning, one clipped for purely pragmatic ends: Ibsen's Method of Self-hypnosis that Really Really Works, which he used to flush his mind after every reading, to convince himself that he'd never heard of Lovecraft. It worked until the next dread Introduction.

So THE TRAGEDY is set. On the left side of the stage, clutching a sheaf of pages, paces Hylam P. Hector, eyes bright, head thrown back in post-declamatorious rapture—a man who looks like the kind of bachelor to live in one of those dark-eyed apartments over the town's drugstore (but who in fact lives in a house too featureless to notice in one of those streets named after numbers).

Center-stage is the dog you know as 'Ibsen'. Luckily for Mr. Hector, the pallid sea of light flowing from the green-shaded lamp laps not upon the shores of Ibsen's eyeballs. Yet if some foul fiend should, in a trice too quick for Ibsen to react, wipe from the dog's brow that rampant brush and shine upon the eyes of the hound, the unswerving gaze of a hundred-watt incandescent—if Hylam P. Hector had looked into his dog's eyes then, he would have been struck dumb.

For on this particular damp and gloomy evening indoors, Mr. Hector's poem, Moon Something-or-other Someplace-else, must have had a dozen lines that in their hysterically romance-tinged paranoia, their frustrating inexactitude, made Ibsen itch as bad as if he'd been licked by a thousand fleas. But he was used to that from 'Daddy'.

No, what finally raised the hair on his spine and made him loll his tongue to keep himself from raising his lip and letting his canines glow, was, not that invidious use of the word that should only be heard in another context, the casually friendly 'hi'. Ibsen's sensitive hearing was bruised every time Hylam Hector read out *hie* (and two *hie*s made Ibsen want to bite). But that wasn't the snap of tragedy's jaw.

An observant master would have noticed the growing furrow under that hedge of brow, but Hylam P. Hector noticed nothing.

And Ibsen, never a demonstrative dog, showed as little emotion as the palace guard with heat rash. The hound was long inured to too many *moon*s, *hideous*es, not to mention the abomination *shewed*; Ibsen, toughened by countless *lurk*s, suffered silently also through too many exotic places celebrated (especially galling coming from this man who wouldn't even walk his dog); and still, Ibsen soldiered on, carrying out his duty, evening after evening after evening, and always interrupted, at that.

Ibsen, on the evening of evenings just ebbing into night, had managed dogfully to maintain composure, forgive his master's interruption (Ibsen had felt that evening, a whisker away from answering the age-old conundrum: Why, when you dig a hole, is the earth you toss out never enough to fill it?).

Anyone really observing Ibsen then would have known that if he were a human, the only interruption he might possibly appreciate: a stealthy refill of his tobacco pouch.

His eyebrows threw deep shadows, but they were twitching with deeper thought when, "Listen to this, Rover!" (*We sense a deep sense of outrage that Ibsen might feel at this common tag, but since he is middle-aged, and a dog at that, this tragedy is a burden that he must have borne so long that he hardly winces.*) "Daddy's most luscious poem of all!"

And forthwith, Hylam Pituitary Hector commenced to read.

While poetising, his eyes were always either fixed on his sheaf of pages or closed, so he never saw the moment when his dog's faithfulness turned from the tolerance of proprietal deference, to bitterly apathetic scorn.

It's a terrible thing to see in a dog, but ask yourself: Could YOU have withstood as much?—the one-and-ten-thousandth "O*!*"!

But for an 'h' . . .

And isn't that par for all our tragedies? If those two had shared a toothpaste tube, the rift would sundered them e'en before Ibsen was old enough to shave.

S° HYLAM P HECTOR. [*triumphantly brushing his fingertips over his chin that he tries in vain to unrecede*] What a treat that was for you, tonight, Rover. [*exits left. sounds of water running, toothbrushing as Mr Hector prepares for bed.*]

IBSEN. [*stands and shakes himself as vigorously as if he'd just been washed. walks off stage left. His steps down the wooden hall are abundantly clear. This dog doesn't get enough walking and has never had his nails clipped. Thuds and scrabble in the kitchen, as Ibsen opens the door and takes himself out, as usual, for his evening constitutional.*]

A nearby sash window opens with a creak, and an inarticulate but musical cry of pleasure is thrown from it by what sounds like a tiny bird, so must be a little old lady. In all modern theaters at this juncture, audiences are wafted with the Pavlovian smell of roast chicken.

ACT II

Outdoors, under the stars, on the lawn at the base of the neighbor's kitchen steps.

Ibsen is eating chicken out of the neighbor's right hand. She looks exactly like the little old lady who Tweetie Pie owns. Like all ladies of this type, she wears orthopaedic shoes that look as comfortable as a muzzle.

With her left hand she gives Ibsen's floppy ear a respectful fondle, so briefly that he almost nestles his head in her palm. She talks quietly to him of many things, but is either ignorant of H.P. Lovecraft or unusually sensitive to Ibsen's sensitivities. He knows she reads, because he of course, has checked out her house, though she wouldn't have dreamed of asking him to stay and he wouldn't have done so, partly for ignoble reasons (sometimes he wishes that his master and her could marry so that she might end Hylam P Hector's poetising days with real romance, and their two libraries would, in combining, vanquish her collection of Readers' Digest Condensed books. Ibsen always thought the person who condenses a book to be quite as much a fiend as a person who clips a tail).

Tonight she talks of honeydew, how pretty the word it is, how extraordinarily ill-chosen by the ignorant compared to harsh reality, the black blight of aphids on roses. Ibsen understands her sentiments, if not the technicalities. He has always been a fine digger, but doesn't have a green thumb. He gives her fingernails a final wash and issues a complementary tail-wag. She stands with many creaks, but as many complaints as an old chair when someone sits in it. They part wordlessly and without looking back. He's off to explore the base of a birch tree or two before walking around the block pretending it's around the world, toward home.

ACT III

If only this were merely a play, but life is unfortunately, life. So the mundane must be reported along with the extraordinary abdication of Ibsen's responsibility for parting speeches, or at least a quip.

Ibsen lies asleep on an overstuffed chair in the same room in which his master uttered the fatal O! —the room a real estate agent would call 'the living room', but Mr Hector calls 'the library'.

A large gasp, like that of a hot water bottle sucking down fluid, comes from the bedroom down the hall. This is followed by an annoyingly pendant silence. Then another gasp with perhaps a hint of shudder and a muffled scream, followed monotonously, by more silence.

Ibsen hears them all, and doesn't raise an eyebrow—all the sounds of normality to him who knows naught else but that all humans sleep as fitfully.

And now that we've ploughed our scene for action, we shall slip into the past-tense, the tense that dresses best bad memories.

SOME THINGS YOU should know about Hylam P Hector

In addition to his father wanting him to be an odontologist or something like that, or possibly because of that wish, little Hylam suffered from attacks of *pavor nocturnus* (night terror) so extreme that he used to sneak into his parents' bedroom when they went to sleep, simply to stay awake. He sat on the bare wood floor in his thin nightshirt, listening to them snore.

Never bold enough to wake them up, he ended this practice one night at age ten when he heard a team of robbers clean out his father's 'rooms' at the back of the house. The robbers had a horse with severe allergies to the flowers in the garden. It never stopped sneezing, and a horse who sneezes could wake a cemetery. But neither of his parents so much as turned over in bed.

He never told his parents about this incident, but it was only one of many that haunted him, before he met Lovecraft's works just after a failed love attempt in his first year of college.

His father was by this time, dead, and Hylam frittered away the rest of his inheritance on magazines that contained Lovecraft, notebooks in which to attempt to write stories like Lovecraft, and blank books with leather covers, in which he wrote his Lovecraftian poetry.

The problem with his taking up with Lovecraft, however, was not just that Hylam became a writer of insufferably frightful verse. He became an undocumented statistic in one of the most dreadful pandemics ever to hit humanity (and as a side-effect, other species).

He could have been the poster child for the disaster which until now has been nameless, but we shall break the code of silence and speak up. At his little upstate college in Horsenail, New York, Hylam P Hector caught *Apnoea Pavorlovcraftis*, an anti-social disease.

Alone in his bed with his eyes tightly closed and his face turning purple from the effects of held breath, he'd inevitably break, issuing those antimacassar-shaking explosions of heretofore pent-up breath.

Every night come beddy-bye, he was so exhausted, he literally fell upon his gaping sheets, having barely had time to don his most beige pajamas. His eyes would close autonomically, and he would instantly be plunged into his first abyssal nightmare. And as everyone knows, now that we've revealed his disease, those nightmares were filled with grasping tentacled monsters and other women who were dangerously beautiful, strange gods with too many consonants to their names, things that lurk, hidden just out of view, more tentacles—and all the while he spent his sleep trying to hold his breath, so that he could not be seen (especially by the unseen). Then the air would blast out of his mouth and all those tentacles would reach out towards him till he made a pillbug of himself in the middle of his bed, holding his breath again . . . and so on, till his saviour, the thing he called affectionately and inaccurately, his 'alarum clock' rang at 8 o'clock AM.

He never felt he'd slept a wink, yet he'd nightmared loud as the Front all through the night.

Such a contrast to his day job. In his waking life, he was a writer, see—and not only that, but the celebrated enough never to reveal himself to his doctor: 'Augusta J. E. Wilson', author of AT THE MERCY OF TIBERIUS (*New.*), INFELICE; or, the Deserted Wife, ST. ELMO; or, Saved at Last, MACARIA; or, Altars of Sacrifice, VASHTI; or, Until Death us do Part, and INEZ: A Tale of the Alamo. (in cloth and paper covers at all good booksellers) "*Who has not read with delight the Works of* AUGUSTA WILSON? *Her strange wonderful and fascinating style; the profoundest depths to which she sinks the probe into human nature toughing the most sacred chords and springs; the intense interest thrown around her characters, and the very marked peculiarities of her principal figures, conspire to give an unusual interest to the Works of this eminent Southern Authoress.*" asks a back flyleaf of the "Intensely interesting" PRICE FIFTY CENTS D.M. Canright's THE MINISTRATION OF ANGELS, and the Origin, History, and Destiny of Satan.

So not only was he a secret Southern Authoress of intense 25-cent mysteries, but he wrote them without a single *O!*, and even at their most terrifying junctures, he bashed away at them with the coldness of a butcher tenderising steak. All day he wrote commercially, but something happened when the lights outside were low, or maybe it was the green-shaded lamp.

Luckily for him, after his failed one-sided love affair the week before he discovered Lovecraft, passion for another woman had been something he didn't feel the need of any more. Nor, fortunately for him, did he wish to have a dog in his bedroom at night. Ibsen had excellent hearing, but no wont to have his night disturbed by his master's commotions, since there was no cure he knew of for the disease.

Ibsen was able and quite ready to tear robbers to shredded meat, should they venture into the house. And Ibsen being a dog who was faithful to his master, was always ready to defend his master against anything a dog can sink teeth into. But short of peeing on his master's face, Ibsen couldn't think of what to do to break the nightmare/breath-hold/gasp explosion cycle.

B ACK TO THE Action
   On this dark but unsuspenseful night, the one in which
Hylam Hector tried too far, the affections of his audience, Ibsen,
as we have seen, had settled himself on the soft overstuffed chair in
the library, as usual of an evening. We thought he was asleep, and
indeed, his eyebrows twitched as if he were dreaming, and his paws
lightly pawed. A careful observer would have noticed, however:
only Ibsen's front paws pawed. His back legs were extended, and
held quite rigid.

He was thinking out the hole problem, and being a dog who
didn't believe solely in theory, was acting the problem out.

From the bedroom came a sound like the hot water heater
blowing up. Then silence. Then another sound, like that of a giant
eggbeater trying to turn a bedspread into butter. Then silence. The
normal night noises. Ibsen pondered on.

In the contrast between the imitative heckle that Hylam P.
Hector wrote and the professionally paced artificial hyde turned
out by 'Augusta J. E. Wilson', we have forgotten to tell how fertile
the man's imagination was, somewhere in his crowded brain.

On this particular night, that imagination had caught fire,
perhaps lit by the one-and-ten thousandth O!.

Whatever, by the time he'd brushed his teeth, gargled, counted
the hairs on his head, and done his chin exercises, his mind was
still full of moon and exotic shores. He didn't fall into his gaping
sheets, but lifted them up and inserted himself between them. And
by this time, his thinking had spread to shadows. He laid his head
on the pillow and glanced out through the diaphanous curtain, at
the pale bright moon. He still wasn't sleepy. The curtain fluttered,
and he thought to close the window, but the bed felt as delicious as
the arms of a beautiful woman who is coming through the window
now, her long hair flowing, and a tentacle reaching from behind her
toward the bed.

His lungs closed, mid-suck.

The tentacle ran its tip over his left ear, then caressed his chin,
what there was of it. And it seemed to find him good. Whether it
was a part of her or some limb from another monster of polypous
perversion, this diabolic limb was followed by a horde of silent
others.

He knew the eyes of the beasts were upon him—beaks ready,
maws opening, bodies smelling of reek from the farthest eaons—

and as each new horror progressed forward, his lungs contracted and his throat clutched harder . . . then released enough to let him scream—the fine high wail of a boiling lobster.

And all the slink and drop and terror was just the first assault and reaction. That first woman and the tentacles, just the first of many creatures, gods, horrors—each freshly risen, driven, called from the unspeakable reaches of hauntingness, which visited him this night.

He held his breath, exploded, screamed, writhed till his sheets turned to cream cheese and his pillow to aged Parmesan—and *still* the dog we know as Ibsen but who Hylam Pituitary Hector called Rover when he called him a name at all, never lifted more than his floppy right ear in the bedroom's direction—and that, merely in a wishful surmise.

If only the fain poet had restrained, just one 'O!'—(or even drafted just the 'O' without also throwing in the perpendicular projectile strapped to its back) think what would have happened. Ibsen would have gone forth to grab and dispatch with a shake of his head, each and every thing that had flown, crept, emanated, and oozed in over the window-sill, even the Tentacled One. And who knows? He might have succeeded. His strong jaws might have made hamburger of even the most dread overconsonanted god.

For after all, he was a brave dog; and faithful to his duty—before the fall-out.

By 3:40AM, however, Ibsen was a changed beast. He felt he was on the cusp of solving the problem of the hole, and just needed to sleep on it.

At 8:04, Ibsen woke groggily. He had always hated that alarum. It was still ringing, an untoward which had never heretofore occurred.

Ibsen marched to the bedroom door, wrenched it open, and beheld what was left of his master—perhaps a spleen, and his pipe. Telltale sucker prints led out the window.

[*Ibsen walks down the hall, trying not to wag his tail, but the observant can see it sway slightly before he exits stage right, in the direction of the kitchen.*]

ACT, THE CLIMAX

In the next-door rose garden, sun shining brightly upon.

LITTLE OLD LADY. [*Her wrinkles look character-filled. She wears a pair of garden gloves and is throwing oaths at something we aren't privy to see on those gorgeous, big-headed blooms.*] Damn you to asphalt! [*She hears something coming up behind, puts a hand to her ear, and her face lights up. Suddenly she turns as if she forgets she is not a young college girl. The object of her affections is the dog we know as Ibsen.*]

IBSEN. [*Drops bone at her feet. He gives her a wag-tail.*]

LITTLE OLD LADY. [*clasping hands in glee, and regarding the dog with upholsterer's eyes*] I wonder. How soft do you like your bed? [*She takes off her gloves and throws them and her secateurs into a trug, which she forgets as she trips up her kitchen stairs with Ibsen at her heel. They enter the kitchen triumphantly, and the door slams behind them, unattended.*]

[*A sound like a small bird singing in a shower wafts from the kitchen window.*]

LITTLE OLD LADY. [*still offstage, singing the words*] I'll put on the roast, but I never asked. Do you like stuffing?

IBSEN. [*also still offstage*] Tail-wag [*uttered with a slight dip of sadness. He already misses the library next door.*]

THE PLAY'S END

B UT THAT IS why dogs don't appreciate plays.

Ibsen, being a dog, didn't waste time in Regret. He walked at the heels of the little old lady, through the kitchen and down the hall.

Ibsen's nose twitched. He realised he'd never been in this part of the house, and a strange, exciting smell emanated from the closed door. The floor boards groaned and grizzled under the LOL's heels. It was *that* old a house. She reached out and tried to turn the china doorknob, but it didn't budge.

She gripped her hand, grimacing, and inadvertently looked down at Ibsen. He understood completely, suffering from a touch of lumbago himself. Up he leapt, and the doorknob didn't dare give his jaws trouble, not while the door itself was subject to his claws.

He'd looked back at the LOL, forgetting not to wag his tail. She went into the room ahead of him and . . . he didn't know what to think.

The walls and ceiling were hairy and scaled with many thought-provoking artefacts, and two walls were lined with bookcases so filled to bursting that Ibsen's tongue lolled. The LOL pulled out one oversize book, opened it and laid it on the floor beside Ibsen.

He'd never known a hole so wide and deep could exist.

Her laugh was a bit embarrassed. "I don't know why I'm showing you a tourist shot. But Frank took it the day we started that trip."

Ibsen nosed the book closed and read the words: Tectonic Geomorphies of the World's Five Grandest Canyons; an Introduction [and the author] Franklin G. Orpington.

A small thin book was placed briefly on the floor unopened and then snatched up again with an embarrassed giggle. But not before Ibsen had had a chance to read, "The Cavnericolous Fauna of the Dambool Region in Ceylon" and author: V. Patchoulevsky.

Then a large ball the size of a watermelon was lowered in her arms for Ibsen's inspection. It smelled like a mouse dipped in shaving soap.

"I picked up this in Trinkamalee. That's in Ceylon, you know."

She actually watched Ibsen when she talked, though he would have said the strange ball was far more interesting than he.

"It was just upcountry from Trinkamalee where I was laid up with beriberi. I didn't want us to leave. After all, we were finding species of bats impossible in everyone else's thinking."

Ibsen was entranced. But why did she keep these treasures here? Of course! he blinked. *They're much too precious to expose to the unworthy.* Without realising it, he sat up straight. His right ear slightly rose.

"Oh!" the LOL said (Ibsen's eyes were misty by then, but neither mist nor hair could keep him from concluding, from a print of a young beautiful woman and a handsome man with a full chin: her name was Violeta Patchoulevsky, *Dr.* Patchoulevsky.)

"You must be suffering terribly!"

Ibsen hadn't noticed, but since she had, he felt like a feather had been shoved up his nose, as the full effect of the camphor hit him.

His head wagged back and forth without him having the faintest control, and in shame and embarrassment, his nose shrunk till it was all wrinkles, and he stopped breathing and his eyes grew big enough that his eyebrow hedge parted . . . and he sneezed—all over the cover of that magnificent book he had opened again and had been greedily reading surreptitiously.

"How thoughtless of me!" she cried. "If you're to live here, we must get rid of these."

This was all too much for Ibsen.

With every ounce of passion in him, the dog who was inexpressive as a barber's floor and as silent as the tomb, rested one paw on the edge of the book, the other paw in the Dr's lap, lifted his head, and *howled*.

Dr. Patchoulevsky was not only *not* a dog, but *was* a zoologist. Even so, she understood.

AT SIX O'CLOCK she served dinner. Since the night was cold outside and sopping, she made him lamb shank stew and noodle pudding with raisins; and she had a bowl of tomato soup over crackers.

After an hour's silent companionable digesting, she put on her coat and a souwester hat, and picked up a large disorderly handbag, and they went for a walk. Not just around the block, no. This walk was a *dog*'s walk. She waited at every tree he needed to inspect and mark, didn't cluck when he squatted and took his time, and they walked past all the streets with houses till they got to the end of town and just past that, to a field.

Then she rummaged in her handbag and found a fresh bone. She gave to Ibsen.

He took it and dropped it solemnly. Then he dug its hole, savouring the pleasure of reaching in with both paws, flinging back the sticky mud, judging depth, slope, width of base. Barking sonarous soundings. By the time he dropped the bone into the hole, he'd never heard such a satisfying thud. And this time, when he filled the hole, he knew exactly why he had to cheat and dig another hole to top up the important one.

All the while, she waited patiently, in the rain. If he had been lesser than a dog, he might have looked back in time and Regretted that his master hadn't years earlier summoned his murderer.

They walked home in the drizzling rain in states of different but equal bliss. Both thoughtfully, of course.

This thoughtfulness was the reason both were unobservant, or they would have heard following them, something which sounded like the inexorable slink of a rotary carpet sweeper fitted with galoshes.

It was the giant tentacled Thing, the murderer Itself—its eyes big as watermelons, fixed upon *them*.

The giant tentacled thing was suffering mightily, having followed the Call all the way from the deeps of Chesapeake where the horseshoe crabs are feastly, up through beach towns rife with crab thieves and souvenir shops, out into the terrible wasteland of New England towns crawling with small but proud colleges, insane asylums hiding behind hedges, and poets.

Onwards the thing soldiered, till it reached the Caller. And though it dispatched Hylam Pituitary Hector as fast as it could gulp, the Thing remembered too late, that merely excising the spleen doesn't go far enough. One must never swallow a fevered brain.

It had suffered all day with dyspepsia. And to kill time till it could decamp, had peeping-tom'd thru the window and espied these now-boon companions, the dog and his mistress. It had watched them all day, traversing the outside of the house silently, its polka-dot sucker-prints washed off by the incorrigibly unsalty rain.

And it shadowed them now.

They reached her house and went in the door, totally wrapped in their world.

Ibsen shook himself in the front room (so violently did he shake off the hot steamy wetness, that the next day every volume of the Readers Digest Condensed books was nowhere to be found. They'd shrunk so tight, all that was left was a scattering of articles popped out onto the braided rug—*a*'s, *the*'s, and *an*'s. Useless as plots, Dr. Patchoulevsky swept them up and boxed them for some purpose which would make itself known some day. About six months later, she wrapped a bow around the box and presented it as a welcome present to her new neighbor, the celebrated fly-tier Buff McInerny. He took them graciously and was touched that she had *tried* to give him a thoughtful gift, so he didn't look down on her ignorance. Trouts aren't smart, granted, but they're not dull. Clearly the woman didn't know fishing, or she'd not have thought anything less than a box of *peripateticallys* would do.)

But the Thing with the tentacles was still outside and the woman and dog had now progressed to the room which had enchanted

Ibsen. If they had been observant, they would have noticed a low regular squeak like that of windscreen wipers, and if they'd looked over at the window, they'd have seen, staring in upon them, an eye flattened across the expanse.

"I'm at least as intelligent as a dog," said the observer to itself. "And I've been to Ceylon."

And though it looked to some, as if it were of morbid personality, it was actually an optimist. So the Thing reached up to the second floor, where it found a crack in the bathroom window. It only needed an inch.

AND TO ITS delight, the dog and woman were as intelligent as it had hoped. The dog recognised the Thing's sucker-prints from the Deceased's bedroom, and welcomed the Tentacled One most heartily into the fold.

And the dog's mistress rustled up a bucket of clams.

LAST SCENE IN THE MOVIE

(although Ibsen insists he doesn't wish to play himself)

Full moon over the Grand Canyon silhouettes on its rim: one Winnebago; and the three companions—a paw, hand, and tentacle poised over each respective brow—the Dog, the Woman, and the Thing each gazing infinitely thoughtfully into the abyss.

CLOSING CREDITS

Music:
  "Craft My Lovethrob" by the Arrhythmics
  "Galoshic Riff" by Thing

Bufo of Oahu: Ukulele Ululatress

The frog wasn't a prima donna, nor was he insensitive, heartless, stupid or lackadaisically cruel (which is more than I can say for some). Nor did he have that ridiculous figure with the long legs and grotesque waist. Nor was he a he. Nor was he a frog. Nor (a point that particularly piques me) did he sing (his voice was dubbed!). He should be infamous, but better yet, unknown, for he became falsely famous for singing, replacing like the understudy who ate the star, the one true Light. As for the high-kick cakewalk, frogs have no shame.

So, Mr. C., you have a golden opportunity to tell the Real Story in what is sure to be a 3D Box Office Hit. My screen play is attached but here is a synopsis of "The Song of Bufo: The True Story of Grammy-O."

The film opens with music reminiscent of "The Godfather" played on ukuleles, and this prologue:

A bulldozer makes short work of a strip of local haunts, including 4Seas Never4Get Tattoos and Kimo's Brunch Shack on Waikiki Beach in order to build in its place, the Oahu Grande. My great great great and something mamma sadly leaves the premises of Kimo's garbage pile.

No more will she be able to catch her fill of Spam cans tossed out the kitchen door by the cook and owner, Kimo Kealoha himself. (This could be said in big type, couldn't it?) Kimo's was her territory. (Could this be stated symbolically in the way the strings are plucked?) It wasn't easy to keep a spot, and she'd needed protection—which came from Kimo himself, big drinker, music lover, master of the strings, all three hundred pounds of him. The local health department would have been the death of Kimo's soon enough, if their notices to end the show unless he changed his style were to be taken seriously. But development struck first and killed this diner and all others with standards that suited our family to a T (a little pun there. Though we know that the *noir* genre doesn't engage puns, this film must have one pun every 12 minutes at least, to keep our target audience enthralled. And to be honest, Mr. C., *noir* has always lacked the color that puns give, as well as shall we say, a certain sleight of tongue?)

So that prelude scene, before the opening credits, shows the tragic ending to a beautiful relationship—Kimo's lightly tossed Spam tins, caught by Grammy's lithe tongue, and licked clean by that most versatile organ. (If you don't know your proverbs, you mightn't know then amongst toads of a certain age: *Maturity means you don't have to swallow everything whole.*)

Then by the light of the moon, Kimo drinking on the back step to the soft lulling strains of Grammy-O's incredible repertoire. It is true she loved above all, Rossini, though for Kimo's sake, she added palm trees swaying in the breeze and the sibilant spurts of gently frying Spam when she sang the "Duet of Two Cats." (both parts. She did have a marvelous span of notes, and could do terriers to a T, too.)

Let's get this straight first. This film is in no way a rehash of that lying piece of trash in which a demolition worker in New York, of all places, finds a cardboard box that had been sealed somehow in a building since time eternal. Then unbelievably, a frog jumps out, after who knows how long without a drink or bite. Next, without stopping to catch a fly, even more incredibly, he (!) sings. Sings! And (don't blame me for the indecency) he kicks up his heels in an unseemly display of legs that never seem to end. And to top all this, he does all this for a person who's never short-ordered a fried egg, let alone tossed a single can of Spam.

And what does this oaf do in thanks? He wants the frog to sing some more, for *others*. And this is the sweetest bit of the deal. He wants the frog to sing for: paper and metal that this jumped up 'manager' wants to stuff into his own yawning pockets.

That the frog didn't cooperate is the point of that movie, the sitter in the center of the pot of plot, the sitter who refuses to focus on the salient matter. But frogs are famous for mentally catching flies while their skin bubbles, aren't they? Even so, why should a frog who has for some unstated reason, been condemned without trial to an unlawful sentence of solitary confinement without food or recreational activities, be expected on release to become a useful member of society, let alone an exploited entertainer? As for the salient matter, let's give the frog who took the role, the benefit of the doubt and say that he had no knowledge that he was an accessory to Grand Theft. How *could* he, how could *any* frog with a sense of self-respect have lived down the sheer shuddering vaudevillianessness of that performance: an act that brings audiences to tears—of laughter? Even a performing elephant is afforded enough dignity not to be covered by a suit, but the frog in the movie even totes a cane and flaunts a hat that he waves like it's some punchdrunk dragonfly.

Of course *you* would have seen through the lame humor and slapstick. You would have separated the bathos from the purported pathos. You'll want to set the record straight, give the public the straight dope. And get that damn frog out of the picture.

About 50% of the rest of the plot can be about the carving up of parking lot, vacant lot, and backyard territories between the Frogs and the Toads along the Waikiki strip. A subplot will follow an uncle's branch that ended up in Australia, taken there in the mistaken belief that we toads (*Bufo Marinus*, but we eschew formality, so bufo to you!) like to hang around canefields and climb cane for beetle grubs. We'd as likely climb Christmas trees to eat the lights! (Sure, we've got a rep that butterflies would kill for, but we're not out for trouble. We just make trouble for anyone who puts the bite on us.) That first shipment of kidnapped bufos, every one of them plucked from salubrious surroundings, was literally dumped in the canefields of that impossibly far-off giant island and left to starve, or else. They died hungry, homesick, and with their ears filled with the memories of once happy, now painfully nostalgic tunes (like "Grease in the Air") but their subsequent generations have lost the taste for Spam, and now thrive in suburbs on canned dogfood when they're not being hunted down and frozen to death in kitchen freezers, "to protect dogs"—a so-called "painless death," I tell you no lies. If we liked to freeze, we would have moved to New York, with fur coats! A creepy existence in a fright of a country, but those horrors are for Bufo II, which screenplay I am happy to send to you if you prove yourself worthy on Bufo I. The scene with gifts from Australia to the newlyweds Charles and Diana is pure Hitchcock—the book's skin glistens. One hopes its resilience couches active poison pores.

Now that you know that you must Differentiate and Distinguish between that Lying "frog" movie and this True Story, I will continue.

Since Grammy could not jump, Kimo picked her up from the encroaching jaws of the bulldozer and took her to his home where they would have continued to live happily together. He was a dab hand at the ukulele and she had a snap-jaw memory for songs—not just tunes but words, in any tongue. At night, he would stroll along the beach with her in his shirt. Her meaty little arms rested upon the top seam of his pocket. Neither the flashy glitter of the setting sun on the baby-blue horizon nor the dancing curves of the hula girls on his breeze-moved shirt could rival the majestic beauty of her great golden eyes—and when she ululated her mouth was the ultimate wave. (slow motion scene here with lotsa music)

One night—a particularly beautiful one—they were strolling with their eyes half closed in pleasure, when along hurried, so fast he almost collided with them, a harried Hollywood producer. He stopped short just as Kimo and Grammy-O had reached that point in their duet where she said "animal, vegetable, mineral" in double-double time, with a Waikiki beachwave beat, and he strummed a note in laid-back Oahuan virtuosity, till his chords evoked the frill of fried Spam's frazzle.

The producer was amazed. He was also hidden from the moonlight by a lazily parked cloud, not that the duettists would have noticed him anyway. But, let this be made clear by the jarring music: he was also slippery of heart and a villain of the Highest Order. He was also capable of deadly deeds, though he had no poison sacks in his skin. Being in monetary trouble, he instantly seized upon a sinister plan to Get Rich. (Show but don't tell: in symbolically significant music as well as in monochromatic lighting of his ugly profile, all nose and chin and legs.)

The producer went back to New York, where the most sinister producers live, and made that movie. In it, he substituted a frog, because frogs will work for tophats. And he used the mean streets of New York as well as New York construction workers, because he couldn't afford Hawaii, not even sunny Hollywood. And New York construction workers aren't chumps like frogs. They got wind of his movie, and they made moves to get in. They've got a union, see? They had protection.

Out in innocent Oahu, out on the increasingly broodingly shadowed beaches of Waikiki where the waves can always be depended upon to pound in the background, my great-great-and-something Grandmamma, our Grammy-O, was none the wiser. Nor was Kimo.

The first thing they know about the Big Cheat is when they're told by some of her kids and grandsomething kids, the ones who hung out at nights at the Old Waialae Drive-In Theater on Waialae Avenue.

It's not there anymore, but you know the scene. Pure degeneracy, nothing like the wholesome graveyard beside it, where sporadic bounties of bouquets of flowers appeared, which attracted a moderate amount of snails and slugs and beetles. and then rotted in vases of healthily festering water so that decent families could spend their time at night sitting on the dark or naturally moonlit silent graves—throwing out their tongues, hauling in the food, then gulping in that way a real toad does, where the eyes get sucked into the face, all in the no-nonsense business of consuming, as serious toads have acted since time began.

The worst thing is, the kids at the drive-in first thought that the movie was funny. (Don't show that. Instead, show them gorging themselves wanton catching moths and mosquitoes, and then one of them and then another being distracted by the disturbance on the big screen by "Hey, it's a frog in a starring role!")

First they think that the story is about a hood who'd come out of lockup, one of the Frogs gang in some far-off land, and gradually they get the drift. That this is the stolen story of the One True Queen of Song—our Grammy-O—and her Kimo Kealoha. The way you'll direct it, audiences will see, up close and pore-focused, the young toads' dawning rage ... and in the scattered glow of lights at the **Old Waialae Drive-In:** projector, cigarette lighters, car cabinlights, Waidelay Snacks stand—lit by all those lights, the sides of one young toad after another grow big and shine blue as their poison glands grow full, and ooze blobs of toxin pure and green as the paste of the best wasabi.

From the music audiences will *feel*, along with each one of these thousand or so youths, the fervent wish that whoever stole this story of Grammy-O would be smitten with a sudden irresistible urge to fly to Oahu, jump in a taxi and say, "Take me to the drive-in," and then, before the people rev their cars to leave, this thieving monster of moviemaking will drop on all fours and scurry forward hungrily to find and then stuff his mouth with one of these willing punks. *Pick me!* they sing together, in the longest song (and dignified shuffle) of the film.

So after the kids wise up Kimo and Grammy-O, Kimo takes Grammy-O (only because she insisted) to the drive-in to see the movie for themselves (she sits silently on the dash, not eating a thing though the mosquitos crowd the car so thick, you'd think they're her fans). After the movie, Kimo takes her home and makes her an impromptu special, what he calls his Queen G Fry-up: spam cubes rolled in his very own mealieworm mayo. (She did, like that other great crooner, have a penchant for processed foods. Just listen yourself to "Love Me Tender" and you'll see how processed foods give added richness and smooth out the lower register.) So Kimo goes out to the back porch and she carries on, sitting pensively upon the lawn. He tosses cubes to her—one by one, only to see them litter the ground like so many wasted lives.

Some of the punks who wised up these two, having secretly hitched a ride to the drive-in and back, are now hiding out at the base of a bromeliad, spying like detectives: (do the close-ups) The corners of Grammy-O's mouth quiver but her lips are sealed, her grief is quiet, royally dignified— Kimo's shoulders heave, his mouth emits heavy blues-sighs, his neck swells as if ready for song. Then, in the *noir* at the base of the bromeliad, caught by a corner of the the harsh glow of the porchlight: the camera pans to the stricken faces of the young toads, pinched with remorse that they had spilled the beans without thinking (but when do punks sit around long enough to think?) how bad Grammy would feel at her Talent being stolen and made into something fit—for Frogs. (The camera flits to Grammy-O, who now breaks into, through closed lips, her heartbreaking "Palyachi of Waikiki.")

Fadeout to blackest *noir.*

Then one night shortly after, Grammy-O wasn't anywhere to be found, even by the kitchen garbage can. Kimo thought she was in season elsewhere, so to speak. He of big heart understood, though when this stretched to another night, and then another, he pined. Soon enough (we'll feel from the music) he'll learn The Bitter Truth.

He couldn't help but sell out after Grammy-O was run over one night (in a hit-and-run) after overindulging with the punks at the drive-in, her great-grandkids none the less, but she was bitter. That movie had made Grammy-O seethe. (Ironically, she had thought this the safer way to blow off steam. She'd earlier contemplated going out to catch cars, something anyone only ever does once— the thrill is great, but short. Even the wisest toad and the flittingest frog can't disengage a tongue from tire, and after one rotation . . . I'm sure you know this stuff already, but you might think a little horror scene of what-if might be a good little piece to slip in if you're lacking something terrifying somewhere—no filmgoer will ever be able to forget the *pop*.)

So Kimo was alone with no end in sight. There was nothing to live for, and soon enough he was a pitiful sight, forgetting to eat, waisted, addicted to solo song. At first it was "Ukulele Ululatress," in every word of which he poured his love, his loss, his admiration. Over and over he sang it, till, like the tides, there was no beginning and no end.

Particularly dramatic, but possibly earning you an XX rating is the scene of the discovery of her body. One of her beauteous characteristics was her size. She weighed as much as 6 cans of Spam, and only fitted in Kimo's pocket because, in that XXL shirt it could have stored a drugstore fruitcake.

So Grammy-O was jumbo—and when she was run over, she must have looked like a steamrollered Kimo Primo Loco Moco Brunchplate Special. (Two deep-fried all-Spam patties under two easy-over-light eggs, on a thick bed of saipan noodles, all smothered in brown gravy topped with two dots of Kimo's sweet-potato-mayo and a big green grin of wasabi hot enough to make your eyes pop.)

She was also unable to object to any suitor. So in no time a line formed that stretched far along the highway, an untidy line composed of libidinous toads from all walks of life who had wanted, admired, listened, looked, tried, but not been able to keep time with her. One after another, they tried to embrace her, to dig their thumbs into her famous formerly meaty sides, But she was too flat to get a purchase. Still, toads are nothing if not determined, so first one became a tragedy, and then another as cars did not slow down or swerve to avoid. Before long, these tragedies became statistics, and then the first car crashed for some inscrutable reason, and then the other car crashed into that. There's lotsa newspaper stories about the crash, but no obituary for her death. Kimo was left with nothing but his own presumption, though he was ever a simple soul, and wouldn't have known that word.

He missed his love to distraction, and he couldn't find a job anywhere slinging Spam, so what could he do but sink to torchsong? Even drunk with love, he wouldn't sully his pure true love by exposing it to an audience, so instead, couched it in a succession of the usual blondes and brunettes, all with horribly smooth skin and teeth that showed all white and—ugh!

I would advise you not to feature any of his subsequent best-selling platters—"On the Beach with You," "You're the Girl for Me-Ee-Ee," "A Slice of Heaven," "Your Golden Eyes," and most especially not "Ukulele Ladylegs." Better to concentrate on the perfidy of tourists, of East Coast Mainlanders, of those who *do the cakewalk.*

He wasn't particular where he sang, so he sang to tourists in the Grande. They loved it, all that syrupy pain that they slurped up along with their rummy coconut cocktails.

Numb with pain, he let himself be signed up by a producer, and with barely a look down upon the Waikiki beach below, suffered in silence during the flight to stinking, concrete-ridden, pesticide-infested Los Angeles, then sang quite shamelessly (show that it was to forget, but he couldn't) in studios with fake caterpillars shoved in his face. He made lotsa money as "King Kealoha" but what's money without love? Like a meal without Spam.

So say some of that but don't take the emphasis away from Grammy-O. Fill in with whatever you think, being the great director you are.

Etc., with lots of songs about Grammy-O, and without anything boring, and *no kisses*, to the End.

Only that is only one End! This blockbuster has, like all the famous ones now, two! The thing is, since this all happened in the days before DNA testing, and since no coroner scraped Grammy-O from the road, no one really knows what her end was, and there are other Theories.

So you must also show the Other Most Respected Theory amongst the Family, and this one will earn you an R rating, at least:

On a back street with no view, the Loha Kabin Kort was rumored to be the hangout of the Mob. If so, the Mob must have been in the wrong business. It was one of those kind of places where you can smell the mildew from the carpark. The story goes that "Pinocchio" Grant, "Eight-fingers" Louie, and Izzy Gillespie moved in to one of the kabins, and proceeded to entice innocent toadlets.

It is certainly true (my mother told me) that Pinocchio would toss from the window of Kabin 3, cigar stubs large as the cockroaches in the Oahu Palace kitchens. Toads have no resistance to cigars, especially from Cuba. And this was in the days when Cuban cigars were still cheap enough for your entry-level contract killer, so in no time, the paved grounds of the Loha Kabin Kort were awash in eager open-mouthed young bufos. Next, Pinnochio dipped the stubs in rotgut alcohol, usually white Burgundy but anything with a proof. Pity the little toadlets. Eight-fingers and Izzy were shovel detail. They did use shovels to pick up the besotted toads. Then the next part is almost too gruesome to show, but do! They took them inside, dumped them in a pot and boiled them. Then they bottled the stuff and shipped it to the Mainland, where it was sold on the mean streets to people who wanted to get high, mostly as a soak for marijuana to induce a special thrill of reefer madness.

That's the truth. And the theory is that one day, in her grief, the Queen herself wandered into the Kort and ended up, eventually, in New York, as a bit part of a marijuana stogie.

We see her in the Kort, snapping her mouth on that portentous cigar stub, then next, being picked up insensate, and when she weakly struggles, being subjected to the worst indignity—rolled on her back and tickled helpless. Then she is tossed into a pot of water. And the heat is turned on. We see the flames of gas play around the base. Only she's a toad, see! She doesn't sit around. Even in her drugged state, she makes to leave, only she's a toad, see. She raises herself as far as her short curved legs can go and lifts her short curved arms up, up, as far as they will go. But she might as well be a human trying to climb up a smooth concrete wall. We see the lid come down upon the pot. It's a pressure cooker! Soon we hear the scream—of the pressure cooker.

And you know the score. If you cook a pink corned beef in a pressure cooker, it comes out heart-attack gray. You might open the lid and have the audience see, through the cloud of steam, her face upended . . .

In one version of this True Story, Pinocchio slaps her awake when they bring her in the Kabin and makes her sing "Ave Maria," which makes him cry. Then he drops her in the pot.

There is yet another version of her end, which you might use in Bufo II. In this version, she is smuggled out of Hawaii by nefarious agents of Kulture, and shipped to Australia where they're short of Divas. She is then used to dub some woman who looks remarkably like her, and who with Grammy-O's voice and this woman's wave-wide mouth, becomes a Star.

As to who plays Grammy-O, it must be a Star who could play a queen. But all the current feminines are grossly leggy, frighteningly waisted, and have necks that belong in horror movies, so we must look to the history of the stage and mix that with modern improvements in technique, to find our lead. You will agree that the character is so magnificent and radiant that only a character actor should be considered. Marlon Brando would have been beautiful. But he is in the place where toads go when they've been run over.

So I choose, to play Grammy-O, some actor who gets into the skin of his character the best these days. Someone who, say, makes everyone call him "Captain" if he's playing Captain Bligh—and not only that, makes everyone want to mutiny, and mutiny only because the script doesn't allow for murder. He can be depended upon to throw himself into the part, and so will use the chili and mustard skin cream we'll supply topped up with heat lamp treatments to achieve a complexion worthy of the part. He will have the right tone of sober, lovely dignity, wiping the public's memory from that froggy frivolity, that waisted look.

For a part like this, the part of his life, he will *become* our Divine Grandsomething Mamma, Grammy-O, the Diva of Waikiki, in the Buformance of his life when he, to try to reach the pinnacle upon which her beauty shined, makes the world see in every closeup, the great emotion and unequaled glory of her huge golden eyes (his will have to be glass).

So, Mr. C., here is your golden opportunity to really make something you can be proud of, instead of the dross that passes for the common box office sensation and your previous Academy Award winning hits. You can relieve yourself of the stress of doing movies about the frankly unmarvelous, more creatures with skin tone created in a computer, more activity that adds up to nothing more than busyness, and (I can hear you sigh with relief) you can shed that most boring part of all in all your movies, those *long pointless chase scenes* (as every toad who graduates from tadpole knows: the wise sit and wait).

I, quite frankly, had my doubts about you being up to this challenge, but you were voted the famous director most likely to want to redeem himself, so here's the deal. You make the film of your career, the musical drama "The Song of Bufo: The True Story of Grammy-O," and right the wrongs of both history and filmmaking. It's a win-win-win, with Bufo II following, and sequels beyond your wildest horizon. You know they'll all be hits if you tell the Truth. And as for critics, just let them try to plague you! The Frogs can go croak. We offer you not only the opportunity of your life but great protection. Like the soon to be Immortal Grammy-O, a Toad isn't just a pretty face.

But don't delay. Once-in-a-lifetime opportunities, like flies, don't sit around to be contemplated. Of course, you could refuse, but I wouldn't advise making us angry.

How Galligaskins
Sloughed the Scourge

So long ago that the roads were topped with the dung of ass and ox, in a land rich in short days and mouldy shadows, in the town of Ranug-a-Folloerenvy, lived a master argufier named Werold but known as Galligaskins for his old-fashioned knee-high socks that (in the heat of argument) he was always hitching up.

In this out-of-the-way town called by the low, just plain *Ranug*, where the bakers sold more day-old bread than fresh, and the tailors worked all night—in this tumbly-down filth-paved town, all the men (save Galligaskins) wore long, leg-hugging fine-skein hose white and delicate as the foot of the petal of a rose. These stockings showed best in winter when the lacily laddered knit exposed a wealth of leg-skin glow—puce, blue, crimson, suet—according to the state of the wearer's chilblains.

Galligaskins' hose were loose and thick, and brown as feast-day pancakes for the poor. And they ended folded over just below the knee, where he tried to tie them fast but they always slid past his garter of a cord—a shocking sight but one that persevered and was accepted as something that must be; as a rainy day, which cleans the streets.

For Werold was Ranug-a-Folloerenvy's only argufier, as necessary as the glove maker. He had much to do with the rich and would have died a slovenly but relatively wealthy ancient, if the rich hadn't got themselves into such a muckle.

It happened this way:

One day a drab nullness of a man called Bladsteth who unnoticed, had left Ranug some time before, returned—a new man—from, he said, far Ghovenir. Or rather, that is what some people *said* he said, and though they knew not this mouthful-of-stones, they did not question where? but tsked and answered with an impatient nod and a quick "So? Yes, yes. Go *on*." For the question wasn't where he went, but what he *wore* now that he'd returned.

The ladies swooned, to be brought to life only with a clod of chicken scat up a nostril. Men secreted themselves, unbuttoned sleeves as fat and slashed and colourful as candied-fruit-stuffed pheasants, and blew their noses into the embroidered cloth. Each man was suddenly as ashamed to be seen in what he stood in, as Adam was in the garden that suddenly wasn't Paradise. Tavern braggarts, cock-strutting swaggarts, lute-picking peach-firm swains, grandfathers with faces like empty sacks, all men alike— each man then counted out his wealth (which took not long) and matched that to his wits to find a tailor to make up, without much lucre, a suit like that which had caused the swoons. Now such a time began!

The children who just a moment ago, it seems, were little versions of their fine-clothed parents, now wandered free, undisciplined, unfed. And in what wear? Whatever rags they pleased. The town's air shimmered with the cries of women, and their tearful honks. Their grief melted the starch in pleats that were once so proud, they could hold the women's heads up from the strength of style alone— till that traveller, Blansthet, blessed and cursed be he, the cause of all this wilt.

Every woman of any worth cursed Blansthet's cheek, for he'd returned alone. No lady did he bring with him, nor key, nor word to what a lady's wear would be to mate the splendour of his cockscomb finery. Not only that, but the menfolk's wear would beggar a dromedary caravan. And the most foudroyantly furbelowed dames, instead of crying, screamed. If only a *she* had come to town, a *Desidora* instead of *he*. For no Ranug man in normal times would risk his health ignoring the gentler sex's cry, lady to lady: *Be mode*

*as me, you wish! On my own man's worth, you shall not be. Be
modish, you who challenge me, as an old dried pea.*

And so, whatwith the men consumed by fashion with no time to
think of else—and the women consumed, first with grief and then
with hunger (for when his tailor took the whole of each man's all,
what man had time to notice women, children, or even his stomach's
need?) whatwith all this, there came to Galligaskins such a drying-
up of arguments that finally, he had None.

Though the town resounded with grief, Galligaskins' sniffs could
pick out not one rumour that added up to a dispute that he could eat
from—not even one petty snivel of an accusation that the greatest
troublemaking miser in the town would have normally ordered, to
be paid for with a promise. As Ranug-a-Folloerenvy's only guilded
disputationist, the doubly-good sums he was accustomed to taking
from both sides of any case were now, many times over, doubly lost
and missed. Starved, his leather inkpot shrivelled till its sides met,
skint as gentle ox's cut-purse. The worthy citizens were too busy.
For the master argufier: a ruinous state.

So Galligaskins spent a coin on a pair of boots so practical, they
must have been pawned by a traveller. Wearing the best (least torn)
of his two mangy shirts, a once-fashionable jerkin that was now a
chest-warmer with one button, and something he considered a cape
but no self-respecting ass would bear tossed over its shoulders, he
left the place he had been born. His hobnails rang on the cobbles in
a mockery of a fare-thee-well.

By mid-day he was so hungry that when he came upon a stunted
medlar tree at the top of a hill, he braved it—a rash action. Being
winter, the tree was bare of leaves. Every fruit that had met the
wind had fallen, and had been eaten in the snow by creatures who
knew not that the fashion for these fruits had ended generations
past.

The tree had one stolid trunk and many arms, their elbows
hooked together like a poor man and wife in front of the landlord.
But the arms of a medlar sport sword-sharp thorns. Galligaskins
bared himself, and wielding his body like a key, he stuck his arm
in. Thorns raked his flesh and pricked his wrist as he stretched his
fingers forth . . . and plucked the last remaining fruits.

Eleven medlars did he glean, a handful. Burnished and dry-
pimpled as Winter's cheeks, as ripe as weeping boils, they smelled of
musty spice. Famished, he sucked them dry, spitting skin and stones

till just after the tenth medlar when his shrunken belly, delicate from starvation, whined at this rotting richness. Galligaskins, mad with rage at this contrariness, madder still with hunger, regarded the last suppurating medlar, the most dangerously swollen of them all. Then he ravished it, swallowing every bit—its weeping tear, its tannic skin, its gassy flesh, its five rock-hard, rough-edged stones.

Now the last medlar was gone. His tongue tingled from the dry sharpness of that skin. He breathed into his hands to catch the last wisps of smell from that rank, sopped, scented flesh. Oh, he regretted his haste. His stomach turned, but as he dressed himself, he paid it not the slightest heed. He was just pulling up his right galligaskin when his gut growled a most unfamiliar note.

And with no ado, the eleventh medlar spoke.

"Walk fifty-and-seven steps," it said, and though its voice was rusty, each syllable was quite precisely paced, "with the sun warming the right side of your face. Then cut across the field till you come to a place where there are five rocks that you can see poking from the soil at the base of the barley stalks. And," said the medlar from deep within Galligaskins, "If you see no rocks because they have walked away or because they lie, then continue as you please until you need to stop and eat.

"Continue on, and one day you will come to another kingdom. You will know this because of the clothing—*keep still! Mind my counsel.*"

Galligaskins rubbed his stomach. If the medlar only knew the stab of *clothing*.

"As I was saying," said the medlar, pausing frustratingly, so like a master argufier when interrupted that Werold held his breath in awe.

The medlar must have felt Werold's admiration. "Mind you," it said, chatty as if they were feasting at juicy gossip. "The people in the kingdom I speak of wear jerkins, surcoats, cloaks, skirts, mantles, codpieces, wimples, bodices, great pumpkin sleeves, guimpes as crisp as toasted eggwhite froth—clothing from top to toe, including galligaskins white as icing—all bought fresh every morning, and served with the morning cup by the serving class. *Thems that serve wears the yesterday's, or the day before's,*" the medlar sing-songed as if it had heard that rhyme ever since it was a bud.

"And them that are too poor to serve," it said, reverting to its russeted professorial cadence, "deck themselves out in the castaways tossed from the same windows as open for the overturning of the chamber pots."

"But!" the medlar rasped. "On your fortune do not ask why there is no water in their morning cup, nor any goblet to hold drink. And though you may smell high, cover yourself with spice rather than take a bath or anoint yourself with unguent—though there be trays clotted with rose petals or rivers flowing with cardamom-scented almond oil, or lakes of water clear as tears, or."

"Or?" said Galligaskins. "Or?"

He beat his stomach, but all he got from it was groans. The last medlar was silent, or maybe silenced. When next it spoke, its words would be lost in the trumpet calls of sooty rye, the worse half a half-rotten onion, that year-old shard of dried-peas pudding. Galligaskins cursed his gut. Now he would never know why, but follow the medlar's orders, he knew he must. For when had a fruit ever spoken? *And speak it did, to me.* And besides, he had nothing else to do, his way to find a crust in that style-fevered town all dried up. He turned around and spat on the ground as a curse and riddance to that worthless, worry-induced peace he'd left behind.

He set out ... and though it took a long time, whatwith his pulling up his galligaskins at every seventh step, and the wrong turn he made at the beginning ... one bright morning, emerging from a dark thicket, he espied a river soup-thickened with fish so fat they floated. He walked on them easy as upon a path ... and when he stepped upon the other bank and saw the people and the land, his nose cried: *You are Here.*

His mouth filled and overflowed as if the river of saliva could run down his cheek, fall upon his jerkin, drop down to his galligaskins, slither down to the toe of his boot, and from thence to the riverbank, where it could surround and drown and pull the catch back up—but how could it? Werold grabbed at his calves, but the fat slovenly hose had slipped down to his ankles again. For a moment, his mouth hung open and glistened, stupid as a dead fish, as he tidied himself with desperate speed in this place of undoubtable good fortune.

That he was always *Here* and never *There* was a lesson he'd learned only too well on this trip. At last, however, Here was where he had been sent, for here was somewhere that only the likes of a lecturing medlar would think real, and not just mischievous leaf whisper.

He bent down and peered at the ground, then picked up a scrap of brown stuff with white stripes. He sniffed, and shoved it in his mouth before he had time to obey his mother's deathbed warning: *Never shove somewhat you dun know in your gob. It's like ter poison your blood and cause your hair to frizzle orf.*

Gingerbread!

Gingerbread with thick white swirls of icing! No one from Ranug-a-Folloerenvy who could have afforded this ambrosial cake would have thought to eat it—not when there were capes to seek, and new lace caps. Their treats were only what could sit from head to feet, on them. Their insides were never seen, so had to abide with day-old-bread made by bakers who made no cakes, and nothing fresh.

BEFORE HE KNEW it, the argufier Werold—weary, starving, workless—-ate so much gingerbread that he fell asleep with an ache in his stomach and a smile on his face—having eaten his way through the scraps of twelve nightshirts, thirteen socks, a filmy guipure sandwiched between two caps, one-half of a too-stale boot, innumerable delicacies of bodices, a stodgy codpiece, a jerkin so padded its owner could stand with his chest puffed out at Cupid. And a slice of a detachable sleeve that truly was as big as (the medlar had foretold true) a pumpkin. Although even the meanest shred of underclothing was the most heavenly food he'd ever stomached, with a smell so divine he wanted never to be out of the presence these rags, he had been able to be picky, being all alone on the bank with not a soul in sight.

When the shadows lengthened, instead of trying to eat all the skirts that lay around, he made a bed of five of them and tossed one into the river where the fish it landed on picked a hole in it large enough that Werold could see one of the fish's protruding eyes, and the profile of its thick lips with a hint of double chin. The river that was visible between the fish was clogged with sodden clothing scraps, much as lichen hugs the rocks in a path. Every few moments, a fish barely moved its body and opened its mouth—encompassing a scrap of used apparel.

It wasn't dawn yet when Werold woke a changed man. He sniffed the skirts and put his hands together in silent thankfulness to the wise medlar. *It must be the cloves*, he thought. No longer starving, knowing that he was sent here for his fortune, he was invigorated and ready to take on any argument. *Versuith aey!* Werold the argument-maker who hailed from that silly tumbledown, fashion-chasing town so far away, was now set for better things. Sharp as a clove, he walked to his unknown destination not caring a jot for the picture he made. *Up!* he commanded his galligaskins, and though they did not obey any more than they ever had, he felt as if they jumped to his raised eyebrow.

The road led to a gated town, but with no one to challenge him. Instead, the path before the gate had a pattern in white stones that said in swirly letters:

Welcome!

The townspeople, though dressed in mouthwatering display, were so obliging that he immediately felt at home. Everywhere he went, people wanted to help.

"I wish to have a sign painted," he said. No one asked him why, but he was taken to someone who said it could be done and took his order, refusing money "for the pleasure" (not that Werold knew what coin they took, even if he had any to hand out).

Werold next sought a place to set up business, and he was led to a narrow but luxuriously furnished shop and room above on Market Square, with a place to secure a sign so that it hung out over the street and would be seen by all. "As if I were a king" he protested in so few words that it would have shamed him, if he had been quoted in his Guild of expert exponential argufiers, but he was assured that he was the first argufier to ever have graced these parts. Indeed, no one had ever heard of argufiers, but all agreed that they must be very necessary, since he was one.

So.

Just before sunset on his first night in what the townspeople were pleased to call Pleasanz, the town's newest inhabitant hung his sign. It said:

for all your
ARGUFIER, DISPUTATOR, PILPULIST, DISCEPTATOR,
LOGOMACHIC, BELICOSSIC, WRANGULUMENTOR
~needs~
Werold of Ranug-a-Folloerenvy, MoA., HLD, GKoB,

From the sign hung three iron rings framing objects finely wrought. In the left ring: a fork-bladed backstabber dagger. The middle held a scene as fine as lace: a man spitted over a small bonefire, flames curling from the eyes of the topmost skull. Suspended in the right ring: a simple vial. Each object in its ring was barred diagonally with a red-enamelled banner.

After Werold hung the sign he looked for a place to eat but didn't find one, nor a place to buy anything to eat. So, lit by stars, he crept out of town and visited the riverbank again, where he ate his fill and made another bed hidden by a hedge, as now that he had position in Pleasanz, he could not be seen to be slumming. *Tomorrow,* he said to himself as he snuggled into the fragrant bedding, *I'll find the measure of Pleasanz.* But just before he closed his eyes, he spied a scrap of bodice within arm's reach, and dropped it into his waiting mouth where it dissolved and trickled down his throat in a manner like gold down a wishfulfilled miser's. *If,* he mused as his throat convulsed on the remains of the taste of its tail, *this toothsome thing is not a Pleasanz cake, what marriage could there bake when a Pleasanz cake and wine, and my mouth meet?* (For Werold was at heart, a misunderstood poet.)

H E WOKE BATHED in sweat, and tried to jump off his bed, but his hands pushed through three skirts and stuck, and his chest pulled away the topmost's elaborate decoration so well that he looked like he'd aged twenty years and grown a mat of curlicued white hair.

He had to use his arms like flails to beat his way out. Torn skirts flew everywhere, hitting the ground with thuds. He ran to the river's edge where he jumped onto the backs of the nearest two fish and bent down to wash the icing off his chest. It was as hard to scoop up unsullied water as gleaning the mice from the rye in an opened barrel. He scraped at his chest, grabbed at his ankles where his galligaskins lazed—and was poised to run back to town, but the sight of the fish kept him longer, longer than he had meant, longer than he would have wished. They glistened in a slow turbulence, gulping their scraps of sodden clothing in such a desultory manner that he could see from the way their lips drew back: disgust. They lay on their sides, each fish's one bulging eye so lacking in expression, it lacked only the flattening that death brings. All these bloated creatures almost still as paving stones seemed to yearn that fate of slow choking in a basket, to lie on a slab at the monger's.

On an impulse, Werold tore the button from his jerkin and threw it out between the banks where the fish were so massed, the river was hidden below them. Before the button had a chance to hit a body, the river shattered upwards. Fish jumped as high as his shoulder. Bodies as big as his arced up and slapped down, roiled the water and rolled in the river, their great mouths snapping, fighting for that button till the banks were slick with water and mucked with sticky, slippery brown bits as shiny and toothsome as a rotting mushroom.

Werold turned away, sickened.

His stomach was now upset as a sober man's. *I ate used clothing, like a fish!*

On dry land, he spent an hour looking for just the right yesterday's clothes, enough and good enough to make an outfit that could pass as fashionable, and fresh. When he finally found shoes modish enough, he next found a plain undecorated cloak. Then he stripped himself bare laying his cape, hat, jerkin, shirt, and boots upon the cloak. He balled his galligaskins and shoved them in his boots. Then with a look back at the fish, who he didn't trust, and a unanswered question about the future—What of the people in this town to come, the limits of their discontent? In case he had to run, he shoved the bundle into the hedge as far as he could reach, at shoulder height. Only then did he dress in his strange but magnificent clothes. These new galligaskins were thick and soft, and stood upright as toy soldiers.

Back to town he walked, no longer needing pause to bend.

The morning was just getting a move on when he stood under his sign, where he was immediately surrounded by curious Pleasanzers— so many that he had to mount a barrel to explain what an argufier does, and what he could do to improve the lives of all who flourish here, in this *most pleasant town, if I may pun*, he smiled. His audience smiled back, but there were some raised eyebrows. "Perhaps you do not pun," he bowed, in case some in the crowd were inclined to take offence. They looked so physically capable—if they spoiled to fight. He pointed out each swirly word in his sign and explained it bare. No one had ever heard or seen an Argufier, Disputator, Pilpulist, Disceptator, Belicossic, or Wrangulumentor.

To illustrate the wonders that his advocacy would bring, he then pointed to the iron-circled red-enamel bannered wrought-iron objects creaking merrily under the sign. His explanation had always worked before because what they showed, and their barring, spoke plainly to everyone who couldn't read in Ranugfolloerenvy (and that meant pretty much everyone). But the people in Pleasanz, though most fragrantly and exquisite equipped, knew nothing of barring, let alone backstabbers, fork-bladed or not (Someone held up a butter knife and asked, "You mean us to use our fingers?"). They smiled and clapped when Werold said "bonefire", and an elder showered compliments at the graceful curls of flames shooting from the topmost skull, but this could not cover up their embarrassment of befuddlement at the bonefire itself and the man slowroasting over it on the spit, which they thought he was clasping, an urge they assured the newcomer they were free of.

And "No wine?" asked one worried Pleasanzer about the vial. Poison was too foreign a something for them to understand.

So Werold ended up saying that these portrayals were too ancient for him to know, but that the work he did was too modern and necessary for anyone in Pleasanz to be concerned about such old ways, *so consider them effuzlements of portriment, he said. That, invermore, by the by when all is said and done* . . .

The Pleasanzers were most pleasant, but they were drifting off. Werold had begun to treat them as he did an argument from a rich man, *by the word impregnable.* Panicking, he employed yet another argument without meaning, but this one contained the word *today*.

The result was faster than a new fashion sighted in Ranug-a-Folloerenvy.

WEROLD LEARNED IN moments that *Today* was the Pleasanzers' most important word, concept, creed, bond, promise, source of panic, pride, and aspiration. Everything in Pleasanz revolved around *today*. So much so that he got so much work that first today, and the next, and the next, that he had never been so busy.

They paid well, too: anything he asked. They didn't want to bargain, never cried poor. Pleasanzers carried wads of paper money that they liked to stuff their clothes with, pulling notes from sleeves and hat brims as often as a pocket.

Within days, Werold the Argufier had forgotten he'd ever been called Galligaskins. He was rich, and not only that—so well respected! Since no one had ever had a dispute here, they left them all to him. He proposed, and they paid. He crafted arguments that spread a web across Pleasanz more interconnected and elaborate than that of the most flamboyant spider. So complex were his arguments, so refined that sometimes he cried reading them, they were so perfect.

Like all perfections, however, this was flawed. Each Pleasanzer wanted Werold to argue: for each, an argument a day. If they could not get him to make an argument, they wanted what they considered the next best things, in the order of his sign: a disputation, pilpulation, or . . . . If he was too busy to make them one of those, a . . . And if he couldn't fit any of those in, everyone settled for a wrangulumentation because, as everyone said within a week of his setting up, "Fie if anyone this side of the firmament is as great a wrangulumentor as Werold of . . . where this Master hails."

Within two weeks he had so much work that he had no time to count his money and no time to buy a trunk, so he began to stuff it in his chimney. He was so happy at first that he had no time to worry. On the twenty-second night, however, for no reason attached to the number 22 as far as he knew, the fault faced him, as big as that crack opens between your feet on the upper story of your house, and yawns wider . . .

Everyone in Pleasanz just hired him to be agreeable. No one cared about what arguments he made. "They pay me to see the pleasure in my face," he grizzled, grabbing a wad of money clogging the fireplace, and tossing it in the dusty air tinged, as always, gold from the Pleasanz dust of disintegrating gingerbread: rye, cardamom, ginger, cloves, cinnamon, mace. Werold guessed the rest, but he had never found any place where Pleasanz cloth was made, let alone where all the gorgeous raiments were created. He never even found a poor, cross-legged Pleasanz tailor. And what town doesn't have a wealth of those?

Though he sought, wandering alone in the hours when the population slept, those places of creation—cloth and clothing—they were not the only places he sought but never found. They were minor searches, to satisfy his curiosity. Sating hunger was something else. Being a prominent new citizen, as everyone assured him that he was—he could not say to anyone, "If you please, where do you buy your meat and cakes?" The market that he stared out at, only sold shirts and skirts and cloaks. Not an egg. Not a hen. Not a fish or cake nor cabbage. He could not find another market.

As to a place where he could drink a drop of ale, that was hidden, too. He could smell, at times, a glorious ferment that insinuated itself past the stench of gingerbread—but could he find a tavern? No. Nor a place to buy a slice of pease pudding or a pig's knuckle; nor could he even hear a woman selling pies. Werold could find not a scrap of food in Pleasanz, and was so well bred, everyone said, that he was too encumbered by respect, to ask.

At night, instead of following Pleasanz custom and tossing all his wearings of the day out the window onto the street below for the rubbish collectors to take out to dump at the river—every night he ate just enough to sate his hunger without causing his stomach to revolt. He had to pinch his nose as he ate. To stare at the beauty of the collar of the day, a lace of crisp rolled wafers hung together with suspended loops of icing—then to break it apart wafer by wafer and shove them in his mouth, where his teeth crunched the brown lace, and the loops melted on his tongue while he tried not to retch. A fine shirt, he bunched into a ball and squeezed till it was a pill that he swallowed. At first, these were the easiest to digest, the thicker clothing being too hard to keep down, but by the twenty-first night, he was so hungry he ate a whole padded jerkin, and then worried himself to sickness at the thought that a collector might notice that he was not discarding his dailies as he should.

Maybe the rumour would go around that he did not dress freshly. Maybe he would be unwelcome soon. Maybe he would starve here, in abject wealth. For he had nothing to spend the money on, except for his daily order of wearables—the richest available, only what was expected of him—delivered as was the custom, on the doorstep at dawn.

Come the next night, the twenty-second, he could not eat a thing. He picked up a brilliant argument and tossed it to the floor.

Then he picked up a wad of money, and tossed that upon the argument. He turned his head to the door, opened it and did not look back. He met no one as he walked out of Pleasanz, and his gingerbread soles made no sound on the cobblestones. Out of the town gate he went without looking back at its great smiling face. Along the road he went, till he reached again, the riverbank.

He stripped, tossing everything into the river, and rolled on the dew-laden ground till the revolting smell of Pleasanz had rubbed off.

Then he reached into his hiding place in the hedge and pulled out his bundle.

Rain had made its way past the thorns and leaves. The cloak had been sopped as bread in milk, then dried as a crust. Then it had split, and its pieces grew a velvety coat of blue-green mould. He opened it on the grass. There were his travelling boots, mouldy but still good for a thousand leagues. Their outsides stunk of gingerbread, but tucked inside each was a galligaskin, the hose soft and thick and unable to stand as ever, and though spotted with mildew, not smelling at all of Pleasanz. His shirt, jerkin, cape, and hat stunk. Though the gingerbread cloak was also green with mould on its inside, the smell of those hideous spices stuck to the clothing like an evil curse. In a fury, he tossed shoes, shirt, jerkin, cape and hat high, over the hedge. Then he sat on the grass and shoved the balled stockings in his face.

These galligaskins were moist and rich with the scents of his unwashed traveller's feet.

He dropped one ball in his lap and tore at the other one till he ripped it into pieces in the more worn and rotted places, the feet and inner calves. He stuffed a piece into his mouth. He sucked it, rolled his tongue around it and through the holes in the knitting. He put his hand up to his mouth so that he could breathe out upon his palm, and inhale.

His eyes were shut in rapture when the moon came up. A sibilance made him open them.

Some fish had come up onto the bank like a pack of eels, and had arranged themselves with their tails to the river and their eyes toward him. He continued to eat the one galligaskin that he had torn into pieces. It was not an easy thing to chew. Though rot softened it, particularly underfoot, its yarn caught between his teeth. This slowed his greed.

The moon showed through to the luminous back of the watchers' eyes, making them into mirrors in which he saw himself eating as he never had—with such joy, and sadness that there was only so much to this meal. The fish took no liberties, nor made any sounds that he could hear, but they must have communicated some way, for soon the bank was so covered with fish, each head pointing in his direction, that he choked.

The first stocking, the one that held extra savour at its crusty top from a time that he fell and tore his knee, he'd gulped the last stitch of, but he could not eat more with these silent lookers-on. Tears stung his eyes.

He ripped the top of the undevoured hose with his teeth so that the knit unravelled on his tongue. Swallowing his excess saliva and his appetite, he pulled the knitting asunder and made a yarn ball, as the fishes watched. Then he stood up, naked as he was born. Walking amongst them, he broke the yarn into pieces and dropped a piece into each of the uplifted mouths.

As he broke and distributed yarn, there was no fighting amongst the fishes, even though, to give each fish a portion, he had to break the yarn into shorter and shorter pieces. When he had fed the last fish, the one whose tail lay in the river, he was unsure what to do. The fishes watched him, but if they'd turned their heads away he wouldn't have been able to see himself in so many mirrors. There he stood on a riverbank—unclothed and without a coin of any realm.

Why did I take that medlar's counsel? he asked himself, striking his tripe-white knees with both his fists till all were red as a maiden's lips. Who should know better the value of what is free? He didn't ask the fishes, of course, any more than he would have asked a mirror. They remained as they were—expressionless but still as a playwright's wished-for audience as Werold hit himself, then wept a bit, then pondered, sitting naked on the grass. The only sound was the slow woosh of gill-moved waters.

Werold became very still and increasingly vacant-eyed, till suddenly he slapped his head. "I know!" He scrambled up, wiped grass and mud from his skinny backside, and did a little dance. "The medlar," he sang, stamping three times. "Valued as most blessed" *stamp stamp stamp* "what *medlars* wish."

Werold's deliberations had led him to this conclusion: Any medlar would anoint itself with the scent of gingerbread if only it could, for that is almost how a bletted medlar smells, but never quite.

Every medlar is rootbound. "But I have legs!"

Werold laughed, an action this master argumentitioner had never been seen to take. Even now, he thought, that goodnatured medlar might be living richly in its imagination, as it travels in the shoes of the traveller it told the way to happiness. Whether the medlar assumed that the scent of gingerbread is all for everyone, is something Werold didn't try to fathom.

He had made up his mind, with no argument that it brought forward. The fish had eaten his galligaskin kickshaws with the same delight as he—not to be polite, not to be agreeable. "We do agree!" he said, expecting not a wriggle of understanding, not a blink of their lidless eyes.

For now it was time, Werold decided. He would meet his end here, as he could go nowhere naked, but could not bring himself to don the litter on this land. "Perhaps you'll find me tasty," he said to them, "you poor creatures who have never tasted worms."

He jumped from the bank.

Werold the argufier will be no more, he thought as calmly as he could, as his nose met the water. He could not swim, so hoped his end would come before he lost his mind.

His toes touched the soft thick bottom of the river, but only once. Every fish must have raced into the water. They bumped up against his chin, hit his chest and legs and back. They flayed the water from the river, from him, using their solid bodies, their lashing tails and fins. One big fish slipped under his feet and flung him free of the river. He sailed into the air and tumbled back upon the back of another giant. Without thinking, he grabbed that fish's fin. It turned its head back toward him, and he saw himself in its eyes. Werold, wearing a smile to rival the happy face on Pleasanz' gate.

The fishes would not let his head slip into the river, but they pushed him so that his body hung in the depths. Then began a procession in which each fish rubbed against him backwards, and they rubbed him everywhere below his head, from his neck to the undersides of his feet. Soon he was as covered with a thick coat of scales as they, though the arrangement was somewhat Galligaskinish—saggy and slovenly next to the tight, neat patterns on the fish.

His coat and leggings needed constant adjustment, but the fish took care of that. His new profession—and the fishes greatly looked up to him—was to lead them up the great unexplored river where he pulled the worms off boys' hooks in every new fishing hole. If there was a fishermen's net poised to throw upon the river, Werold stood up, on a long sinuous fish's back (this was the only treat the fishes still squabbled for) and dazzled and intimidated all the two-legged landlivers with his shining raiment. Whenever fishermen saw the wondrous man of the river with their own eyes—the man who was coated in a fish's rainbowed mail—they rushed to their huts and then back to the river, where every fisherman emptied a bucket of offerings. The waters swirled the most at worms, but also liked were pig's knuckles, roasted hens, buttons and buckles and belts, soft slippers, and the lees of ale. The action of leaping fishes and man was so looped and wet and active that no one could say for certain whether the man ate worms or only hens and bacon.

Two-legged landlivers watched, drool-mouthed. And that night in the house of every civil citizen who saw that the man was not a myth, everything wearable though it be new as the morning egg, was ripped and cursed and piled in a heap—from gold-embroidered shirts to hose as fine as spider webs. On fine streets, it was impossible *not* to hear the rich men wail, and grizzle, answer their ladies' cries with sharp replies; and kick their dogs, and moan and keen and weep.

In rude huts, fishermen tore their hair, worried over whether their offerings were rich enough; whether the visitors had gone their way sated or having left a curse upon the nets.

The glittering vision on the river, the unattainably clothed man— though looking just the same from year to year, from sighting to sighting—left fashion in a leap.

So this is almost the end of this true story, except for what I pass to you.

At night, those days, only scoundrels and the wretched were not in bed at home. At campfires along the river, fierce arguments flamed over what the man on the river droned, for on moonlit nights the one they called Silverlips was seen to sit on the back of a fish, spouting a stream of endless words. About one thing though, every loud-mouthed vagabond agreed. That each word might have made some sense in some other order, but the arrangement from the mouth of Silverlips made "nonsense".

My great greeaaaaat grandfather, a wretched poet, watched the fire and held his tongue, but while others were sleeping, he'd slip to the riverbank and cup his hands around his ears. The river was slow and deep, never a babbler, so when one violet dawn he heard a drone, he knew it was Silverlips. He caught the stream coming from the river, answered back in like, and penned the story with the quill he carried, and his own hot blood. A fine procreator, he passed down his talents and this tale.

There is no Rice Pudding in the Sea

The cat surveyed the city from the roof's spine. Though its fur pierced the gilded evenset, only two eyes noticed such beauty. They belonged, of course, to an itinerant. His eyes were busy, having surveyed this square from the gutters up while their owner rested one foot against the inside of a knee, his long staff making its footprint in an oddsods swirl of fluro-coloured muck.

"Hyu!" A curse on him, as his staff caught the edge of a coat. His stillness was a nuisance here, where the end of day brought out as much movement as in a kitchen at night.

The itinerant uncrooked his leg. He had noticed in particular, one river in the crowd. He dove into it with a determined stride, making such a splash of noise with his bright-tipped staff and hobnailed clogs that two squeaky-soled hurriers slowed enough to notice him and frown.

The river flowed around the corner and through a doorway. A smell he had thought he'd prepared for shoved itself up his nose and down his throat, suffocating him to dizziness. Retching and wheezing, he was pushed all the way into the place where the food was dished out into shiny red rubbery bowls.

Then the river flowed to the eating area, standing room only. Each person to a space wide enough to eat with one elbow out.

He ate with his staff held tight against his side.

It tasted as it smelt—of dishcloths. The texture was worse. It took all his willpower to keep it down. There was a technique to eating here. No utensils. Gulping it down, a gob went down the wrong way. Exclamations puffed around his ears.

There was nothing to drink. The itinerant tried to remember: *Do they drink with their meal?* But he could only remember the words of a song of theirs. *Cocoa at sleepityme.*

You had to eat fast. Some of the stuff sloshed on him when his bowl collapsed. Like everyone else, he ate it and wiped his hands. They had white kerchiefs. He had his clothes. The bowl taste was hooves and something more indefinably horrible.

The river moved on and around, and dispersed into another square where he looked up and around, and there! That cat, stark in the moonlight.

A bell clanged once, and again, and again and he checked against his timepiece, and the last clang rang out at three minutes and forty-two seconds after seven o'clock. Sloppy time here.

Around the edges of the square, booths were being set up. These people with the slow clock were keen rushers about, and they often jostled. He found a nook where he could watch, undisturbed and undisturbing.

By the third clang at something after eight o'clock, the booths were ready for customers, but law forbade trading until it allowed it, and the allowed time was eight o'clock by the town's bell. He chuckled to himself. Curious thing, time. It always races away when you aren't looking.

No time now to waste. The itinerant raised his staff and pointed it like a finger, "There is no rice pudding in the sea," he said.

His staff grew to the size and shape of a bull-elephant's trunk, and grew—

"And no tin mice on rooftops."

In no time, the itinerant held what looked like a forgotten carrot.

The cat on the rooftop! The itinerant glared up at it.

The cat didn't move a whisker.

The people in the square had seen neither the growing of the staff, nor heard the cat, nor seen the even more miraculous shrinking. They were held in the grip of anticipation, each watching some particular booth, each looking ready to pounce. But not for long. Time waits for no one, except a clock.

The itinerant closed his eyes and concentrated. "There-is-no-rice-pudding-in-the-sea!" he said in one long breathless word. He opened his eyes and imperiously, pointed the withered carrot.

"Obviously. Nor catnip."

This had never happened before.

"What are your demands?" demanded the wizard (for he was really a wizard).

"Demands?"

"You are a cat."

"We are not all greedy." At this point, any normal cat would have licked itself, but this cat remained as still as steel.

"If I release you, will you hold your tongue and let me get on with my work?"

"So little imagination," sighed the cat. "What makes you think I want that?"

The wizard was considerably flustered. Time was moving without him being any the richer for it. The hold on this populace was tearing its fibres as he dallied, waylaid by a contrarian cat. If only he had the right bag . . .

"For shame! Thoughts like that will get you nowhere!"

A mind-reading cat! There was no time to waste. "How may I be of service?" he asked, careful not to look at the cat. Maybe then this cat would quit its teasing.

"I wish to be the instrument you hold."

"This? I mean—" The wizard was incredulous.

Why would the cat want to be the something that the wizard now hid under his robe? It was supposed to be doing its job in a manner to strike awe, but—he dug his fingernails into the flabby thing.

"Wizard," the cat purred. "I watched you since you arrived. Just say 'yes' and I will stop tormenting you. Of that, you have my word."

"And what is the word of a cat on a roof who can't move but talks wildly?"

"Better than that of a wand who listens to the wrong commands. And better than that of a robot. You have robots, do you not, doing the work you find demeaning or too complex to understand?"

The wizard had never in his long life been so embarrassed.

"Yes!"

The abused and sweat-soaked carrot in his hand leapt to his former command, parting the sides of his cloak like an army parting the seas. He held out his arm with it, and out it grew, to the size of a bull elephant's trunk, and then wider, and longer, and it moved with a sinuosity that was genuinely cat-like (though the cat remained unmoved on the roof's spine). When the thing that the wizard held had grown so large that all the people in the stalls and all the people waiting finally noticed it and pointed and frighted with awe and the dogs ran cowering, the wizard said:

"Neglected unwanted unbidden unsmitten kittens mittens socks clocks toys that break artificial-fruit cake—" the bell clanged again, and he wasn't half finished. Quick!

"Returned spurned burned . . . "

He raced through the incantation but he wasn't two-thirds finished when the tongue of the bell licked the side of the bell for the eighth time, and he had *no time left.*

Time! The wizard's flamboyant instrument was supposed to have snuffled up everything on the stalls and whatever else the wizard might value amongst the crowd, and return to the wizard looking like a mere staff, ready to disgorge itself in the privacy of the wizard's quarters where by his timepiece, he should have already been poring over the booty. But the staff did no such thing, as he hadn't had time to finish the incantation. Completely discombobulated, he looked at his timepiece yet again. Four minutes and five seconds *to* eight. *Never* in all his days! A clock was slow or it was fast. But it could not be slow *and* fast.

The cat!

"You did this!" The wizard shook his staff up at the rooftop, for at the last peel of the bell, the great snuffler had shrunk once again to the size and shape of a staff, not even a forgotten carrot that had some shocking aspect of indescrepancy to it. No. The wizard's awesome instrument looked no more than the ordinary staff of any pretend wizard. An identical staff to those that lean against windows in pawn shops, beside the musix and magic rocks and diamond rings and cytrons and genuine rolex watches. His might as well have been those, but this was worse, because this staff was his. The woodlike staff of an eccentric old bugger.

He threw the thing onto the cobbles. He stomped on it. He picked it up and tore off the bright tip with his teeth, and crushed it flat between his great yellow molars. He was so angry that he made himself angrier, and *that* made him so wound up that he gripped his staff—that instrument so formerly capable of flamboyance and his source of pow —he gripped it at both ends between his freckled fists—and broke it over his knee. It bent like an old carrot, then creakily tore itself in two.

The crowd around him laughed. Trading had commenced, but he was more entertaining than shopping.

Not only had he accomplished nothing here. He was stuck here for twenty-four hours! And worse than what he could face, it was twenty-four hours by the reckoning of a cuckoo clock.

There! Mocking him, the bell struck again . . . nine times, and real time was just after eight. Compulsively, he checked his timepiece again. It couldn't be wrong. It was, after all, a chronometer rated automatic calibre 9997 movement—

"No catnip."

He whirled around, throwing his right hand out reflexively before realising that he held no wand, not even a staff. He was just a silly old man. The crowd remembered the fun of shopping again.

The wizard shook all over. He could do nothing without his wand here, and he'd broken it. That temper. How would he ever—

"If I ever catch you!" he shouted at the cat.

"Not even rice pudding," the cat repeated, but this time, just behind his elbow.

A little boy! Not even a magical cat.

"Haven't you ever met a ventriloquist?" The boy's accent was pure black cat.

The wizard grabbed a handful of his beard and stuffed it into his mouth.

The boy crooked a finger at him. The wizard bent down, his kneecaps cracking. The boy looked around. They were alone. "Would you like to come home with me . . . " He glanced around again—"for my mum's rice pudding?"

The wizard shuddered.

"It's *wantable* rice pudding."

The wizard stayed in his uncomfortable bent-over position. He felt too cowardly to straighten. His knees, and his back . . . "Everybody ate their bowls to the last drop. I saw that." Even the memory brought on nausea. Without his staff, he felt weak. A sweat broke out on the top of his head.

"That's the law," the boy said. "Eat what you're given, or you'll get it—"

"The-next-morning," the wizard said quickly, a wave of nauseated saliva rushing into his mouth. "Thank you kindly, boy. Now run home."

"If you promise not to snuffle it up with that great thing of yours, you can have some rice pudding at our house."

"I'm old, boy, and I don't have to where I—"

"But you'll want to eat this!"

The wizard didn't know if he was being cruel, but if he didn't stop this boy, he feared for his own health. Everything here—"Nothing's wantable here," he said.

The boy's face reddened. "My mum's rice pudding is. So wantable you'll want to snuffle in the bowl forever."

A trap. But maybe the boy doesn't know. "Do you have a real mum or a romum?"

"A real mum!"

"And what makes you think you want to share anything wantable with me?"

"Because you want our unwantables." The boy's eyes were like marbles that get lost. They found the dark places in the wizard where he held his secrets.

The wizard reached out and the boy bent his head. The wizard felt behind the boy's ears, down the middle of his back, in his armpits. He was a real boy.

"And you can have strawberry jelly."

"I've never had that," the wizard said. "Made with real strawberries?" Now, that was *really* something, something from a time and place the wizard had never found.

"Of course not," the boy said. "This strawberry jelly is *wantable!*"

As they left the square, the wizard looked back and up, but the moon and the cat had disappeared.

Ay! The boy was disappearing, too. He was fast as a cat. "Wait, son," the wizard called. "Slow for an old man."

He commanded his muscles to move faster, but they obeyed him as muscles respect old men. *Oh, for an old man's cane!* The wizard's clogs rang irregularly against the cobbles and the trash. The boy, being a boy, could only slow so much.

The wizard was slowed by his mind which acted now as an ordinary man's, not able to rush and think at the same time. Hwah!

His clog caught on a cobble. He took off the other one and tripped after the boy in his stockingfeet, hoping with the dreams of an old man tired of being a wizard, for this not to be leading into a trap.

He had to stop. His chest heaved, and he took great breaths. His lungs sounded like an ancient musix. The boy happened to looked back, and stopped. The wizard put his hands together, lifted them in thanks to the boy, and cursing his body, carried on, but after only a few steps, his hopes slowed him once again.

He—a wizard who had everything, who could have made his own wantable rice pudding, little boys, their mothers, cats that obey, bubblegum that pops forever, Anything!

He wished for the end of this journey to find: a real mum for this real son, and a house that suited them. He wished for good smells. He wished for that wantable rice pudding and the red "strawberry" jelly that he'd stopped believing existed except in mythology. And he wished on . . . a cat? A boy? A moon? He didn't know, but he wished suddenly with the passion of a wizard without a wand, a man with old knees and no cane—if it weren't utterly impossible, could he eat his rice pudding and red "strawberry" jelly from a real white china bowl, please, ringed in blue?

Dreadnought Neptune

Molecules of Old Spice, bundt cake, hot wool, sauerkraut, machine oil, beaver dusted with snow, and of unadorned excitement melded and rose to the ceiling of the round-shouldered compartment, only to swirl silently back upon the masses. Translucent windows turned into mirrors as night fell, brightened the surgical light within.

"Dreadnought Neptune," Eugene Thomas said, just loud enough.

His father Jules, stifled a shiver of guilt. *I should have stopped, bought him a candy bar or those Red Hots he likes.*

Oh yeah, you big sap? And why didn't you run home for his toothbrush? Like everyone here, they came as they were, carrying what they had. *It's hard on a young boy.*

He bent his neck down, examined the naked, tender place on his son's head where the whirl exposed soft white. *Myself at his age? Eat?* His heart bumped. He heard it. *They're so much younger than we were.*

"Neptune Dreadnought," Eugene repeated. Jules regarded him soberly. The boy was speaking to himself. *He doesn't feel it. Undeveloped?*

"Hm," said Eugene. "Hm hm hm."

"Hm," Jules chuckled. *Quit your Agnessing.*

He would have liked to take out his handkerchief and mop his head, take off his hat—but his elbows were pinned by the crowd.

"Crowd" doesn't quite describe the people packed into the little metal craft. "Crush" was more like it.

THE THOMASES HAD been lucky. When Jules lowered his son from his shoulders and stepped into the portway, he glanced back at the writhing snake of a crowd, the end blurred by scuffles loud as a barroom brawl.

An hour it had been since then, Jules estimated. He didn't have a watch at the moment, his habit of overwinding being a 'trial on the family.' *The past.* He shoved that niggle out of his mind. *Six* hours is nothing of a wait, for *this.*

Inside here now, the heat—tremendous—*only to be expected.* A faint whirr stirred the air, but with perhaps seventy people standing in a space little larger than a broom closet, and everyone dressed like polar bears, it being February, sweat slicked every face.

There were a few families here, but no babies. Two boys' high voices rose at times, like two wasps, but they were an exception. Mostly, there was so much silence that the few remarks people made to each other cut into only the cottony muffle of overdressed people breathing.

A little growl, and then a muffled pop sounded next to Jules, and then the pop's smell wafted up.

Eugene looked up at his father, mortified.

Jules cringed inwardly, but only for a moment. "The price we pay, son," he whispered. "Too little time to rig up suits." Could a suit have been rigged? he thought.

"You mean?"

"We'll be there in a jiff," Jules said. "And we'll fill up that gas tank," he joked, as he always had when Eugene's stomach let it be known that the boy needed food. But Jules curled his shoulders inward, awaiting the outraged yell, or a punch in the kidneys.

At Jules' reassurance, Eugene's digestion lost all modesty, erupting loudly and more aromatically than that first gentle waft. But oddly enough, a few other digestions replied, and then people began, in little jerks and blusters, to talk to each other. Jules looked around and just in time, grabbed his lower lip in his teeth. This was no bridge night or church social. *This is not the time to break the social ice*, let alone let loose with alota fool talk. He dropped his eyes. *Live these momentous moments. Listen to the future as it becomes the now, so unknown, and yet so familiar.*

Eugene smiled up at him, and his heart jumped with pain. *My smile at the same age. My son. My stars, and the cow jumping over the moon. Eugene and me, riding the cow together. And rockets soaring and comets flying across the skies, their tresses snapping in the eyes of the galaxy watchers, daring all who dare to fly across the face of the heavens.*

Jules gazed at his son and his own years dropped away. He felt that electric , incurably impatient joy of being seven again. His eyes stung with awkward tears that he couldn't wipe away, but just then maturity stepped in, smearing the smile on his face, crooked as a blind-man's peanut butter sandwich. *Eugene is me at seven all right, with—nothing to blame the boy for—a dash of Agnes.*

He squeezed his son's hand. *Nobody else needed*, he thought powerfully just then, in a way that he hadn't before. *No one complaining, warning, hesitating, practicalling, nagging, questioning. No Agnessing.*

The flurry of socializing died down, everyone nursing their own thoughts.

Jules was reminded of all the vegetables—spinach, rutabaga, broccoli Agnes made his son eat. *It's worth the trip just to get away from broccoli..* The smell in the compartment was now thick enough to slice, but oddly enough, there was no complaining, no whining at the crush; not like there'd be, say, waiting for a picture show, *which just goes to show*, Jules nodded, *what even a boy's capable of when he hops into his dream and is only waiting for Opportunity to stomp on the gas.*

A cough cut the air, a couple sighs and a grunt, and then there was silence again. Eugene lifted his face to Jules and earned a reassuring wink, and boy and father played a game of silent squeeze-rhythm, their clasped hands riffing jazz tunes, syncopating time, while time slipped along in front of Jules' dreamy eyes; but to Eugene, didn't pass.

"Ｈow long more d'you think it'll be?" Eugene asked.

"Can't tell, son." Jules considered that it might be hours yet, perhaps timed by an aural emanation, a Neptunian countdown now being received somewhere in the shiny works, the bug-shaped silver-shimmering craft warming up its tubes to leave. Listening, he could hear a faint wheezing.

"In its own good time, of that I know," he reassured his son.

"Here, liddle boy," a big man beside Jules said. He pushed a small package into Jules' free hand. "For your son," the man smiled. "Broughd id in case dere's any brats, bud dere ain't. He's a nice boy, so's he mighd as well ab a chew."

"We're much obliged," Jules said, passing the packet to Eugene's sweaty grasp.

"Gee, thanks!" said the boy. "I wonder if it'll still have taste when we land."

"The name's Thomas," said Jules.

"Jodes. Jay oh ed ee ess."

Jules was momentarily sickened by the harsh pink smell of bubble gum layered over everything else.

"Dond mean do be nosy," Jones said. "Bud dond you hab a wife or sum'n back home?"

Jules' face contorted momentarily, then smoothed. "Visiting her mother."

"Sorry," Jones said.

Eugene twisted around so he could look up at Jones. "I'm not, Mister Jones. What mom would let me go on this?"

Sure enough, the few women here didn't look like they possessed a glove between them, nor a wish to have a nice day at home away from unhealthy excitement, nor—from the moment she spotted this ship—did any of these women look like she would remember if she *had* a little boy.

"Why're you here?" Jules Thomas asked.

"All year climad control. No crowds."

"You mean that's not one doozy of a cold?" Jules asked, "And crowds?"

"Wish id were. Adenoids. And cornds."

"Sorry to hear." Jules shuffled his feet so that there was no chance of stepping on the man's toes.

"Graed nambe, ain'd id?" Jones commented.

Jules had been thinking almost that very thought, and found himself faintly annoyed to have it brought up by this unhealthy character with the big red nose.

Perhaps his son felt the same, for just then, Jules felt his hand squeezed. He just wanted to be left alone to live to the full this once-in-a-lifetime experience: the Waiting Period Before Embarkation.

Plenty of people might think they had the guts to do it, and the number of people trying to get in was in the hundreds. But in a city as big as Chicago, it was still a lot less than the turnout for a ball game, or the crowd that rubbernecked the Hula Hoop Derby that made Page One of the *Tribune*. Sure, you had to have sticktoitiveness to wiggle your way to Hula Stardom, but after it's over, what's it add up to? A fancy banana split and a night of bad-dream indigestion.

But this! *This ain't no ball game*, Jules said to himself, feeling so free, he talked to himself like that coarse man would, the one with the adenoids. Everyone had just dropped their life fast as a handful of hot tar. *Pile in! Take off! So long, Earth!* Jules laughed to himself, thinking of front pages to come.

The day had boded well. Taking Eugene to the toyshop on Saturday afternoon had been Jules' plan all week. The rocket kit in the window was something they would have to take out of town to fire off, but then that would be yet another day of excitement.

It was when they turned the corner of Elm Street the block before the toyshop, that they saw the shiny bug-shaped vehicle. It didn't have recognizable wheels—just a shimmer down below.

"What the—" Jules mumbled.

"It's the Dreadnought Neptune, Mister Thomas!" a splotchy boy said, running away from the thing towards the Thomases. "I've got to tell the folks."

Jules grabbed, but the gangling boy slipped through easy as a drop of mercury. "No time!"

Jules took Eugene's dry hand in his clammy paw and ran two steps—like dragging a fire hydrant.

"Dad. Dreadnought Neptune?"

"The ship to take us, Eugene. There's no time. You heard George."

He jerked Eugene loose and they ran, him a shamble of short legs and heavy coat, the boy skittering but no longer a drag.

"That proves it," Jules said. There, in the midst of the human ants swarming by the entrance to the craft, was old Mr. Schlumpfer, without his hat. With George gone and Mr. Schlumpfer there by the craft, there was no one left at the toy store on Saturday afternoon, its busiest time of the week.

"It's the Dreadnought Neptune, all right." He knelt and put his hand on his son's seven-year-old shoulders.

"Want to rocket, son?"

Eugene's face at that moment reminded Jules so much of his own, inside and out.

"There won't be any trees there?" Eugene asked.

"Hard to tell."

Eugene picked a scab off his knuckle and ate it. "I suppose it depends on what they've prepared for us."

Jules looked at Eugene and thought that he had not considered that far. His son was just that little bit different. Suddenly Jules could not think of a grown man he would want more as a companion.

"Guess we'll find out what they've prepared—"

"When we find out," Eugene finished—the end to a favorite bedtime story—when the boy was two.

Jules was shaken, he didn't know why. So *what?* "There's no time, you know," he said, maybe a bit portentously.

"George said," Eugene said.

"And Mom?" Jules kept himself still, slowed his words. "There's no time for her. We don't have to go."

Eugene's eyes were so steady that for a moment, it seemed as if he couldn't blink. "No," he said.

Jules swept Eugene up onto his shoulders and pushed their way into the front of the most crowded mass of men and boys. Mr. Schlumpfer was working his way to the door at a remarkable rate for a little old man. Jules was just wondering how, when he saw a man jerk away from Schlumpfer with a little cry. Well, well! And here I thought they were party tricks. He wished he had thought to carry such a party trick for eventualities. Gently but ever so insistently, he pushed a smaller man to the side.

Eugene wiggled. "Hello, Mr. Schlumpfer!" His feet beat a tattoo on Jules' chest "Mister Schlumpfer's coming, too!" but the old man was busy.

"Steady, first mate!" Jules ordered. "We'll meet him on the other side."

All around, "Dreadnought Neptune" were the only words you could hear distinctly, but those words positively hummed.

In his pockets, Jules carried five dollars and fifty cents, a half-full pouch of tobacco, a comfortably battered briar pipe, a half-full box of matches, and a power-ten loupe. He suddenly wished he had brought his nail clipper.

Now, when it must be at least 6PM, just as Jules' knees were beginning to say *There's no place like home*, Eugene squeezed his hand. Jules had thought Eugene had been sleeping against him, standing up, but maybe not, because the boy's voice had an edge to it.

"Dad," he whined. "Did you see any sign that said 'Dreadnought Neptune'?"

"No, Eugene," Jules said, surprised to hear the snappishness in his voice.

"Can you hear that pounding, Dad?"

"Yes, Genie." Jules was careful to modulate his voice. It *was* a long wait for these soft boys of today. "But don't you remember? People have been pounding the outside to get in almost since the doors closed."

"I saw id," Jones said, now awake. He had spent the past interminably long time snoring against Jules' shoulder.

"What?" Eugene asked.

"The name."

"See?" Jules craned his neck to smile down at his son, then turned to Jones. "I was too busy getting us through the crowd."

"Dee ded," Jones said.

Eugene giggled. "What?"

Jones looked like he was having second thoughts about the boy. "Indishuls," he snapped.

"Initials, Eugene," Jules chided. "Dee En. Be sharp."

"But Dad!"

"Hmmm?" Jules growled.

"I'm not smart alecking." The boy's eyes glittered. "Dee En could stand for anything. Did you see the name?"

"No son, but George—"

"And Mister Schlumpfer." Eugene interrupted. "I know."

The 'I know' sounded just like Agnes. Jules wished he could slam the door to his study and light his pipe. "Yes, Eugene," he managed to squeeze out from between his teeth. "So?"

"And us, Dad. We're here."

"And me," Jones added.

"And me," said a man none of them could see, but it sounded like close behind.

As if a switch was flicked, the low decibel level of conversation, mumbles, and grumbles suddenly increased, and began to spike.

"Deadbeat nincompoops!" yelled a teenage boy.

"Dratted nonesuchers," an Englishman drawled.

Laughter broke out, amidst a flurry of deep-voiced, but stoic grumbles.

"Taking its own sweet time taking off, isn't it?"

"Least that proves this train ain't run by Mussolini!"

The guffaws shook the craft so much that a high-pitched voice needed to add a two-finger-in-the-mouth whistle, to be heard:

"There's something scratched here!"

"Give him room," a deeper voice commanded. "He's got to bend."

The crowd scrunched till heads and shoulders looked awfully mixed up.

"Deadlock Neptunium!" a reedy voice rang out.

"Neptunium, neptunium. What the hell?"

"Is it Russian?"

"Don't be crackers!"

"Did he say Communist?"

"Shud! Up!" boomed a voice that sounded experienced, or maybe just fed up with the wait.

A moment of silence pervaded the atmosphere. And then a laugh that made Jules' hair creep.

"It's elementary, Watson," chuckled the laugher with a polyester-English accent.

"Nep-*Tun*-ium—" a woman's voice rang out, as if everyone should have known.

"The first synthetic transuranium element of the actinide series discovered," said the man who'd done the stagy Holmes bit, in a weary tone that didn't sound convincing. "The isotope was produced by McMillan and Abelson—"

"in 1940 at Berkeley, California," the woman who'd said Nep-*Tun*-ium, cut in.

"as the result of bombarding uranium with cyclotron-produced neutrons," the man finished in a flurry so fast that he sounded this time, pure American. And then he drawled, "Hi, Maud."

"Hi, Frank. What you doing here?"

"Here?"

"Of course not here. Chicago."

"A different nest."

"A fine nest you've made for yourself," Maud laughed, meanly.

"Speak for yourself, Maud. Netherby stole your work, too?"

"Excuse my French," an older man interrupted. "But hell if we care about your Netherby. Cut us in to your know, why don't you?"

"I'm afraid, young man," drawled Frank, now in his world-weary "English" voice, and there was a quick shuffle and the sound of a punch.

At that, the crowd erupted in recriminations till a piercing whistle stopped the noise. "Quiet, please!" screamed the reedy voice again. "There's a big fat button here, by this panel. And it's got something scratched on it."

"Let him look! Get back!" the most authoritative voice commanded, and everyone scrunched again.

Outside, the Chicago wind howled through the city, but the human banging on the outside of the craft had stopped hours ago. Inside now, only the faint breathing of the air mover could be heard.

"It's crude," the reedy voice announced, and people craned their necks to see the speaker, a thin-haired youth with a neck like a wrung chicken. "And it looks like it was scrawled real fast. But yes. It's an eff. A capital eff."

"Whad's that mean?"

"Press it!"

"No! Don't!"

And a whole lot of other things, screamed at the same time, till no one could hear what anyone said, till one woman's voice soared above all the tumult, and it was Maud's. "Just open the damn door!"

At that, the crowd pressed forward toward the door, but either there was no way to find the opening mechanism, or the wild panic that ensued when it didn't open directly caused too many people to shove against each other, and then slip on the shiny floor, and they became bodies that were trampled anyhow, as others stepped on them and stroked the walls, trying to find a latch, anything that stuck out, and there wasn't any, and the walls grew wet with sweat, and more people fell, and there was so much punching and yelling and unholily high screaming, you couldn't hear a thing.

In two uncountable minutes, half the people were dead in a pile, and Mr. Schlumpfer lay against the opposite wall, his face poking out of his coat like a potato out of a burst sack—and as grey.

When the door finally opened, half the rest of them killed the others in the rush out.

F EW OF THE living ever questioned how the door opened, or cared to mention their participation in the incident, and it is a shame that experiments as fruitful as this have been besmirched by so-called ethical considerations.

The inventiveness and bravery of Maud Pickett and Franklin Hoffstedder in undertaking this psychological study have never been fully appreciated, except by Professor Eugene Thomas who followed Pickett out the back way as soon as she disappeared, leading his father, who in trying to wrench his son toward the door everyone was pressing toward, was himself crushed to death almost, and would have been if Eugene had lost his grip.

Without discussing it between them, Jules and his son came to an agreement. Agnes, Eugene's mother, Jules' wife never got the goods on the story of what happened to Jules' coat (and his right arm, strained at the shoulder) the night her son and husband were gone till way past a boy's bedtime, let alone a husband's duty to home. And Jules refrained from saying anything to back up Agnes' insistence that Eugene eat an even larger pile of vegetables every year he lived at home. Eugene would eat his reeking pile of green in silence, his face letting on nothing of his thoughts, his disgust, while his mother regarded him with consummate pride. Her other friends' had sons they couldn't control, one who, when his mother found him pouring his glass of milk into the aspidistra, gave in to his hate of milk and stopped making him drink his allotted dose. Agnes roiled at that lack, enjoyed a well-earned gloat. Her son wouldn't end up as a delinquent, uncared for, unguided.

As Eugene ate, she smiled at her plate. It wouldn't do to smile at him, giving him the sin of pride.

And as Eugene ate his spinach, Jules, his father also hid his smile. He knew, though it would make Agnes unbearable to live with, that he owed his life to spinach.

And when Eugene moved to California to be an important scientist, Jules spent his days waiting for the hours when he was let out of the apartment for some errand, when he'd roam the streets, looking. Never to anyone, not even to the memory of Mr. Schlumpfer, would he have said For what. Certainly not to Agnes— nor, to his everlasting regret, to Eugene, his once-so-promising son. For the older Eugene grew, and the greater Eugene grew, what Jules saw was something he tried so hard not to think about, but he had to just accept. Eugene's strength was his weakness. His solid mind, that lack of imagination, that willingness to succumb to the hard cold dull-eyed fact, to grasp an explanation, that addiction to the real. It *hurt* Jules. Hurt him in the stomach, like eating a cold, hot-mustard slathered sausage.

Yes, Eugene turned into a brilliant scientist. Everybody said so. But with too much Agnes, he would never see Neptune, never feel the comet's tail snapping in his face as he rides that cow over that big old so-close moon. Always be himself, weighty as an encyclopedia, stodgy as mashed potatoes.

One day, Jules thought as he turned the key in the apartment door and said, "I'm home dear. I had to go to 59th Street (or '48th Street', or 'Park Avenue', or 'the third hardware store I tried'), sweet, to get a fitting for the lamp (or 'the replacement' or whatever the errand was for, and sometimes he forgot and got in quite a stink of trouble)—One day, he thought especially at that time when he missed Eugene the most, and remembered just how the boy's hand felt in his when they were riffing their jazz, waiting for the shining moment—the lurch of takeoff!—If, when I turn a corner and see another spaceship parked and waiting, I'll have to board alone.

The Shoe in SHOES' Window

The shop says SHOES because that is what it sells, just as the bakery next door says BREAD. When milk jumps out of a cow's eyes, it would make sense to call a shoes-shop "Liliana's" or "Mode", but that, incredibly, is what is done in those places where chaos reigns.

Truly, where chaos reigns, even at night, nonsense and evasion shine where people look for straightforwardness, but where they look for inspiration, something beyond the realm of daily existence, they are then shown only things, and who can feed his soul with that? For a tired man or mother, a few moments of my treatment is like taking off socks and shoes and dipping your feet into a cool stream on a hot and stinking day. I restore the mind and nourish the soul—myself and my colleagues, I should say: window dressers to the People.

I dress the windows of SHOES, as well as the shops FOOD, STATIONERY, CLOTHING, and TOYS. This year I won the Hero of Culture Award for SHOES, but my most consistent triumphs, I think, have been in TOYS.

For years my days have been filled with the dual necessaries of life: creativity and undisturbed peace. That is a state unachievable to the workers in the shops, disturbed as they are from shop opening to shop closing, by constant interruption. It is impossible to do a proper inventory! But I am glad to say: that is not my problem.

I have cordial relations with them all—or *had*.

Today SHOES was in an uproar, and I was dragged into the middle of this unpleasantness.

A man came in last week, who wanted a shoe in the window.

Not only did he want a shoe in the window, but someone told him (was it the young girl from the provinces, or sour old Luka?) when I would be coming back to work on the window: this afternoon.

He appeared at my elbow after I had unlocked its shop-side door and just as I raised my leg to climb up. He wanted a certain shoe in the window, he said, and he said this with such audacity that I banged my knee turning toward him.

He has one leg.

I was so startled that he spoke to me, that I acted stupidly. "H'm," I said, as if this *h'm* meant *yes*. I climbed up into the window and locked myself in, but he had disturbed my creativity so much that my hands shook.

He waited for about five minutes while I sat on the floor of the windowcase. He pounded on the door, but I was safe inside. Then he ran outside and attacked me from the pavement, using his eyes and one finger. But he could do little from the pavement unless he wanted to become a display himself. He left the ranks of the window gazers—a curious old woman and a girl whose eyes were only for the window.

I thought that I had taken care of him, so I felt it was safe to climb down.

I was met by the whole SHOES unit who had called an urgent meeting. Though I am technically not part of their unit, I had no choice but to attend, the window being the source of unrest.

EVERYONE WAS IN the most vile of moods, the air thick with the bad breath of people who need to eat and haven't since their mid-day soup at the canteen.

I argued: I cannot have my materials stolen. What would the window look like then?

Then I asked the meeting if anyone had tried to interest the man in the shoes in the shop. No one had thought of that, but why would they have anyway, several argued. They could not sell the man one shoe, and he—*"sensibly"*, he had emphasised, didn't want to pay for what he didn't need. When he added *"patriotism"* to that argument, no one knew what to do with him.

The meeting discussed needs, and I had to defend myself against accusations that I hadn't discussed materialism with *him*. "That would have rusted his face," Kishov said, his head bent as he shook dandruff from his hair onto the floor in front of him—a contest he played constantly with anyone, even himself if no one wanted to compete.

Naturally, the meeting first tried to pin the blame on me—an outsider. But I'm not an artist for nothing. Next, they turned on the girl from the provinces, for it was she who broke off counting shoes to listen to a person who was not in her work unit, a person who just came into the shop like anyone who comes into the shop looking for shoes. She didn't seem to understand even when she was asked, "Do you let the dust disturb your concentration when it blows in?" Instead, stupid girl, she began to cry. It was decided that she would henceforth be housed with Luka.

But that only solved the problem of the *maker* of the problem. The problem itself was still to be dealt with.

There were some in the meeting (those going grey at their temples) who just wanted the problem to go away, and were willing to do it the underhanded way. "Sell him the shoe," they advised.

Others recoiled from that idea, the very young and the oldest. "What if we get caught," one young woman asked. "We will, surely," an old woman said.

"He will, not us," dandruff-head said, meaning me, and was nudged in the ribs by his middle-aged superior.

I didn't need *him* to tell *me*. The shoes in the window are there for their beauty, as is the painted sled that's in there now. They are not there to sell. If I allowed the shoes to be sold, where would I find shoes to put in the display?

Of course I could not sell a shoe from the window, I told the meeting. They are not mine to sell. They belong to the window.

"Then give him the shoe," one voice said, I couldn't tell whose. The necks I expected would bend up and down, bent up and down enthusiastically, as none of their heads were mixed up in this business.

Luka laughed, which surprised me, as I had always thought she was ready to report me for something she might think she found.

Suddenly she was on my side. "Can't you just see this hero walking down the street, wearing a shoe from *our* window?" she said.

The cinema-scene that played in various minds at Luka's instigation produced titters, scowls, and paleness.

Next, the meeting turned to the topic of who this disturbing man could be:

A spy sent to see what we would do?

A person who was so uncultured that he had never been in a city, and thus had never seen shops? He has a strange accent, but then so many people in this city do.

After further fruitless speculation (the hungrier everyone got, the more peevish and argumentative the meeting became) a decision was finally reached. The problem of the one-legged man who wants to buy a shoe would be solved by myself, the most cultured and also the most lettered, by writing a Directive to Address Irregularities.

I WROTE THE Directive, and it properly addressed, I thought, every possible permutation of irregularity. I framed it and hung it behind the front counter, where it was admired and read out to those who could not read.

It explained that the stock in the shop was for sale.

It exhorted all workers to do their duty, and not be waylaid by people from outside the unit who would not have the unit's productivity as their goal, or might even be saboteurs.

It made clear the inalienable difference between the shop and the window. *Each to its purpose, and each to its needs.* (I would no more think of taking shoes from the SHOES shop to put in the window than I would steal a man's hair from his head, though his hair might look good under a hat in my CLOTHING window. His hair serves the man's head. The shoes in SHOES serve their inventory.)

The Directive went into finer detail than perhaps you have patience for. But by the time that the nail was banged into the wall and the Directive straightened, there was no fault in understanding amongst any of the workers in the unit, even the young girl who had never worn shoes till she came to the city, let alone seen a shop.

A state of peace and equilibrium reigned again.

IWAS AT SHOES today, hanging shoes on a painted vine that sprouted a red shoe, a blue one with white laces, and a patent-leather boot, when an insistent knock on the door of the window broke my concentration and made me fumble the shoes, the precious shoes.

I knew before I opened the door, that it was him.

"I wish to buy that shoe," he said, taking hold of the door and pulling it open. Not only that, but he insinuated his long body onto the base of the window floor and stretched out his long arm to point to the shoe he wanted. A left-foot shoe half hidden under the dropped patent-leather boot: a green shoe with yellow laces and a punched design along the toe. I leaned my body out over his, partly to push him back and partly to see what he was wearing: the same drab lace-up as every man who had bought shoes in this city for the past three years.

I pulled back into my window and stood upright. He stood upright also, supported by a cane in his left hand—a respectful distance from my window door.

He puffed out his chest to make sure I saw the stiffness of medals. So this was to be a test of wills!

I fought in the Great War, too, though I was not, like him, a pensioner, if that was what he was. He was either that or something more sinister, as he clearly wanted to turn my life upside down.

I used the classic defence, which usually works: pointed disinterest. I went back to my work, shutting myself away from him.

He tapped on the door with his cane.

I called out: "Luka, please ask for this hero's identity card. We will have to report him as a attemptive supply liberator."

"Comrade," I heard Luka say, and I could see without looking, that perpetual bubble of spit grow large and pop at the side of her mouth.

Then I heard Luka cry out some primitive peasant *Save me!* curse. The supply liberator must have had a shock of a card.

"Comrade window-dresser!" the man called. "Come down, by order of the Ministry of the People's Welfare."

I had known in my bones that he was a spy. Others would have had wet their legs at the word *Ministry*, but I had nothing to fear.

My feet met the floor with a steadiness none of the SHOES work unit felt. They stood around comically rigid. But I had comported myself faultlessly throughout this trial.

The man leaned on the counter. Luka snatched the abacus out of his elbow's range. "With the exception of "—and here he pointed with his cane to the couple of middle-aged men—"Unit SHOES, Hero Boulevard has performed with distinction." He elaborated for a moment on the pride he felt in seeing a unit that—and he wiped a tear from his eyes, which brought tears to many.

He was not finished. *I am to be awarded another medal!* I wanted to sit at that announcement, I felt so weak.

The man from the Ministry continued. "There is a need," he said, "for high-class shoes for heroes with one leg. At the moment, there is no unit detailed to carry out this function."

That is true. There is the manufactory that makes shoes for windows. There are manufactories that make shoes for shops. But his Ministry had identified a need, as yet unfilled.

I therefore now announce to you what he announced to us at that moment that I can still feel, down to my toes: There will be a manufactory of high-class shoes for heroes of the left foot. Our unit will make those shoes, and I will design them. None of us has ever made shoes, and I certainly have not designed shoes before, but that has never stopped any worker, once there is a plan.

I am filled with joy, as this is recognition above my previous recognitions. I am drunk with joy. And so is all of my new work unit, except for a few middle-aged men. We shut SHOES to celebrate. The chair was dusted off for the esteemed posterior of our benefactor from the Ministry of the People's Welfare. I feel—I feel it still—a warmth of comradeship such as I have never felt with another. There is the unspoken promise between the Ministry man and myself (his eyes shined with approval towards me) that if this manufactory fulfils, there will be yet another manufactory established with myself as designer, for high-class shoes for the right foot.

In the glow of ruddy cheeks and shining eyes, bottles appeared from nowhere and glasses were filled. The first toast! We all raised our glasses, and the man from the Ministry inclined his glass with a little rakish tilt towards me . . .

The man from the Ministry proved to be a hero indeed. When the party was over, the SHOE unit members were as firm-legged as boiled turnips, but he took his leave, rising like an oak from his chair. He walked down the block and disappeared in the murk of a broken streetlight. Even with his cane, he walked with the tread of a true leader—a leader who that fine green shoe looked cobbled for, as soon as it met his foot.

The Emperor's Backscratcher

A long time ago in the kingdom of Ch'u, history, one day, stopped. So said the Lord High Chief Philosopher, Hwang Tu Soh, who declared that everything worth discovering had been discovered; all stories that could soothe the evening's fears and the daily boredom, written; all enemies crushed to insignificant grains of sand; and the peasants of Ch'u as stilled forever in their place as the light of darkness in the deepest well in Ch'u.

The Emperor, though godly, was surprised to be apprised of this intelligence—and pleased.

The place was the Throneroom, the time was shadowfree, and the news made the Emperor's stomach jump. How he hated the daily Conferring! But since his head had reached his father's knee, he had been forced to attend. Conferrings had always made him ill. All that advice gave him headaches and sometimes dulled his appetite. All the problems he had faced in his five years on the throne had wearied him. Which advisor gave the best advice? Whose path should he take? How could he ever sleep at night entirely free of care with all these advisors pestering him, and a frightening world outside the walls? But now, at last, a Conferring had brought him joy. While the blood of his last enemies still perfumed the air in the Chief Historian's account, the Chief Philosopher in the land now brought him news that he, the Emperor, had accomplished what no other ruler had. He had slain the biggest enemy of all: history itself, whose lifeblood was change. Now nothing ever would.

He sat for a few moments, pondering Hwang Tu Soh's pronouncement. His stomach began to tingle as it filled with joy.

"Tsioh!" A sound like the cough of a tiny bird cut the pendulous silence.

The Emperor sighed. Sometimes he wished he could just forget about the Empress. He wondered at the curse for doing away with her. Was it true?

He turned and raised an eyebrow.

The Empress was, as always, timid with him as a fox, and as beautiful. Would locking her in the Tower of Perpetual Sorrows invoke the curse?

"Dear Godly One, dear Magnificent Golden Staff, dear Emperor-Husband Whose Glow Blinds my eyes," she began, as she always did. And she leaned sideways so that her head came close to his, but not close enough. He had to lean towards her to allow her to do as she clearly intended. He leaned, heaving a bellow of a sigh.

When he was close enough, she whispered in his ear . . .

The assembled Lord High advisors heard nothing except their own hearts beating. They stole glances at the Lord High Chief Philosopher, who for his part, regarded the Imperial couple as an ancient father does, his lovable but dimwitted child. Not that he could actually *see* them as anything but magnificently coloured blobs.

While the Empress talked, the Emperor remembered, yet again, why he kept her at his side as he ruled the world. Annoyed, he waved his hand and she straightened in her chair—a painted doll again.

"So what has happened about the money?" he snapped, so loudly that pigeons exploded from the roofbeams. He examined his fingernails as he asked his question, the exact nature of which was as easy to pin down as a cup of water poured upon sand. This habit of his was extremely distressing to his counsellors—all except one. Hwang Tu Soh remembered this Emperor's father, whose skill at terrorizing with a few vague words was artistry itself.

Several Lord Highs felt their hair follicles contract, but said nothing. Had there been a theft? A fire? Had taxes not been adequately collected?

The Emperor rose slightly in his chair, turned his head with magnificent slowness, and spat. His aim was excellent.

"The paper money, the paper money," piped an UnderLord from the Treasury. "We are still looking for a solution." He spoke as if he would have liked his hand cut off rather than make that admission. Well, the hand might still be cut off.

The Godly One, Magnificent Golden Staff was not pleased. "You have had four days to find a way to make paper notes that no one can match," he pointed out, with chilling calmness. "Four days more that I am losing wealth as the counterfeiters work."

The Emperor's anger was rising fast, and now it switched direction. "Hwang!" he snarled, "What's this about history being over when this very task hasn't been carried out! When, for every counterfeiter I order flayed, more fake paper money is made in some other corner of my land?" The Emperor's voice now took on the sound of steam escaping from a kettle, as he reached a thin, high scream. "You told me to stop the loss of metal through this change to paper, and I did. For what? For you to bankrupt me?"

Hwang Tu Soh, the Lord High Chief Philosopher, stood as if deaf and blind, or turned to stone.

The Empress imitated the little bird, and the Emperor waved his hand impatiently at the same time as leaning over to hear her whisper . . .

Now, the Emperor was even *more* annoyed, but she had to be right. She always was. He turned to the Lord High Keeper of the Treasury, who had tried to hide behind a department scribe.

"Fan Fa'h!" the Emperor roared. "It was *your* advice. Do you covet my coins now useless in their caskets? Speak!"

The Lord High Keeper of the Treasury's eyes showed their whites like two fried eggs. A few sounds escaped his throat, but none of them were words. He was equally terrified and outraged.

The problem had started in the distant past, but by the time this Emperor's mother died and he came to the throne, the lack of fresh sources of metal had become serious. The custom of burying the coinage of Ch'u with the dead to pay officials in the Afterlife not only stole the coins from legal circulation, thereby stealing them from the Emperor, but took them out of the Emperor's hands should he want their metal for another purpose. The Palace had continuous and unpredictable needs, and it was silly to use good metal as symbols of worth, for anyone to trade in return for what they wanted. The Emperor wanted metal, and therefore, it made sense for people to trade something easily supplied and almost worthless—paper—

when all the Imperial Palace had to say is: "This little piece of paper equals this much silk, or rice or meal." And the dead would have their own special death-bribes printed, too. The supply of paper was vast, mulberry trees growing wild and tame throughout the realm.

Thus, the Edict of the Coin had been declared, and all coins held by the citizens had been handed to the Palace's representatives, in exchange for the new paper money made in the Imperial Treasury's Paper Money Manufactory, two buildings of venerable age and dilapidation in the Treasury compound, only steps from the Imperial Kitchen itself.

But soon there was far more wealth in the Kingdom in paper than there ever had been in coin. The advanced state of civilization needed many artisans with superior skill—far too many in the very trades of papermaking and printing that paper money required. So every advancement that the Imperial Manufactory achieved, to make its paper stock more distinctive, the printing on its notes more elaborate—was quickly copied faithfully enough that even the Emperor's workers in the Manufactory could not tell the difference between the products of their efforts and a plethora of impostors. A locust plague of artisans had descended on the challenge of making money for themselves, and succeeded brilliantly, despite the punishments and the many inspectors roving the realm— inspectors who could well be profiting, too. The urgency of creating a counterfeit-proof note was imperative. Imperially imperative!

A ND NOW, IT had been four days, or it was the fourth day? No matter. Every day was another day of theft from the Emperor, and now the UnderLord stood there like a gibbering ivory statue, saying that he *still* had no solution to offer.

Disgusted, the Emperor turned again to Hwang Tu Soh. "How can history have stopped." he asked, "if there is still this problem?" His molars squeaked against each other, his teeth were so tightly clenched. "How can you say, *Chief Philosopher*, that everything is perfect and there is nothing more to know, and nothing more will *change*," and here he pounded his throne, "when this most important problem is still not solved?"

He glared at the old man, who gazed back with the expression of an egg in its shell.

"Are you saying that this won't change?" the Emperor yelled. "That I'll be thieved from *forever!*"

The Lord High Chief Philosopher almost imperceptibly shrugged. He had been old in this Emperor's father's time. All Emperors enraged themselves over matters of little consequence.

"Dear Emperor Husband." The Empress didn't try to whisper, but used her speaking voice, as delicate as the breeze from a passing butterfly. "You know he's so forgetful, and—"

"The answer is easy," the old man said, cutting off the Empress if indeed he heard her at all. "Make a paper so special it cannot be copied."

He'd said it so simply, as if he were above all, bored, that the Emperor raised his own hands to clap them in unbounded glee—and stopped. The Treasury's people would have discounted that already. There were no rare trees in the Palace grounds from which paper could be made. Everything, in fact, used to make the Emperor's money came from outside the Palace, and was plentiful, even the pigments. So was the old man trying to talk in riddles? The Lord High Chief Philosopher was a trying character, but this Emperor's father had instilled respect for the man, so the Emperor stilled his anger as he remembered: *Hwang Tu Soh is the Chief Philosopher, and though his body is earthly, his mind is in the clouds, it is so superior.*

"And how," the Emperor asked, with impatient patience, "do you advise us to make our money paper of such incomparable uniquity that it cannot be copied?"

"By including in the wood mash, the macerated hearts of all the Royal Writers and their attendant scribes. They are no more wanted, as we know everything that can be known, and have written everything that can be written, including every story that can ever be. And the Royal Historian, after he records today's events, which mark the end of history."

The Emperor expelled a great sigh. This little wizened man had again proved why he'd been the Lord High Chief Philosopher for forty years. Against his brilliance, his forgetfulness was a gnat to a dragon.

The Emperor approved the plan instantly, and the Emperor's Guard escorted what amounted to a quarter of the assembled away, and seized the rest of the required from their chambers in the vast Palace complex.

THE PLAN WAS carried out exactly as advised, but a little more so, because after a little something in his stomach and a little sleep in the afternoon, the Emperor woke gloriously refreshed, and in that state of restfulness and active mind saw almost blindingly, the glow of glorious freedom that the end of history had brought.

No more need for daily Conferrings, for everything was fixed. There would be no more strife, no need to counteract, no more subterfuge, no more thieving of his riches, no more war (which gladdened him because war wearied him), for he'd vanquished all his enemies. There would be no need to refer to history books, or science, or philosophy, no need to read books at all. So the magnificent bindings of the Palace's library could become the stuff of jewellery and furniture, and collars for his menagerie of boars and peacocks and fish. And there would be no more need for advice.

So he issued the Very Last Edict of History, a little after the fact of its End, but in terms of history, only a moment late—a gnat.

His edict improved on the Lord High Chief Philosopher's advice. To the pulp mash used for the Emperor's counterfeit-proof money, the Emperor ordered added: all books and learned works, and all the macerated hearts of all of the advisors in the Imperial Kingdom, including and especially Hwang Tu Soh's—to add incomparable uniquity to the mash and because there was no further need of them.

The bodies of all those whose hearts were used, except one, were donated to the citizens for their pigs to fatten upon. The Lord High Chief Philosopher's bodyflesh was cut into little strips and dried as treats for the Emperor's menagerie, and the long philosophical fingernails were mounted on the end of an ivory stick as the Emperor's backscratcher, for remembrance.

When the macerated pulp contained everything ordered in the Edict, the next parts of the royal command were carried out. The Treasury's Paper Manufactory produced the special paper in one huge, irreproducible batch—making enough paper stock for all the money that the Kingdom would ever need. Then the Treasury's Printery printed all that paper, and sliced in into many thousands of pieces, and with that last task, the pieces became money. Then the workers destroyed all the equipment they had used to produce the money, according to their orders (an afterthought of the Emperor's, not in the Edict), and then (another afterthought) the workers were destroyed by the Emperor's Guard, according to its orders. And then the Emperor handed the Very Last Edict itself to Thunder, his favourite tusked boar, who relished it.

AFTER HISTORY STOPPED, the Emperor could do anything. The Palace was bared of all but his servants and slavegirls and Guard. Because he could do anything, the Emperor watched his peacocks strut and cry, dallied with Thunder, teased his hawks, and fed his carp. He slept whenever he wanted to, which was very much, and he ate with the same abandon. He was delighted not to have to concern himself with the past any more, but even more excellently delighted not to have to concern himself with anything outside the Palace grounds. So, for instance, though he never disbanded the Imperial Army, it wasn't because he thought he might need them. It was because they didn't matter any more, so he just stopped paying them. Whether they knew that history was over was not his concern. They'd learn soon enough and adjust, as he had.

Day followed day, for a week, or maybe as much as two. Exactly how long, the Emperor didn't know, and was relieved not to have to care. All the calendars had been destroyed as unnecessary, and he had never needed to look at the moon. The Empress couldn't tell him. After all, she'd been his most intimate advisor. Regarding the decision to include her in the mash, the Emperor had wavered weakly briefly, but in the moment of wrenching himself free of superstition, he felt old Hwang's spirit of approval warm him as the long fingernails scratched his back.

As for all that new, uncounterfeitable money, the Very Last Edict had decreed that all old money had to be handed in to the Imperial Collectors (some of the Emperor's Guard) and was worthless for trade otherwise, and the Collectors would calculate oldworth and hand out the new notes in return, and anyone caught using old money for any other purpose would be paid in death. That was last part of the Very Last Edict, but after the Emperor visited the Treasury's most important room and saw all the stacks of new notes, pillared from floor to roofbeams, he was loathe to part with this precious wealth, minted at so vast a price. So he commanded his Guard to guard it and not to let any out.

So when the people of the Kingdom handed in their oldworth paper money (as they had once done, their coins), they were handed notes in return, which said, "By Imperial Decree" and nothing more. They looked so official that, since most people could not read, they couldn't tell that there was no value whatsoever to the notes they now owned. But soon enough, within days, the message got around. Your old money is worthless and you won't get any new. Old money was therefore used to cook with and to stuff in mattresses or in draughty cracks. The new money was an egg, traded for a piece of wood, a pig's foot for a cup, a horn for a jug of milk. And for those with nothing to trade, a grumbling belly for an answering grumble from the lips. And the army traded blows and death for anything they could get their hands on.

Since the Emperor's accounts were all on long-term credit, his money lay untouched, its incomparable smell delighting the Imperial Nostrils in his daily visit to his hoard.

One day perhaps three weeks past history, a woman slipped into the army's garrison and asked to see the Commander there. The soldiers who hadn't deserted gave her a knowing leer. She was delicate as a little bird under all that grime. She was, however, escorted to the Commander, more out of amusement than any other reason. He, however, wanted nothing of this whore, till she lifted her filthy hair and pushed the rags of her garment down her back till her shoulderblades were exposed.

Instantly, the Commander threw himself to the ground. This woman bore the Imperial Tattoo. Only the Palace tattooist had those pigments—and his heart had gone into the mash, along with his pigments for good measure. This woman's heart beat strong, and though the Commander had heard she had been slain by Imperial order, His order must have been weaker than Her something in the hand, and vanquished in the expectancy of more to come.

The Commander's prostration was partly the result of the plan he had just been working on, on a scrap of bark on the table top. The Empress glanced at it.

"There is an easier way," she said, her commanding voice belying her delicate form. "You may rise."

AND SO THE garrison, what was left of it, marched, one by one, like a band of thieves, and entered the secret passage that the Empress told them about, and the Commander knocked the special knock on the thick wooden door at the end, and furthermore, said the secret code word and delivered the message of deliverance to the Empress' faithfully bribed retainers—and slew the Emperor's Guard who were all sleeping because the Emperor was, had a merry time with all the slave girls and the cooks, and remembering their allegiance (the Commander was a commander, he knew in his heart—no ruler) marched out of the Palace Gate with the Imperial palanquin and returned with the beggarwhore in style. And in the midst of all this, they of course, slew the Emperor. And also, in the midst of this, though the blood that flowed of the Guards and such was very much and very wet, somehow the Treasury room in which the pillars of money were stored was quite dry. Dry as tinder, which the money resembled as it caught fire, and burned with a unique stench, till all it was, was commonplace ash.

And later that day, the menagerie entertained the Commander and his troops as a magnificent feast.

Thus, like a gong that has been silent but is hit again, that which had stopped, started again, resoundingly. The sounds of it reached the Palace's outer walls and beyond, where the townsfolk had gathered, listening to the sounds within. When the Palace Gate opened enough for a body to be thrown out and then shut, a few brave souls approached. Its heart looked the same as theirs. Although it was naked, they recognized it as the Emperor from the peculiar hair, and the legendary fat. As more townsfolk gathered, peasants who had come in from the countryside joined them, watching as His Imperial Godliness was fought over by two sows.

Crowds formed. The Palace owed them all, and all the soldiers, now inside those gates, were thieves . . . But there weren't as many soldiers as there were townspeople and peasants . . .

And so history, from that point, raced madly, like a horse kicked at the starting gate.

And that state of madness lasted for a while, but how long is unknown. It is said by some, though I cannot prove it, that in the peak of the best time in Chu's history for its pigs and some of its citizens, a warrior army raced down from the north, surprising pigs and citizens alike, slaying as many as the visitors could pack into a few days of unbridled joy. And as this horde lived on horseback and valued no sleep nor stillness, they used their time in the Kingdom to destroy its very trace.

And so, for Ch'u, history ended, as Hwang Tu Soh had declared. And it ended so completely that it is debatable whether it ever began. As for the Lord High Chief Philosopher, his accuracy *was* a little faulty, to be sure, but as he often said, a little time is of little consequence.

—⊕—

King Wolf

CARRETT,

Selwyn Lovelace Wilde "Leary" Passed away at the Sisters of Mercy Nursing Home, Sunday, January 9, 2012.

Aged 98 years young
Gone to God
Got new feet

Dearly beloved husband of the late Rose. Cherished father of Sister Mary Elizabeth, Nigel (dec'd), Maurine (dec'd), Ronald (dec'd), Cyril (dec'd), and of Silvia (nee Carrett) Pennycuik (dec'd). Beloved father-in law of Ethel (dec'd), Maria, and Cyril (dec'd). Loved grandfather and grandfather-in-law of Joan Carrett-Wong and John Wong, and Alexander Carr (ne Carrett) and Simone Dodd. Loved great-grandfather of Jack and Julie, and of Safire, Emrald, Wolf and Lovage.

A Mass Service for SELWYN will be held at the Sisters of Mercy Nursing Home Chapel, 2158 Pacific Highway, Tempe, on Thursday (January 12) at 11AM. On conclusion of the prayers following the Mass, the funeral cortege will proceed to Kurringah Memorial Gardens Crematorium.

Sydney Love & Care Funerals
Sans Souci   **All Suburbs**
9538 9087   **0413 879 733**

Hour after hour the car sped on, the last town with multiple turnoffs being Wollongong. Now the signs were for turnoffs. Old Erowal Bay, Sussex Inlet, Beachside Lots Just Opened. Swan Lake Caravan Park, a surf shop. Signs on the road with nothing to show for them but trees. Yerriyong State Forest, Luncheon Creek Road, Manyana . . .

Crows jumped out of the way of tyres just fast enough to miss being hit, but there were rich pickings—wombats, wallabies, a few rosella parrots caught with their heads down into seeding weeds, and magpies that also picked the kills but weren't as quick as crows.

Now the traffic was erratic, thin, nothing local—car and truck smashing into the slow-spinning clouds of mating flying ants. Windscreen wipers already sticky from acacia fluff worked hard to remove greasy showers. A few cautious drivers turned their night lights on.

Inside the car, air-con stirred the sultry coolness.

"You don't get that report to me by Monday, I'll serve your balls to my dog!"

In the middle of the middle-back seat, Lovage Carr leaned over in her child-restraint seat and whispered to her oldest brother, Safire, "What dog?"

In the back seat, eight-year-old Wolf unbuckled his seatbelt and turned around till he was looking forward, his head between them. "What balls?"

"Tennis balls," said Safire, aiming a punch backwards.

Wolf laughed. "Come on, he muttered. "Tell Lovie about our dog. Dad's such a family man."

Emrald, Safire's twelve-year-old twin, twisted awkwardly against her seatbelt in the cramped space on the other side of Lovage. "Don't."

"What'm *I* doing," Wolf whined. "We shouldn't let her get her hopes up. And besides, you know what Mum has said about dogs carrying hydatids."

"Like what Dad does about kids carrying childhood," Safire snickered. "He's right, Em. They hate dogs. And if she asks one more time . . . "

In the front passenger seat, their mother pulled out an ear bud and a faint tinkle of étude leaked. Then she put her ear bud back in.

They were talking so low that Lovage didn't listen, and anyway she was thinking of the dog. She had been playing with Pobblebonk, pretending he was a frog prince, but dropped him when she heard *dog*. Maybe Daddy was angry at someone who was supposed to deliver a dog to meet her as soon as the whole family got home. And she and the dog—she'd already named him Lion—would go in the back garden where Lion would bend his head so that she could ride him, and then they'd parade in front of the flowers till the blue-headed ones bowed to her, and she'd slide off Lion's back and he'd raise his right paw, and they'd play tennis.

The car speeded up, passing a truck. On both sides of the road, the trees looked like dark smudges.

"Fuckin *fuck* you!" their dad yelled. "I don't care if you've got a tumour the size of a fuckin *stadium*. Monday at nine, complete with charts. And ex the excuses." He slammed his left hand against the steering wheel. "Bastard!" His right clutched his phone, and though no one in the back seats could actually see, they could all imagine his thumb working away.

Lovage started shaking. But maybe he wasn't as angry as he sounded. Sometimes it was hard to tell. He was always so busy that he was 'short' as he sometimes said when he apologised, as sometimes he did after he'd scared her and he and Mum had had a fight.

She clutched her lower lip between her teeth.

Safire unbuckled his seatbelt and turned sideways. He stroked her fine golden hair. Her face crumpled. He leaned out over her. "Em?"

Emrald had been desperately punching the remote control, and finally, the screen lit up.

Narnia!

Mute, but that didn't matter. They all knew every word.

Lovage put her thumb in her mouth. At four, she should have outgrown such habits, but she should also have outgrown wetting her pants.

Safire gave Emrald a thumbs up and slid back to his seat, though his legs were even longer than Emrald's.

"Saffa," said Wolf. "Any chips left?"

"No."

"You selfish pig," Em whispered furiously. She leaned out over Lovie and snatched the bag of Smiths Salt and Vinegar off Safire's lap. He grabbed for them and they both pulled. Only the size of Saffa's feet muffled the shower. But they were such experienced fighters that none of this could be noticed in the front.

Wolf had already soundlessly buckled himself in again. No one else liked facing the road they'd been, but then no one else had an incentive to avoid seeing Narnia. Wolf was not only eight years old but with thick dark thatch and deep dark eyes, looked so much like the selfish little brother that he hoped Lovie would outgrow her fantasies of the four of them being special royals—Kings and Queens only lacking a kingdom waiting to be rescued by them, with him being the slimy, sweet-loving sinner so that they have someone they can nobly forgive.

He'd read the book version to see if it was just as bad. Although the book didn't have any mug shots of him in it, he resented the story so much that he took revenge—and his crime made him feel good and bad at the same time, like going to bed without underwear.

It was a *library* book. He buried it in the sticky orange peels and gritty coffee grounds in the wet-food garbage bin. And the next day he confessed, when she was alone at the counter, to the nice librarian with the nametag that said Ursula. He told her that the book had slipped from his hands into the school toilet. He expected to pay for the book. That didn't worry him, but to be banned from the library . . . But she leaned over the counter, smiled and whispered. "I did the same thing once. Don't you worry. We'll just adjust . . . " And she turned to the screen and tapped a bit.

"There," she said, tossing her bright grey hair. "That copy never existed. But don't go away." She reached under the counter. "I pulled this from the withdrawn books before it could reach the sale table. I've kept it here for you. It'll cost you, though! Twenty cents."

It must have been one of those books that the librarians who don't trust people had kept in the dungeon, saved from the shelves, but then it became just another old book adding to their piles.

On the cover, two dancing birds spread wings edged with feathers that stuck out like long, black-gloved fingers. The base of each wing bore a big lopsided yellow square—like trucks do on their back doors. The book had a strange, never-ending name—Animals and their Colors: Camouflage, Warning Coloration, Courtship and Territorial Display, Mimicry—and it was by Michael and Patricia Fogden. The publisher was Crown, Wolf was happy to note. There were publishers he favoured and others he thought untrustworthy.

He rushed home with it to look up, first, the meaning of yellow. He'd already read that yellow means *Don't eat me!* in frogs, so he supposed that the yellow signs on trucks meant *Don't get close.* But when these birds flash their patches, what could they mean but *Come closer! Admire my beauty!* Wolf had hoped to find out why yellow was his favourite colour, but he never did.

That was six months ago already. He looked down at his T-shirt printed with the kangaroo in the middle of the big yellow road sign and the unnecessary words: Kangaroos Crossing—a Christmas present from Em. He would have liked to wear it on an island with just her. The stupid words annoyed him. And he hated everyone looking at him, saying it suited him. But he didn't want to hurt her feelings.

He always felt even more left out when he saw how much Saffa and Em played along with Lovie, always acting as if they were just putting up with it, not getting any ego trips themselves. "Lovie needs to play Wardrobe," they'd say. So he had to play along, being the bad brother in this cruel world of make-believe that trapped him. He had to play or he'd be branded the selfish brother in real life, the one who made Lovie cry.

And though he didn't want those know-it-alls, Saffa and Em, to know, Lovie's tenderness always broke Wolf's heart. He dreamed of Lovie, of a real big bad wolf slinking up behind her as she walked a trail of yellow bricks. And from out of nowhere, faster than an arrow, more toothy than a shark, he'd come running after that wolf. Just as that wolf that slathered after Lovie was ready to pounce on her, he'd leap. His long claws would slash that wolf's hide down to the bones. That wolf's spit would splat against the bricks on the path as its jaws shattered under his, Wolf's! body, heavy as a load of rocks. And at that moment in Wolf's dream, Lovie would turn around and notice that there was a big bad wolf spatted almost dead, under her brother Wolf, who had saved her. And she'd catch her lower lip in her teeth. And then he always woke up.

Wolf reached into the chest pocket of the stained and smelly jacket his mother called his second skin. He pulled out a book with a waterproof cover, opened it to a stray page, clipped his book light to it and turned the device on. In the grey light of dusk he watched the light unfold like a mutant finger, or god, and point its holy light down to a page. He glanced at it, closed his eyes and mouthed the words. "Treatment for a broken shoulder . . . "

"Would you fucking credit it!"

Alex Carr hit the steering wheel so hard with his left hand that he dislodged his earpiece. It dangled loose over his right ear.

"Would you mind?" Simone removed her earbuds. Piano streamed from her lap. She took off her reading glasses, placed them in the case on her lap, and lowered the screen she'd been looking at.

Her husband stopped in the middle of readjusting his earpiece. He threw up his hands. "You and your Darcy!"

"We've had enough of your histrionics, thank you," Simone said, looking straight ahead, not at his hands waving free of the steering wheel. "I've got work too, may I remind you, and you just juggle team members and money. If you had to place and juggle kids! One day in DOCS and you'd be begging me to trade. Besides, we're time poor and you waste it on what, your sainted grandmother nun you've never met before? This house you say he has, had, in Hunters Hill? No one else turned up except that funeral vulture. I *told* you it wasn't worth the inheritance to drive from Melbourne to Sydney."

He'd been humming to himself, tapping his phone, but stopped. "You wouldn't know worth if it—!"

She turned to him. "I *learned*." And she bowed her head and picked up her glasses case. If she was trying to conceal her smile, she was failing.

"You learned shit!" His earpiece fell onto his lap . "So you read free ancient romances! on a pad I gave you! So you groove to Chopin. How refined! You wouldn't know worth if—"

She picked up the pad. "I learned what someone isn't worth."

He picked up the earpiece and threw it at her pad. It bounced off, falling onto her lap.

She brushed the earpiece off as if it were a spider, and stamped and ground it into the carpet.

He throttled the steering wheel with both hands. His face crimsoned as he drew a ragged breath. Then he stamped on the accelerator and turned the wheel.

With the power of a turbo-charged V8 elephant, the SUV's wheels tore gravel, clipped a drainage ditch and flattened five metres of brush before it hit the tree. The shrieks of metal shear and crunch of glass shatter were smothered by the explosions of four airbags. They puffed out clouds of white powder.

Without the airbag in front of her, Simone would have gone through the windscreen. Instead, her neck snapped. Her head tilted roofwards.

Alex jerked in his seat. "Fuckin airbags!" He leaned toward his wife, but his bucket seat and . . . "Fuckin gear shift!"

He raised his hand to adjust the rear-view mirror, and just then the over-arching bottom limb of the dry and brittle scribblybark tree cracked, tore and fell, punching through the roof above Alex like a fist through paper.

The children's screen hung at a crazy angle—its glass a knife.

Somewhere near, small birds chittered. Maybe they'd been disturbed in their going-to-sleep arrangements. At another time,

Wolf would have loved to explore and explain it all to anyone who might have been interested.

"Guhghhhh," went someone in the front. It was a gurgle, like at the dentist right before you spit. But when this gurgle ended, Wolf sniffed. *Yup. Just as the books say.* His belt already unbuckled, he knelt on his seat, looking forward.

Lovie gasped, then started coughing. He stroked her head. "It's okay," he said. "Hang on a sec." Her scalp was hot and sweaty, and a sweet smell of pee drifted up from her.

He reached out and squeezed what he could of Safire and Emrald—a shoulder and a hunk of hair. Em was scrabbling at her eyes. "Everybody out! Poison."

"It's only baking soda or something," he said, feeling sure he'd read it somewhere.

"Fuh ckin shit," Safire mumbled. He unstrapped Lovie.

She banged her face into his, sobbing convulsively. Her lips wet his ear. "You're making noise. We're not supposed to move."

"It's okay," said Wolf.

She raised her head and stage-whispered, "They're *really* gonna get mad now."

"I'll tell them it wasn't your fault," Em said, pulling Lovie onto her lap.

The doors were locked. They held their breath while Safire positioned himself to kick out the window with both feet.

"No!" Wolf hissed. Behind them, gravel crunched. "Shut up and play dead. Someone's coming!"

Safire sat up. "You nuts?" Lovie squirmed in Em's arms.

"Get us help," Em said through gritted teeth. Above, the heavy limb creaked against the roof. Outside, car doors opened.

Safire carefully turned himself around and knelt on his seat. "Here!" he yelled, waving his arms.

The seat jerked, and Wolf sprang up in front of Safire. From Wolf's open mouth close enough to kiss, a sharp, hot, wordless shriek plunged through Safire, whose body reacted by shooting a blurp into his pants as all the terror that had been lurking in Lovie, emptied from her lungs.

The two people, a nice young German couple touring Australia in the strange continent's summer, took to their heels so fast that she stumbled and fell, and he tore her sundress pulling her up. They drove away as fast as the aging rental van let them get away with.

Em and Safire looked daggers at Wolf.

"Lovie," he said, and pointed to Safire's window. "That's cracked. Bash it out, Saffa. Talk later."

There was something in Wolf's calmness that made his brother drop back and kick the window with both heels. It didn't come straight out. He leant over and opened the eskie on the floor, taking out a tinny of Mother that his dad had packed so that he wouldn't need to be spelled on the thirteen-hour drive home. Safire scraped a circle on the window with the aluminium rim. Then he king-kicked, and heard the glass showering. Then he slithered out the window. Falling onto the broken glass wasn't as bad as the broken brush. One torn twig whipped across his eyelid. He stood and looked to Wolf, who motioned him around to Em's side. She scooted out holding Lovie with some difficulty, but Safire helped, so there were the three of them standing there beside her door. Wolf was nowhere—

"Here!" he called, running out from some bushes a few metres away. "C'mon Em. Saffa. let's get our stuff out of the car."

Safire let Wolf direct. They both carried, but Safire took the heavy stuff. Soon they'd cleaned out the car, including Lovie's old blanket and their mum's and dad's laptops.

Em had settled Lovie on the car blanket and sat beside her. At nine o'clock already, way past Lovie's bedtime. Lovie curled up and stuck her thumb in her mouth. But she wasn't going to go to dreamland yet. She sat up. "Where's Pobblebonk? Pobblebonk is hungry."

"He just ate a grimple," Safire laughed. "It's his bedtime."

"No it isn't."

"Well, tell him a story. He's hungry for a secret." Behind him Wolf was making frantic *Tell him to Shut Up* signs to Emrald, who took the cue.

"Here's a Messenger from Pobblebonk."

"Thank you, fair Queen," said Wolf, who bowed and unfolded a pretend scroll.

"From the far-kingdom of Scrumply Gumps, I bring this letter, to be delivered to the fairest Lovie in the land."

"That's me!" Lovie laughed. Her green eyes gleamed large as a nightbird's.

"We ask her gracious Lovieness if we may entertain Pobblebonk for a . . . it's hard to read this . . . oh! A kwunth."

Lovie took her thumb from her mouth. "What's a kwunth?"

"A scrumble gumpsian month. And they say Pobblebonk loves their fly pies. So yes? Please yes?" Wolf stood on one leg, and fell over.

"Yes!" Lovie shouted. "But only for a grumble gumpskwillion what ever you said month."

Beside her, Em gave Wolf a thumbs up with her right hand and wiped an eye with her left.

"Mr Sleepy awaits you," she said. Lovie curled up against her and within a minute, they could hear the snuffly snore of a child who'd cried without anyone having said, "Now blow your nose."

Wolf never told them, and they didn't ask, but finding Pobblebonk had been one of his first priorities. He'd found a leg of the soft stuffed frog under the front passenger seat, but it was stuck. He pulled, and it squelched into his fingers.

He bit his tongue then, stopping his scream, but not his vomit.

FIRST, WITHOUT ANY discussion, Wolf opened the suitbag, rifled through it and some other bags, and did some bushbashing till he was a ways away. He used a bottle of water from the eskie to wash off, and a splash of his dad's aftershave to deodorise. He used a pair of his dad's socks to dry off, slapping biting flies off his bum and his wet legs. His underpants hadn't leaked, but he dumped his boardshorts anyway, and pulled on his black school / funeral pants. He didn't have any other choice.

The night was as mild as January on the south coast of Australia often is. A light smell of honey from the blossoming hakeas made them seem well disposed to visitors in their kingdom. Wolf and Em talked quietly while they waited, and when they caught the strongest whiff that confirmed their suspicions of why Safire had needed time to himself, Wolf explained that those evil bushes that spelled so good and that had left their marks should be dubbed Your Spininesses.

Em nodded, then shook her head. "If they were human, we could dub them Your Fakeries."

When Safire came back, Em opened the eskie and took out a tinny of Mother. She opened it and they passed it around.

"I won't sleep anyway," said Safire, after he had a gulp.

"Neither will I," Em added, passing it to Wolf.

Wolf raised his lip. "I snuck some of Dad's a year ago. Didn't you know it tastes like shit?"

Safire leaned over and grabbed the can.

"What you want with it?" Wolf demanded.

"I'm just gonna toss it."

"Not in the bush!"

Safire stood to his full height, that of a full-grown man. And he threw with all the graceful force of a practiced athlete. They heard an audible clunk, surprisingly close.

"Fuckin forest!" He knelt and punched his brother hard in the back. They rolled off the blanket, Wolf's teeth in Safire's shoulder.

"You wanna wake her?" Em held up a heavy stick and wagged it. "Okay, Mr Know-it-all. You must have had a reason for screwing up our rescue. Out with it."

"That's all I wanted," mumbled Safire. "An explanation. And it better be good."

SAFIRE RUFFLED WOLF'S hair. "If only she were some little bugger like you."

"He doesn't really mean that," Em said, smiling at Wolf and crooking her eyebrows at Safire.

Wolf smoothed the carpet beside him. "Saffa's right, Em. But even if that were true, we'd still have the problem of us being four."

"Four wards of the State," Em said. "You know the kind of people Mum has bitched about, the foster-business pros."

Saffa sighed. "I tried to ignore her bitching."

"I don't know which she hated more," said Em. "The foster parents or the problem of the kids who need placement."

"Yeah, I guess," said Saffa. "I felt bad for those kids. I think she kinda hated them."

"Not as much as she hated us."

Em said it. Safire had been looking down, but his head snapped up.

"I didn't mean that," Em said. Her mouth hung open.

"Dad too," said Wolf. "We cramped his style."

They were silent long enough that Wolf finally said, "I didn't hear an owl hoot."

Em broke into a short burst of laughter, or sobbing, that ended in hiccups. "On re . . . consid . . . eration," she said. "Mum didn't hate us."

"Not personally," said Wolf.

"She loved the *idea* of children," laughed Safire.

"Which gets us back to Lovie first, said Wolf. "And keeping us four together. It'll be daybreak before we know it."

Saffa punched Wolf lightly. "Friday the thirteenth evening by a spooky outback forest." He whistled (poorly, but no one laughed). "You clinched it, but hell. I would have run from those screams at any time anywhere."

Wolf turned to Em. "You really think this Auntie Joan you talk about might take us?"

"I don't know. I only know that she's his sister and that she married a cardiologist that Dad hated on principle."

"The principle being that the cardiologist helps people to get healthy hearts and Dad bled people dry as a corporate banker because he never had a heart and . . . "

Em held up her hand. "We've already held our Mass for Dad. No sermonising." She turned to Wolf. "They live in London or Manchester or something. And Dad and his sister never got along, so I think that's a dead end. Sorry."

"Besides," said Safire. "We can't take the risk of turning ourselves in. And besides . . . "

"Spit it out," said Em.

"No. Maybe I'm wrong. It happened here, in New South Wales, and that's across the border from Victoria."

Em grabbed him in the back of the neck and squeezed. "Now you're being stupid. Speak up."

"Okay! What if when they find the car, they find out that it's Mum and Dad. So they crashed. But what if they find out that we were in the car too? Sure it's school hols now, but in two weeks it won't be, and even though we moved and we'll all be in new schools, someone's gonna twig sooner or later. And then they'll be onto our parents for why we're not in school, and then they'll link it up with some crash far from home, in the middle of nowhere, on a dark and scary night. Then they find out that our parents were tomato sauced. And flickity flack. They'll have a new motive to find us. Murder!"

"Like, we murdered them?" Wolf rubbed the small of his back.

"So forget I said it."

"No."

"I agree no," said Emrald. "Dad was a bastard and Mum was a—"

Safire held up his hands. "You endethed the sermons!"

"Social worker." Wolf said it straightfaced. They all broke into giggles so loud that Em shushed them and looked to Lovie, who didn't move.

"D'you know where we are?" Wolf asked Em. "Not exactly, but I remember the sign that said Fishermans Paradise. That was a ways back, but I think we might have just passed a dirt road before we . . . "

Wolf lifted his head. "Listen."

Safire and Em closed their eyes. Wolf shivered and reached down the back of his shirt. "Not the bongers. Listen past the insects." He waited while he admired the dull gold iridescence of the Christmas beetle in his hand. Its feet almost hurt, they were so prickly. It was just sitting there doing nothing when it decided to open its wings and fly.

Safire whirled around and punched air. "Fuck off! God, they're spastic. And fuck your quiz."

"I hear it, Wolf. The wind in the trees."

"There's no wind, Em. It's the sea."

Safire punched air. "Holiday houses! I get you."

"Saffa," said Wolf. "I only meant the beach."

"But see, Wolf, if we're lucky, Saffa's right."

"We leave at dawn," announced Safire.

"I'll scout first," said Em.

Safire swung an invisible bat. "Then I'll break and enter. There must be a holiday house we can hole up in."

Em stretched her arms out to them, piling her hands together. "My dear criminal family."

They piled their hands on hers.

"Wait," Wolf whispered. "We've got to vow that we'll never let anyone split us."

"Of course we vow that," Em snapped. "D'you have anything new to add?"

Wolf looked hurt. "Of course I do."

"Sorry."

"That's okay. It's just that we can't take chances. And Lovie is so friendly We can't hide forever and we need to give ourselves new identities, new names. Something Lovie can't stumble on, if she talks to someone."

"A no-brainer for the names," Safire said. "And you're brilliant, little brother. Lovie will love being permanently Lucy. And . . . " he crinkled his eyes. "You should love being Edmund."

"No!"

"C'mon," Safire teased. "Edmund the sleaze, for a good cause."

Em stood up and kicked Safire in the bum. "Enough of that. "It'll be Ed. Okay? And by the way, when and if we all get out of this and land with someone good and kind, of our own choosing, to be family, I vow that we'll rename you, Wolf, King Wolf the Cautious."

"I accept." Wolf seemed partly mollified. "If Saffa is King Boofhead."

"Had you thought of a surname?" Safire asked Wolf.

"As a matter of fact, I had, and Em reminded me. Cosa. It'll be easy for you two to remember, and Lovie never learned more names for herself than Lovage, Lovie and Lucy. So she'll learn this easily."

"Why Cosa?" asked Em.

Safire looked at Wolf with a question in his eyes. "I think I know why. Because it's cosy?"

"Good try, and almost there but not all the way. I was thinking of the family. Our family I'd die before betraying. That's the code of the cosa nostra. I saw it in some movie Dad had on one night. I'm willing to bet that cosa means family, from cosy, just as you said, Saff—er, King. And nostra is *our*."

Wolf was in full flow, his angular face flayed by tree-sieved moonlight. "I'd be willing to bet that when they hunt for us, we'll be called the Car Kids on the news. Nobody'd guess."

Safire punched Wolf's shoulder, in a friendly way.

Em kissed the top of Wolf's head. "You're my favourite Italian crime boss. And by the way, Saffa. Fuckin's dead.

"What you mean, Miss Fox? I know you—"

"That's not what I meant, Saffa. We've buried the fuckin shit with Dad. You're not a younger him. Wolf, it's way past your bedtime."

"Amen," said Wolf.

Em laughed. "It's way past your bedtime, anyway, you little brown-noser."

"You're both too smart for your own good," said Safire. "Now both o' youse. Sleep! I'll take the first watch."

"Okay," said Em. "But you need more sleep, so wake me in two hours."

She lay down, stuffed her backpack under her head, and closed her eyes. Some nearby tree must have been in blossom. Bats were squabbling in the leaves. She wasn't any sleepier than they. "Saffa?"

"Yoh?"

"What you think this funeral thing was all about? And why'd you think Dad made us go when no one had anything to do with him in real life?"

"I dunno, Em. But *I* met him."

Emrald vaulted herself upright. "When?"

"When he was alive."

"I figured that, you idiot."

"When we still lived in Sydney. I must have been about Wolf's age. No, a year younger. It was the day after my seventh birthday, the one when Dad gave me my first pro racquet."

"Well?"

"Well, Dad said that now that I was growing up, he should introduce me to his grandfather. The place was some big stone mansion in a street of them."

"Cool."

"It was pretty weird. It was huge, you could see from the outside, but like, the front hall had a crack in the wall that you could put your hand in. The whole place stunk of tobacco and—"

"What was he like?"

Saffa closed his eyes. "You know our nose? Dad's, mine, and yours? It's his. He must have looked ace when he was our age. But he still was pretty amazing. Sitting there when we arrived, like an emperor. And his hair was grey but there was still lots of it. He had these incredibly bushy eyebrows."

"So what happened?"

"Some chef guy answered the door and let us in, where he sat in the lounge with us while Dad and the old guy talked for a while. Then the chef picked him up and took him up the stairs to his bedroom—"

"A male nurse."

"I guess. So we all went to his bedroom where I had to wait for another long time while Dad and he talked or fought. It was hard to tell. And then we left."

"That was it?"

"Yeah."

"No wonder you never told me."

Safire heard her flop down on the blanket.

He rolled his neck, beginning a stretch routine, remembering . . .

The walls. Covered in paintings with carved gold frames and hundred-year-old grot. But their darkness didn't hide the scenes of naked men and women, some holding cups but all in one humungous gropefest. In the loo, the taps were gold dolphins and the tub stood on lion's feet but standing in the tub was a chrome-frame chair with a blue plastic toilet seat.

The walls of the bedroom were mangy red velvet. Its fur was sticky.

But it was the painting over the bed that Safire had dreamt about ever since that day. On a hill with odd trees like asparagus, a beautiful naked woman writhed on a cross. On her head was a garland of roses, their thorns cutting into her forehead, which streamed with blood. Her hair hung in thick dark ringlets, sprung also from under her arms and between her legs. A crowd of men reached up to her, some touching her feet. All of them looked up to her, their eyes shiny, their lips open, thick and shining with drool. You could only see the top portion of them, but enough to see that they were not all old and some were good-looking, but they were *all* leches.

For years he had nightmares, especially about that hair. But a week ago he had another dream about her—she was a pole dancer with red high heels. And he was in the audience.

He also didn't tell Emrald that halfway through the visit, their great-grandfather of the imperious nose and noble head, took out his teeth. Then his mouth became a terrifying slash or hole And that his clothes were a white shirt and grey(?) pants that St Vinnies wouldn't accept. And his voice was rough and breathy, and he kept pressing a stained scarf embroidered with mermaids to his neck. And that Dad had said to Saffa after they left, that the reason for the scarf wasn't that Great-grandfather was an artist or anything like that, but to cover the hole in his throat.

And he never told anyone that when Dad went downstairs to the loo just before they left, Dad's grandfather told Saffa to come closer. And when Saffa managed to, the old man pressed a little box into his hand and told him to save it till he was grown-up and in the meantime, never show it to anyone. He never did. His pants pocket was too shallow, or the other stuff might have crowded it out. By the time he got to his room at home, he pulled out only a box of Smarties.

A T THE FAR edge of the blanket, Emrald woke and listened to Safire's deep, measured breaths. The cloth jerked under her. Probably, Em thought, he's doing another ab routine from *Men's Fitness*. After what must have been fifty situps, he stopped.

"You asleep?"

"No."

"I'm sorry about your violin."

Em was sorry, too. She missed it already.

"You'll never be able to play violin again, you know."

Em sat up. That hadn't occurred to her. "Why?"

"You're too good at it. You'll be recognised."

He was serious. She grinned at him, not knowing if her face was a black mask. "This is the first time you haven't called it stupid. But what about your tennis?"

"I've always hated it."

That was a surprise, but then he'd been pushed into it from age three.

He stretched out and began counting pushups.

She lay on her back. They had not talked about who they'd find to be family. Who would not only want them, but be able to support them? Most important of all, who could they trust? She discounted type after type—the-more-the-merrier Christoids, friendly paedophiles, men cracking onto her as a babe. She considered hacking into some IVF registry, but dumped the idea when she remembered how so many of those 'successful' parents were like her mother—loving the *idea* of kids.

No one will want us. And we can't trust anyone. She was lost—until *gay guys!*

She knew she'd have to explain it right, or Saffa would dismiss it with *Poofters!* But a nice old middle-age couple of say, 50, would be past their wild sex days. And besides, he could beat them up if they tried. As a stable couple at their age, they'd be smart and able to appreciate Wolf.

The idea grew on her as she thought of the couple. They'd be well off, cultured, so they'd love good music (I could switch to harp). They'd always been cruelly deprived of having a family—a family they'd always yearned for. Now they'd have the whole shebang including a dog (and all gays love dogs). She would of course be able to have them as friends. She smiled to herself as she imagined it all, knowing that the most important quality was in the bag. An old gay couple would have spent more than her lifetime keeping secrets, pretending they were someone else to the outside world.

There was only one problem. Would this beach that she could hear waves pound on, be the kind where old gay guys stroll? That could be a problem. At least it wouldn't be Fishermans Paradise. Gay guys don't fish.

She drifted off to sleep and within the hour, her legs as well as Safire's were splayed anyhow over the hunting ground of countless creatures of the night.

A MONSTER WITH wet lips was eating Wolf from the head down. The monster had Wolf's shoulder in its talons. Wolf opened his mouth to yell for help but could only rasp—

"Wolf!"

Lovie's lips tickled his ear. She'd worked her way into him till she was almost under his body. "Something's coming to eat us."

Not far away someone seemed to be practicing guitar, plucking one string— pobblebonk male frogs competing. That couldn't be it.

She blubbered into his neck. "Shut up," he said, sitting up, irritated and scared.

Something *was* coming. Something heavy, with a slithery tread.

Picking up Lovie as best he could, Wolf stood, trying not to make any noise.

The darkness ahead exploded in branch snapping, leaf rattling flurry. Then a long hiss dropped down to them from one of the trees ahead. He couldn't tell which—when he saw the side of the closest tree change its profile, at about a storey high.

He lowered Lovie—she was too heavy—and pointed. "See that tree? Up there's the big brother of my Mr Lizard."

"Really?"

"Not only really, but you know how much Mr Lizard likes you to give him banana?"

"Oh!" she said. Her whole face transformed. Wolf loved her and hated her so much in that instant, that his breathing stopped. Why was Lovie when she was happy, Happy at a level that he could never hope to reach? Why did she make him want to kill for her? Why, when she didn't even appreciate his love, and when she was going to grow out of being Lovie in when—a year? Two?

She took his hand in his-*to torture me?* Her disgustingly beautiful eyes looked to him with perfect momentary trust. "Do you think his big brother would like banana?"

"He'd love them, Lovie, but not tonight. Now let's go back to sleep."

She surprised him by not becoming a problem, agreeing to settle down next to him on the blanket. But it was a while before he could sleep, and then it was another nightmare—Mr Lizard waiting fruitlessly.

Em woke first, scratching an itch. I smell disgusting was her first thought. Then she opened her eyes. Dawn had come and gone. She was facing Saffa, the zombie till noon. Wolf was also fast asleep, but woke at a touch. In fact, he was the one who really woke them up, as soon as he sat up.

"Where's Lovie?" His stomach felt like it had dropped out onto the ground. That goanna. He hadn't given it a moment's thought, except to admire its mansize length.

No one could move. They were all too panicked. Emrald and Safire couldn't look in each other's eyes, let alone Wolf's.

"Goooood lion. Lion hungry?" Lovie walked into the clearing, holding a little white and black dog. When the dog saw the other three, it trembled against her.

"Shh," said Lovie. "They won't hurt you."

THE JACK RUSSELL refused an orange that the rest of them shared, and lapped as much water as it could from Em's cupped hands while Em held it. The little dog didn't want to leave Lovie's arms, but did allow Em to attach a makeshift leash to the red, dog-tagless collar. Em stroked the trembling body till the little dog licked her hand.

Em turned to the others, her mouth hard. "She's a Christmas dump dog. And she's just had puppies. Could have walked from the Fisherman's Paradise turnoff. She's starving and her teats are sore."

So now they were five.

Wolf called to Lovie, but she ignored him, either playing with Lion or wanting to be cuddled by Em. That was always how it was with her and Em during the day. Then he didn't exist. Only at night when she was afraid.

"I shouldn't have stuck around," he mumbled. "They're never gonna be able to adopt parents now." He pulled his books out of his pack. All from that library. All due a month ago, now technically stolen, since he hadn't turned them in before the family'd moved.

"Ursula would have taken me."

"Who's Ursula?" Em said, sitting next to him.

"Nobody!" He filled his pack again and stood up. "Aren't we going?"

"Going where?" Lovage looked to Wolf's clouded face, and to Emrald.

"Let's get a move on," said Safire, sweeping up child and dog. "I'll carry them."

Lovie squirmed till Em had to catch her, and the dog jumped out of their arms.

Wolf caught the dog's lead, but he didn't need to. It was only waiting to rejoin Lovie.

"No," she cried, sobbing hysterically. "Don't!"

"She's hungry," said Em.

"Don't what?" said Wolf.

"Don't go home. Let's play Wardrobe."

"Why play Wardrobe?"

"We won't get in trouble!"

"She's not making any sense," Safire said.

Em smoothed Lovie's hair. "You wouldn't either, if you were hungry and four. Let's go!"

"No!!!!!" She fought being in Em's arms, which made her sister hold her harder. Her screams must have been heard on the highway.

Wolf touched Lovie's arm. "Hey Lovie, I've got an idea."

Blessedly, the sound stopped.

"Let's never go home again."

The dog stood and peddled against Em's leg, wanting up.

Lovie stared at Wolf. "Never go home again?"

"Never?"

"Not to Daddy?"

"Not to Daddy," said Safire.

Out of Lovie's line-of-sight, Em waved to Safire: *Shut up!*

"You mean Lion can come with us?"

"Of course," said Wolf.

"And you promise Daddy'll never find us?"

"How could he? He's never gone with us before when we played Wardrobe, so how could he now, when we're not playing?"

She considered, and it seemed to make sense to her. But then she remembered something.

"And Saffa and Em would protect us on our travels?" She reached down for the dog. "After all, Lion's just a baby, and there might be a bad queen you leave us for."

"He wouldn't do that," said Em.

"Shut up," said Wolf. "Saffa and Em would protect us, Lovie, and look how much Lion already loves you."

He nodded to Saffa who held out his hands to Lovie with *I'll take it from here* assurance.

Wolf knelt and rummaged in his pack, hiding his tears. He felt stabbed in the heart.

"I could find us another daddy," Lovage said to Safire. "I nice old man in a bathrobe."

"Brilliant," he mumbled. "A flasher." But he was shaking his head and grinning at Em, who hadn't heard.

She was watching Wolf. *Sometimes!* thought Em, I wonder if Lovie even *has* a heart.

Gladiolus Exposed

The weekend at Thoreau's Retreat was Katie's idea. Wilder Benn & Ho had just picked up the account. She was elaborately casual when she pitched this togetherness jaunt to me. It's free, she said, and it might be "sorta fun in a perverted way." "I'm perverted," I laughed.

The ads for Thoreau's Retreat offer a Revive the Mood "Two nights' accommodation for two. Complimentary nonalcoholic Vermont-grown champagne, resident sensei on call 24/7. Complimentary pocket guides to Vermont wildlife, use of Zeiss Conquest binoculars so you can spot, without disturbing, our natural wonders such as the Great Spangled Fritillary Butterfly and the rare Stinkpot Turtle; and a host of surprises."

Thoreau's Resort is conveniently close to Killington, a fact left out of the literature. After Killington, Katie talked a bit as I drove. *What stinks? the promotionals? ads? Thoreau's Retreat?* I didn't answer, as that would have been interrupting.

I had my own theory about that come-on Thoreau quote next to the rates in the brochure—"*Why should we be in such desperate haste to succeed?*" —but I kept my thoughts to myself. Katie does not appreciate comments from people who don't know anything, unless they are in a focus group.

As soon as we arrived, there was a clash of shoe wear. Katie's calves won't tolerate flats, and her feet are naturally pointed. The looks I got were worse than those directed at her, as if I'd bound her into those high heels. I like them, but my taste is only a coincidence. She ignored the scorn but lost her above-all-this composure when the unpaved grounds sucked down her stilettos. The Revive the Mood Special didn't come with complimentary Dr. Zen shoes.

As to the romantic atmosphere supplied by the sight of other guests, I had forgotten how much even people of wealth, can, left au natural, age to resemble black-and-white films. The gray-and-white, ultra-wrinkled couple checking in before us offended me. "What's your excuse?" I wanted to yell, but because of Katie, I behaved myself.

We had to walk from the carpark through the commons to our cabin, which welcomed us with a rag rug, two rocking chairs, art over the bed in the shape of the largest picture I've ever seen of an asparagus spear, tastefully shot, captioned in faux nineteenth-century handwriting, "THINGS DO NOT CHANGE. WE CHANGE."—HENRY DAVID THOREAU; and the pièce de résistance of surprises: a jar of Metamucil cookies. The bathroom romanced us with a toilet, douche, stand-up shower, Japanese-style straight-sided cube of a tub, and a notice about the evils of laundering. The toilet had no paper seal to break. I dreaded the bed, but it was the saving grace of the place. Katie flopped on it with a historical romance, grimly determined to last out the weekend, but no way wanting to compromise herself by experiencing more than she had to. Lucky for her, she didn't have to dread the resort's idea of food. It was no worse than her usual. I drove to Killington, where I got a pizza made by someone who thinks that ketchup is Italian. By the time I got back, Katie had found out that Thoreau's Resort offers no decadent room service, so she was waiting for me to lead her on another expedition over the grass to the "Commons Lodge," her heels aerating the soil, me helping to pull her free at each step. I sat with her in the restaurant while she ate. Despite and because of her condition, she stuffed herself full of celery-root *au jus*.

I won't tell you what Thoreau's Retreat offers in the way of small-screen adult entertainment. For once, I went to bed before ten o'clock. Katie was asleep before eight. Horrorville it was, but two days without decent food wouldn't kill me, and the weekend was a good idea. I felt a twinge of nostalgia for a time when I considered walking in the mountains to be exercise. Now, a break for forty-eight hours was good for me, as it was so rare; and we needed to have time together enforced upon us, otherwise it never seemed to happen.

THE NEXT MORNING at dawn (the quiet woke me) I was taking the mountain air, perfuming it with a contraband Cohiba while I picked wildflowers for my pregnant wife, when a sparkle of dew caught my eye, and I noticed the gladiolus—not some flopsy yellow common garden flower, but a *gladiolus*, commonly called the "body" of the three-part bone. The sternum or "breastbone" as it is commonly known. I laid it on my hand and it looked as if the bone were formed for me: exactly the length of my wrist crease to the tip of my middle finger.

Bones, like the salt-and-pepper granite stones in Vermont, rise to the surface of fields each spring when the ground thaws. Sunlight glinted in the sharply defined facet for the third costal cartilage. The convex curve of the lateral border of the gladiolus faced the sky, two facets rising free of the earth.

My mouth flooded with cigar juice as my fingers nosed the ground all round what I estimated to be the dimensions of the whole sternum. Then as delicately as I could, I dug with the tips of my fingers in the sodden but surprisingly hard ground—under the gladiolus, that broad blade of middle section, till it looked like a bridge over a valley. A fist-sized rock had to be pried from the sticky soil before I could get to the manubrium. (The articular surface for the clavicle emerged, surprisingly for such dense bone, as a complex splinter surrounded by dark clumps of soil salted with frustratingly bonelike pieces of quartz.) The knees of my weekend chinos were so stained by this time that they would have made a homeless person blush. My fingertips felt abused, my nails looked disgraceful, and my back was sending urgent messages to my brain. Time was passing, though, so in a spirit of no rest for the wicked, I tackled the other end of the bone, the delicate xiphoid process . . . and spat a cigar stub that looked like a wad of cud when I pulled just wrong and snapped the delicate filliped point.

From my first sight of that tiny pool of dew in the bone facet, I knew this to be, not the normal bones that pop out in thaws:

cattle, sheep and deer. That glimmering facet made my heart race. A human breastbone is unmistakable, and anatomy was my favorite subject in med school, however much I love urology. I knew as soon as the gladiolus was exposed in all its length that it had belonged to either a small adult male or a female about the size of Katie.

What finally lay on the palm of my hand—stretching from my wrist crease to the top of my middle finger—was the breastbone itself, the sternum. The body of it was a perfect gladiolus, but both ends of the sternum were damaged—the superior end intriguing as hell; the inferior, a blunt accusation.

Ever since scaring myself as a kid with stories I read by flashlight, I've fantasized about finding someone, and here a someone was. Odd to find this, but then I suppose in real life, it isn't skulls that people "find," but bones that the average person would never know were human. How many people in, say, Brattleboro, let alone Killington or Thoreau's Retreat, would know a human bone from wildlife? I felt a frisson at the thought of finding this before it was stepped on by an ignorant hiker. Chakra charts don't teach diddly about bones.

I dug till my fingers said they'd sue me, and then I had to leave. With no tools, I couldn't dig deep, nor far. I found no other bones, though I expected to find at least the tip of a rib. And I had hoped to find an answer to the mystery of the shattered manubrium, one of the toughest bones to fracture in the human body. I held my breath when I found a bit of metal. A bullet . . . But once I cleaned it with spit, the bit was only a pebble that I had mistaken for something important because it was time to go. Although I was in sight of the resort, the actual site was featureless, so I pushed the dirt back into the hole I'd made so it would all look like a marmot or somesuch's rooting around for food, and I hid my Piaget under the fist-size stone that I planted in the middle of the site.

In the five-minute walk down to our cabin, I remembered the flowers, but it was too late to pick new ones. Instead I swept into the Commons Room and spotted a crystal bowl of crocuses. Perfect, so I took it. If you know what you're doing and don't explain, you can do anything.

Katie was conveniently asleep when I got back. I placed the bowl by the bed and went to our bathroom where I wish my dentist could have seen how gentle and effective a cleaning can be. I used my toothbrush and Katie's whitening toothpaste.

Job completed, the manubrium was intellectually appealing, though aesthetically flawed. I couldn't look at the xiphoid process because it annoyed me. But the gladiolus was simply beautiful. I dried the sternum on my towel, rolled it in my clean shirt, and packed it in my suitcase while Katie snored—and I remembered to change my slacks just before she woke, just in time for brunch.

She didn't object when I said that we needed to leave by two o'clock. I said that I had forgotten about a case I had to check on at Mt. Sinai, but I really wanted to get home because being so close to the bone site frustrated me. I needed equipment better than my fingers and some Thoreau's Retreat Commons Room spoon. And I didn't want to have to think, on my next dig, whether Katie would be awake.

Monday morning I was back at the clinic, and she was back at the agency. She rang me at eleven o'clock.

"Tell me all you know about incontinence pads." The first time she'd ever shown an interest.

A TYPICAL MONTH—WE didn't see much of each other, and there was no way I could get right back to the site. First, I had a rushed week, then it was off to England, to Freeman Hospital Newcastle Upon Tyne, where Haslam's **"Imaging in Loin Pain Best Practice" would have had me seeking him out during coffee at another time, and David Tolley's** Stuart Lecture, "The Changing Face of Urology—Are We Prepared?" was not obvious. As to my own paper, the topic of urological forensics is a well without end of fascination; but I wished yet again, as I presented my findings, that Katie's verve were mine when it comes to communication.

But I had to get back to Vermont. Katie was by this time obsessed by Etheria (latest focus-group fave name, Katie said). She wanted me on tap, but not at hand.

Finally, I left work at seven pm one Friday, in a rented Land Rover. I slept somewhere as downmarket as Vermont goes, where I was unlikely to meet a bottle of anything de-alcoholed. Before dawn, I set out with the gear that I bought along the way: a collapsible shovel and a metal detector.

Not being a Daniel Boone sort, I had thought I would never find the place again without the metal detector, but I knew it even in the moon-distorted light, and through the haze of pain I felt when I twisted my ankle between two rocks while I focused not down, but ahead. *Approaching . . . almost . . . there.* Logically, I should have known that I would recognize the spot, considering the number of times I had dreamed the find over the past weeks.

I didn't expect my watch to be as ruined as it looked, but I'd already claimed it on insurance.

When I began to dig, the only sounds I heard were owl calls.

By the time I had dug a hole big enough to bury a Yeti, the garbage truck was hoeing down its breakfast in Thoreauland.

I found nothing but bittersweet-chocolate-colored dirt and enough quartz pebbles to light Hansel and Gretel's walk to the wicked witch of Mars. I unearthed nothing else. No ribs, vertebrae, skull, no bullet, bit of iron, wooden cosh—no implement or agent of death; and not even a sliver of shattered bone.

Yet even the telltale heart had an explanation.

I HADN'T TOLD Katie about the bone before, and didn't plan to tell her. She is conventional about things like insurance and laws, and she would have expected me to alert someone. *I don't know. The authorities*, she would have said.

And then I would have given up the precious thing for no reason, and it would be officiously boxed and lost, buried where no thaw would ever expose it.

A couple of weeks passed, busy as ever for both of us, but one Friday we were both able to knock off work by six for a little romantic dinner at a place I thought she'd like.

"Feel like going back to Thoreau's Retreat?" I asked.

"As paying guests?"

"I guess so," I said. I abhor wasting money. "What's wrong? They too cheap to give you another weekend for research?"

"We lost the account."

"Oh," I said. I knew she'd feel bad about it, so I changed the subject. "What happened to Etherea?"

"Etherea?" Her fork split an asparagus spear down the middle. Her brow would have creased if it could have, as she separated a sliver of cheese from the vegetable as carefully as if she were boning a fish.

I couldn't watch her eat. I hoped the baby wouldn't come out looking like it had spent its time in her dieting for life.

"The incontinence pads," I said.

She dropped her fork and knife on the white expanse of plate. "Do you have to do that?"

At that point in our relationship, our chemical attraction was something we could remember, but she didn't choose to and she made it hard for me to put that attraction above the way she feels about my work, conveniently forgetting how we met. *Why is what I do, of the two of us, the unmentionable?*

She was at five months then, and a couple weeks later, suffered a miscarriage. I'm not surprised, but she was. It was incredibly tough. She'd planned for that baby. We both had. All the emotional capital she'd sunk into it. We almost split up after that but were so busy, it was easier not to.

In that post-expecting period of adjustment we made time to make some resolutions together.

1. We would try to rediscover each other again;

2. She would try not to be patronizing about my work, and

2a. I would quit smoking the cigars that she said she smelled on my breath.

DURING THE NEXT stage in our relationship, Katie and I stayed home in the evenings and watched movies together. I found the gladiolus invaluable as an aid. I used to sit with it. The facets for the third, fourth, and fifth costal cartilages fit my fingers so perfectly, the gladiolus felt like part of an intimate garment. As I touched the hand-warmed bone, I imagined what had happened. All sorts of lives and deaths danced as the movies played. Greta Garbo and Robert Taylor Camilled in black and white, to the happy tears of Katie while I fondled the bone. *The English Patient*, something that would previously have had me crawling the walls or snoring in relief, played all the way through while I dreamed with my eyes open, sternum in hand. *Thelma and Louise* drove cross-country while the bone submerged itself in flesh, grew attachments, developed a life and personality, found an accident waiting to happen, or a murderer. Katie could put anything on, even *Fried Green Tomatoes*, and I sat through it, rapt.

But she found a new annoyance to complain about.

"Where'd you get that hideous bone?"

I'd already planned what I would say if she asked. "An anatomy kit."

"Can't you use a rubber ball?"

I said I liked the bone. It reminded me of med school.

She came home one day with a squeezy in the supposed shape of a brain, a stupid promotional that I can't imagine why she thought I hadn't seen. It insulted me as much as if I had proposed a name for that disposable urinary collection device that she of all people had as an account.

She began to work late again and through the weekend, and so did I.

We rarely met, but when I was in her presence, I found that touching the bone soothed me. I could tolerate her presence.

One evening while she was watching, a few drops from my glass of water fell on the bone, magnifying a section. When I wiped it dry, light fell upon it in just such a way that I noticed something I hadn't seen before, but I wasn't sure of what I saw. The next day I was able to confirm. The anterior surface of the gladiolus was shallowly adorned with the faintest and finest of carvings—a Victorian monogram, scrolling frills, the finest of lines. Only five millimeters in diameter, I couldn't make out the letters under any power of magnification because they were both too fanciful and too patchy; but I think there were three (and one of them was an *L* or a *J*) surrounded by a garland of flowers (forget-me-nots?). I cursed the cleaning I had done, so harsh I almost missed this.

The mystery of no other bones was now partly solved, though new mysteries leapt into my mind with the swiftness of bandits leaping upon a lonely Victorian coach.

The monogram could only have been carved by an expert, I am sure. A skilled engraver. This confirmed some theories I had wanted to firm up.

Now, the more I felt along the gladiolus, the more I knew that its size was exactly Katie's. I hadn't thought of her sexually for some time, but now I was drawn to the wide space between her breasts. Her aversion to fat revealed far more of her now than when we met. The attachments of the muscles of her third costal cartilage were so visible that in some lights, they were shadowed as if they had no epidermal cover. She loved her muscles showing, so I could gaze there (when we were together) to my heart's content (and imagine it at other times). When she was in the mood, as she sometimes still was, I could run my fingertips along her flesh. At those times, we were more powerfully aligned than ever before. I imagined her gladiolus, undressed and gleaming, curving seductively from damp earth . . .

I wasn't obsessed or anything. The bone stayed home. Too risky to carry with me—nosy security, luggage loss, the off chance that I'd leave it in my hotel bed during some red-eye packing rush. Anyway, during a conference, I thought about the paper I'd deliver, and then about how I was. When I got home, sometimes Katie was home, too. But always, the bone was there to greet me.

One night I came home about five am from a conference in Vienna. Katie was in bed. Vienna had been bad. I'd had twenty-two hours to think about how boring I was, how I wished that Katie could sell my ideas. I undressed and got into my side, reaching for the bone on my night table, but my table was bare. It took me shining her light in her face to wake her up.

I had to ask three times before she woke sufficiently to understand. "Sorry, the cleaner threw it out," she said. She flicked off her light and pulled the sheet over her head.

I can't express sufficiently, how *bad* I felt. *Bereaved.* Breathless. Heartsick. I moved my pillow so I could see better. I needed to wake Katie up enough to make love. I looked down at the shape of her face under the sheet. She was very still.

Too still to be asleep.

Cleaner, my ass! She was holding her breath, the bitch. As Poe said, "Years of love have been forgot, in the hatred of a minute."

Adventures of Discovering the Ellemehnopee

(a true story)

He came first once, then twice a week, exactly at 7:30 pm, in a clean torn shirt topped by a gnarled sweater, his smile eager and shy, his hair still wet from the bath. He always came bearing gifts. A box of apples, their skins still covered with the cataract of bloom, a bag of grapefruit smelling like tonic water and stink bugs, some flame-red persimmons, always picked that day.

His ringed notebook was clutched in an armpit, filled with his former and latest assignments. At first I asked him whether he wanted a mug of tea when he arrived, but I soon stopped because it would sit getting cold, and then he would drink it all at once because I had made it.

He knew how to sign his name, but could not read the letters, so we started with the alphabet. Starting with A, B, C. In printed form, both capitals and lower case, in four alphabets. Century Schoolbook because of its nostalgia to me, but the practical reason is that it's a good serif font for reading any of these complicated squiggles and other impertinences that were part of all letters before type artists knocked the little hooks and noodles off to become the simplified, increasingly used, but harder to read *sans serif*— William's second alphabet to learn. I chose Gill Sans, a late 1920's font originally based on Edward Johnston's alphabet for the London Underground, but which seduces me with its uniquely elegant and legible proportions. Besides the pleasure of looking at it, I chose this second alphabet because of its resemblance to his third alphabet, the one that his hand had to form by printing. The fourth, of course, was cursive, and he was surprisingly eager to master it, the form he picked out to learn being a classic, 45 degree angled copybook style, generously looped, somewhat fancifully capped.

The alphabet, though, presented the first problem. In order to remember the letters and their peculiar order—why, for instance, are not the sounds grouped—I chose to teach it as a mnemonic. There was only one that I know, and I hesitated, then told him honestly that it was the first long song that I memorized, and I still say it in my head to be able to use that book of mystery and magic, the dictionary.

So we sang it together, and to my delight, he felt the delight that I do in this simple learning aid. He thrilled at the plot. The deliberateness as it begins its march, only to stop abruptly at G. I could feel his sense of suspense. Then we set out again, only to stop again poised but breathless after P. Then with the same sure tread as when set off on our expedition, we approached the end of our journey, which always sounded like a thud of a let-down to me, but didn't to him, because I grew up with the reward of rhyme at the Zee, but here in Australia, Zee is Zed, which doesn't work. Not to me, but to him, it worked "a treat", as he would say. Because it meant that he had seen all the letters and remembered them.

I thought that being a song, it would be easier for him to remember each letter, but I was pleased that he also felt additional pleasure from the arrangements of sounds they make, and the relationships of the letters to each other rather than just abstract symbols in sight and sound. I never discussed it with him, but could see from his joy that he also felt something about the exoticness of it, especially when we came to the part of our journey where we meet what I always have thought of as the rare spotted forest-dweller, the ellemehnopee.

Once he learned what the letters were, we began to practice the sounds they make. I could not find any books suitable, but could remember my mother teaching me how to read after school when I was in the first grade. Sight reading was just coming in, and my mother wanted her children to know how to read, so she ordered some books and taught us by herself.

The diphthongs and paired letters were the key to it. And they are what I started with. I made a large card deck—cards with single letters and cards with combinations of two, three, and four letters.

We started out playing cards. CAT. HAT. CH + A + T. That sort of thing. For it wasn't as if we could have started out with ONE, TWO, THREE. Besides, with his rather old-fashioned Australian dialect (in which cockney plays a large part), "one, two, three" comes out as "one, two, free," which meant that both the "th" and the "f" were building blocks that we stumbled on, though not pyramid-sized.

He also had the problem of "d" and "b", "p" and q".

But they were not insurmountable either. Far from it.

Because this man, a very successful farmer, had left school early because the forest was so much more interesting. I only found out about his illiteracy in a slip-of-the-tongue by his wife, saying something about him wishing that he could read so he could enjoy what I so clearly enjoy. So I offered to try, for it would be a joy for both, and so we began our lessons. He knew words in the way that children learn words now in too many places in the English speaking world—as specific words, by sight.

Soon after William and I began our hopeful experiment, I began tutoring an 11-year-old boy who was unhappy that he couldn't read. I saw his plea in the local paper, and in my naïve enthusiasm, I was eager to help. He had passed every grade, indeed, got average grades at school. When he came for his first lesson, I gave him a children's book about lizards, so I could hear where he had problems. He looked at it and me. He did not know the alphabet. He was not able to read *Cat in the Hat*. His parents wanted to help but didn't know how this could have happened. I asked to see his report card, and he brought it to me. It explained the problem. Such a good boy. No trouble at all, So quiet. His reading was "good". The comments were written in a semi-literate hand, and the spelling would not have passed any test, except a school system's like this one. I visited the local schools' office and asked what their policy was. Pass everyone. Failing makes children feel bad.

Because Luke had such immediate problems, we scheduled several sessions a week. Easy for him because the teachers have so many days off for preparation, and then there are so many days that the children are out of the classroom doing some sort of visit somewhere, like the park in town or somewhere baby-sitting-on-the-move from the attitude of the teachers; and then there are so many breaks for holidays, he always seemed to be on holiday. His parents said that it didn't matter if he went to school or not. He didn't learn anything. He did know some words. He'd say, "I know that word. We learned that word." But it was like a drizzle of memorized hieroglyphs, with no logic to connect them.

I tried to make it as much fun as possible, and he tried to concentrate as well as he could for a normal boy of eleven with so many fun animals outdoors, and the sun on the paddocks. Sometimes we adjourned to the outdoors and did lessons there, with him spelling out loud and building words in his head, and saying them out loud. He especially took to rhyme, which suited me down to the ground.

Luke was a charming boy, not at all dim-witted as his parents and he were wondering about. We would have gotten somewhere beyond, yes, the mastery of *Cat and the Hat*, except for natural inclination and pity and laziness. His mother felt sorry for him, and didn't believe me when I said that he had to do the homework I made for him each lesson and settle down for an hour every night, or it would never sink in. The bicycle came out as soon as he came home, and then, at each lesson, we would almost have to start all over again. It reminded me of taking Rosie to her school once a week, and us both rolling our eyes at the other people who were still saying "Sit. Sit. Seeyiiit!" month after month forever.

Finally, I told the parents that if he did not do the homework during the week, I could not put in the enormous effort it was to craft these lessons specially for his interests. His homework, by the way, was with the deck of cards I made for him, in which you got points for making the words and building from them to make new ones, like in Scrabble, so more than one could play. They also now had Junior Scrabble itself, and there were simple rhyming and sentence construction exercises in addition. But the bike was more fun, the mother not wanting to be hard on her child, the father at work, trying hard not to be laid off because of an ailing back. So Mrs. ended the lessons by telling Luke that I "didn't like him any more." I only found this out later, after the family split up. What Luke is doing now, I don't know. But he has been cheated in life, for what boy does want to work, especially when he's come home from school, in those crucial years that he is cooped up in "school" and the school gives him an education not worth a splat of birdshit?

William was different. He was exhausting. He did two hours at night every night, minimum, for the pleasure of it. Because he had never known how to read, and always had to hide it, he remembered EVERYTHING. He didn't need silly mnemonics because he had never had the luxury of anyone teaching him elegant little sayings to help him remember. His memory was built from sheer willpower, then the ability that comes from the practice of flexing the muscle of memory. By the time he came to me, he was a truly exceptional man, with no knowledge of his exceptionality, other than that of being an illiterate—and painfully shy and insecure because of it. He soaked up my lessons, both written and spoken, so well that I had to become extremely pedantic in making absolutely sure of every tiny point that was said to him. I had to LEARN like crazy. He forced me to think, and then to think again, such as no teacher had ever forced me before. His mind picked up exceptions to rules like rose thorns find tender skin.

He adored diphthongs. He thrilled to their different personalities. He was awed by the concept of silent letters. He was amazed by the illogic, or secret codeness of having a word with a whole lot of silent letters huddled together in it.

He loved watching the action of the ink coming out on the paper. And he used black ink. Pencils were below him. He would write a whole page perfectly, and if it had a mistake, he would write it all again, correctly. When we got to sentences, he felt masterful at being able to punctuate them exactly, to put the comma in where it belongs. To indent for a new paragraph. To think about what constitutes a sentence, a phrase, a paragraph, an argument itself. The logic of thought unfolded in his mind as he played with the building blocks of language itself. It wasn't as if he could not think before. But seeing words on paper and knowing what they meant opened up a feeling that then he could explore new thoughts, whole books, something that he had always wanted to do.

We began to use the dictionary, and he found intense joy in first, figuring out how to find the word, and then, seeing the definition. We even went through the symbols for pronunciation, because he hated not knowing what they meant, and when he knew, he always liked to pronounce the word as the suggestions said, sometimes surprising suggestions.

He bought his own dictionary, and told me that he enjoyed spending an evening with it, reading.

We read out loud, and with his mild dyslexia, and his eagerness to please, he had a tendency to run ahead of himself. I had to say, "Slow down. Read that again . . . See. Now you are reading it right. It says 'Not to be used within sixty days.' Not 'To be used within sixty days.' " Because, of course, we were not reading *Dick and Jane play with Spot*. We were reading poison pamphlets.

For "graduation" he wrote a letter (his handwriting, his composition) to the Mayor, about something that needed to be done in the region. The mayor wrote back immediately, saying that he had been unaware about this issue till this very informative letter, and so the Council had been directed to fix the problem immediately. And the Mayor was telling the truth. He did get onto it immediately and pulled his weight to make sure the Council workers did, too. To my gobstopped surprise, that was the quickest and most successful political request and action taken that I have ever seen. William just thought that that was the treatment us letter-writers are used to.

As for William, another family, another culture. Less beautiful nature outside the jail-of-a-schoolhouse doors, and who knows? Thinking of today's many-lettered elite, William, with his innate abilities, would have had no problems being their peer. But as for them being his peer, I would rate them to him as a red delicious apple is to an honest, crisp, flattened ball of an apple, netted with the rusty veins that only those in the know, mean the mark of the truly delicious: the russetting. The mark that makes your average person throw the apple away.

THE ALPHABET UNCOVERED IN ITS HABITS

At fifty-five, this farmer, grizzle-haired
with eyes pale soup from too many skies
met and discovered the alphabet
and it wrapped its letters around his head
the H and P and O and T
and all the others in their riotous abandon.

Wild they were with their own associations
and he gawped upon, uncovered at last
the marriage of the G and H and the quick
divorce with no hard words, then new
flirtations with other lovers for just a moment
G and U and H and T and then, more fluid
matings! Couplings airy in their flightiness
amoral in their joyousness. Laconic in their
messageness. The bible and a poison pamphlet
same U and G and H and T and just as many
liaisons, even though the one says thee.

His filmy eyes, with their magnifying specs
watched and learned, and memorized the varied
combinations, till he smiled when he saw the T and H
together, and the O and U meant that G and H could make
a foursome, and the nonconformist letters and the nonconformist words? Stolid dogma helped him to remember,
like a prayer and a marriage and the shapes that made
his name, the name of fifteen letters, that at fifty-six
he learned.

And now he's fifty-eight and so
his story ends as pear trees grow
when left alone —
without an end.
For him, the letters, to the scarcely seen,
are not cold tools, or means to read
that book. Communication only? No!
Yes: living, leaping, singing, naked friends.

His thinking, ex-espaliered, spreads now
branching, budding, blooming to the yet unread
of lichen-covered borer-riven dogmas down below
as he, the farmer, reaches to prune his fruit trees,
diphthongs, word song buzzing in his head.

Pococurante

The whole town sucked in such a big breath, a fly would of clutched its throat gasping. Would Pococurante raise a sweat to stay alive? We waved flies away with more effort. Yet at a flick of his wrist, grown men ducked. Dad said a word he shouldn't of in mixed company, but nobody cared.

Astride the town's great river red gum on that blazing day in February, Pococurante didn't defy death. He humiliated it.

When finally he landed head up, feet exploding dust, I cheered like I never did before, nor since. Dad made strange sounds like rain hitting dry ground. He was *crying!* And he wasn't alone.

Smooth as a cold beer, Pococurante passed through the crowd and down the street, the gold letters on his shirt-back slithering.

The next morning I asked Dad, "What's Pococurante mean?"

He must of been thinking for breakfast, because he answered right off. "The god of thunder, I reckon."

That made sense to me. Before Pococurante, a bullock whip was just a bullock whip.

As for the circus, I forget its name, but it was a mangy thing. It didn't have a tent so it wasn't any more than a man who rode a horse with his head in the saddle and his feet in the air. We could do that before we were six. And a woman with a beard and hairy arms, and a clown who was only funny when he pulled the red nose off his face to sneeze, and a lion who wanted to sleep and a lion tamer who doubled as the fancy-talk introducer, and Pococurante.

As for the town, it was mangy, too. One of those unloved border towns that straddle two states, where the people on both sides think life on the other side is better but it isn't, and before you notice, everybody's slipped away including you, feeling guilty but bloody relieved, like how you leave a funeral.

As for Pococurante, I had a theory I carried around inside me till I saw my first action in war. I did think, you see, till I really shouldn't of, that this Pococurante *was* some sort of god. That my dad had nailed him good, but at the same time missed. My dad, you see, thought Pococurante had named himself in imitation of. But Mrs Fletcher at school said there weren't any gods named Pococurante, and she reeled off all the ones there were. Plain God, who we knew. And to some, his son, so that took care of two. And Zeus and Mars and Pluto the dog-god and Neptune with his hayfork, and Tor the blond, and some more that I can't remember, but Pococurante? No.

Pococurante, I'd say each night. I knew he wouldn't like frilly stuff, so I talked to him straight. *Be a sport*, I'd say, all under my breath. *Toss me some of your bravery. You've got bags of it to spare. Make my face as still as yours. You can do it, but I can't on my own.* I certainly couldn't. *Make me look like I don't give a cuss what people think, like you. Tell me what you want from me and I'll do it. Anything.* He never answered directly, but he was the last god on earth I'd of expected to answer anyone like me.

Before Pococurante, if you'd of said that anyone in my town would ape a man with an embroidered shirt, spit your teeth goodbye. I imitated his walk, which is funny looking back on it. But every boy did and many men, so it wasn't funny with everybody and his dog doing it. And even though two boys killed themselves trying to be Pococurante, no-one wished otherwise any more than they wished that the good years didn't come because of the bad. But there was a limit. When Ridgy Bray was heard whistling *Nobody Cares for Me*, he was given a friendly punch-up for putting on airs. I thought it was sacrilegious.

One day when a kick in the stockyard punched my kneecap so my leg folded front to back, I bit a hunk off my lower lip rather than scream. *Pococurante!* He gave me the strength to be a man, but he was as mysterious as weather.

And then I went to war and saw another Pococurante, and another. I saw four by the war's end. I felt shy around them. Lots of men did.

But to Pococurante. He'd gone to that war my dad did. Dad never talked about his war. But when I saw Pococurante's face again on other men, and I saw that walk—all that I copied but knew was never me—I knew then, the original wasn't a god, but what a man could be.

When the war ended, I asked one of the Pococurantes to be my business partner—the one who saved my life. I thought I'd have to beg him, but he said okay. Just "Okay."

I was so taken aback, I couldn't answer back, but he didn't seem to need that. I was honoured that he thought me good enough.

He didn't have any plans so I made up plans for us both.

WE OPENED A dry cleaning shop in Adelaide. I named the dry-cleaners *Pococurante*, after he said he didn't care what it was called. It had a classy ring to it, the young girl at the business registry said.

"About time we had some tone here," she declared. "Adelaide's such a sleepy place."

I didn't know what she was talking about so I shut up. My partner leant over the counter and looked at her, and I thought she'd die right there.

"Poco," she said. "Little! and cur-ahhn-tay."

She clicked her fingers and cocked her head. "Greased lightnin! pronto, current, see? I might work here but . . . say!" she said to my partner (I was a flyspeck on the wall). "You haven't by chance, seen the film at the Odeon?"

"Yar," he said, giving her a ghost of a smile.

So *Pococurante* the window said, in swirly gold script, close but not quite the same as I remembered.

IT WASN'T AS if my partner didn't work. He did. But the business didn't thrive. He was so attractive that the counter got mobbed, but he was hopeless with ticketing clothes. So, though we lost some love-struck women who'd been coming in bearing clean twin-sets just to see him, I took over the counter and he worked in the back. But he didn't seem to get the knack of cleaning and pressing, either. Pleats came out cock-eyed, buttons were torn off, and if I'd of wanted a wedding dress to look like the next morning after a night at the pub, I'd only have to give it to my partner, Po. Yes, I'd named him that in the war, and it stuck.

Faithful, many of our customers were. They tried so hard to stay with us. "Jiffy's open closer to my busstop," one said to me. "But you're the only ones who treat us like intelligent beings." She was the girl from the business registry, our most fervent customer. And she had one helluva big mouth. Everybody thought of us as some classy Jiffy, though a dog could of slept on our jobs and done a better job than Po, and I couldn't do everything. I used to come in during the night and redo Po's work, so's he wouldn't know. He never caught on, though thinking back, he should of.

But Po never noticed. He pitched up every morning on the dot, never took sickies, never loitered at the counter with his many admirers who came in to catch a glimpse of him. I'd say, "Just a tick, Miss Timble," and ring a bell. "Po!" I'd have to yell, to get my voice past the muffle of clothes, and through the racket of the tumble machines. "Look who's here." Po would push his head between the cello'd garments and give the customer his ghost-smile, "Yar," he'd say and disappear again. "Hard at work, poor boy," Miss Timble would say, "Just give him this," and she'd leave a little package of lamingtons she'd made, and flee. Or Miss Crumb, or old Mrs Methuine.

Even the old birds weren't immune to him, though he was immune to all.

I married during the first year, and my wife was a mystery as big as Po. I asked her early on why she wasn't stuck on him instead of me and she asked me back: "What's there to be stuck on?"

SYLVIA HELPED IN the shop the first few months, trying to teach Po how to press, but he never learned, and then she couldn't help because the Stoddard Solvent made her sick, and she was sick enough anyway. And then Po, our first, came. And then of course she couldn't help any more, except for bookkeeping, something that Po and I'd been hopeless at.

Syl liked Po, too, but "He's a sadsack, isn't he?" she asked one night after I got home at midnight from my moonlight fixup job at my own place of business, "You're nuts," she said. She was peevish, Po being such a teether and her with a bun in the oven ready to come out.

"Sadsack!?" I regret I snarled. I opened the fridge and found only a chicken and a bottle of milk. Not one damn beer.

"And where's my bloody—"

"Pull your head out, Mal!" Syl wasn't a simperer. "You don't even listen to the radio in that place."

I didn't. It slowed me down and there was so much work.

But her voice did something to me now. I was never one for a fight, but she could knock me out with a word. "Sorry, Syl," I said.

"That's alright," she said. "Hey, let's not wake Po. But really, love, any man who doesn't know a beer strike's on is a man with a problem to solve."

"Beer?"

"Four days now," she said.

"Strewth!"

"Turn around," she said, and when I did, she stuck her big stomach into the small of my back and massaged my shoulders. "They're stiff as coat hangers."

"The books look worse than you," she said.

"Hmm," I said, knowing she was right and wanting her hands to stay doing that, and not wanting tomorrow to come. *Please don't say another word*, I silently implored her.

"He's not—" she said.

"I can't."

"No, you can't."

WE COULDN'T, YOU see. We couldn't split the partnership. I couldn't imagine Po, Big Po, being on his own, out in the cold. Sure, there was a billion women who'd of liked to spirit Po away, but even if one succeeded, then what?

"I owe him," I said, and that was that, certainly since Little Po. For though Po wasn't god, ("That's for sure," Sylvia laughed, and though it was irreverent to him, I had to laugh, thinking of how I often I'd say *You bloody gorilla!* while I fixed his jobs at night)—

though he wasn't god in the dry cleaners, he was godly in the ways that count. Me being alive proved that. And certainly Po as a failed god would damn our newborn to something . . .

"It's not like we're superstitious," Sylvia said, "but."

Sylvia always could put words in the right place.

So we had to do something, but what? We couldn't abandon Po, but we couldn't keep the shop going like it was. "Is he good at anything?" she asked.

It was already two in the morning, so she ignored my "Lotsa things" and went for the kill.

"What, precisely?"

Little Po woke for his twosies. I'd slept through them before, but this time I watched her feed him.

When she got him to sleep it was almost three a.m., and I had nothing to say except "Nothing particular," thinking of something very particular.

"I suspected that." She sighed and shifted her stomach. "You're soft as a cream bun, Mal. He still living in that working men's hotel?"

"Where else would he bunk, except with us?"

"Horrid places, those."

"No they aren't."

"You hated them."

"Yeah," I admitted, snuggling up to her. "But I like my comforts. I guess he doesn't care."

"Yar." She did him perfectly! I laughed till she hit me. "Wake Little Po at your peril!"

At that, it was impossible not to wake him, and we did, right and proper.

SYL HAD THE idea of branching out instead of giving up. "There's a ton of new migrants we can choose from. Let's find us a nice little tailoress. We'll add Dressmaking and Fashion Advisory to the window, and get little cards printed up."

So we did. Mrs Kamensky even spoke a bit of English, and she certainly could sew. She had a very Parisian air to her, the customers thought. Unlike lots of Adelaide men who didn't talk about it, the women and girls had never been over there, so any Pole could of fooled them. Every Tuesday night was a free-to-all fashion advice evening, and it sure was attended.

I asked Po to come to the nights and sit in as security, but Syl had her own devious reasons and they worked a treat. When fashions were modelled before tea and cake was served, the natural thing was to look to the man in the room. When Mrs Kamensky said "This is the way to do so-and-so" eyes would always turn to Po. He brought a great deal of juh nuhsay quah, as Gloria, the girl from the registry office (now Mrs Braverman) said.

Shortly after the fashion nights began, a group of brickies' labourers came in one Friday lunch hour, their beery breath making me miss my bachelor days. "Where's this Po bloke?" said the guy in front, plonking a fist the size of a pumpkin on the counter.

"What you want him for?" I asked a bit too loud.

To my relief, Po suddenly appeared at my side.

"You Po?" the head bloke asked, looking a bit shaken.

"Yar," said Po.

"You got a ball and chain o' yur own?"

Po just looked at them.

"He's single, matey," I said, "but what's it to you? He pinch your sheilas?"

"Not likely!" said someone.

"What's your gripe then?" I demanded, Po lending me bluster I didn't own. I felt good defending him against whatever they wanted to accuse him of.

"He go to these ladies' nights?"

"Would you want to?" I asked.

The room exploded in laughter. Even Po smiled at that.

"What a man's gotta do for a quid," someone muttered.

"You're alright, mate," said the lead brickie, and they walked out.

The sessions brought us so much business that I could finally hire a girl to do the cleaning and pressing. She didn't speak much English, but she could put a knife pleat in a bowl of custard, that girl. She was so good that Po didn't need to do anything. He took to doing only the ug-type work, lifting dirty loads and such, and otherwise sitting on a stool in the back, unless some customer wanted to say hello or ask his advice. His advice was always the same, it seemed to me. He gave them what they wanted, as far as confidence-building went, his smile letting them know that they knew best. But the women who liked him never noticed that. I won't say I understand women.

Then he'd go back to his stool. He wasn't a reader, so him sitting on that stool most of the time bothered me. He looked lost. I thought back to the war and remembered his spoons, so the next day I pinched two from home and gave them to him.

"Are these right?" I asked. "We could use some music."

He started out rusty, but it only took about a day for him to loosen up, and then those spoons clacked out all kinds of songs, and he played better than I remembered. It was okay, seeing him slouched over the stool, banging those spoons against his knee. The girl, Majka, liked his playing, though it was hard for me to hear with all the moaning and hissing and tumbling of the machines.

Those were good days. I slept so well that even the twosies of little Beatrice didn't get me up.

The Pococurante fashion evenings became so popular that we got a half page write-up in the *Adelaide Telegraph* as the place to be if you want to be in mode, with a big photo of the window:

Pococurante Cleaners

Dressmaking & Fashion Advisory Service

The article was feisty: "A poke in the eye to all those who think of Adelaide as not able to hold its head up with the major cities, as far as style is concerned."

I framed the page and hung it in the window.

The next week Jiffy Cleaners closed, and within days, I told Majka to bring in an offsider, we had so much business, so she brought in her younger sister. Now there were two girls working in the back of the shop, and Po mainly playing his spoons. It would of been odd if it were anyone but Po. And his songs were so full of life.

About a month later, I heard two screams and fought my way through a crush of cello'd suits to find Po holding up a red-bellied black snake with one hand and picking up a wedding veil with the other.

"It want kill me," Majka said, her hands on her heart. Her sister half hid behind her—their eyes big as oil stains.

Po dropped the snake into the middle of the wedding veil, pulled up the edges and knotted them. The snake squiggled but it couldn't get out. Po had bagged that snake so smooth, you'd of thought he bagged a snake a day before breakfast. I'd wondered before where Po came from. He never said.

He looked to me.

"Take it away!" begged Majka.

Her sister pointed. "No that."

I agreed. I pulled a set of Alfred Hotel drapes from their laundry bag and handed Po the bag.

He dropped his improvised sack into the laundry bag, gave the girls one of his ghost-smiles, and left out the back door.

The front door bell had tinkled several times and the counter bell was berserk, so I left the girls with a "You okay?" and their uncertain nods. As soon as I could, I joined them in the back and they told me the story. The redbelly had come out from a pile of musty woollens that looked like they hadn't been worn for years. "It want kill me!" Majka kept saying, and her sister acted like one of those jerk dolls where you pull the elastic to make its head nod. I didn't laugh. They wouldn't know that the snake just wanted to get away. I did say I'd never seen another snake in Adelaide, and then showed them from the style of clothes in that pile and their sheepy smell, that the customer was a cockie, and since they didn't know that word either, I had to say *farmer*, but they didn't understand till I said *Baaah!* And then they smiled.

Then I said so that they understood, regardless of whether they believed the rest of what I'd said: "You tell. No work." They both understood that. We couldn't have our lady customers thinking snakes were lurking in the Pococurante, eyeing their high heels.

Po didn't come back that day, but was security at the fashion night that night, reliable as ever.

The next morning when Majka and her sister arrived, they carried between them a huge old case made of something that looked like leather. They ducked to get it in the front door, and took it to the back. Po was already there, playing his spoons. The shop wasn't OPEN yet, thank goodness, or I would of had to close, I was so curious.

Po stopped playing. We watched as Majka undid the buckles while her sister held the case upright. They opened the hinged lid together and Majka brought out what looked like a taxidermied snake from some Land of Giants, but instead of fangs, it had a little brass cup for a mouth. Majka's sister laid the case down and stood beside her in front of Po.

"You take," Majka said.

"From us Papa," said her sister.

"Wahzsh" or something like that, Majka said, "Snake." She pointed to the thing.

Po nodded to them, no smile at all. He got off the stool and took it from their hands like it was a baby. He inspected it as thoroughly as I've seen him check a gun. It proved to be some weird musical instrument. Black, thick as an anaconda, and in the shape of an S that then snaked down into another S. He found finger holes in the horizontal places of the snake, and put his mouth to the mouthpiece. He moved his lips around experimenting like you do with a new girl . . . and blew.

At first nothing happened, so he wet his lips again and stood up straighter.

He got a gurgle out of it like a toilet in an apartment house. His eyes crossed, looking at the mouthpiece. He shut his eyes and took a big breath and settled his lips again.

"*Bwaaaah!*"

I hadn't heard that since I left the place where I grew up. Take a six-month-old calf away from its mum, and if it doesn't make that bellow right off, give it time and it'll blast you to the next shire with that sound, and if it doesn't, you're deaf, guaranteed.

The Pococurante is a small place. I stumbled back, holding my ears and would of fallen but for the press of hanging clothes.

The girls were prepared. They giggled but didn't take their hands from their ears.

Po grinned.

He took a breath and tried again, producing a more civilised sound. I looked at my watch. I had to open the shop. The girls tore their eyes from Po and the great snake, and turned their equipment on.

THE DAY WAS punctuated with the call of the hungry calf. And it was funny, the reaction.

"You got a bull back there?" asked most.

I had a great time instructing city people on the particulars of bull calls compared to calf calls. "That's one hundred percent calf," I said. "You think a bull's got a great deep voice like that, don't you Mrs O'Brien? Mrs James? Mrs Braverman? No, a bull's got a soprano, beautiful and thin and high as a lady's. Like yours!"

"Get away with you," said Mrs Braverman, waving her hand with its flashy wedding ring. "You're pulling my leg."

"Po," I yelled, but he couldn't hear so I had to step back and beckon him through. His eyes were closed so I had to get Majka to put her hand on his shoulder.

He didn't come immediately but when he did, "I was telling Mrs Braverman here," I said, "that a bull's got a high voice, nothing like that calf-call you're making, isn't that true?" Ever since that redbelly, I reckoned he must of come from a place like me.

"Yar," Po said. His lips were curiously red and swollen and he had a faraway look in his eyes.

A little pleat formed between Mrs Braverman's eyes as she regarded Po.

"Let's see you play," she said.

I bowed to her and turned to Po.

He went back and returned, struggling through the clothes racks with the instrument in his arms. At the look of it, Gloria Braverman's pleat deepened but Po's eyes were closed by then, his lips pressed to the mouthpiece.

"Bwaaaah!" yelled the giant snake with the voice of a hungry calf.

Mrs Braverman fled.

It was so funny, I laughed till I cried. But I didn't tell Syl.

FROM THAT DAY on, Po played only the snake instrument. All day. After a while, he could play like the wind in the grass, so soft that the equipment overpowered him, but the girls didn't like that. They liked him to make the calf sound. "Bwaah! Bwaah!" they'd urge, and "Bookat!" or something like that.

So he made up songs that sounded like they were yelled by a hungry calf. They loved them and they accomplished so much work that they were oftentimes standing around with their hands on their hips, waiting. By the end of a month, I think he could of made that snake whisper, but he didn't. It only yelled.

The first intimation that I had of anything wrong was when I noticed that women had stopped asking for Po.

Then one day when I opened the door, I found an envelope that someone had shoved under the door. It was an article clipped from the *Melbourne Daily Courier*.

A DELAIDE CULTURE TAKEN to the Cleaners In a Word

"In the mushroom culture that is Adelaide, your correspondent has come upon a delicious morsel of farce in the centre of town: The Pococurante, where those with fashion at heart come every week, and the crème of Adelaide have their clothes created and cleaned to a T. This centre of culture is run by two strange blokes, who must be laughing up their sleeves at the cognoscenti who don't know their pococurante from their frankly-Scarlett,-I-don't-give-a-damn. They serenade the beauties that flock to this denizen, with Mozart. Not quite. Follow the sound of the angry bull, and you'll hit the bullseye."

All day I drove myself insane. What was the article on about? Some nasty anti-Adelaide bit of snideness? That's something that Melbourne and Sydney do, but I was trying all day to figure out what to do about Po, who really had to stop playing that snake thing, at least like that.

I'd never read the *Melbourne Daily Courier* before, and don't imagine that any of our customers did. But that article could of been slipped with the ink still damp under the pillow of every Adelaidian, such was the response we got. We hadn't been this slow since the old days, and the people who did come in, came in with silly questions, not things to clean. I could *feel* the city's anger.

In the back of the Pococurante, Po played his snake for the girls, who were getting through the work faster than it was coming in today. Po hadn't mentioned that I didn't call him to the front any more, but then Po never mentioned anything.

My one comfort that day was that Po didn't know about the newspaper article.

I DIDN'T WANT Sylvia to find out about it either, but when I got home, she met me with "What's the bull? And what's this all about?" And she shoved an open book at me and pointed.

The dictionary. I didn't need her to point. On the left hand page, something was circled in angry red crayon.

I read it.

"Why didn't you just punch me in the eye?" I asked.

"Why didn't you look it up?"

"It was a name, not a word," I said. "He was *Pococurante!* I told you. Would you of looked up a name embroidered in gold on a bloke like that's shirt?"

"Huh!" she said and without taking her eyes off me, yelled "Beatrice! Get your teaset off the hallway floor this second or—"

I heard a scuttle and a whimper, while I looked at the thing in my arms and wondered what to do with it.

"I don't know," she said to me. "But honestly . . . perhaps not."

Sylvia and I were just inside the front door. I walked past her and dropped into my chair. I couldn't decently strangle the dictionary, so it sat in my lap.

Syl walked over to me, picked it up and flung it against the wall. "There," she said, "You can put it in the bookcase later." She rested her hands on her hips.

"Now," she said, "I asked you about that bull."

"It's a calf," I said. Syl was born and bred in Adelaide.

"Get on with it."

"It's only an instrument that Po practices in slack times," I said. "Sometimes it sounds like a calf . . . only a calf."

After a while she said "Mmm," and then, "Must feed the kids."

She put them to bed as soon as they'd eaten. Then she fixed two tall, stiff drinks: brandy and water without the ice and without the water. She put the glasses on the table by my easy chair, shoved me into it, and sat on my lap.

"You can't change the name now," she said, "or everyone'll think they've got you. You must tough it out." Then she kissed me.

"I don't deserve that," I said.

"Too right you don't," she said, and kissed me again.

She talked, and we drank on empty stomachs, and I felt after another of her drinks, that I could tough it out. But then there was Po.

"You must face Po," she said. "Buy him out."

"Yar," I said, but we didn't laugh.

I knew I couldn't do it.

THE NEXT DAY we might as well of been closed as far as customers giving us jobs went. The ones who picked up jobs were cold as a witch's tit, excuse my French. But in the late afternoon, a reporter came in from the *Adelaide Telegraph*, just as Syl had told me to expect.

"They've picked a fight," she'd said. "And they'll get it."

So I was ready, I hoped.

I laughed at the Melburnians' *snideness* as Syl told me to call it, and shrugged my shoulders at *Pococurante*, saying that if Melbourne people didn't think that Adelaide people don't know what it means, that just shows Melbourne's unworldliness.

"We can snap our fingers to what they're obsessed with," I said (something else memorised from Syl). "We've got juh nuhsay quah." I added. That, I'd remembered from Gloria Braverman, who had said it alot once, and Syl said that I should repeat that, too.

"I bet the reporter will ask you to say that twice," she said. And she was right.

"And about those sounds of an angry bull?" the reporter asked.

"You ever been to an opera?" I asked the reporter, and he laughed out loud as he wrote that down.

I laughed with him, but didn't feel any too good inside. Po hadn't come in, and didn't pitch up all day.

THE ARTICLE IN the *Adelaide Telegraph* came out the next morning, and it was a triumph. Melburnians were *"jealous sourpusses, as anyone would be with their weather . . . According to Oxford professor W. K. Lister from the Royal Academy of Music, who is visiting his sister here in Adelaide, from descriptions of the instrument being played by Mr Pococurante"* (I distinctly told the reporter: *Clarence Braithwaite*, so I don't know how this mistake occurred) *"the instrument is a Schlangenrohr, otherwise known as a Serpent, invented hundreds of years ago to be played in churches as a choir enhancement. It is a credit to our city, and possibly of quite venerable age. It is extremely difficult to play. The professor said he would be honoured to meet . . . "*

Customers came in all day waving the *Telegraph* like a flag. "Hooray for us!" they crowed. "Where's Po?"

Po didn't come in all day. And what's more, the snake-serpent-whateveryoucallit had disappeared. I'd been too preoccupied to pay any attention to Majka when she'd asked about both the day before. Po had always packed it in its case and left it in the shop before.

WHEN I GOT home Sylvia was there to meet me at the door, a frothy glass in her hand and a smile as big as a house on her face.

I pasted a smile on my face, but couldn't face the drink.

The next day the girls were frantic. Still no Po. I served the crowd of customers at the counter and then told the girls I'd go find him, and to take the day off.

I closed the shop and walked the three blocks to the rooming house where we'd both lived till I got married. The manager went to Po's room at my request, but Po didn't answer the door. He was paid up to the end of the week so it was like pulling nails from ironwood to get the manager to open up his room, but finally he did when I said I'd leave and come back with the coppers.

Inside, a neat room greeted us, with nothing personal in it except what he left in the wastebasket: a magazine of physical culture—something of a surprise. A powder-blue envelope with no writing on it, but it had once been sealed. A balled-up clipping from, you guessed it before I did: The *Melbourne Courier*. And a dried-up applecore.

I felt sick.

While I scouted round the room, I remembered what it was like living in the one next door. Alone in your room, you'd hear other men breathing, turning the pages of magazines, and the rest. The back of each door had a sign on it that said, "NO women" topping a lot of other NO's. The view from the window was a brick wall with a painted ad: Bonds.

I went home to Sylvia, not knowing what to do. We put the kids in the old Morris and drove all over Adelaide, even out to Snake Gully, looking, like lost farts in a haunted shithouse.

"He's gone," I said after two hours of this.

"Where would he go?"

"How should I know?"

We took the kids back. They were crying. I left her and them in the house, and went out again. I didn't know where, but I had to go out.

I walked till my feet were blistered. I hadn't walked this much for years. He could walk, I remembered. He never groused like the rest of us at the length of those tramps in mud.

When I felt so lost that my eyes were getting misty, I made my way back to my own house, and Sylvia.

Our stereo ran hot that evening so that music took the place of talk. We didn't have too many records, so she had to play her Benny Goodman twice. That was fine by me. Any noise would do, because nothing would do.

We went to bed early and I looked at the ceiling for hours. I wanted to strangle whoever those people were—the nasty ones. He had protected me, and what had I done for him?

"You need your sleep, Mal," came Syl's voice through the darkness. She'd been pretending to sleep, too.

"I'll be right," I said to Syl.

"Shh!" she said.

"I was," I said, miffed. It was Syl who had spoken, not me.

"Shut up, Mal. Listen!"

I heard it. A voice—high and thin as the night. One long note. It swelled . . . and then died away.

"How beautiful!" whispered Sylvia. "Shh!"

She didn't need to shush me. I felt my ears stretch, I was straining so hard to hear.

Again and again—that voice, and each time, further away.

"There's no words," she whispered, "but then there aren't really in opera, are there?"

She wasn't wanting an answer, so I didn't give her one. She shut up again.

"If only I could sing like that," Sylvia finally sighed when the voice was too faint to catch any more.

When dawn came, I heard her ladylike snores.

WHEN I OPENED the door of the Pococurante only a few hours later, Majka and her sister came in as usual, but we each had our jobs to do, so we nodded to each other and got on with it.

A crowd of customers was already waiting, sounding like a flock of galahs: "Did you hear her too? My word! I wonder who . . . "

And they must of breakfasted on radio waves to come up with *Call of the Soprano, Phantom Lady of the Night, Dame Melba's Ghost, Heavenly Disturber of our Peace* and such rot.

Well, Sylvia had been taken in completely, but I couldn't let it stand. All the customers got an earful of my correction, as I explained that the *lady* was a bull. After about an hour of this, an old guy who was quietly waiting, holding a hoary jacket, backed me up. "A bull's call is unmistakable," he said.

Finally, at that slack time just before noon, I was alone in the front, so I went to the back and told the girls that I was sorry they'd been too far away to hear that bull, living in their migrant camp, but they said that just around dawn the whole camp heard it, too.

"Papa say no bull," Maj said. And just then, a ghost tweaked three sets of lips.

The Age of Fish, Post-flowers

Just when you think you've killed them all, others impossibly wriggle over the wall. Or bore through it, some say. Or worse—though this might be another rumor—breed within.

As for the sounds, there's lots of speculation, some of it pretty noisy itself. Are the sounds some new tactic to get rid of the orms? We in the corps have argued about that, most of us too scared to want to talk about it, or to want to hear it discussed; but (and it could be a pose) a few loudmouths insist on spouting daily assurances that the Sound, as they say it Capitalizedly, is the Newest Advance in our age. This might be convincing if they, the optimists, weren't doing the mole act along with the rest of us, and running downstairs as fast as they can when the first sounds rumble in the distance every forsaken morning. They answer *collateral damage, possible risks, someone will tell us, never you mind* and the sun will come up sunny one day.

Today we got another report closer to home. An orm, a relative baby though thick as a man's thigh, its dorsal fin tall as his waist, and its mane thick and coarse as cables. Just a block away, it was caught in the act of engorgement, two legs waving from its maw.

The story goes that a man in blue shot it with his harp-net. The orm's tail wasn't properly caught, and smashed the guy's stomach to pulp, but the mib had already called the orm squad. The person in the orm (unknown sex) was already a lost cause. That orm would feed a hundred New Yorkers, maybe plenty more from outside. That's what Julio says because he saw someone who saw the squad load it into their omni. All just speculation on my part. I'm not a knower, and I don't know anyone who is.

The sounds and craters are something else. The sounds come always at dawn. In them are elements of rumble, drag, shear, and I would imagine earthquake, all in one indefinability, just the sound to make you wake shaking from a dream, though this isn't one. Correction: wasn't one before. The real has exceeded dreams—former dreams, that is.

The sounds have patterned our waking. We all run down to the drypit (though none of us has slept enough) and huddle there feeling the building tremble (or is it just us?) till the day calms, relatively.

IT'S STILL RAINING. We passed the forty days and forty nights mark long ago, thankfully longer ago than anyone in our corps cares to harp about. No one left amongst us is the quoting type. I don't remember the last time the moon shone.

Two levels of underground carpark in our building are now nicely filled with water. So we don't have that to worry about. Power could have been a problem but for our resident genius, an arrogant creep otherwise. Julio is the only person who can relate to the guy, but as long as Julio stays with us, we're laughing. (Must keep Julio happy!)

Julio is a genius, too, but a different kind. He named us "The Indefatigables" but that is really he. He found it in a book, he says, in his self-effacing way, but he is the one. I have never been able to figure him out. I thought perhaps it was love, and of who else but Angela Tux? But she left almost at the beginning and Julio stays. He says we give him purpose and that he loves the Brevant, and maybe we do and he does. I certainly must give him purpose, as I don't think I could live without what he's done for us.

The Indefatigables, properly the coop of the Brevant Building, "the corps" as we call ourselves, would be happy as clams these days (no irony intended) if we could only get more dirt. George Maxwell goes out for it instead of just wishing we had more. He went all the way to 51st Street yesterday to find a dirtboy with real dirt.

He was so upset he didn't mind the danger, he said. I think that he was so upset he didn't *think* of the danger. I've never sought a dirtboy. Too frightened of being killed for my seeds. George, though, is a big guy, played varsity in Yale (people say it's still around, where the knowers are). George is one of those guys whose muscles get more tough with age as does their stubbornness. We've got quite a collection here now in our little group, none as brave as George or useful as Julio, but we like to say *each has something to offer.* The building used to be filled with useless types—hysterical, catatonically morose, or verbally reminiscent, but they died out or disappeared. I'm proud and I admit, lucky, to be part of our corps now.

From Julio, the super, we hear rumors. He was the one who told us to fortify, though in the end, it was only him and George Maxwell who stuck broken glass and angle-edged picture frames and sharpened steel furniture bones into the outside wall, one man sticking, the other man guarding the sticker with a pitiful arsenal of sharpened steel. For the steel, it surprised us all how many of us had Van der Rohe chairs. I got mine at a ridiculously cheap price from a place in Trenton, though the delivery, by the time they were all installed in my apartment (I had to get three at the price) was ridiculous. I was glad to donate the chairs. They had always seemed to unwelcome my sitting in them, and gloat when I left them alone. Until the defenses project, I had never been able to part with them, but the prospect of them being torn asunder into ugly scrap gave me the best day I could remember in this age.

So few diversions. The Wall now, you'll want to know about. Walls, really, I don't rightly remember when. Sometime in the first years of the age. The orms were only part of the reason then, but the part that motivated public pronouncements on the Wall project. Where the orms came from, we'll never know. Norwegian cruise ships were blamed for dumping the "freshets" as the spawned babies are called, with the ballast, in both Miami and New York. The Norwegians protested, saying *these are not orms*, and anyway, theirs are mythical (though plenty of Norwegians disputed that). But the mayors and the President said "orms" in their announcements, and so that is what we've called them since. It doesn't matter about the name any more anyway, nor how they got here, nor to us, how far they have traveled inland. There are rumors that they reached the Great Lakes long ago, and the Mississippi, and that they can travel overland for many miles before they need water. We used to speculate, but as George pointed out, why? We're probably the safest in the country because we protected first, and we have the most organized (not to mention mechanized) protection force in the country, as far as we know, and also we still have both wall-workers (we hear) and men in blue.

The Wall. The first place of building was the hardest: New York Harbor. Then the Wall encompassed more and more of the boroughs, then out to formerly exclusive burbs. The greatest achievement of mankind—it can be seen from outer space. It had massive public support, and became a focus of both civic pride and hope. I remember the feeling.

The Navy sonared the sea to bejesus, both the harbor enclosed by the wall, and out to three miles. Then the army electrified the Wall wherever it was land-based. We slept easy for it must have been close to a year.

Then the first orm was found *inside*. I remember the headlines in the old *New York Times*: "Mib loses fight to orm; Mayor vows to beef force." Eleven feet long, it came up through a toilet in Flushing (yes, Flushing got in, though I don't know why, but maybe it wasn't Flushing but they said so because it *is* funny, and let's face it. Anything funny runs like a nose in November). By the time the orm was hacked to death with a broken plate glass window stuck to a love seat (by the wife, a weight-lifter, I remember, but again, I don't know if this wasn't any more true than Flushing) the orm had (supposedly) bitten through the middle of a tall and muscular dry-waller (but again, he could have been a flabby accountant). Whoever-it-was's middle was found in the orm on occasion of the orm's post-mortem (orms were not then eaten by anyone). The fact is, an orm killed in a safety zone.

A massive eradication campaign was launched to kill freshets within the Wall and anything that had gotten into the sewer system. The subway was sealed, the vent covers replaced by cement plugs.

There was maximum publicity for effort and minimum information of results. Then media stopped, as there was thought to be no further public benefit to be gained from it. The orms kept coming for a while and then as far as we heard, died off. Julio says they never died off, which is why we and anyone else of wealth isn't connected any more to the sewer or to any other municipal system (if indeed, there's anything left).

In one respect we feel secure. Now neither people nor orms can climb our walls, nor gain entry through our two doors (our genius designed that protection).

"Be prepared"—our motto for when we do have to leave the Brevant. Each of us has to on a rostered basis, for at least a little time. George (the health nut) makes us. "You need the air," he says. He doesn't add, *You need gut-building*, but he could. Both muscles in the gut like George, and some of the guts that gave him the courage to fortify our building. Each of us has to deal with the dealers. That spreads the load. And sometimes, one of us doesn't return. We all mourn the loss of the corps member and whatever it was that was lost as pay to the dealer. The most valuable pay is of course, seeds. Dealers being who they are, there are those who think only of a shot of energy—and they want meat.

Next to seeds, the next most valuable commodity for forward-thinkers, is dirt. The dirtboys are just that—boys, and dirty. They are the second fastest natural things in the city. They are the only ones who know where dirt is. Mibs kill them if they can corner them because dirtboys dig holes in the Wall to go outside to get dirt. That's what's said. I don't know, but they carry the dirt in their clothes. They strip and you've got to put the dirt into *your* clothes. Tied-off pants and shirt arms are a giveaway, so there's many ingenious ways that dirtboys hide their load. If we're caught with dirt, we don't get killed, but we do get drafted to volunteer. I've never known a volunteer. Part of Julio's job is to keep us from being volunteers, and so far, the Brevant has been left alone. What we have that is valuable to the mib besides our seeds, I never know but Julio does. He usually asks us for old electricals: a shaver, some extension cords, a bread-making machine—and we always give the him the stuff. Someday maybe we won't have the means to pay, but so far we do. Why the mib don't just take what they want, I don't know. Maybe they are designed to serve.

Lately I've been thinking of other things. Like these craters Julio told us about. Every crater open to the sky is a breeding ground, he says, and he also says it is a matter of time. Since the orms adapted to the electrification of the wall, the electricity had to be disconnected and sharp spikes mounted porcupine-style all over the wall. And this means that with rain, danger is increased, as the streets are slick and every pothole is a pool. An orm and you and water—and as soon as the orm feels your presence, your body will spit like a frozen freedom fry dropped into boiling oil.

The craters are the most recent crisis in our age. I've never seen a crater, but Julio has, blocks of them on the Grand Concourse in a stripe that is so fat it took away the Jerome Avenue El. Poe Park, he said, is now a *much* bigger park (and he laughed in a spine-crawling way), and that little house is gone, he said, which is too bad, but the El being gone makes a much nicer vista, he said. How a whole elevated "subway" could disappear along with all the buildings, we were trying to comprehend when he said it all made the neighborhood look much better, and he laughed again, *even with the craters* where all those stubby brick apartment houses had been. *Alexander's final closing down sale finally finalized*, he chuckled, and then he nearly choked himself pointing to us and cracking up, doubled over like some comedy antique. It was rude of him to make a joke that only he understood. But then his happiness is infectious and we all ended up laughing anyway. Julio has a way that can bring you out of your cares! He always looks on things in his own way. I wish I could, as I had nightmares for a week from that trip of his to the Bronx, especially the *where did everything go* part.

George saw a cleared area in Queens with lots of holes where basements were; and oddly, so did Fey, who once traveled further than anyone. Must have been his daydreaming that let him get that far, and luck that brought him home.

I could worry during my waking hours, but where would that get me? That sounds heroic, stoic maybe, but I can only worry about so much, and at the moment what I worry about—what keeps our whole corps awake at night, is this: Does anyone know about our sunflower?

The corps celebrated when this sunflower took—the only one of five precious seeds from George's last (strictly illegal) seed expedition. (The only trade that is legal is to work for "food" as a volunteer. I can't eat that "food" from what I hear of it, and I don't want to sacrifice myself to the Wall any more than anyone with a smitter of choice left.). Perhaps these seeds came from the botanical gardens in the early days of the Transition. George assures us that, as he was assured, this sunflower plant will grow to have a flower with real, fertile seeds. Regardless of the pictures in books in the

Brevant collection, we have to see those seeds to believe them, and then we have to see *them* make new seedlings. Our books are all *old*, bought way back when because they *were* old, even then, when seeds were seeds for the generations, and books with pictures were for collecting and not trying to get some information, *any crumb of useful information* to live by.

Mrs. Wilberforce's ancient poodle paid for the sunflower seeds, and we were lucky that that dealer was crazy with hunger, or he would have asked for the poodle *and* seeds in return.

Orm. You'd think it would have a nightmarish name, but it doesn't need to. That horse-shaped head. The mane, its congealed, tangled mass; the gasping mouth, as wide as a garbage bin and fringed with triangular, razor teeth. The eyes of a shark, pitiless. A voracious appetite for flesh. Just to see it move is terrifying. The humping fleetness of it over walls, up brick, galloping across intersections once so clogged with people, buses, cars, honking yellow taxis. That was in the early days when there were pictures of them in the news. I've never seen an orm in real life.

But back to the sunflower. Our future relies on this plant—our fortune and salvation. Few people have the water, the dirt, and the power to grow indoors, and also, have the social organization to not destroy their riches. We have all that, which makes us *very* rich, potentially. Seed dealers are low-quality thinkers. They think only of the present. Meat gives them a present. We want a future.

We are not alone. There are a select few who think as we do. Which is why there are dealers, thank goodness. We paid our last meat for these sunflower seeds, if no one is brave enough to hunt orm. Even Julio and George aren't that brave. "Yet," says Julio.

Our cucumbers failed again. Sterile seeds again. Or maybe fake. The mushroom spawn won't take. That was a terrible (and costly) blow.

None of us have gone sidewalk-harvesting. Too much danger for too little reward. The little shoots of grass that spring up are so small by the time they get picked. The other weeds disappeared years ago. Didn't get to bud stage. As for the parks, they disappeared early, their danger recognized and paved over. We'd read that we could eat bark, but all the street trees were burnt that first winter.

Everyone has responsibilities. Old Mr. Vesilios has the dwarf apple tree, as he was allowed to keep it. It was his to begin with. He loves it. He calls it "my wife." And what would you expect someone with the name Luthera Treat to have? And by the way, she looks like her name. I thought "prunes" but it was chickpeas and something she calls black salsify. How would she have gotten chickpeas, ones that weren't sterile, let alone salsify, you ask? She grew them in her windowbox back when we kept windowboxes. She says she got the chickpeas from a trip to Egypt when she was young, and had kept them for luck. She says luck, but I am positive: romance. She says she planted them because she couldn't stand the look of any more flowers, but if that's true, then I'm the Easter Bunny of Times Past. The chickpeas are nutritious, but they're *beautiful*, and she turns red if anyone asks her about their origin. I can't complain about Luth, though. By the way, she hates being called that, she says, but we call her that because George says she secretly likes it. Actually, I'm sure she hates it, and furthermore, wishes she were a Genevieve or Helena and a beauty—her outside matching her inner soul, which is truly beautiful. I would say that even if there were still beautiful women left here, because it's true. Luthera's manner fits *Luth*, though. With her looks, it wouldn't do for her to show romantic notions, thus her embarrassment over the chickpeas (and their carved, exotic windowbox). She hardly needed to be interested in food crops on a personal level, even if she was big in the funding of some food-donating NGO, as Julio once said.

As for the rest of us, we've had to learn to like to eat "purple pillow" and "espresso" geraniums (tasting like a pillow of mothballs and nothing much respectively (certainly not coffee), clove-tasting carnations, revoltingly sweet violets, fartish marigolds, tulips that look like candy canes and almost taste like food, *almost*— all that flowerbox stuff that distinguished the Brevant. It was once recreational to eat ornamentals, Luthera said, and when she did, I remembered a time when philanthropy dinners stunk from what looked like soggy, forgotten corsages dropped into every course. At that time Luthera "in revolt" threw out her tulips and lobelia, and planted her windowbox with salsify and those chickpeas. More than any other person's efforts in our corps, her revolution has kept flesh on our bones. The salsify, we particularly have grown to enjoy, though the yachties used to complain that it tastes too much like oysters—"oysters dying over the beach fire, and the juice running down salty arms, bottles of beer, and sun." The yachties are all gone now, thank god, having left in a group. Luth's sourness is more popular than the yachties' reminiscences any day.

There are other crops now, also. We have never been able to get potatoes that would grow. We tried, even though the dirt cost was phenomenal. We haven't been successful with any of our so-called organic wheat grains, brown rice, lentils, or any other of the healthy stores that most of us had in our pantries, mostly untouched before they were recruited as crop seeds. We grin and bear other ornamentals, and they haven't killed us, like when Kate in 4C gorged herself on her own impatiens, rather than give it up to the corps.

For generosity, the prize if we had one, would go to that gray-skinned shaking relic of a rocker, Fey Klaxon. Real name John Smith *really*, he told us the day that our corps got down to its present number, eight.

At the end of our first corps meeting (25 present) to set up the new order, he told us to please wait, which was unusually polite for him. We were so shocked, we did. He soon appeared staggering under a huge potted bush. Its leaves are only plucked on special occasions (and then, only a precious few), such as when anyone leaves the building, and when we are all huddled in the drypit listening to those sounds. We tried to propagate more with cuttings, and failed. Our attempts to grow from seed have failed also. For my money, this is the most valuable possession of our corps, though Fey's food store would be more sensibly considered the biggest valuable, now almost vanished.

It seems that all of us have in our own ways, liked good buys. The Moores on the first floor collected Ming but what they paid for each piece was their biggest joy. It wasn't how much. It was how little. Unusual in the art world, but then Mr. Moore's business was smell-alike name brands. For Cordell Wainer, it was shoes. For Mr. Vesilio, it was olive oil. He used his wine room to store olive oil, and hated wine. For me, it was canned goods. Not having any guests, I had lots of room. I shopped sensibly. Delivery was a problem, so I stocked the spare room and the bath in one delivery. When the first intimations of a new age began, I decided that the dining room could again be put to use, and filled it, too. It was a comforting sight—all my cans. It was crowded again, like when I was a child and my parents filled the rooms with guests and laughter.

I received my last can from the corps about a year ago, but it made me feel good thinking how long my can supply lasted everyone with good management (my own, as I have been from the first, in charge of the food stores).

Fey did better than I, though. He had become chronically shy. I would be, too, if I looked like he, and had looked like he had looked. His health was a constant worry to him. He had been on Dr. Etker's mucousless diet for years, and that didn't do any good. His colon troubled him. Crystals didn't work. He worried about fungus. He didn't trust practitioners any more, so he devised his own regime. He stocked up and then planned not to leave the building ever again. What he bought was canned English-style custard powder "with pure vanilla and pure cornstarch." At the time of our first coop meeting, he had lived on that as a pure food, just adding water, for six months. His apartment is larger than mine, being two joined together for rampageous entertaining. One, he had filled with his provisions. The custard ran out last month.

We are all still healthy relatively speaking, though no one carries excess fat, and you can count everyone's ribs and vertebrae, a little more delineated each day. We still have a varied diet, though it needs to improve pretty fast now, as nothing miraculous has turned up. Everyone but Fey admits to craving meat. I know I do. None of us has tried orm. We don't talk about what other people outside the Brevant eat, although we know that rat is traded practically legally. I could *never* eat rat! Orm at least, is a fish.

The sunflower is our most valuable possession now. It is our future, should no better future shine upon us.

— **II** —

We do think of a better future, you know. Not for our children. The Brevant is not for children. But because, why? Mr. Vesilios gave a beautiful talk last night about the number of colors he has counted in the blossoms on the apple tree, and his talk gave me a dream that I didn't want to wake from.

It is now dawn again, when most of us habitually wake. That sound is beginning. I should rush down to the drypit.

The sunflower. The sunflower, though still a sprout, is breathing in, exhaling oxygen or whatever it is plants do. In, out. Just like us, but the sunflower calmly breathes all day and sleeps all night, every night, in its rare earth. And is loved. To be so loved.

That sound. Its muffled quality only makes it more terrifying. I always make a racket of noise rushing to get down the stairs as fast as I can. I make as much noise as I can, to cover up the sound. Today, for some reason, I listen—don't let myself move.

One of Fey's leaves. Is it possible to imagine chewing a leaf? A gob of them? The bitter spit, that pinch of plaster that Fey and Julio figured out as the strange accompaniment to the leaf. The leaking of ease and happiness into my blood, my heart, my thoughts. It lasts such a short time, but in that time, even the sunflower doesn't matter.

I listen, and imagine being George Maxwell. Being Julio. Being more than them because they rush down to the drypit, too. I imagine being like someone in the old days—strong, brave, heroic. Like men in blue were back when they were real men in blue.

The sound is louder now but still far away, I think. Crashing bangs and slides? I'm sure if you were underneath, you could only feel, not hear, because your eardrums would explode.

I am going. I am going. I wish I hadn't stayed in bed this long. Moving is all the more difficult. Usually I run, but now it's all I can do not to flatten myself and crawl, hugging the walls. Ashamed, I force myself to walk calmly, an insane compromise.

In the vestibule, a tiny opening high in the barriered window lets in the dawn light, pink as a young rose. When did I see this light before? It's been so long. Back in the time of roses, when I used to wake to pigeons cooing against my window. Then, on with the tracksuit, out to the park. One lap, and a cool-down in the rose garden when the dew lay in the petals.

Now, roses in the sky just makes it all the worse to dive like a mole as day breaks. My stomach twists. Wouldn't it be funny to describe the reasons why, as in the old days. *Doctor . . .*

And the solution to my problems? Clumps of cintered powders.

That sharp bar of rose-colored light enters my right iris. I should be a mole-rat now, huddled in the drypit with the rest of them. Eyes, unnecessary, as we sit out the monotony of our daily terror.

Perhaps it is my stomach, or maybe the color of the rose.

I lower my head and quickly perform all the tasks needed to open the small exit door.

Its *swish-clunk* at my back speaks for me. I can't hear it, but I feel it against my body. Felt it.

Dawn is dead.

The Sound that blanketed the Brevant's door-thud, is *alive*. So, alive, it runs between my teeth like a mouse. There is nowhere to go. I threw off my moleskin when I touched the door, so I do what I imagined—step into the street. Now's the time to lift up my head . . . and that feels *good*.

Searching the skyline, where is the source? The Sound is so loud now that it crowds into the me-ness of me, or would *like to*. It is so loud that I can't tell which sounds I hear. Originals or echoes.

The sky is now the color of wet cement, with a slick of blood in it. Peer as I do, I can't see anything through the murk.

Looking out . . . looking up . . .

Something.

Two thin cables (?) though each could be at least as thick as a city block. I can't tell distance.

They fall parallel from a point of infinity to a jagged horizon.

Scrapes and crashes. Distinct. Sharp. I saw for a moment, but all that's left is the Sound now, as the cables disappear in the wool of a grey sky again.

I haven't heard of anyone installing anything above the city, but I told you already—I don't know any knowers. It would be so much safer up there. Maybe they didn't want us interfering, and that is why they make that noise. What are they doing? Maybe this is the cleanup they spoke about. They took their time!

Even on my tiptoes, as far as I can see, I am the only person watching. My whole life, nothing like this.

This is the best thing that has ever happened to me.

Wallace Evian Sturt IV. Little Wally. I'm not little. It's just the fate of IVs. My great grandfather would have sunk all his money, spent it all on whores and horses if he knew that it would have trickled down to the likes of Dad, and I'm no throwback. There was something to the grands. More than just living to make contacts, make money. I've overheard people refer to me as "nice" back when my parents were alive.

I need to concentrate on what's happening. They promised us years ago to do something, but never specified, and then they didn't bother to make announcements any more because all we did was complain.

Well, we *did*.

The Sound pummels the air now. It's rising in shudders from the ground. It's personal now, like when a dentist punctured the roof of my mouth. I can feel the Sound from my soles to the roof of my mouth, to the roots of my hair. I can't properly *see*, dammit.

A smudged cloud rises and then falls and as if it never left us, the sun comes out and shines down like the sun once did. The sky in the area of the chains is now old-fashioned innocent-flower blue, and that grayness is unmistakably clouds not made by moisture, but made by what we've made, for they rise from where the chains disappear into the skyline. I am *not* going to move.

The cables (or chains?) are even bigger, and the grinding crashes get closer and I stand where I am, chewing on the inside of my cheek till I can taste metal. My own blood. But I can coolly taste it and report the taste to myself.

Another cloud puffs, and then a spate of crashes, crisper than before, closer than ever. My cheek twinges, awash with blood.

I can see the end of the cables. They are attached to what looks like a giant open mouth of a net. They're pulling the net upwards . . . full. Fat power station cooling towers bulge out the shape, bits of highway, buildings, spires poke through the holes. What must be bridge cables hang down from the bottom like the angel hair spaghetti of my childhood hung from a fork. As the bag rises, more of the mass becomes visible. A ball—that Earth sculpture that had once been so big. Huge unmistakable broken blocks—the Wall!

Bits fell at the beginning of the pull. Those were the last crashes.

I wonder how many orms they caught in the net.

Now there is no sound. Rather, there is a startling reverberation of hush as the bulging base of the bag is hoisted high. I can see that its enormous bulge at the base would be wider than Yankee Stadium. Many times wider. The long, long bag ascends—into the brilliant sun. I couldn't see where they ascended to, for the glare. And now, though it is blue where I've looked, raindrops stab my eyeballs—a monkey's wedding, I think it's called. Sun and rain. It's over for the day, anyway, I know. So I uncrick my neck and turn around for home.

I didn't even think about an orm, that whole time. I don't even know how long it was.

That was close. I do know that. I have seen.

I will tell about it, and I know I won't stutter even once. Wallace isn't a good name, but it's better than Little Wally, and a darn sight better than Luthera. Maybe my name will be changed.

Others could have been me. There were rumors, but no one believed them. I didn't, and Julio laughed. George said it didn't matter. He just said, "Get out. Get your air."

Build guts? Did George know, but had undeveloped guts himself when it came down to the choice of being a mole every morning, or throwing off that shameful animalness and striding out as a man, biting himself to bravery?

Now, at least somewhere, there is no Wall. That must be a good thing—the breakthrough we've been waiting for, but were too cowered to realize.

Anyway, I will tell of what I saw—I who ventured.

And what to do, now that the Sound has been identified? I would advise: As long as we go underground, we should be protected during the sweep.

Can I insulate myself with painted canvas and make myself a spear, or have we used up all our chairs?

What does orm taste like?

What would Luthera think if I brought one home? *When* I bring one home. I hope they don't clean up everything before I catch one.

But there I go again. Might as well have been stuttering still, such was the Little Wally mindset. Sure, it would be great to be the hero of the corps. But throughout history, any man worth his sword thinks higher than a Luthera.

Tap

It seemed rather friendly at first, the polite thing to do.

"'Scuze me."

"'Ave a mo'?"

"You busy, Simon?"

"—"

Always without warning, always when I was deepest into work. *Tap*, invariably on the right shoulder.

Nowadays, when we're dismissed by email, human touch is precious.

Anthony Brough, my supervisor at CJP, first made me aware of it. He loved to call me into his cubicle by email, and then put his hand on my knee while he went over my deficiencies. Then either someone had lodged a complaint or when the floor went open-plan, I can't remember, he took to the gentle tap. Just once. I'd turn in my chair and he'd nod his head backwards towards the area with the retro beanbags, where it usually took him only about ten minutes to make my hands sweat and wonder how I'd make it through the month because he always left no doubt that the evaluation would end with a smile like a curse, and his knell of "Best wishes. Better luck next." Yes, he never said "time"—saying it would cut into his valuable t . . .

His tap could come at any time, sometimes several times in one

day. He seemed to know when I was hardest at work to beat a
deadline. When you're concentrating in front of the screen, your
shoulders rise, the bones poking up like a hanger with your slack
bod hanging slumped.

Tap.

Then I'd be in a panic to SAVE before . . .

Yes. There'd be about a 3 second max delay.

And if you think I took it silently, I'm ashamed to say you're
wrong. Just like when someone cut in front of me in a queue, I
couldn't shut my gob. At the feel of Anthony Brough's tap, I'd blurt
"Sorry."

Every effing time.

Even if the room didn't have the ambient whir of 50 terminals
and sealed-in-freshness air con, I never would have heard him come.
The carpet was minimal, but in addition to affecting the "I'm too
busy to shave" look, he padded around in his "I could have slept
here" socks.

His commute? When he arrived at the office, he always gave out
such long-have-I-suffered vibes that I imagined it as a long silent eye-
avoiding, touch-averse sojourn in a first-class carriage from God's
own countryside south of London to this fashionable Docklands
corp-sit overlooking the Thames, CJP's HQ. He could have actually
lived in a squat near Heathrow with a bunch of undocumenteds for
all I really know. Not that I didn't speculate.

He never raised his voice; indeed, had this soft-spoken way of
attack that he could have perfected with *au pair*s before he was
school age, making them cry and bribe him so he didn't tell his
parents; or maybe his parents both worked at shit jobs and would
have tried to save if they could have resisted his sweet persistence.
And he also had this way of sneaking up that was so tomb-silent, he
might have been trained by being starved of his bottle as a crawling
toddler if he made enough sound to wake a dustmite.

And me? Contrary to what you'd expect from my qualifications,
I commuted from a south London suburb distinguished by
an embarrassing name (that probably hurt my employment
opportunities), a civic building styled as "brutalist" deliberately
designed to be ugly (as if there is contrast needed); and for
public sculpture, a giant biodegrading cat of fibreglass. In that
neighbourhood there is much warmth of human contact, and a
certain etiquette. When a man speeds up to walk beside you and

extends his hand, you shake down your own pockets to fill it. The rent is cheap, for London. With work being such long hours and such low pay, I didn't see the downsides when I signed the lease. (I did hope to be able to afford to move to a nice cold neighbourhood soon, as soon as I got another supervisor and recognition of my worth.)

CJP was no worse than other companies, or maybe I was too squeamish to want to put myself through the torture of job-hunting, so I just tried to get down to it at CJP. I am, if I do say so myself, rather an expert, and worked in the hope and expectation that I'd be noticed by someone above Anthony Brough.

But he seemed to have a sixth sense for knowing when I really could not take a moment away, when I was so worried about losing time that I almost didn't care what the fuck he was going to say to me or what the fuck he *did* say in all his polite, undermining way.

Sometimes he must have seen a spark of impatience in me, an uncricking of my neck, because on those days, it could be an hour after he'd said, "I'm glad we had this little talk. I'll put in a word for you, that you'll try harder,"—it could be minutes later when I'd be back in my chair, picking up the pieces of my lost concentration, when *tap*.

On the night after the day he did it three times and I missed a deadline I'd been looking forward to, I had my first nightmare about him. A sharp pain in my right shoulder woke me. I'd been on my stomach and must have been flailing my arm around. The tossed bedclothes were like a limp salad. The sheets were wet with sweat, my hair was matted, and my pillow was soppy with sweat, drool and I think, tears. I flipped myself on my back and pulled the covers up tight around me.

Three stories down, the street was buzzing with the usual 2am ambience, a fight that no one was going to stick his head out the window over. Glass broke, probably preparatory to someone getting his nose sliced off. It was all so open, loud and vivid down there— so *normal* on this street that the screams, taunts, "I'll kill youse" vows and sounds of collateral damage to windscreens and whatnot soothed me. They were so fully occupied with each other that they were reassuring as a dog fight on the other side of the door. Who would think to come up here and enter? I fell asleep again, but it was only a snatched nap.

Just as in the day, the tap came without warning.

I woke feeling the nightmare as if I was still in it—every detail as real as the cold sweat I felt from my head to my fish-cold feet. I'd been sitting in my chair at work and *tap*. I whirled around and could only see my workmates, all hunched over their own chairs, heads aimed at screens, all too far away in body and mind to have done anything. They weren't even pretending not to notice, so it had to be just nothing. Nothing more than, say, talking about fleas and feeling itchy. In the dream I thought it out so rationally, told myself to have a laugh at myself and a healthy rush of hateful wishes toward Anthony Brough. I took a swig of water, focussed on the screen and felt—*tap*. Not some little itch but a jab to my lightly flesh-covered shoulder bone—ever so polite of course, but insistent, as if this were the end of the workday and my bone were the lift's DOWN button.

In the dream, I knew there was a deadline. I tried so hard to work. I bent forward toward the screen. Tap. I slid down into my chair. Tap.

Tap.

I turned my back to the screen and put the keyboard on my lap. Tap.

I tipped the chair over and stood with my back to the desk. Tap.

I haven't mentioned the big difference between me and those DOWN buttons. They don't say "Sorry" but in my dream I *wanted* to say something real. Wanted to so bad. Instead, Sorry would come out of me like he'd press my button and watch me shit my pants.

The sound or pain of my neck cracking in the act of turning woke me. I remembered that, too, as I lay in bed waiting for the sounds of traffic to grow to a roar.

It was almost noon when I got to work, my right arm in a sling. I rode past my floor in the lift, and gave notice to the Human Resources Supervisor. She was surprisingly sympathetic to my complaint of sudden RSI, but when I left the building without seeing Anthony Brough, I realised that the sympathy was only corporate. Because I hadn't bothered to get a doctor's evaluation before resigning, I had no claim. She'd fly through *her* next evaluation.

That day I didn't look towards the future, just avoided it. My neck really did hurt but I dumped the shoulder sling as soon as I was out of the building, and spent the rest of the day being a vegetable. Ate a meal in the local Indian, then watched stuff till I was mindless, and went to bed with my teeth luxuriantly unbrushed, at something past 2AM.

Woke screaming.

The tap nightmares weren't all the same, of course. In one, I was standing on the edge of what must have been the white cliffs of Dover. Green grass, and then nothing, like standing on the top ledge of a dodgily built skyscraper. The very roots of grass sticking out from the precipice looked like ancient fingers of the dead, reaching in frozen hope. The toes of my shoes were hanging off that edge, and *tap*. I couldn't whirl around. I could have crumbled the edge where I moved. But I didn't need to look. There was no one there.

I'd be at a supermarket in my dream, and I'd feel it. Or not in my dream. It was no time before there was no difference. The tap could come at any time.

On the toilet. In the shower, of course.

I took to having a crap as fast as I could. To not having showers. Soon after the openness of pavements became too much, and me hugging walls and shopfronts as I progressed down a street had attracted so much notice that I'd been talked to by police, I realised that going out at all was just not on.

And what about Anthony Brough? I did mention the bastard to a friend early on, an old schoolmate who is now a solicitor specialising in petty crims. He said, "Why don't you find out where he lives and throw a brick through his window? Or can't you hack into his terminal at work and plant porn on it, and then, like, you know." That's when I knew there was no solution.

One thing good about the police experience. I was taken into the "forensic physician's room." I know because I looked up what it must have been and found it in a neat little guide, "Health Care of Detainees in Police Stations." It's the room with the cabinet of goodies. Funny, that. You'd think 'forensic physician' meant someone who evaluates dead people. Anyway, he was as sympathetic as you could expect from someone like that. "Have you always been a depressive?" "It's common to feel anxiety, but you mustn't let it control you." He left me in the room for a while and then came back. Thank god the two cells were already full. "Sorry," he said when he returned. "I'd rather you stay till tomorrow, so this will have to do. Take one now . . . " So I walked out richer by two little sample-size bottles, one of "something to help you sleep" and

Xanax "for anxiety." As if I didn't know. And advice to contact the NDP (National Depression Programme). As if I would.

I tossed them both on the way home. Only an idiot would want something to make him less aware, unable to protect himself. Bovine.

You can get stuff delivered for a while, but eventually you need more money, you need stuff you can't get by delivery. You begin to look too disreputable, I guess. You start to smell. The flat did, that's for sure. I couldn't do the dishes, not with my back exposed. I couldn't get rid of the rubbish.

The only thing for it was to cut off that shoulder. I drank all that I had one night, a cocktail of stuff left over from a few parties, stuff that girls had brought over (since that was all I had left). An almost full bottle of elderflower liqueur, half a bottle of peach schnapps, and two creme de somethings, sweet as the stuff in chocolate centres, and a full bottle of Smirnoff, which always tastes like nail polish smells. Two mugs of it, and I got going. I used my thirteenth birthday present, the electric fretsaw from my dad.

There was less blood than I expected, and I was very proud of my work. Of course it hurt so much that I had to do it while sitting, not standing, against the wall, but the safety release worked as it should have when I passed out.

When I woke up, I sprayed it all with betadine and sprinkled all the wet stuff with betadine powder. I had read that air was best for healing so I left it open to crust up naturally.

Then I polished off the rest of the booze and fell asleep for a while. Woke up sick as a dog, vomited the crap out of my system, cleaned up the floor with my left hand and a dirty shirt or something, and threw myself in bed. The shoulder was pounding with pain, good searing agony.

Somehow, fell into sleep. He, or it, came upon me while I was running, and then I could only run slower.

Woke.

Opened the window. So much sky. Had to try to fall with my back to the building.

I left instructions that I be laid on my back.

I WAS, FOR a time. Didn't imagine being burned. Did anyone tell you that your nostrils fill with stink? That your body bloats, oozes, pops, creaks, that your fat screams; that your bones sigh like whoopie cushions before they fall apart, partway. And after your 15 minutes of flame? Does anyone tell you that you don't end up as some tidy pile of ash, but more like the scrapings from a fireplace in a city where people scrounge wood from condemned buildings.

And as for the tasteful urn for your eternal rest, dream on. I can swear that I was thrown, not even into a cardboard box, but the same old black plastic bag whose sisters, like hookers, decorate pavements from the poshest addresses to the worst, and lean against the railings in front of so many collections of flats so equal in name—'. . . Mansions'—that this equality could only have been doled out for the purpose of dispersing without favour: the best medicine.

Leaning up against me, digging *into* me is a crowd, I never asked *who* any more than I knew who lived above, below, beside me in my building. Hearing them was quite enough. At least there were walls there. This might as well be me at work. No privacy, no dignity. No future.

No future, stretching out endlessly.

After a long trip, I'm pretty sure I've ended up as landfill, with everyone pressed even closer, no one looking at anyone else, not a friendly word or smile, no more welcome human contact than you'd get on a city bus.

It's ironic that there's all this pressing, because you wouldn't think you'd feel, but oh you do. This isn't like some guy who gets his leg blown off and afterwards, can feel it itch. This isn't phantom limb, some syndrome for physios to heal.

I can feel my body. As in toes, fingers, nose, my itchy arsehole. And by feel, I mean that it is here. I can't move, of course, not even squeeze my sphincter.

And so I'm stuck with these neighbours all around, detritus people and the detritus of their lives. A syringe leans against my thigh, a used sanitary napkin (I can smell it) against my mouth. Receipts, the acrid remains of a cell phone, a melted wad of coffee cup; someone who might have been a supervisor at the local Tesco or an accountant, not that I care, push against me—all in that sticky façade of familiarity as if we were in some email-mandated 'party' to celebrate the company's success—or worse: a Council-organised televised meet-the-neighbours, with the same amount of warning. Your eating habits and filthy socks are "no problem" but you have to hide your rage and shame.

At least here, there is quiet, you might say, and that is true. And there is time, you'd add. And *don't* say *All the time in the world* any more than you'd like me to ask you with a laugh, "How's changing the world going for you today?"

No rush indeed, but time. Time to think down here. That's another myth.

Just like I was thinking yesterday maybe it was, that you've got to be mad to top yourself in a city. Go on a cruise, have a bit of fun, run up a bill that you'll never need to pay, and on the third night out when the sea is choppiest, jump. You'll have a good quick drown, and a lovely clean end. Be chomped by fish and worms and that, and be part of the Cosmos.

I'm amazed I got the whole thought out, and doubly surprised to do it now again for you. Extraordinary. Honestly, I've got more chance to win Lotto than get a whole thought in again. Even that one was so rushed that maybe it made no sense. I don't think I was scatterbrained up there, but here, I think I'm losing the ability to be me.

Here—I didn't tell you the worst of it. And who's to say. Maybe you'd like it here. After all, are you doing your nut about where you are now?

So maybe it's just me, and for your sake, I hope so (not that I care really, but).

You know how everyone and everything is crowded round me. Well, in this rubble there's one place that they are not. There's an open space, a kind of bubble of air, around my right shoulder.

And though you might think my phantom body probably some common syndrome of the dead, a figment of my imagination, you know: fear is real.

Not a whole thought can I finish. Nor seriously mull, ponder, calculate, cogitate fantasize, drift off, forget, relax, plan, mentally escape or resign myself to anything. And if you think that I'm emotional, that I'm telling this to you in a wordy flow, then remember that I've had to train myself to piece together my broken thoughts. The effing *building* that I worked in could be archaeology by now.

And you already know: I can't turn around.

Whoever or whatever you are: *I know you're there.*

To have killed myself for *this*. Want some advice? Of course not. And I wouldn't have, either.

But I never thought that worse than the tap would be: waiting, possibly forever.

Up top, maybe there's a lid of concrete already sealing all this off, and a block of flats.

Down here, it's so clammily cold that I advise one other thing. Wear something that'll wick away your sweat, unless you can expect, hah hah, to lay at rest.

—⊕—

Bowfin Island

5 Nov, Fri

'sublime but commanding! poss see me immed' Hear texted, possibly trying to warn me off because he followed that immed w 'poss prefer gdd tour italy?' I seriously don't think he meant the 'commanding' to be a come-on.

When I found him yesterday, he said that what I asked for was impossible. Something about the locals mustn't be after the tourist pound, and there's only one possible place to stay there anyway, and it's only got one room, and it's booked years ahead, and it costs more per night than a sensible person would ... No reasonable person would ... besides, there are plenty more places in the North Sea, and why not pick someplace warm and sunny anyway blahblahblaaa.

He's an odd duck, so out for my safety that it's a wonder he doesn't try to sell me a tour of my flat so I don't run the risk of leaving home. But he knows what he knows. I found him in the outer reaches of the Web, almost like he didn't really want to be seen, let alone be an agent. Hear Outer The Way Travel. But then, most clients have web presences before I work on them, that look like they don't want to be seen.

Someone was literally watching my back when I repld YS! NO! B thr! Then I might have screwed up someone's web page, working on two at once, Margate Council's Incontinence Support site & the Smoking Bum Cigar Lounge. I was THAT anxious the opportunity wouldn't slip away before I could seize it on my lunch break.

Luckily, Hear was only a block away, though my bum still hurts from slipping in the rain. That rain must have stopped anyone else coming. He was all alone. I don't know what people are coming to these days. A drop of precipitation, a bit of wind, and they're all inside, only giving their thumbs exercise.

He raised a hand and nodded and motioned me to the chair, but it was a full 2 minutes of anxious waiting for me, while he worked away on his keyboard. I would have said something, but my little mistake of adding Man About Town gents cotton protective pants with concealed waterproof liner to the menu list of the Smoking Bum and pasting the Hoyo De Monterrey Epicure #2 in the Council's IS Bladder and Bowel links stayed my tongue.

Finally he finished and frowned at me. He looked like Mum whenever she saw that I was going out to play. Where's your nicky-tams, she'd say. She never understood why a string tied around your leg just under the knee won't keep your trousers out of the mud. And when in uni, I bought cycling clips, she was downright obnoxious with her Oh now, Mister size 11 boots. You see that I've been right all along but too proud you are, to admit it! and her raised eyebrows and teeth clicks at the extravagances of those clips, followed by two sentences: How long d'you expect your money to last? As long as a piece of string?

I never got a chance, nor did I try to say that my pair of Ice Toolz Plastic Trouser Clips with reflective Scotchlite Strip was only £3.50. *Only*, she would have said, like a gust of wind fit to king-hit the chimney—for my lashout of £3.50 was 100 times, no, an infinity of multiples of what two pieces of string cost, since she even washed and saved the string that held the paper on fish-wrapping.

All my personality comes from Dad, so how could either of us feel guilty for, after she died, throwing away without discussion, her most treasured possession, the framed wallpiece that her gran had embroidered back in prehistory—I can see Great Gran now, embroidering with one hand while with the other, she is darning with cord that lasts, the toes of socks, all the while not letting her feet be idle, those that whip up stinking mounds of neeps and tatties that are, of course, not meant to be eaten for pleasure.

'*Caution* will seldom guide ye wrang' said the thing on the wall. I never did understand my parents' marriage. I did see Mum's mother once, and she was the opposite of what Mum's gran must have been. She wore more makeup than the Harlequeens who played the pub down the street when I was so young that I thought them beautiful, in a scary way. She had the kind of voice those men were trying to ditch. If you closed your eyes, however, the huskiness did have a certain 40s Lauren Bacallishness to it. The fag hanging off her lip didn't. Mum didn't approve of her, and she conveniently died suddenly of some complication, I think a truck.

So this agent had that look on his face, that *Mum* look. Then he added, 'Dreams don't make good trips, but bad trips last forever. It is my professional responsibility to advise you against peradventure.'

I hadn't noticed before, but he even sounds like Mum, and on his desk is one of those tourist plaques, probably made in China, but he must have bought it because it flattered his ego: 'There's nane sae deaf as them that winna hear.'

Without turning around, he pointed to the poster behind him. "Mr Hear," I said, "I must be back to work soon, so please, no games. Don't let anyone Scotch ye might mean something to you, but it's beans to me."

"T'other," he said, jabbing his thumb back to the left.

"See Skye afore ye Die"? Not worth reply.

Then he put his hands on something on his desk that he turned my way: a garish tabloid brochure fronted by a group of t-shirted girls looking ready to shag anything.

I stood up and took off my anorak. Now, staring at him from my t-shirt were the words, 'Twitch and Tick'.

"Bowfin," I said.

"A penny saved—"

"Is a 500th of a cup of coffee," I said. "Now Bowfin. Or Mars."

"All that money," he said, as if my spending it would hurt him. There was something positively Calvinistic about the douchebag. He was, in short, getting on my tits.

"A young man like you should be saving for—"

"There's nae poackits in a shroud!"

He smiled grimly. "Single?"

"Of course."

"Then," he said, "I can offer you from Friday the seventh, three days at Puddock House."

Whoa! That, as this diary shows, is only 2 days away.

"Only because of a cancellation due to premature death. It'll be filled—"

"Book it!"

"It'll cost—"

"Book it!" I screamed. My thumbs tingled with intended tweets: eat yr hrts out! Bowfin Is! Try 2 find on map! 1 Siberian Chiffchaff

I was fucked if I was going to miss this chance. I'd already stuffed the opportunity of going to Sula Sgeir back in May and possibly sighting the Red-necked Phalarope, and I lost my lunch one hot day in June when Geoff Pingly tweeted: South Uist flck of 127 btG.

NO ONE is gonna get between me and the possibilities on Bowfin Island. That place that I'd never heard of before Hear, but couldn't miss once I knew. Sure, he's a pain in the arse): but isn't that why good destinations, like good travel agents, are well-kept secrets:)

Not but he's weird! And here's the strangest part of that strange encounter, the thing that stopped him trying to put me off. My comeback. 'There's nae poackits in a shroud.'

Hell if I know where that came from. It was like, coming from someone inside me, someone I've never met let alone listened to. I might as well have been speaking in voices. But then it's the same when I'm writing code. My programming skills always seem to come from some unknown computer inside me. It's a crowded house in there.

I shouldn't complain. Hear's insides might be filled with caution-preaching vicars yearning to be mums—but inside me, I've got, atop the bank of supercomputers, some yelling hairy Scotsman with a wild sense of adventure that matches mine, and hey—he's human!

Meanwhile, at work:

The office has an automatic dobber-in on every galley-slave's chair that counts the seconds that a bum isn't pressing on it, working. You might as well have electrodes wired to your skull. Pressure pads sense just which muscles are tensing up, so the system aces the status quo, plain vanilla CCTV in all its costs. No one has to watch this. You just get shocked if you're deviating, and it's nothing light. After a treatment of this, a man's balls feel like cold falafels. And the system feels wetness just as well, so Felicity Quimper, after her alarm went off for jumping out of her chair, went out and got a supersize Hot & Sour Soup that she took back to work and threw into the little room filled with servers. Defending herself later, she supposedly said that she thought it was an invasion of her privacy to be shocked for having thoughts. Her defence would have only cost her more money, what could she expect? She had committed thoughts during work hours.

I don't know why I wrote all that down. Maybe just for vanity. Will my next place of work be hopelessly behind the times technologically? Fat chance. The only thing that stays the same is that progress just changes the way slaves are punished. But then, that's in the office. One thing I love about twitching is that we tick off our subjects. We're in control. And there's not a damn thing the birds can do about it. They exist, so that we tick. Off hours.

During work hours, struggling is as effective as a wren caught in a net. Order me around, I say. Just pay me heaps. I'm lucky that I can work with my brain tied behind my back. I'm so good at my work that I skill up without having to work at it. If only it weren't all so BORING! I do suffer from interminable terminal boredom. But isn't that the scent of an office? Oh de zzz. Not that my smell is like the other galley-slaves who pong of fear, justifiably scared as rabbits in a fox coven. They're all so eminently *imminently expendable*. Not me. It must be my competence. Always ooze confidence! It would be nice though, to sit in a workchair and merely be passively observed ruining sight and spine and any sense of being human.

Anyway, I got back an hour late and tossed a hot moist bag already looking like it was made of waxed paper into Cooper's lap. THAT stopped him mid-yell, momentarily. He shouldn't complain. He loves samosas. Then I ignored the galley-slave corpsicles cracking their neck bones as they tried to watch yet keep their glute maxes and all their other little bum glutes absolutely dutiful . . . while I cleared out my desk and left, warbling over the alarm as effectively as a Hume's Leaf W trying to best a screaming plover.

The pay there was as usual, more than I'd put in a bank. And somehow I don't think I'll get a rec fr there. And I just spent my savings on the trip. But we're only alive once, some of us. The rest aren't alive at all.

As for those who are working without pay, Great Gran, since you must be hard at it making yourself useful up there in your unheated heaven, here's a job to get on with:

Embroider it in red.

Every job's shite.

And since you must have a carpenter up there, too, please get it framed. Ta! And tally-ho, if you're looking, Mum!

6 Nov Sat

Exhausted already. 6am London to Glasgow flight inexcusably delayed 5! NOTE FIVE hours by snowstorm somewhere. No snowstorm in London. No one fed us anything while we waited, the plane food was an insult, and the rest of the trip so far is a blur. It's 3am, and I'm supposed to be trying to sleep in a freezing cottage built of stone and romantically roofed with straw, like some effing fairytale. My head feels like a pummelled steak from the interminable howling wind.

I got here by degrees. A ferry to one island, then a wait with no time given to when some boat would take me to the next place, so I couldn't get anything to eat or have a decent crap, but three hours of that and the ferry pitched up, only something that took me to the next island. I thought it was someplace named Muck, but I think I thought that because I read some funny article about the Laird of Muck. Anyway, wherever it was, was just a stop along the way. Someone met me yet again, don't ask me how they knew. And then I was taken on a fishing boat to this place.

This journal smells of chunder. The fishing boat rolled like half a lemon in a punchbowl. I was the only passenger, said the captain. Yes, he called himself the captain. He tried to make the journey pleasant, plying me with slices of white bread. I tossed each overboard when he wasn't looking. Couldn't keep anything down, even though there was hardly anything in my stomach.

This journal makes me gag now. I shouldn't have tried to write in it on that tub, but I had to keep my head down, couldn't look at the flipping horizon. Cleaned up what I could then with the only thing I had, the sleeve of my anorak. The captain was bloody useless. He offered to toss buckets of water over me, and kept saying, 'You're bowfin.' I know I'm going there and so does he, but it's a bit rich, him treating me like luggage. I had to tell him to fuck off. The journal's been washed by rain since, and some of the pages are stuck together, but I can't throw it away, not after all I've put in it! When I get to Puddock House, will tell them to desanitise it somehow. With what I've paid, they should have a slave who could lick it clean. Part of the big adventure!

Somehow, just writing this makes me feel better. Can hardly feel fingers, it's so cold here. Light is from candle stub, must go.

7 Nov Sun

I HATE BOATS.

8 Nov Mon
10AM

THE WORST TRIP I've ever had ended last night when I was rowed to a beach the size of a g-string, and left. I didn't know how long I'd be waiting there in the pitch black with only the sound of waves to keep me company, but was vomiting too much to demand an answer. Finally, a few minutes or an hour later, someone came. I expected, for the money I've shelled out and the exclusivity, a porter who'd also climbed Everest and cowed everyone with his yachting skills at Cowes. He would, of course, carry me to Puddock House and deliver me to the tender attentions of my personal butler, who would have my bath ready. God, I stunk, and never want to see a slice of white bread again. Even the thought of white bread makes me retch.

Puddock House!

It's no old manorhouse. It's just a stone cottage, no bigger than a cell that someone would get housed in if he broke into a convenience store.

Its heat is a fireplace.

Bath: tin tub.

Cold water, or water from sleeve in Aga cooker.

At least that's what Macman says.

I thought that Agas were only decoratively archaic, like gas fires with ceramic logs.

He says this one needs fuel, and there isn't any I can see. There is in place of a basket of coal or logs, a basket with clumps of dirt.

This place should be called Siberia's Siberia.

Macman is a scream, if only I were warm, fed, clean, and watching him on a screen.

He's full of stories. Here's one:

It's said, he said, *There's nae poackits in a shroud*, so that is why every man on Bowfin Island was buried with his everyday clothes on, even if they are bloody, torn to buggery, or mockit in the crotch as would give you the dry boak.

Oddly enough, I understand him, even to the dry boak. And it's eerie that he used that line about the shroud. He couldn't be taking the piss out of me, but I do suspect that he used it because he heard that I had when explaining my extravagance to the first captain on this journey. Nosey parkers, they're all fascinated by everything about me. So along with me, the saying has been passed on along the line of people I've had to interact with.

I must make do with the man. He's all I've got. Besides, if I pause to think anything less than good of him, I don't think I'll be able to last until tomorrow. This place is

9 Nov Tue
10AM

FIRST THE GOOD. There are birds here that I wouldn't have believed, even in my wildest. The place is a bloody twitcher's paradise. Yesterday as I was writing this, a Siberian chiffchaff flew into a bush not three yards away. I stress here that this was not a 'possible Siberian Chiffchaff'. It didn't call. Grey and olive above, it had a very Siberian-like head pattern. It was, I stress, no straightforward *collybita*. Definitely not the common. It also has quite a lot of yellow across the breast. It was also unbanded! I would say with certainty that it was a definite sighting. Of course I dropped this journal, and I was trembling as I dug in my pack for my virgin Outer Hebrides Bird Checklist. It wasn't there! Bugger! I must have left it home. There was nothing for it. I would have to make one up in the journal. An annoyance, but that was only the lead up to the main show! Imagine how prophetic my imagined tweet had been: *eat yr hrts out! Bowfin Is! Try find on map! 1 Siberian Chiffchaff*

I don't think I've ever been so excited, so I fumbled reaching back into my pocket, and had to stand up. By then with all the commotion, the bird had long ago flown off, but it had served its purpose. Anyway, my phone wasn't in my back pocket, but then I remembered that I'd put it in my anorak, but it wasn't there. It wasn't in my pack. I ran back to the hovel and it wasn't effing ANYWHERE. Macman was peeling potatoes and I asked to use his, but he said, What phone?

NO PHONE! For the whole time I'll be here. And here I just had the best sighting of my life, and it's gone to waste!

I wanted to choke Macman, but instead, I must be civil. It's torture, but he heated the water and washed my clothes and wiped my anorak down and made a pretty good stew, and—unbelievable, but it's true, sleeps in Puddock House too, on the other side of the room, a hellish blessing. More about 'Puddock House' later.

The torture continued. I went outside to cool off, and as soon as I got there, a male Dotterel pitched up. Then a female Ring Ouzel teased me, and flew off. A Ring Ouzel! Here! I was so upset that I tromped off and within five minutes, saw a spectacular pair of geese, as unbanded as everything here. I felt a sense of choking, I was so excited. But I didn't know for sure. If this was a pair of Bean Geese, that means that I was the first person to sight one south of North Uist in 20 years. But I had to check. It would be awful if I twitched Bean and they were, say, Richardson's Canadians, which sounds ridiculous but all of a sudden I was uncertain about everything. It was all so extreme!

So I dug out my Birds of Scotland, only to find—an apple. That's it. An apple. Oh, and The Source, my waterproof-covered journal where I store my passwords and a lot of code I've written. It's my stone-age backup, the only place I trust to keep these things safe, and now I remember. I took it with me so that if my flat is broken into, no one steals it. And here it was, able to slip out of my pack. I could have lost it at sea along with my phone while I was spewing my guts out over the side, or when I was shitting over the side (did you know that small fishing boats don't have loos? It should be illegal).

So HERE I AM. i cant twitch, i cant tweet. i might as well have stayed at work for all the good this crazy waste of time has been.

Tomorrow can't come soon enough. I dread the return trip, but soon it'll be history. In the meantime

2PM

MACMAN IS USELESS. I told him that he didn't wash my stuff enough. They stink. He said, *You're* bowfin.

I had to walk away, because I couldn't afford giving him my mind. He's unbalanced enough. Still, I was fuming. He had no excuse, treating me like luggage. I mean, on that boat, the 'captain' had a bit of one, and I can even laugh now at the image of someone like him getting laid out as a mattress for telling a passenger "You're LAX."

But say there's another explanation, some New Age slop—'Be one with Bowfin. Om.' I reckon Macman will spout that on the day he takes to dreadlocking his ear tufts. So he's not only useless but inscrutably mad.

Still, I can't get the smell out of my nostrils. A mix of vomit and something sweet, that kind of sweet of something dead. Nightmare sweet. I can't get it out of my nose.

3pm

DARKNESS IS COMING soon. I finally got Macman's name. It's Peasgood. I don't know the spelling, but it's Mr Peasgood. And he's got a sort of sense of humour. Remember what I told you, he said, when he saw me trying to scrape away the smell from my bare arms. He led me to an area where he said the smell came from, a very stony place where he repeated his story of the inhabitants having been buried with their clothes on. The ground was practically all stone with a covering as thick as an op-shop's Oriental carpet. He picked up something and told me to open my hand. It was, he said, a vertebra. !!!!!

The smell he said, comes from all those bodies. It's come and never gone away, though they were buried here that many years ago. I couldn't get out of him WHEN. That's why this is Bowfin Island, he said, and the penny dropped. Stinking Island!

Does that explain the sounds last night? Puddock House felt alive in ways I couldn't bring myself to say here yesterday, but I never before thought I'd ever be glad to have a roommate who's an old man. If it weren't for Mr Peasgood, I might have died of fright. There isn't room in the place for rats, but all night it sounded like the walls were streaming with rats. The place is made of stone. It's impossible.

Now that I know where the bodies are buried. Now that I think of the sounds, they were like fingernails, long toenails. I wouldn't sleep alone if I was told that I could live forever, and with no need to work again, if I only slept here alone for one night.

I asked Mr Peasgood why the people hadn't been buried in the deep dirt here. He was horrified at the thought. That's peat, he said. We need it to burn. So that's the big Oxo cubes of dirt by the stove.

Did I say before that he has a pet? A huge toad! It can't be native. He talks to it.

A month later?

SNATCHING A MOMENT to say something for posterity here. I've learned how to make a fire in the Aga. I'm learning how to cut peat, and make a stew. Actually, cook it. I've also learned how to cook porridge. As for Mr Peasgood having a pet toad that he talks to, the toad is actually giving him instructions. I know how that sounds. I can only tell it like I see it. I can't tell you what the toad says. You couldn't cut his accent with a knife. You'd need a giant's cleaver.

Which leads to the birds.

When I'm not doing chores, I'm allowed to watch the birds. I've never seen so many. Some small bird with a red breast and short tail was singing this morning, and it was so beautiful in the way it tilted its head up and wagged its tail when it hit some notes. The birds here are fascinating. They do the most interesting things, and their songs!

Last year I downloaded Birdsongs of Britain thinking it might help me spot. It was useless. Now I know why. Some bird with, say, a red breast and a yellow cheek is gonna look the same each time you spot it, but its voice isn't like a ringtone. It's unpredictable, and I think, moody. Sometimes after the rain, you'd think it's won Lotto. But the same bird can also sound petty, lonely, frightened, morose, and I swear, horny.

At dawn and dusk, that's when I love to listen. Those are always busy times for me, when I should be setting the fire then or boiling water, or other chores, but instead of dobbing me in, Mr Peasgood always smiles indulgently, sometimes offering up a saying. He's got so many. My favourite is Listen at a hole, and you'll hear news o' yoursel. Aye, he has an accent. It's not like Mum's, but then I don't know what Mum's was, exactly. She was always vague, born in Glasgow but then she says she moved around. She must have, to meet Dad. I've lived in well-heeled London suburbs all my life—didn't know they were 'well-heeled' till I went to work and talked with other galley slaves—and Dad was plain vanilla pom.

So Mr Peasgood sounds a bit thick, but understandable. I had to literally pull up my socks here, learning how to dress. He's always wearing his tweed jacket, every rip always neatly darned.

No stubble allowed here, though no electric shave. 'Twitch and Tick' is now a cleaning rag. Shirt tails that are seen get dipped in salt water before being shoved down my underpants against my bare bum. As I said before, I learn fast, so that only happened once.

He's something of a stickler, but you have to be to live here. And about another thing, like everything else that I couldn't believe at first, but learnt soon enough that he was absolutely right: Bowfin Island only smells to foreigners. It's lucky for us that they never come here. I expect I'll find it enough of an interruption when he gets his half-yearly delivery of oatmeal and his few other treats. He asked if I wanted more paper, another journal that I can write in, but I don't really see the need any more when this is full. It is an affectation, isn't it? After all, who will care to read this, really? I wouldn't read yours, whoever you are if you read this sometime somewhere in the sometime future.

I'm grateful and kind of amazed that Mr Peasgood didn't just murder me or something for intruding upon him. It was unforgivable, what his nephew did, even if Hear did it out of caring, a sense of responsibility. So what if a man chooses to live someplace you wouldn't? So what if he likes the dead more than the living tweeting chirping never-shutting-up masses? So what if he wants to live in a place that smells so bad that you have to get used to it to bear it. No one tries to stop people spending their working life, which is, like, all their life, in hair and nail salons, or reeking restaurant kitchens.

So what if Mr Peasgood is getting old. He's got so much company here that he will never be alone.

And dropping me on him wasn't exactly charitable, was it?

Luckily, he's a good sport. My invasion of his personal space has been treated by him with more grace than I've ever seen in an office.

The dead are less accepting, but he's been there with me all the way, by my side.

I had no idea till yesterday that he also intervened on my behalf, saying that I shouldn't be put to death, that I wasn't a hostile invasion force of one, and did not seek to claim this Duchy for my own. I found out all this when I was formally brought before the toad. I was told to kneel. I did, of course. The toad didn't say a word to me, but no one could stand up to his look. He's got an eerie calmness, a majesty, that comes from, all I can think of is: assurance. He's never undermined by social networking, that's for sure. He has only these subjects under him, and doesn't seek for more.

I couldn't help but be awed.

Mr Peasgood could have been a great lawyer.

Spring

JUST BEFORE I toss this into the sea for who knows who to find, I must say how happy I am that I've proved myself. Laird Puddock has appointed me Assistant Chief Minister!

Oh happy days!

As Mr Peasgood says, Let the dunlins sing!

I must ask him what a dunlin is, but there's only so much time in the day.

Cover notes

Front:

PHOTOGRAPHIC PORTRAIT OF the *Sigesbeckia*, whose reputation has been completely trashed.

Back (and Hardback—with flaps!):

COVERED WITH 100% genuine lightly treated photograph of green-olive brine and air-bred mould (that netted stuff). As with the *Sigesbeckia* on the cover, both spent the whole of their natural lives in honour and I hope comfort, at my place.

The flaps of the Hardback cover hold the world's FIRST AND ONLY TRAVELLING EXHIBITION OF MAGNIFICENT INSIGNIFICANTS. I hope you find the exhibition enjoyable and irritating. May you itch to discover more!

And now, congratulations! You have reached

THE END

of this book.

notice to readers, from SADS:

PEOPLE SAY YOU don't want to know more, not here where you deserve a gold star and release. *They* say it's because you'll be bored, but *we* say they're overfeeling your capacity for pain.

PUBLISHER'S WARNING: Although we've compromised by allowing the founder of SADS to post "a little something", the following contains autobiographical detail, adverbs, and more than 'a little something'.

Why? Why? Why?

The detail of *Sigesbeckia* is in pride of place on the cover, as the finest example I know of a 'discovery' I've made. *The closer you look, the more there is to find.* I put 'discovery' in quotes because that maxim is obvious to anyone who's ever looked. Those extraordinarily flamboyant but minute flowers, the shining pearls held out on multicoloured shining stalks on the clothing of the flowers themselves, the soft green pelt on leaves and stems, the combination of offence/defence that this plant employs. The host of wildlife it supports, from lynx spiders hunting to caterpillars munching, and today, a glitter of shield-bugs mating. Then there are the insects who seem to be stuck fast, possibly acting as food for a plant that is botanically omnivorous? This uncelebrated thing is a shining star in the firmament of curiosities I've been exploring— discoveries that lead to questions—curiosities of the unnoticed, cures for incuriosity—what I call *Magnificent Insignificants*.

The day I saw it, really *saw* it for the first time, I was so excited, I had to share some of its revelations with someone special—an artist whose inventive mind has created wonders such as this. So this was my note to Marc McBride:

> attached, my present favourite. I've never seen a plant that makes music before, but this one does in my mind. Do you also see it as Elizabethan? All jingling bells, puffed and slashed sleeves, kicking lonnng-curling-pointed toe-in-velvet shod feet. And a fine voice for heresy that makes the crowd smile. I've never seen such a little extrovert, and when I say little, it is so small that I only knew this as annoying little sticky things that got caught in Rosie's [my dog's] hair.

Being merely an enthusiast but no expert at anything, it took me some time to discover even the name of this plant, but when I did, I was astounded, writing to another friend, Jeff Sypeck, who is also my favourite medievalist as well as being quite a wonderful poet:

> I need to start a Sigesbeckia Anti-Defamation Society, as there is so much scullilous "fact" spread [Note: The devil of a rage made me do 'scullilous'], much by people in positions of authority who have been quoted and never questioned, that the reputation of this incredible plant bears no relationship to its real character... [blah blahh by gods, do I go on!] enough in it to start whole fields of enquiry and worlds'ful of discoveries, not to mention being the most beautiful plant I've ever seen, combining something that Ibn Battuta would have reported as the jewels and turbans and incomparable wealth displayed, with the aesthetics of Queen Elizabeth's both in the nicnacs she surrounded herself with, and the jewel-coloured harlequin foods such as tarts filled with a variety of colours of preserved fruits.

Yet the *Sigesbeckia* has a different reputation to so many. This plant that astounded me so with its beauty and complexity (and took me months to find out what it is), is, in the highest echelons, derided—Why? It serves a need, the need to make a topic palatable by turning it into human interest story, and what can be more delicious than a tale of revenge?

The *Sigesbeckia*, unknown as it is to today's most prominent experts, suffered collateral damage—all due to this anecdote, itself full of fertiliser.

There are funny aspects to all this *Sigesbeckia* trashing. In almost every case, the denigration is finessed by an exclamation mark, even in dry reference books that in no other listing, contains anything worth repeating, let alone reading unless to help one sleep. The evolution of referring to the plants as 'stinky' could be fun for anyone into 'name and shame'; 'stinky' has evolved into ever more derisive terms such as 'foul smelling' and even 'spiky', yet the original mistaken typo must be from a mention by someone who actually knew something for the flowers are like little beads of honey. So sticky>stinky—why bother correcting, especially if you know, as the crude say, *dick*? In varying the plagiarism of this anecdote, a pejorative race has increased the put-downs—*ugly, common weed, useless, unpleasant*—all terms that are not only unscientific, but merely points of view. (To a hungry snail, a computer chip is as useless as a dress designer. If you fall into a patch of *Sigesbeckia*, you'll come up flowers to examine, but a rose is a rose. The first human guinea pig for antibiotics died because there wasn't enough penicillin to treat his infection caused by a rose's prick—unpleasant! *Weed* is as much a POV as *up* or *yuck*. And as for *common*, hahaha!

As for the oft-repeated *insignificant* . . .

For my sin of smugness at that interesting put-down, I suffered indigestion, so I fomented to yet another tolerant friend:

> [rumbles, seismological farts, lava flow] *my favourite non-human inspirer* [raining ashes] *societal shallowsplashiness. The Sigesbeckia could have a film done about it, or at least make millions of pounds in British courts, so shockingly has its reputation been trashed, based on lies, all lies. And the juiciest part of this is that the people-gossip part of this, of which the Sigesbeckia is just damage, is itself, a made-up froth retold so many times that it is 'true'.*

The truth is that the plant was named by Carl Linnaeus, the man who devised the system of classification of living things that is still in use today. He was also a man with a personality fit for today. He wanted to be famous, was constantly grooming his public profile, wanted to be rich, and (before nabbing a wealthy wife) networked assiduously and sucked up to those he hoped to turn into a patron or source of patron, not to fund expeditions. He was no Maria Sibylla Merian. Linnaeus liked to find his plants in a civilised garden/herbarium in some refined place in Europe, and he liked his explorations deskbound. So, one cushy position ending, he needed another, fast, and he was still busy building his reputation. Thus ensued a torrid Facebook-style romance with a man who also saw benefit in friending Linnaeus, whose connections had seeds. It was in the throes of this mutual affection that Linnaeus employed what is often recommended to the aspiring: flattery. He'd been hired to write the *Hortus Cliffortianus*, a catalogue describing and using his new naming system, of all the plants in the exotic garden/

herbarium of amateur botanist George Clifford, a rich banker/East India Company executive. Linnaeus' dedication in the listing of our maligned star reads (thanks to Jeff Sypeck, who translated the Latin from a poor image):

I named the plant in honour of Johann George Siegesbeck, professor of plant medicine at the St Petersburg Botanical Gardens, who with such great ardor abundantly offered [?] to pursue [research?] the Catalogue of Medical Plants of St Petersburg.

Linnaeus also honoured Siegesbeck by choosing this plant as one of the few to be illustrated with a full-page plate. That Linnaeus missed an 'e' wasn't anything to be embarrassed about, so *Sigesbeckia* is forever *Sigesbeckia*, unless someone overcorrects, which people who aren't even 'everyday people' do.

In addition to Linnaeus' other qualities, he possessed a 21st century sense of being wronged—so sensitively tuned that he could find offence where others would say the evidence was insignificant, and he loved getting back at people. So when he found out that Siegesbeck was going to criticise Linnaeus' theory of plant promiscuity (a theory that Linnaeus subsequently dropped)—*after* he'd already dedicated the plant to Siegesbeck, and after the illustration had been done (from life) by the best team in the business—when he found that Siegesbeck!—*omg#$!!!!*— the maxim "It's never too late" is fertiliser. The book that all this networking folly was to commit to immortality was an unmovable milestone in science. Linnaeus learned the lesson many today consider the most important in Life. There is nothing worse than publicly praising someone who turns out to be a critic. Linnaeus couldn't erase the record. He couldn't cry "Exterminate!"

The damage was done. His networking had been wasted time, his Facebook-type friendship gesture a cruel farce which would be thrown back in his face for posterity, and people would laugh at him forever, for the evidence was plain to see.

But who looks? And history? Insignificant!

H ERE'S A DELICIOUS example of how things change:

2007 was the tercentenary of *Systema Naturae* by Carl Linnaeus. Of course, talking about a book like *Systema Naturae* is hardly going to keep people awake in commemorations, but Linnaeus=celebrity.

So Steve Mirsky, in his *Scientific American** podcast celebrating Linnaeus posed a game:

Here are four science stories; only three are true. See if you know which story is TOTALLY BOGUS.

Story number 3 is true: Linnaeus took revenge on people he didn't like by naming unpleasant species for them. Carl Linnaeus was not above jabs at personal enemies by naming certain species for them. For example, he named a weed that produces a nasty smelling fluid, Siegesbeckia, because he had a grudge against German botanist Johann Siegesbeck.

Far be it for me to advocate such a waste of time, but people with petty minds could have delicious fun counting the un-trues.

A ND SO ENDS this—

But hold on, you say. *This isn't finished. Not with two more mysteries of motivation to solve.* Why would George Clifford have wanted this weed in his garden/herbarium, and why would Johann George Siegesbeck, professor of plant medicine at the St Petersburg Botanical Gardens have sought these weed's seeds?

Sigesbeckia, called many other names including *Hsi Ch'ien* (in China), has long been valued as an important part of the pharmacopeia throughout Asia and the Indian Ocean, the whole plant being used for a range of medical conditions, from skin conditions to rheumatoid arthritis to mastitis.

Anyone with an interest in archaeology can easily unearth much from the BISE (Before Internet-Scholarship Era). Digging in my own catacombs, lo! I came up with two finds that feature *Sigesbeckia*, both

---

* "What's in a Latin Name: The Legacy of Linnaeus" by Steve Mirsky, *Scientic American* podcast, December 26, 2007, http://www.scientificamerican.com/podcast/episode/0afc0a72-af9d-cce6-d93ba3f6e131f8bb/

from the 20th century: *Potter's New Cyclopedia of Botanical Drugs and Preparations* (a British classic that has undergone many revisions—my edition is from Jain Publishing, New Delhi, 1984); and that great 1970 Chinese public health production, *The Barefoot Doctor's Manual* (I have the 1974 translated edition published by the U.S. Department of Health, Education, and Welfare.)

The happy ending here is that anyone can discover the most wonderful things, *anywhere*, because every good quest ends with discovery which reveals yet more mysteries leading to more quests, *everywhere for the looking.*

Story Acknowledgements

These stories first appeared

"The Oyster and Alice O." — on Rudy Rucker's *Flurb* #12, edited and illustrated by Rudy Rucker, Fall [Northern Hemisphere] (2007).

"Lab Dancer" — in this collection.

"Strange Incidents in Foreign Parts" — in John Klima's *Electric Velocipede Issue 9*, edited by John Klima (2005).

"Marks and Coconuts" — in *Postscripts #30/31: Memoryville Blues*, edited by Peter Crowther and Nick Gevers (PS Publishing, 2013).

"The Walking-stick Forest", edited by Ellen Datlow — on *Tor.com* (May 21, 2014).

"The Jeweller of Second-hand Roe" — in *Subterranean* #7, edited by Ellen Datlow, (Subterranean Press, 2007).

"High Life" — in this collection.

"The Eye of Nostradamus Summit" — in *Andromeda Spaceways Inflight Magazine* Issue 44, edited by Simon Petrie (July 2010).

"The Old Testacles" — in *The Cascadia Subduction Zone*, Vol. 4, No. 4, edited by L. Timmel Duchamp (Aqueduct Press, October 2014).

"Rocket Fantazyor" — as the slightly reticent "Wiseman's Terror Tales" in *Jews vs Zombies / Jews vs Aliens*, edited by Lavie Tidhar and Rebecca Levene, Jurassic London, UK, 2015.

"Sincerely, Petrified" — in *Lovecraft Unbound*, edited by Ellen Datlow, Dark Horse Books (2009).

"The Dog Who Wished He'd Never Heard of Lovecraft" — in print and podcast on Mike Davis' *Lovecraft Ezine*, Issue 13, April 2012.

"Bufo of Oahu: Ukulele Ululatress"— in this collection.

"How Galligaskins Sloughed the Scourge" — in *Andromeda Spaceways Inflight Magazine*, Issue 46, edited by Mark Farrugia (August 2010).

"There is No Rice Pudding in the Sea" — in *Fantasy Magazine* #3, edited by Sean Wallace (June, 2006).

"Dreadnought Neptune" — in *Asimov's Science Fiction*, edited by Sheila Williams (June 2010).

"The Shoe in SHOES' Window" — in *Interfictions: an anthology of interstitial writing*, edited by Delia Sherman and Theodora Goss (Interstitial Arts Foundation, 2007).

"Baad-hin'jan and the Chickpea" — in this collection.

"The Emperor's Backscratcher" — on *infinity plus*, edited by Keith Brook (2005).

"King Wolf" — in *A Season in Carcosa*, edited by Joseph. S. Pulver (Miskatonic River Press, 2012).

"Gladiolus Exposed" — in *The Del Rey Book of Science Fiction and Fantasy: Sixteen Original Works by Speculative Fiction's Finest Voices*, edited by Ellen Datlow (Ballantine Books, USA, 2008.

"Adventures of Discovering the Ellemehnopee" — on Anna Tambour's blog *Medlar Comfits*, 21 Jan 2006.

"Pococurante" — in *Logorrhea: Good Words Make Good Stories*, edited by John Klima (Bantam Books, 2007).

"The Age of Fish, Post-flowers" was originally published in *Paper Cities: An Anthology of Urban Fantasy*, edited by Ekaterina Sedia (Senses Five Press, 2008).

"Tap" — in this collection.

"Bowfin Island" — in *Caledonia Dreamin'*, edited by Hal Duncan and Chris Kelso (Eibonvale Press, 2013).

"Cover Notes" — in this collection.

ANNA TAMBOUR's *novel* CRANDOLIN *was shortlisted for the World Fantasy Award in 2013.* THE FINEST ASS IN THE UNIVERSE *is her second story collection. She lives in the bush in New South Wales, Australia.*

thank you

The publisher would sincerely like to thank:

Elizabeth Grzyb, Anna Tambour, Jeffrey Ford, Marc Laidlaw, Kaaron Warren, Cat Sparks, Lisa L. Hannett, Donna Maree Hanson, Robert Hood, Pete Kempshall, Penelope Love, Nicole Murphy, Angela Slatter, Karen Brooks, Jeremy G. Byrne, Felicity Dowker, Kim Wilkins, Marianne de Pierres, Jonathan Strahan, Peter McNamara, Ellen Datlow, Grant Stone, Sean Williams, Simon Brown, Garth Nix, David Cake, Simon Oxwell, Grant Watson, Sue Manning, Steven Utley, Lewis Shiner, Bill Congreve, Jack Dann, Janeen Webb, Lucy Sussex, Stephen Dedman, the Mt Lawley Mafia, the Nedlands Yakuza, Shane Jiraiya Cummings, Angela Challis, Kate Williams, Kathryn Linge, Andrew Williams, Al Chan, Alisa and Tehani, Mel & Phil, Hayley Lane, Georgina Walpole, Rushelle Lister, everyone we've missed . . .

. . . and you.

in memory of
Eve Johnson
Sara Douglass
Steven Utley
Brian Clarke